I0561316

Bones of Earth

Heir to the Firstborn, Volume 3

Elizabeth Schechter

Published by Elizabeth Schechter, 2020.

Bones of Earth

Copyright © 2020 Elizabeth Schechter

All rights reserved, including the right to reproduce this book, or portion thereof, in any form.

This is a work of fiction. Any references to historical events, real people, or real locales are used fictitiously. Other names, characters, places, and incidents are the product of the author's imagination, and any resemblance to actual events or locales or persons, living or dead, is entirely coincidental.

Published by Raven's Wing Books

Previously published as **Bones of Earth** (Elizabeth Schechter, 2020)

Editor: Michael Schechter
Cover design by GetCovers

Raven's Wing Books

ravens-wing-books.com
ISBN: 9781952598012

Table of Contents

To M and J, always.

To my Patrons, who've supported this whole crazy venture
from the word "Go."

CHAPTER ONE

T here was a definite taste of spring in the air, for all that the wind off the ocean was still brittle-cold. Owyn stepped down off the front stoop and shoved his hands into his coat pockets, heading toward the center of Terraces and the healing complex. He needed gloves, he reminded himself. He should really stop by the dispensary. He made a mental note, and then promptly forgot all about gloves as he started to review his running checklist.

Finish the assessment of which houses had been too badly damaged by the winter storms to be immediately habitable. That should be finished today.

Determine which of those houses could be repaired, and which needed to be demolished. He'd told Jehan that he could have that report ready within a week of finishing the assessment. So far, he expected to be on time.

Arrange repairs on those houses that could be finished first. He needed to work with Marik on that — he had a better idea of who could do what in Terraces.

Seal off the houses that were going to be demolished. See what could be salvaged from them. That needed to wait for spring and warmer weather, he thought. So did the repairs. But having a list of which to do first would be a good thing.

Convince Aria that she was wrong. An ongoing project, and one with no end in sight.

Find Aven. Another ongoing project.

1

Overthrow Mannon and see Aria on the throne as Firstborn.
Tabled until he finished the last two.

He sighed and hunched down into his coat as a cold wind trailed down the back of his neck. It had never gotten this cold in Forge. He'd never seen snow like they'd had this past winter. Or storms, for that matter — one right after the other, with no respite to repair damage or bring in supplies. There were still a lot of people living in the shelter caverns beneath the healing complex because their homes weren't safe. And they'd stay there until he finished his job. Which meant that he needed to get to work.

He sighed again, his breath billowing and reminding him of the smoke in the vents where he'd learned to dance. Reminding him of Memfis, who was Mother only knew where. Still alive, Owyn thought. He hoped. He looked up at the icy-blue sky and thought of spring. Spring meant that Aven and Del would be coming back soon. They were only supposed to have been gone for a season. So they were coming back soon.

They had to be coming back soon. The houses in Terraces weren't the only thing falling apart. He turned at the marker and headed for the healing complex. They'd changed houses after Aven and Del had left — Aria couldn't stay in Fourteen Southwest, not without having screaming nightmares. And she'd refused Owyn's offers to hold her while she slept, the way he had on their first night in Fourteen. So he'd arranged with Jehan and Rhexa for them to move. They lived now in a slightly larger house that faced Rhexa's own, on the first ring of the Northwest spoke. It was closer to the healing complex, which was convenient for Treesi and Alanar. Aria had insisted that her Earth had to live under the same roof with her, and since Treesi was no longer a student, she could live where she liked. But she'd refused to let Alanar live alone, and had dug in her heels until Aria had invited the other healer to join them. Privately, Owyn was glad of it — he shared a room with them, and they listened to him when he vented his frustrations at how things were falling apart.

Rhexa listened, too, and offered advice. Aria had been hurt, and was trying to protect herself so that she wouldn't be hurt again. Owyn needed to give her time. Which he understood — he'd been there. He knew what Rhexa meant. He could give his Heir the time she needed. He could give her the support she needed. He could give her any damn thing that she needed...provided that she let him. Which she wasn't doing. She wouldn't talk to him, wouldn't listen to him. She hadn't spent any time with him since the Turning, when they'd welcomed the new year with gifts. She'd made him this coat, and he loved it. He thought it meant that she'd forgiven him for letting Aven go. But since then, the coat had been the warmest thing he had from Aria. Lately, she wouldn't do more than say good morning to him when he came into the kitchen, and she would leave immediately after.

She was making it very clear that she didn't want to be around him, and didn't know how to tell him to go. Not that she really could. He was her Fire, after all.

Things were falling apart, and he was seriously starting to doubt that he'd ever see the last item on his list finished. Not that he'd tell anyone that. He wouldn't even say that out loud to Trinket. Saying things out loud made them real. If he didn't say it, it wasn't real. And if it wasn't real, it was safe to keep trusting Aria. To keep loving her. Because she wasn't going to leave him the way everyone else had.

He swallowed and looked up. Right at this moment, he wasn't sure where Aria even was. She hadn't been in the house when he'd gotten up, which was unusual — he got up early to make sure everyone else ate before they went off to their duties. But when he'd gone to see if he could make breakfast for her, her room had been empty. She might be with Jehan or Rhexa. Probably. There was just so much to do! He headed into the healing complex and waved to the assistant at the front desk.

"Morning, Malani," he called, keeping his voice low. "Where is everyone this morning?"

"Senior Healer is in his office, and I believe the Heir is with him. Healers Treesi and Alanar are on their morning rounds." Malani looked past him and smiled. "And Administrator Rhexa is standing behind you."

Owyn turned and smiled as Rhexa stepped forward, her arms open. He was still getting used to being hugged multiple times a day, but it was a good thing to get used to. She stepped back and studied his face.

"You're not sleeping," she pronounced. "I can see it in your eyes."

"Too much to do, Auntie," Owyn answered. Too much worrying to do was closer to the truth, but he wasn't going to say it. She nodded.

"I understand. How is the assessment going?"

"I should be done today," Owyn answered. "Assuming it doesn't snow again."

"I hope it's done," Rhexa said. "I think we're finally past that point. I hope. Except for late snow. If it's very windy at night, it comes in off the water. But that sort of snow doesn't tend to stick." She snorted. "I think you have to be born here to understand the weather."

"And even when you are, every winter is a surprise," Malani added with a giggle. "This year has been pretty awful, though. But spring is coming."

"Yeah. It is. And I have a lot of work to do before it gets here. So I need to run." On a whim, Owyn leaned over and kissed Rhexa's cheek. At least someone was happy to see him in the morning. "I'll see you later, Auntie," he said.

"Come for supper," she called after him as he hurried away. He waved to show that he'd heard, then turned the corner and headed toward Jehan's office. It was more central than the offices that Rhexa and Risha had kept — Jehan said that the Senior Healer needed to be accessible to everyone, at any time. So his offices were right off the entryway of the healing complex, just around a corner. As Owyn reached the door, he realized that Malani had said that Aria was with Jehan. So he did something he hadn't done since he'd left Forge — he stopped outside the door and listened.

"I can't convince you otherwise?" Jehan asked in a gently voice.

"No," Aria answered. "I've made up my mind."

"At least tell him."

"You know what his answer will be. I cannot."

Owyn swallowed, suddenly sorry that he'd listened. He knocked on the door and waited until he heard Jehan call, "Come in!"

He opened the door and looked in. "I'm not interrupting, am I?" he asked. "Malani said Aria was here." He smiled when he saw her sitting in one of the chairs that sat in front of Jehan's desk. "I was wondering where you were. You weren't there when I came to see what you wanted to eat this morning."

She looked up at him, but didn't smile. She looked impossibly sad, and he was torn between the need to hold her, and the desperate urge to scream at her until she told him the truth. "I was up before the sun," she said. "I needed to fly this morning. Then I came here."

"Then you haven't eaten?" Owyn asked. "We can go back. I can cook something for you. We have that cheese you like." He hated that it sounded as if he was begging, but he knew that he really was. He knew that what he was really saying was "Let me back in. Let me take care of you. Love me again."

If she understood that, she gave no sign, shaking her head. "No, thank you," she replied. "I really am not hungry."

"Aria, you're not eating," Owyn pressed. "I'm not entirely sure you're sleeping, either. You never sit down with us. You never talk to me anymore." He forced the words out. "I'm worried about you." He looked down, shoving his shaking hands into his coat pockets. "About us. About everything."

He heard her get up, but didn't look up. He couldn't look up. He hadn't meant to say anything. Saying it made it real. Now...well, it had been real before. But now he'd said it. Now it was really real.

"Owyn."

She was standing in front of him. He could see her boots, her legs, and the bottom of the long coat that she'd made for herself. He couldn't look higher, and shuddered at the touch of her cold hands on his cheeks. She raised his face, met his eyes, then kissed him gently enough that he wanted to cry.

"Owyn," she whispered his name. "I'm sorry. I've been horrible to you."

"You needed time—" Owyn stammered. She kissed him again, silencing him.

"This is something different. And I will explain. But not now. I ask that you trust me."

He looked at her golden ember eyes and nodded. "I trust you. Just..."

"Please."

He swallowed, not moving as she moved past him and out of the office. The door closed, and he closed his eyes and shook his head.

"I..."

"Sit down, Owyn," Jehan said softly.

Owyn shook his head. "I...no, I'm not going to be long. I...I'll have that assessment done for you tomorrow. That all right?"

Jehan nodded. "That's fine. But I thought you'd have it done today. That's what you told me yesterday."

Owyn nodded. He took his hands out of his pockets and rubbed them up and down on the quilted cloth covering his chest. "I...I need to take a ride. I'll be back in a few hours. So I might have it done today. But more likely tomorrow."

Jehan frowned slightly. "You're going out to Serenity Bay to see Danzi?" When Owyn nodded, he sighed. "I was wondering when you'd go again. It's getting on to being spring. He'll be coming back soon."

"He needs to come back now," Owyn blurted. "Before everything falls apart!"

Jehan closed his eyes. He licked his lips. Then he nodded. "Don't be long," he said. "The weather can change in a minute at this time of year. I don't want you caught unprepared."

"I'll be careful," Owyn said. "Jehan? He is coming back, isn't he?"

Jehan didn't answer.

BEFORE HE LEFT, OWYN needed to talk to Treesi. Which meant finding Treesi — the assistants pointed him in the right directions, but all of them were one or two steps behind her, until at last Owyn bumped into her as she was coming out of a ward room. She brightened immediately when she saw him. Until she looked at him more closely. Then her eyes widened, and she grabbed his arm and dragged him into an empty room.

"What's wrong?" she demanded.

"I'm going up the coast," he answered, not answering the question she asked. "I'll be gone a few hours. I wanted you to know."

She frowned. "Something happened?" she asked. "Owyn, tell me what's going on, or I'll put you to sleep and tie you to the bed."

"Save that for later, and do it in reverse," Owyn answered automatically. The mock-threat and response had become almost rote, and it usually made them both giggle. This time, though, there was no laughter. "Treesi, we're losing it. We're losing everything. I can't get through to her, and I don't know what to do!"

"Her. You mean Aria," Treesi said. "Owyn, you talked to her?"

"Just now, yeah," Owyn answered. He ran his fingers through his hair and winced when he hit knots. "Well, a little while ago. Before I came looking for you. She was with Jehan when I got here. I offered to cook for her, because she hasn't eaten yet today. And...yeah, I told her I was worried about her. And about us."

"What did she say?" Treesi asked.

"She asked me to trust her." Owyn looked at Treesi, then turned away to look out the window. "And I do. I do trust her. But...Trees, she's closed me out, and I can't...I don't know what else to do!"

Treesi came up behind him and wrapped her arms around him. "Owyn, I wish I could be more help. I feel like I'm not helping at all."

"She talks to you, though," Owyn said. He turned in Treesi's arms and put his arms around her. "She talks to you. So maybe it's just that she can't talk to men?" He frowned. "Or she's still mad at me. I thought we got past that."

"She's not mad at you," Treesi insisted. "She was hurt when she found out. But she's not mad. I don't think she ever was."

"Easy for you to say. She didn't throw things at you." Or stop talking — it had been weeks before Aria had spoken a word to Owyn after she found out that he'd been there when Aven and Del had left for the Water tribe. What had finally broken the silence was Owyn's gift to her for the Turning — a rose made from finely worked iron. Owyn had traded his labor at one of the forges in Terraces for the materials and the time to make it, and it had been worth the early mornings and the late nights to see the look on Aria's face. She'd cried on him after, and apologized. It should have been over. But it wasn't. It still felt as if nothing would ever be the way it had been.

However, Aria kept the rose on her dressing table, in a vase that sat in the circle of the cord of Aven's water gem. Also in the vase was the gray pearl that Aven had left behind, the one that he'd told Owyn he meant to give to Aria the morning after their first night together.

Treesi sighed and rubbed her cheek against his shoulder. "Owyn, I understand. I do. You show people you love them by taking care of them. And she won't let you. But that doesn't mean she doesn't love you."

"I do what?" Owyn asked. She giggled.

"You take care of us. You fuss at us to eat, and you make sure we sleep, and you keep the house in order. You make sure that Alanar has the lozenges that he likes when he gets a cough, and you make me the tea that I like when I have to be up late reading." She kissed him gently. "And we're not even going to mention the bread."

"I like making bread," he protested.

"You do it every morning, no matter how late you've been up the night before. You're always up with the sunrise, so we have fresh bread for breakfast." Treesi met his eyes. "Owyn, you show us how much you love us by taking care of us. And it's killing you that Aria won't let you do for her."

Owyn took a deep breath and blew it out. "I'm going up the coast. I want to see if the Water tribe traders have started coming in. Marik said they'd come in the spring. It's spring, mostly. I need to see if I can get a message out to Aven." He closed his eyes and rested his forehead against Treesi's. "I...I can't fix this. I think I might be making it worse. But maybe I'm not supposed to fix it. I'm not the Heart. Aven is. He can fix it. We can all be the way we were before. But he has to come back."

She sighed and kissed him again, then stepped back, out of his arms. "I'll walk with you to the stables."

"No, Trees," Owyn said. "Not that I wouldn't mind the company, but you have work to do. Go on, tell Alanar where I am, and that he's not to worry about me. I'll be back by the evening meal. Auntie Rhexa says to come for dinner."

"I'll walk you to the door, anyway," Treesi said. She took his hand, lacing their fingers together. "Owyn, be careful out there."

"I'll be careful."

"Take your whip chain."

"Yes, Treesi," he said with a laugh. "You take care of me just as much as I take care of you."

"And for the same reason." She squeezed his fingers. "I love you."

They stopped in the entryway, and she stepped into his arms again. "It'll be all right, Owyn," she said into his ear. "You'll see. We'll be fine."

He nodded. "Keep telling me that, love. I need to hear it. I need to hear it until I believe it."

She shifted and cupped his face with one hand, kissing him deeply. "It will be all right," she repeated. "We'll be fine." She grinned and kissed his nose. "Now go, before it gets so late you're coming back in the dark."

CHAPTER TWO

O wyn still wasn't used to coming and going in Terraces. Leaving meant that he had to find a tunnel guide to take him through to the stables and then out. Thankfully, the first tunnel guide he found was Marik.

"Going to visit my ma?" Marik asked, smiling at Owyn. He pushed off from the wall where he'd been leaning and looked up. "The swallows say the winds are good. Warm up high. So it'll be a nice ride. Mind if I tag along?"

"Mind? Never," Owyn said, and meant it. He honestly liked Marik and enjoyed spending time with him. They started walking, with Marik taking the lead through the tunnels. Owyn stayed on Marik's right — despite Pirit and Jehan's best efforts to save it, Marik's left eye had been too badly damaged in Teva's murderous attack. He was still getting used to it to the loss, and the patch that he now wore.

"You're going to check and see if he's coming back yet?" Marik asked. "The winds have changed. It should be soon."

"Keep saying that, will you?" Owyn said. "Maybe it'll come true. Because Jehan won't answer me straight when I ask him."

Marik took a deep breath, and slipped his hands into his pockets. "He'll come back. He can't stay away. He's drawn to her like a magnet draws a compass needle."

Owyn snorted. "I like that. It's accurate."

"That being said, she's being a bit of a bitch," Marik continued.

"Hey!"

Marik shrugged. "She's my Heir. I do care for her. But she's treating you and Trees like dirt, and she's done worse than that to her Water." He turned to look at Owyn. "You told me you liked it when I was honest with you."

Owyn scowled. "I just...wouldn't have called her that. She's been through a lot—"

"We've all been through a lot. We've got a lot more to go before she takes the throne." Marik shook his head. "She'll get there, if she stops reacting and starts thinking again." He turned to Owyn again. "Uncle Jehan says she's a little spoiled. She's used to getting her own way. He told me about how they convinced her to learn to swim."

"She hasn't told me that story," Owyn said. "Neither did Aven."

"Aven threw her into deep water," Marik said. "And then had to save her when she panicked. He broke his own change cycle in doing it, and Uncle Jehan had to put him into trance because he was in pain."

Owyn stopped short. "You're telling me that Aven did to himself the same thing that Risha did? And it was Aria's fault?"

"Not quite what Risha did," Marik answered. "He hadn't finished changing from land to sea, and reversing it in the middle is painful. At least, Uncle Jehan says it is." He shrugged again, and started walking; Owyn hurried to catch up. "But what happened after is that Aria was so contrite over hurting Aven that she did exactly what they needed her to do. So..."

"So if she finally sees how badly she's hurting the people she loves, then she'll start thinking again?" Owyn asked. "And here I was thinking that yelling at her would be a bad thing."

Marik laughed, the sound echoing off the tunnel walls. "I don't think yelling will do it," he answered. "I think it's going to take a long, hard conversation."

Owyn nodded. "I...yeah, she has been avoiding me. Maybe that's why. All right. I'll sit her down when I get back. Tell her everything."

"If you need help keeping her in one place, I can be there," Marik offered. Owyn shook his head.

"I think this needs to be the Heir and her Companions. Me, Treesi and Aria. But thank you." He looked around. "We're almost there, right?"

"I'll make a tunnel guide out of you yet."

They reached the stables, and had to wait while horses were saddled for them. Owyn laughed when he saw his horse. "Freckles!" he called, and took the reins from the groom. He let the horse sniff him, then scratched Freckles' forehead. "They treating you nice, yeah?"

"He eats his head off," the groom says. "And doesn't like to be saddled. He'll work on a lunge, though, if he feels like it. And if there's an apple in it for him."

"Really?" Owyn clicked his tongue at the horse, watching Freckles' ear flick toward him. "Hey, behave yourself. And no fussing at the grooms. They're taking care of you."

"I think he misses you is the problem," the groom said. "Right, old man?" He slapped the horse on the shoulder. "He wants his man."

Owyn grinned. "Well, we'll have a good long run today, on the way back. What do you say?" He stepped to the side and swung up onto Freckles' back, following as Marik led the way on his own horse, a big gelding named Hurricane. They made their way through the tunnels and out into the sunlight.

"You said something about wanting a run?" Marik called.

"On the way back," Owyn called back. "I don't want him to strain himself on the way there."

"Fair."

They rode in silence for a while, then Owyn drew Freckles up next to Hurricane. "Marik, do you really think he's coming back? Really? You're not just saying it to make me feel better?"

Marik looked over at Owyn. "You know him better than I do, for all that I'm related to him. Yes, I think he's coming back. You don't?"

"I don't know," Owyn said. "I really don't. I...it broke him, I think. What happened, and then having Aria turn on him like that. It broke him. I don't know if he'll come back because I don't know if he can." He looked down at the reins in his hands. "He promised he'd be with me. With us. We promised each other, the three of us. And...she broke the promise."

"And now you feel like you're bailing a leaky boat."

"And my pail has a hole in it," Owyn added.

Marik grimaced. "Owyn, I can only tell you what I know. And from what I know of Aven, he'll be back. He just needs time to heal. The same way Aria needs time to heal. And when he comes back, that might be the thump that she needs to start thinking again." Marik shrugged. "Which is why I'm coming with you. He needs to get back here before she does something really stupid and alienates the entire tribe."

"You don't think she will, do you?" Owyn asked. "I mean...what would she have to do?"

"Not a lot, to be honest. Aria is walking on eggshells already, especially outside of Terraces where people don't know her, they just know that the Heir has wings. The word is getting out about her, now that we're not locked down. When I went for supplies the last time, they were talking about her down south in Cliffside. Mostly good, but there are still people out in the tribal lands that think that Air folk aren't human. Risha set those seeds in Terraces. And you've seen the results. It's like a strangle vine. You can pull it, but it keeps coming back."

Owyn let the thoughts churn around in his head for a while as they rode. They were just coming over the last ridge before the long trail down the sea and the village when he spoke again, "I'll talk to her when I get back. And...here's hoping we'll have some good news when we get to the village."

THERE WAS A CERTAIN rhythm to how things worked in an Earth village — even in a blended village like Serenity Bay. If you were there for reasons other than market day, you arrived, and were greeted by the highest ranking person — in this case, Marik's mother, Danzi. They welcomed you to the village, and you sat down with them for a welcome drink, usually a pot of tea. If the weather was fine, you sat outside, where everyone could see you. If the weather was foul, you sat in the visitor's hut, which had large, wide windows so that everyone could see you. While the water was coming to a boil, you discussed the weather, the state of crops or the height of the snow. While the tea was steeping, you discussed the advent of whatever season was next to come, and tallied births, deaths, and marriages. And when the tea was finally poured into cups the size of your average thimble, you made polite, nonsensical small talk until the pot was empty.

It was enough to drive Owyn to distraction. It was nothing like the way things were done in Forge, where you made decisions and agreements in the forge and sealed them on the Master Smith's anvil. Usually, he could contain his impatience long enough to at least enjoy the tea, but this time? As Danzi set the kettle over the flame, he cleared his throat.

"Could we...maybe not do the whole ritual today?" he asked. "It's...I don't know if I can sit still that long."

Danzi smiled. "I can tell. The kettle isn't the only thing coming to a boil." She took a seat across from him at the table. "What troubles you, Owyn?"

He took a deep breath, and the words came out in a rush, "Have you had any news? Any word from the deep water?"

Danzi folded her hands on the table. "Traders with gossip. Nothing more than sea foam, as my man would have put it. There's word of an army being raised on the waves. A war leader. But nothing that I can point to and say that this is certain. And I haven't heard anything that speaks of my nephew by name." She frowned. "I did hear that there was a canoe of Arana's line beached further up the coast. There's another village. Shadow Cove. It's about three hours ride north along the coast. Less than that by canoe, but I seem to remember you don't go by water?"

Owyn shook his head. "No, I don't. Three hours?" He'd have to overnight there, or come back in the dark. But if there was someone there from Aven's family canoe, someone who might have more news. Who could carry a message...

"You're going, aren't you?" Danzi asked. "I'll have something put together for you for the road."

"And tell Marik to go back. I'll go alone," Owyn said, still ordering his thoughts. "I don't want to worry them. I won't be able to make it there and back before dark. I'll have to stay the night."

"I'll send a letter of introduction with you," Danzi said. "I'll put it together now, so you can get underway. And I'll tell Marik to bring the message back. Do you want to leave a message with the traders that are here?"

"Yes, please," Owyn said. He looked up and smiled. "Thank you."

Danzi led him out of the visitor's hut and down to the shore, where there were several canoes, and a number of very large men. One of them glanced over, saw Danzi, and came toward them. He bowed slightly.

"Mother Danzi, we should be ready to sail with the tide. Thank you for your custom."

Danzi bowed her head slightly. "I've one more thing to ask you, Huri. To carry messages." She gestured to Owyn. "This is Owyn Fireborn, Companion to the Heir. He seeks to get a message to a son of Arana's canoe."

Something flickered in Huri's eyes. "To whom?" he asked.

"Aven, son of Aleia," Owyn answered. "If you'd be kind enough?"

"If I can, yes," Huri said. "What message?"

"That he needs to return to the Heir. We miss him, and we need him back. Stress the word 'need,' please, when you tell him? Maybe grab him and shake him?" He mimed shaking someone. "We need you back!" he said, and looked at Huri. "Like that?"

Huri grinned. "I'll do what I can. Mind if I don't shake him, though? If it's the Aven I've heard of, he'll put me on my tail."

"You've heard of him?" Owyn gasped. He looked at Danzi, who shook her head. "What have you heard?" he asked.

"Hunter. Warrior. Navigator. Right hand of the War Leader. Short temper," Huri answered. "If I can reach him, I'll tell him. But I won't shake him. I like living."

"If you've heard of him, then have you heard of Del, too?" Owyn asked.

Huri smiled. "Him, I've met. Del the Silent. Very canny trader."

Owyn grinned. "Really? I wouldn't have thought it of him. Well, tell him he needs to come back, too."

Huri nodded. "I'll pass the message on, Fireborn. As soon as I reach their waters."

Owyn offered his hand, and clasped the trader's wrist the way Marik had shown him. "I appreciate it. Can I do anything for you in return?"

Huri looked thoughtful for a moment, then shook his head. "If it's for the Heir, then there's nothing more I need. War Leader says we follow the Heir." He grinned. "We don't argue with the War Leader."

"Sounds like it might be painful if you tried," Owyn agreed. He let go of Huri's hand and looked at Danzi. "Thank you. Now, three hours north, you said?"

"Follow the coast road. Your supplies should be ready by now."

Owyn smiled. "Thank you." He headed back up toward where the horses were being tended to. Halfway there, Marik caught up with him.

"Three hours north?" Marik asked. "Why?"

"Because your mother said there was a canoe from Aven's family beached up in Shadow Cove."

"So you're going off to Smugglers Cove," Marik asked. "Just like that?"

Owyn stopped and turned to face him. "She said it was Shadow Cove."

"Shadow Cove is what's on the map. Smugglers Cove is what we call it," Marik said. "And that's because that's what it's been for years. So if there's someone from Arana's canoe there, then there's definitely something wrong. You're not going alone."

Owyn shook his head. "You're going back to Terraces. Someone needs to tell them where I've gone."

"We can both go back, and go to Smugglers Cove tomorrow. We'll be able to be better prepared—"

"And they might sail on tomorrow morning's tide, and I'll have missed the chance," Owyn said. "No, I need to go now. I'll be fine, Marik. But you need to go back so that Treesi and Alanar don't worry about me."

Marik frowned. "Not Aria?"

"Marik, I'm not sure she notices when I'm there. I don't think she'll notice if I'm gone."

Marik's jaw dropped. "She loves you, Owyn. She's just...mixed up."

"And that's why I need to go. So I have some chance of unmixing her before it's too late!" Owyn dragged his fingers through his hair. "I need to go. I've got my whip chain. I'll be fine. And if I don't come back by tomorrow night, then you can come looking for me."

"Because a trail that's two days cold is so easy to track," Marik grumbled. He rolled his eyes. "Fine. Be careful."

"I'll be careful," Owyn assured him. "Remember, I grew up on the streets. I can handle myself."

Marik snorted. "There are no streets here, Owyn."

"You know what I mean!"

"And I know you've gotten the shit kicked out of you, so be careful!" Marik shook his head, then squeezed Owyn's shoulder. "If something happens to you, Alanar will take me apart. You know that, right?"

Owyn grinned. "You're scared of Alanar?"

Marik looked confused. Then he nodded. "You haven't seen him really angry yet, have you? He's got the most patience of anyone in Terraces. Until he snaps. Yes, I'm scared of Alanar. If he wants to hurt you, you will know exactly what hurting really means."

Owyn blinked, completely taken aback. "We...we are talking about the same Alanar, right? He gets that angry?"

"It takes him a while, but yes," Marik said. "Teva used to tease him, back when we were all young. Alanar put up with a lot until Teva went too far. He set up a prank. If it had worked, Alanar would have gotten a bucket of muddy water dumped on him. But it got cold and the water froze, and Malani triggered it. She ended up in the healing complex with a broken skull. Alanar found out and got mad, and Teva learned the hard way that it's not a good idea to rile up a healer." Marik folded his arms over his chest. "Owyn, he broke both of Teva's arms. Just by touching him."

"What?" Owyn gasped. "He didn't!"

Marik nodded. "He did. He got into so much trouble with Gran. He said he'd do it again, too, if Teva ever tried something like that again." He frowned. "I don't think I could even imagine what Alanar would do if he ever got his hands on Teva now."

Owyn's eyes widened. "I...fuck. That's a scary thought. I've seen a lot, and I have no idea what he'd do. I can't even imagine what he'd do. That's scary."

Marik grinned. "Isn't it, though? In a good way. I don't have any clue what Alanar would do, but I'd love to find out." He shook his head. "But for now, I'll carry the message back. You go see what you can find out."

Owyn nodded. He held his hand out to Marik, and pulled the taller man in for a quick embrace. "You be safe," he said as he stepped back.

"You, too," Marik said. "Now go on. The sooner you get there, the sooner you'll be back."

CHAPTER THREE

It had been a long time since Owyn had last had three hours alone and silent. Working with Rhexa meant that he was meeting with people all day, and in the evenings, well...any house with Treesi in it was rarely quiet for very long. He hadn't been alone with his thoughts since...

Since they first got to Terraces. Since he'd left the house after arguing with Memfis. Since the last time he'd seen his father in the flesh.

Memfis was alive. He was certain of that. He wasn't sure where, but he was sure that Memfis was alive. Maybe he should add that to his list — find Memfis. It was a good idea, but he also wasn't sure of what would happen after he found Memfis. He wasn't sure if anything would be the same anymore. No matter how much he wanted it to be.

"Maybe it won't change too much," he said to Freckles, watching the horse's ears pivot toward him. "He'll grovel. I'm pretty sure he'll grovel. And...yeah, I'll forgive him. But it'll be weird after. Because I'll forgive him, but it's not like I can forget what he said." He scowled down at his hands, then looked up. No one on the road. Nothing but snow and gravel and birds overhead. "He needs to explain. That's what I need. I mean, Rhexa's ideas about him being afraid he was going to start drinking again make sense, but I need to hear it from him."

Freckles sneezed and shook his head, and Owyn grinned.

"Yeah, I'll deal with that when we find him," he said. "I've got bigger worries to deal with right now. I really don't know what to do about Aria." He fell silent, listening to the birdsong and the sound of the wind whistling through the cliffs. "I love her, Freckles, but I don't know how she feels anymore. I thought she loved me." When was the last time she'd told him that she loved him? He wasn't even sure anymore.

Had she ever, really? Or was it just that the Mother was pushing them together because there was no time?

"You know," he said to the sky. "If that was your plan, it failed miserably. We're not together anymore. We're not doing anything anymore. We're falling apart. We're supposed to be a whole. We're not. And we won't be until we have Aven and Del back, and until Aria changes her mind. So maybe you can help me out? I'm trying my best here, but nothing makes sense." He sighed. He'd danced, but his visions had been jumbled, as clear as mud. "I know my best probably isn't much," he continued. "But that's all I've got." He looked down at his hands, wondered if he should say anything else. If he'd said too much. If things were already too far gone.

No, there had to be something. There had to be something else he could do, something he hadn't tried. Something none of them had tried. Or maybe, something that someone else could try.

It all came back to the fact that the Companion bond had been shattered. And...who else could reforge it but a smith? He just needed all the pieces.

"Think we can go a little faster, Freckles?" he asked. The horse snorted, and picked up his pace.

TREESI LOOKED UP FROM her charting to see Aria in the door. She smiled. "I'm almost done. Come in and sit down."

Aria nodded and came into the charting room, taking the chair where Alanar usually sat. Alanar was currently in a conference with Pirit, and had told Treesi to go on ahead and get her charting started.

Treesi looked down at her paperwork, carefully wrote out the last few lines, then closed the folder and put it into her bin for the Senior Healer to review. She cleaned her pen, set it aside and corked her inkwell. Only then did she look across at her Heir. Aria had lost weight. That wasn't good, given everything. She looked pale, and there was something strange about her wings.

"Aria, are you losing feathers?" Treesi asked softly. She glanced at the door, then concentrated. No, there was no one within earshot. Good. "Is that...normal?"

Aria shook her head. "No. And yes."

"It's not normal to lose feathers, but it is normal?" Treesi frowned. "I don't understand."

Aria met her eyes, then looked away. "I am not losing feathers. I...I've been preening too much."

Treesi's eyes widened as she remembered something Marik had told her once about birds when they were under too much stress. "You're not pulling out your own feathers? Aria!"

Aria looked down, and her voice was quiet. "Treesi, I...I need to go."

Treesi got up, came around the table and knelt down next to Aria. "Go? Go where?"

"I need to leave," Aria whispered. "And...I need for you to come with me."

"What? Leave?" Treesi gasped. "And go where?"

Aria turned in her chair and took Treesi's hands. "We're going to Forge. To my grandmother. I need to be someplace where I can think. I...I can't do it here. I need to be away. I spoke to Jehan. He doesn't like it, but he won't stop me. And I need you to come with me because I need someone who I can trust."

"Are we all going?" Treesi asked. "You, me and Owyn?" Aria lowered her eyes. It answered Treesi's question more clearly than words. "You're leaving him behind? Aria, why?" She shook her head. "You can't. It's already hurting him so much that you've closed him out—"

"I know," Aria said softly.

"You're going to lose him," Treesi pressed. "You're going to lose him, too."

Aria shuddered. "I'm losing everything. Everyone. I'm losing myself. I...I need to find myself again. That has to be my first step. And I cannot do it here. I have to go." She looked at Treesi. "I asked him to trust me."

"He needs to know you still love him," Treesi said. "He's been trying to care for you. And you're pushing him away..." Her voice trailed off as she realized something. "Aria, you haven't told him, have you?"

Aria shook her head. "No. I wasn't sure..."

"I told you weeks ago!" Treesi protested.

Aria continued as if she hadn't heard. "Once I decided I needed to go, I knew that if he knew, he'd never let me leave his sight." She smiled. "He'd wrap me in blankets and smother me to protect me. And I can't do that, Treesi. I need to take a step back, and find my way again. Before I can't."

Treesi squeezed Aria's hands. "He's gone to Danzi's village, to look for news about Aven. You should wait for him to come back. Tell him. Tell him everything. He'll understand. He'll understand that you're scared. We're all scared. You can't just leave him in the dark. He'll shatter like glass if you abandon him. If we abandon him, since I'm going with you. Tell him what you told me. Tell him everything. And once he understands, if you ask him to, he'll let you go. He might insist on riding with us to Forge, but he'll leave you safe in your grandmother's house. That's more than I can do. I'm not a fighter. He's your warrior."

Aria looked thoughtful. She took a deep breath and pulled her hands out of Treesi's. "If he returns before we have to leave, I will tell him."

Treesi nodded and got to her feet. "All right. When are we leaving?"

"Tomorrow morning at dawn," Aria answered.

"Then we should go and get something to eat. You've got a long talk to have, and you'll need to sleep." She held her hand out to Aria. "Come on. Owyn made soup last night. I think there's still some left. You like his soup. And there's bread from this morning."

Gently, she coaxed and goaded Aria out of the healing complex and back to their house, making her sit at the table in the kitchen. There, Treesi added a log to the stove, and put the soup — a thick vegetable and grain stew — to heat. She cut bread and cheese, and set them both in front of Aria. "You're going to eat. You're not eating enough. If you don't eat, we're going nowhere."

Aria stared at the bread as if she'd never seen such a thing before, then picked it up and took a bite. A second bite. A third, and Treesi turned back to the soup, stirring it so that it wouldn't stick and scorch.

"Who is going with us?" she asked as she stirred the soup. "We aren't going alone, are we?"

"I don't know yet," Aria said. "Jehan said he would have riders go with us, but not who."

Treesi nodded, and started ladling soup into bowls. Maybe she could have a word with the Senior Healer and make sure that one of those riders was Owyn? It was a thought. She'd have to find him sometime tonight. Maybe she could ask Alanar to stay with Aria while she went out.

"Anyone home?"

The familiar voice echoed down the corridor from the front room. Treesi turned and looked at the door.

"Marik?" she called. "You're inside? We're in the kitchen!"

A moment later, Marik appeared in the doorway. "I've been looking for you," he said. "I went down to visit my mother with Owyn. She had some news for him—"

"What news?" Aria demanded. "What did she say?"

"That there was a canoe from Arana's line ashore up in Smugglers Cove. About three hours past Serenity. He couldn't not go. He asked me to take the message back to you, that he was going. He'll be back sometime tomorrow, he says."

"Tomorrow?" Treesi repeated. "Oh, but—"

"Thank you, Marik," Aria interrupted. "I appreciate that you came to tell me." She turned and looked at Treesi. "Is the soup ready?"

"Not...not yet," Treesi answered.

"Then I have time." Aria rose from the table, smiled at Marik, then left the kitchen. A few minutes later, Treesi heard a door close. And, no doubt, if she'd been closer, she'd have heard the click of the lock.

"I'm missing something," Marik murmured. "What just happened?"

"Possibly a disaster," Treesi answered. "Marik, if you would please go find the Senior Healer? I...I'm not sure what to do right now. I need to talk to him."

Marik looked over at the door, then stepped closer to Treesi. "What's happened?"

Treesi shook her head. "I just need for you to find the Senior Healer. Please."

Marik nodded. He closed his eye for a moment, then smiled. "He's outside. I'll be back in a few minutes." He turned and hurried out of the kitchen. Lacking any idea of anything else to do, Treesi went back to stirring the soup. She ladled it out into bowls, set them on the table, and sat down. She should probably call Aria to eat. But then she'd have to wait to talk to the Senior Healer, and she needed to do that now.

She heard footsteps, and Jehan came into the kitchen, closely followed by Marik. Jehan looked worried. "What is it?"

"Aria told me that she's leaving tomorrow morning," Treesi said in a soft voice. "That we're leaving tomorrow. I managed to talk her into waiting so that she could tell Owyn the truth. She was going to do it when he got back. But he won't be back until late tomorrow, and now I don't know what to do!"

Jehan looked startled, turning to Marik. "Where's Owyn?"

"He went north. Smuggler's Cove. Ma said that there was a canoe of Arana's line there, and he went after it."

"Arana's line? This close to shore?" Jehan snorted. "It'd never happen. She'd never allow it. Can you ride out? Bring him back?"

"Only if I want to be laid on my arse," Marik answered. "He's pretty set on going. Senior Healer, he's got it in his head that the only person who can fix what's ailing our Heir is Aven."

"He might not be wrong," Jehan muttered. He slumped down into Aria's abandoned chair. "You got her to agree to wait?"

Treesi nodded. "Maybe I can convince her to wait until Owyn comes back?" she said. "Jehan, if she leaves him behind, it'll kill him. He's already feeling abandoned, and she hasn't even left yet."

"Why is she leaving?" Marik asked. "And where is she going?" He frowned. "And who exactly is we?"

"Aria says she wants me to go with her," Treesi answered. "She said Jehan would pick riders. Can you...not?" She turned to the Senior Healer. "Can you tell her that we need to wait until the day after? Owyn will be back tomorrow!"

"No," Aria said from the doorway. "I am not waiting. I am going. I am leaving tomorrow. And if you do not come with me, I will go alone." She folded her arms over her chest. "I am already failing. I have already destroyed what I was set to do. Why would it matter if I turned away from all of you?"

"Aria," Jehan said, his voice gentle. "You haven't failed." He got up and went to her, resting his hand on her shoulders. "Aven is going to come back. He loves you—"

"And I broke his heart," Aria interrupted. "I was stupid, thoughtless, and heartless, and I broke his heart! He thinks I do not love him anymore, that I do not want him anymore. And he left me. He left his gem behind and he left me." She stepped back, away from Jehan. "I turned away from him, and from Del who has caused me no harm, because of something neither of them can control. Because of who they were born. It makes me no better than Risha. I need to go and be alone. I need to think. I cannot go back to my mountains, so I am going to my grandmother."

Jehan shook his head. "You're nothing like Risha. The fact that you're regretting your mistake now shows us that." He smiled slightly. "You didn't tell me where you were going. Or that you met Meris. I didn't even know she was still alive."

Aria smiled. "I like her. Very much. And I think I will be safe with her, so that I can think and best decide where to go and what to do from here. And if Aven returns while I am gone, he knows the way to come and get me."

Jehan took a deep breath. "You can wait a day. For Owyn's sake."

Aria shook her head, and spread her wings. Outspread, the places where there were feathers missing were very obvious.

Jehan's jaw dropped. "Aria!"

"I cannot wait," she said. "I have to go, before I damage myself beyond repair. You cannot make my feathers regrow, Jehan."

Jehan sighed. He held his arms open, and when Aria stepped into them, enveloped her in a tight embrace. "I didn't realize it was so bad," he said, just loud enough that Treesi could hear. "I'll make the arrangements. I do wish you'd wait, though. Just one night."

"I don't have the time anymore," Aria mumbled into his chest.

"Uncle?" Marik said. "I'll go with them."

Jehan looked over his shoulder at Marik. "I'm not sending you, Marik. You're not fully acclimated to losing the eye yet."

"I have eyes," Marik insisted. "If there are birds in the sky, I have eyes."

"And if you're attacked on the ground, you have no depth perception. You're still learning how to fight without it," Jehan countered. "I'm not sending you out to get hurt again, Marik. You're still not fully recovered." He shook his head. "You're staying here and training, at least until summer." Jehan turned, keeping one arm around Aria's shoulders. "Marik, I know you want to help. But getting yourself killed won't help anyone." He ran his other hand over his face. "I need to decide who I'm sending."

Treesi moved toward them and held her hand out to Aria. "The soup is ready, and you need to eat."

Aria followed docilely and took her seat, but didn't pick up her spoon. "I want you all to know something," she said. She didn't look up, staring at her bowl. "I have decided that it is best for me to take myself out of Terraces, and away from everyone, so that I can better recover from what happened and decide what next I must do. If there is no one to ride with me in the morning, I am still going to leave." She raised her head. "So there will be no juvenile 'I have no one to ride with you, so you must wait,' ploys to make me wait for Owyn, in the hopes that he will be able to talk me out of leaving."

"You're not being fair to Owyn," Marik protested. "He loves you. He just doesn't know how to help you right now."

"He's right," Treesi agreed. "If you leave him, I don't know what he'll do. He's getting more depressed by the day."

"He has Alanar," Aria says. "He seems to prefer Alanar's company."

"Because you won't spend any time with him!" Treesi snapped, and Aria jerked in shock. "You've been closing him out ever since Aven left. He's convinced that you hate him because he let Aven go. If you leave him now...you might lose him, too." She swallowed and looked at Jehan. "He's gotten so dark over the past months. I don't think he'll hurt himself, but you'll have to watch him."

Aria's face went pale. "He thinks that I hate him? And you're worried he might hurt himself?"

Treesi sat down. She buried her face in her hands and tried to collect her thoughts. Then she folded her hands on the table. "When you came to Terraces, it was very obvious to me that you and Aven were the center of Owyn's world. When we came to get you, when the storm was coming, and he found you were gone, he panicked."

Aria nodded. "He does that, yes. It is hard to calm him. You saw, after he fought with Memfis."

"I did," Treesi agreed. "And this time, he calmed himself. Because you needed him. Because you called him your warrior, and he needed to be that to save you. He is who and what he is now because you needed him to be that. He's a warrior, and yours to the tips of his fingers." She sniffed, and touched the brown and gold gem at her throat. "We all are. The Companions. You are our reason for being. And when you close us out, yes, it hurts. I'm not as bad as Owyn is, because he's had you longer. But you're pushing us all away, and Owyn isn't the only one who feels it. Do I think he'll hurt himself if you leave him behind?" She shrugged. "I've been watching him get more and more quiet, and nothing I can do brings him out. He brightens a little, for Alanar, but not much. And the rose...He worked for weeks on that. He started over twelve times, because it wasn't good enough. He told me that he hoped it would be enough. He didn't explain what enough meant, but when he gave it to you, and you smiled at him? It was like you gave him everything he'd ever wanted, all in a basket with fancy silk cushions." She met Aria's eyes. "And then you didn't talk to him for a week. You avoided him at the table. You didn't even touch the bread—"

"What does bread have to do with anything?" Marik interrupted. Treesi ignored him. She looked at Aria, and saw only confusion and hurt.

She didn't understand.

For a moment, Treesi wondered if shaking her Heir would be considered blasphemy. Instead, she closed her eyes and got up from the table.

"Eat your soup, Aria," she said softly. "If we're leaving in the morning, I need to pack."

She left the kitchen without another word.

SOMEONE TAPPED LIGHTLY on Treesi's closed door. She didn't answer, but they didn't leave. They tapped again. Then the door opened and the Senior Healer came inside. He closed the door behind him and stood with his arms folded over his chest.

"Why didn't you tell me you were worried about Owyn?" he asked softly.

"Because we were handling it, Allie and I," Treesi answered. She set down the tunic she had just folded. "When he was working, he was distracted. It was only really at night that he started getting dark, and we were handling it. And the closer we got to spring, the more hopeful Owyn got. Because Aven was coming back, and Aven would fix everything." She turned to face him. "Aven isn't coming back, is he? We're broken beyond repair."

Jehan shook his head. "I don't know, Treesi. I want to say yes, he is coming back. But there's never been any kind of test on the Companion bond before. Not like this." He took a deep breath. "I know my son. I know how much he loves Aria. I don't think he'll come back because she's the Heir. I think he'll come back because it's Aria." He snorted. "And is he ever going to have a surprise when he gets here!"

Treesi rolled her eyes. "Aven's surprise isn't the problem here. It's Owyn. He's fragile right now. When he comes back and finds we're gone, he'll shatter like glass, and I won't be here to put him back together. It'll be on Alanar." She frowned. "Where is he, anyway?"

"Mother had some specific training she wanted him to take," Jehan answered. "Which, knowing my mother, means that she's instructing him on the art of putting broken Companions back together."

"It might have been nice if she'd started that months ago," Treesi grumbled.

CHAPTER FOUR

Three hours, Danzi had said.

She hadn't considered the state of the roads. Or the lack of them — there was an entire section of the coast road that could only be called a road if you were being very, very generous. Owyn ended up backtracking, then leading Freckles over an area of rocky terrain that was entirely too close to the cliffs for Owyn's liking, and that left them both sweaty and shaking. They stopped for a rest then, and Owyn sat and ate some of the supplies that Danzi had sent with him, looking at his map. He wasn't looking forward to the ride back — maybe he'd be able to go further inland. He'd have to find out once he got to Shadow Cove.

In the end, it took Owyn nearly five hours to make the trip, and the sun was touching the horizon when he finally rode into the town. There was a welcome party waiting for him — he'd seen the sentries in the rocks, so it wasn't a surprise. He dismounted, and took the letter of introduction that Danzi had written from his belt.

"My name is Owyn Fireborn," he called. "I've come from Terraces. Danzi from Serenity Bay sent a letter." He held it up. "I've come looking for information."

A man stepped forward. "Fireborn isn't a common name," he drawled. "Only used in certain circumstances. One specific circumstance, if memory serves."

"Your memory does indeed serve," Owyn answered. He tugged his coat open, and pulled his scarf down to reveal the Fire gem at his throat. "This would be the one. I am Owyn Fireborn, and I serve the Heir to the Firstborn. Aria, daughter of Milon and his Air Companion Liara."

The man's eyes widened. "Well, looks like the gossip is running true for a change. Welcome to Shadow Cove, son. I'm Barsis, and I'm headman here. Let's go have us a drink, and I'll look at Danzi's letter." He gestured to one of the other men. "See to his horse."

"Freckles, you behave yourself," Owyn murmured to the horse, who snorted at him, then let the other man lead him away. Owyn followed Barsis. "Do you think we can dispense with the whole tea ceremony thing?" he asked softly. "I don't want to offend, but—"

"Tea ceremony?" Barsis interrupted. "Danzi's still doing that?" He laughed and shook his head. "No, lad. I'll give you something a mite more warming than tea to get the chill out of your bones, and you can tell me why you came all this way. We're not much on ceremony here in Shadow."

He led Owyn into a stone house with a low door. Inside was a single large room separated by hangings, surrounding a central fire-pit. Barsis gestured to a bench next to the fire-pit. "Have a seat. I'll pour, then I'll look at that letter." He picked a clay bottle up off the table and filled two cups, then handed one to Owyn and took the letter from him. Owyn sipped the drink, which proved to be a surprisingly smooth alcoholic something, and waited while Barsis read the letter silently to himself.

"Danzi says you're looking for information. What sort?" Barsis said as he lowered the page.

"Our Water went out to the deep for his season. It's nearing time for him to come back, but with the weather we've had, we're not sure where he's coming ashore. Danzi said that there was a canoe from his family line beached here. Arana's line?"

Barsis looked startled. "Arana's line? Son, you're chasing sea-foam. Arana's folk, they don't come to shore. And if the rumors are running true, Arana's gone back to the Mother these past few months."

"What, she's dead?" Owyn gasped. "Oh. I...we hadn't heard."

"That first big storm, from what I hear," Barsis continued. "I'm sorry to be the bearer of bad news. Now, what's your Water's name? Maybe I've heard tell of him?"

"Aven, son of Aleia. She was—"

"Waterborn before him. I know from Aleia," Barsis said as he picked up his own cup. "She wasn't but a little slip of a thing when I met her, though. Years and years ago." He nodded, sipping his drink. "Aven is her boy?"

"You've heard of him?"

"Heard he stands with the War Leader of the waves. Not sure how much of that I believe. War leader? Out there?" He nodded in the general direction of the sea. "It'd be like herding crabs."

Owyn snickered. "All I know from crabs is that they bite. I mean, pinch."

Barsis grinned. "Trust me. You can't herd them. And getting all the canoes out there to join under one War Leader? That's about the same." He shook his head. "Sorry you came all this way for nothing."

Owyn swallowed his disappointment. "Thanks. I couldn't not chase the rumor, though. If I hadn't come, the whole blasted canoe would have been here, wouldn't they?"

Barsis laughed, sounding like a braying donkey. "We'd have been up to our armpits in them! Good thing you did come, then. I'd have had no place to berth all of them!" He looked around. "This is the guest house, son. You're welcome to pass the night here."

"Thank you," Owyn answered. "I appreciate that. It wasn't the best road getting here. I'm going to need to know how to get back without using the coast road. It's gone in a few places."

"Is it, now?" Barsis frowned. "It's still too early for us to start sending trade goods down to Sanctuary and to Terraces. I'll send some runners out in the morning. There's another road. It'll take you further inland, and closer to the blasphemer's patrols, if any of them are out there. Sure you want to risk that? We can run you back to Terraces on a skiff."

Owyn fought back the urge to shudder. "I can't," he managed to say. "I can't leave Freckles. He and I have been through a lot. We'll be all right."

Barsis studied him for a moment. "Not a seaman, then?"

Owyn grinned. "No. Not a bit."

"I understand. I'll send a runner with you. Make sure to keep you clear of any patrols." He nodded toward the door. "Come and have some food. Folks will want to hear about the new Heir and her Companions. How many do you have?"

"Three of the four," Owyn answered. He finished his drink and stood up, following Barsis out to meet the rest of the village.

It was a small village, and they gathered around a central bonfire for a shared meal and news. Owyn told them about Aria, about Aven and Treesi. He told them about what had happened in Terraces, about Risha and Teva and their attempts to murder Aven and Aria. He told them that there was a new Senior Healer in the Earth tribe lands, and heard their murmured approval when he named Jehan.

"He's another one I met, back when he was still so new to his gem that he was uncomfortable wearing it," Barsis said. "Good man. But then, if you're called to a gem, you have to be a good man. Or a good woman. What's our Heir going to do now, Owyn?"

Owyn considered the question, and how to answer when he had no real idea. "We're waiting for Aven to come back from his season," he finally answered. "Then...once the weather turns, we'll see. We've a lot to do in Terraces before we leave there. The winter hit them hard, and we've been throwing in to help the people there before we move on."

"The winter hit all of us hard," someone in the crowd called. "How is she going to help us?"

Owyn looked around the fire, unable to tell who'd asked. "How have you been helping each other?" he asked in response. "Because...you honestly don't think that she's going to snap her fingers and everything is going to be wonderful and kittens and puppies and double-yolked eggs, now do you? She's the Heir, yes, but she still has to work to make things right. So do we all. And we have to do it together." He looked around again. "That's the problem with what Risha was telling people, you know. That there was something different about the people who didn't look like us. That they weren't even people. She doesn't want us working together. She wants Water and Air gone, and she doesn't care who she hurts or kills to do it. She's no better than Mannon. They want what they want, and fuck the rest of you, and anyone who gets in their way." He looked around, saw Barsis nodding slowly. "So we can't be like that. We need to be together, work together. Work with each other. We need to be the Mother's children, all of us. And that means helping each other. Don't ask me what Aria's gonna do to save you. Help her save all of us."

He jerked in shock at the cheer that went up around the fire, and stared for a moment before turning to Barsis. "What was in that cup you gave me?"

Barsis just laughed. "If that sort of wisdom was in any brew of mine," he said. "I'd be at the bottom of the keg every day. No, I'm seeing why you were chosen, Fireborn." He turned to look at the villagers. "He's right. We can't be looking just for ourselves. We have to look out for the others. For all of the others. If we're not fighting for all of us, then what are we fighting for?" He stood up, which seemed to be an unspoken signal — people started moving away from the bonfire, heading back to their homes. Barsis came to stand in front of Owyn as he stood up.

"You'll do just fine, Fireborn," Barsis said. "Come on. Mornings come early here."

"Are there any canoes ashore?" Owyn asked as they headed toward the guest house. "Anyone I can send a message out with?"

"Someone from Tersera's line," Barsis said. "He was going to leave with the morning tide. We can go over now, if you want."

For a moment, Owyn couldn't remember why that name was familiar. Tersera? Then the memory of the body in the cave came back in a rush. "I...yeah, I should talk to them."

"You've gone white as a sheet, son," Barsis said. "What is it?"

"Just...I'll have to pass on some bad news, too."

Barsis led him down to the shore, where Owyn could see a long canoe pulled up on the rocks. There were several people moving around the canoe, and as they approached, a woman came toward them.

"Barsis, we're good to sail with the tide," she said. She looked at Owyn and arched a brow. "Newcomer?"

"Visitor from Terraces," Barsis answered. "You've got a boy there, don't you?"

Owyn shuddered. "I...you're Virrik's mother?"

"His aunt, actually," she answered. "You know him?"

"Not...not really," Owyn stammered. "I...I know of him. From his roommates. They told me about him." He paused, looked down. "I...I'm sorry. I shouldn't be the one to tell you this. Virrik's dead."

"What?" the woman whispered. "What? How?"

"I..." Owyn swallowed. "He...he was killed. By Risha. Because he was Water. We...we found him. Our Water took him back out to the deep. We didn't know who he was, or why he was there, but...but Aven did what was right for him."

He looked up to find the woman staring at him. "Because he was Water?"

"You'd best explain, son," Barsis said. "What you told us at the fire. Tell Ketti."

Owyn nodded, and repeated what he'd told the others. He went into a little more detail about what Risha was planning than he had at the fire, and saw Barsis' face grow stern. When he finished, Ketti was silent for a long time.

"And what's being done about her?" she asked softly. "About this murderess?"

"When we catch her and her partner? They're the Heir's to deal with." Owyn cocked his head to the side. "Unless you want her? I think I can talk my Heir into letting you serve justice. But I get Teva, though."

Ketti blinked. Then she smiled. "That's very generous. Are you certain you can make that offer?"

Owyn shrugged. "Not entirely. Aria's really angry at Risha, for what she did and what she tried to do." When Ketti arched a brow, he added, "She tried to do the same thing to our Water that she did to Virrik. And, if you don't mind, I'm not going to tell you what that was. It was..." He stopped. Shook his head. "No. Not saying even that much. What I will say is that it took four healers working in tandem to save Aven. So trust me, Aria wants Risha's head on a plate."

Ketti's eyes had widened when Owyn mentioned how many healers it had taken to save Aven. "So be it," she murmured. "But if the Heir just wants the head, would she mind if I claimed some other parts?"

"You and she can discuss all the gory details later," Owyn said. "When I'm not around. Because I don't want to hear it."

Ketti laughed. "No stomach for it?"

"Nope," Owyn answered, shaking his head emphatically. Ketti laughed harder.

"So be it. We'll discuss it away from your delicate ears." Ketti looked out over the water. "He was given back to the deep, you said?"

"Aven did what was needed," Owyn answered. Ketti nodded.

"Thank you, for letting me know. I'll let the rest of the canoe know he's gone back to the Mother." She looked at him. "You didn't come all this way just to tell me he was dead. You had no idea I was here."

"No, ma'am," Owyn answered. "I came because I heard that there was a canoe from Arana's line beached here, and I was hoping it was Aven, or someone who could carry a message back to him for me."

"Arana's canoes usually stayed deep. They're not now, but I don't know if the new clan mother will go back to being quite so militant about it. I can pass on your message, when we get back to our waters."

"Tell him that it's time to come back," Owyn said. "That we need him. Please."

Ketti nodded. "I will tell him. Thank you, Owyn."

Barsis rested his hand on Owyn's shoulder. "Come on, son. You've got a long day ahead of you tomorrow, and you need to sleep. Ketti, I'll come see you off with the tide."

KETTI WAS GONE BY THE time Owyn was awake the next morning. He ate with Barsis, accepted a pack of food for the road from one of the village women, and set out with his guide, a young man named Gan. Gan didn't seem to be one for small-talk, which Owyn was grateful for. He wasn't in the mood to chat.

Aven had gone back to his family, not knowing that his grandmother was dead. Had the new clan mother welcomed him, or rejected him?

Had he even gone back to them at all? Why would he have?

Two people now had mentioned a War Leader. And that Aven was supposed to be working with whoever that was.

Was *Aven* the War Leader? The idea seemed ridiculous. But at the same time, he wasn't sure. Maybe Jehan would know.

"Fireborn, this is where I leave you," Gan said. "Take this trail straight south. It'll meet up with the coast road in a few miles, and head straight back to Terraces."

"So soon?" Owyn asked. "Where...we've come a long way, haven't we?"

Gan grinned. "You've had an awful lot on your mind. I understand. It must be hard, doing the Mother's work. I don't know if I could. But I can help this much."

"And I appreciate the help," Owyn said. "Ah...they packed more than I can eat. Have a bite before you ride back?"

Gan shook his head. "I've my own supplies. Thank you, but I need to check the coast road and see where you mentioned things were bad. Go well, Fireborn." He turned his horse back the way they'd come, and rode out of sight. Owyn turned Freckles to the south, and urged the horse on.

"We'll stop in a bit," he said. "Once we're on the coast road."

The roads met just where he thought they would — there was a small bridge over a stream that moved fast enough that it didn't freeze. He dismounted, and let Freckles drink, then dug through the pack that the women in Shadow Cove had given to him. In with the food for him, there was a small bag of grain for Freckles. They were just finishing when Owyn heard a horse approaching from the direction of Terraces. He looked at Freckles.

"Were you expecting someone?" he asked. The horse sneezed at him, and Owyn grinned. He packed the remains of his food into his saddlebag and took out his whip chain. Just in case.

The rider came into view, and Owyn tucked his chain away and waved. "Marik! What are you doing out here?"

"Looking for you," Marik answered. He sounded out of breath. "We expected you ages ago. And you told me to come looking if you were late."

"I didn't think I was that late," Owyn said. He looked up and frowned. "Well, maybe a little. Thanks for coming after me."

Marik nodded. "Come on. Let's get back before it gets too much later."

Owyn mounted his horse, and rode side by side with Marik. There was something odd about the other man, something...uneasy.

"What's wrong?" Owyn asked. "You're acting like you're ready for something to jump out at you and bite you."

Marik turned and smiled weakly. "Uncle said I wasn't ready to come out on my own. I should have listened. It's really strange not being able to see on my left. And the birds don't help as much as I thought they would."

Owyn nodded. "You don't know until you get out, though. Now you know what you need to work on."

"Yeah. Owyn..." Marik paused for a long moment, long enough that Owyn started getting nervous.

"What?"

"Owyn, I'm warning you now. You're not going to like what you find when you get back. And...we all tried to stop her."

"Stop her? Stop who?" Owyn's heart lurched. "Aria. What's she done?" He reined in Freckles. "Marik, if you tell me that she's dead—"

"No!" Marik gasped. "No, she's alive. But she's not in Terraces. She's left."

"She...she left?" Owyn repeated. "She's left? And left me behind?" Everything stopped. His breathing, his heartbeat. They all stopped, then started again in a strange cadence that just felt wrong. "Why? Why would she do that? Why would she leave me behind? I mean...I'm her Fire. She's my Heir. I'm her warrior. She said so. I'm supposed to be with her. I'm supposed to take care of her. She...she's not supposed to leave me!"

"Owyn—"

"No," Owyn interrupted. "No, she can't have left me. She can't. Who knows what's happening? Jehan?"

"He knows."

Owyn nodded. Then he kicked Freckles into a gallop. He heard Marik shout behind him, but he didn't care.

His Heir, his Aria couldn't have left him!

Could she?

CHAPTER FIVE

For the first time since he'd come to Terraces, Owyn made it through the tunnels from the stables to the healing complex without a guide and without getting lost. He doubted he'd be able to do it again — he didn't remember a single step he took from the moment he dismounted Freckles until he barged through the door into Jehan's office.

"Where's Aria?" he demanded.

The Senior Healer didn't look surprised to see Owyn. He gestured to the chair in front of his desk.

"Sit down, Owyn," he said.

"Fuck that," Owyn snapped. "Where is she?"

Jehan's mild expression turned stony. "Sit the fuck down, Owyn, and I will tell you," he snapped back. "I will tell you where, and why. But you need to listen to me."

Owyn blinked, shocked out of his fury. "I...don't think I've ever heard you swear before."

"Because I don't, usually," Jehan answered. "But you needed to hear it. Now sit. We'll talk."

Owyn licked his lips. He took his coat off and draped it over the chair, then sat down. "All right. I'm sitting. Where's Aria?"

"She and Treesi have left Terraces. And she asks that you not try to follow her. She needs time to think."

"That's what you and she were talking about yesterday, isn't it? You were trying to talk her out of going. And she wouldn't even tell me herself. But she took Treesi?" Owyn said. "She took Treesi, and left me behind, and she expects me not to go after her?"

"Yes," Jehan said. "Owyn, she needs to be out of Terraces, and out of sight." He paused. "She's been pulling her own feathers out. She's done some damage to her wings, and if we didn't let her go, she might never fly again."

"But you couldn't make her stay, or at least wait for me?" Owyn asked. "Why did she leave me behind?"

Jehan looked down at the tabletop. "Aria is feeling the weight of her responsibility. To us. To you. To everyone. And she's bowing under it. She's close to breaking. She's been hurt, and she's made some stupid mistakes. She needs to take herself out of the picture so that she can find her footing again, and start again."

"Why leave me, though?" Owyn demanded. "Why not let me help? I'm not Aven, I know that. But I love her, too."

"And she does love you, Owyn. She wants you to know that. But right now..." Jehan took a deep breath. "Risha did more than just try to maim her, Owyn."

Owyn went cold. "What? What happened? What don't I know?"

Jehan met his eyes. "Aria told me that the night she and Aven were taken was the first night they'd slept together. Because Aven didn't know how to put a contraceptive block in place."

"Yeah," Owyn agreed. "And they had that night because Risha—" He stopped. Stared. "Oh, no."

Jehan nodded. "Aria is pregnant. I've examined her thoroughly, and it appears that all Risha did was enhance her fertility. There's no other damage, and she'll bear a healthy child. Treesi noticed first, and she brought Aria to me. She thought that it might be easier for Aria to hear it from me." He frowned. "She didn't take the news well."

"She didn't want a baby yet," Owyn said. "Because it wasn't safe."

Jehan looked away. "I know. And when Treesi brought her to me, and I confirmed the pregnancy, I asked her if she wanted to terminate it. Because her reasoning is sound."

"You'd do that?" Owyn gasped. "But—"

"I know. It's my grandchild. But it's not my choice. It's hers. And...she won't. She wants this baby, because she is deeply afraid that she'll never see Aven again because he's completely rejected her. And at the same time, she doesn't want a baby. Any baby. Because she feels like she'd failed, and that she's only putting the child at risk. She's tearing herself apart, Owyn, and she knows it. What she has demanded, and what I had to agree she needed, is time to recover, and time to find her footing again."

Owyn closed his eyes. "Where is she?" he asked, opening his eyes and looking at Jehan. "Where did she go?"

Jehan hesitated. "She asked me not to tell you. But I'm not listening. She went to Forge." He held one hand up, and Owyn swallowed his protest. "Sending her to Forge was better than having her go back to the mountains. If she went there, we wouldn't see her for a year and half."

"What? Why so long?"

Jehan nodded. "Something non-healers and non-Air don't know about the Air tribe. It gets harder for Air women to fly when they're pregnant, and about halfway through a pregnancy, they lose the ability entirely. When an Air woman enters her final trimester, she molts. Flight feathers don't grow back in until after she delivers the baby."

Owyn frowned. "So she's gone back to Forge. To Lady Meris, I'm guessing? And...does she think I'm not going to follow her there? I know the way."

"She's asking you not to follow her," Jehan said. "Give her the time she needs. She'll come back."

Owyn shook his head. "Of course she will. Just like Aven will. Right? He's coming back?" He looked at Jehan, who didn't meet his eyes. "Are we done?"

"Tell me what you found in Shadow Cove?" Jehan asked.

"Another story about a War Leader on the waves. More rumors about Aven being part of that. And I met Virrik's aunt. So she knows he's dead." Owyn got up and picked up his coat. "Right. If you don't need me, I'll be..." He stopped. Frowned. "Someplace. I guess I don't really have any place I need to be now, do I?" he turned and walked out of the office. Out of the healing complex, and down toward Three Northwest. No one should be home...

He was wrong. Alanar was sitting in the front room, doing something with cording and beads on a tray balanced on his legs. He raised his head when Owyn came in.

"You're back," he said, and set aside the tray. "I was starting to worry."

Owyn made himself answer. "I'm sorry I took longer than I should have. The coast road is out, and it took a lot longer to get to Shadow than Danzi said it would. And...you know?"

"About Aria and Treesi?" Alanar nodded. "I know, blast them."

"What?"

"You're not the only one they didn't tell that they were leaving," Alanar said. "Pirit had me taking special lessons from her, and I didn't know that Aria and Trees were going until they'd been gone for hours. I came home at midday to an empty house." He rubbed his hands over his chest and stood up. "I could feel it was different, so I went back to the healing complex and found the Senior Healer. I've known...maybe two hours?"

Owyn took a deep breath and let it out. "Have you eaten?" he asked.

"No," Alanar answered. "I'm not all that clear on how you and Treesi set the kitchen up. You usually chase me out, anyway."

"Come on," Owyn said. "I'll make something for you, and we can talk. I need..." he paused. "I don't know what the fuck I need right now. Maybe just a shoulder to lean on."

"I've got two of those," Alanar said. He walked unerringly to Owyn, who took his hand. Alanar smiled and tugged Owyn into an embrace. "I'm sorry. I didn't know. I'd have told you—"

"Did you know Aria was pregnant?" Owyn asked. Alanar blushed.

"That, I did know," the healer admitted. "It's kind of hard to keep that a secret from a healer. But she's not my patient, and when I asked her, she said she'd tell you herself."

"Yeah, well, she didn't," Owyn snapped. He clenched his jaw, took a deep breath, and shook his head. "Sorry. That was uncalled for. I shouldn't be biting your head off."

"You can bite me if you need to," Alanar said. "Whatever you need. I'm fine with anything so long as it doesn't leave visible marks."

"What?" Owyn turned to stare at Alanar. "No! No, I'm not taking it out on you. Not at all. So stop that. Come on. Let's get some food."

"Have you eaten?" Alanar asked.

"Yeah, they packed a meal for me to eat on the road. But I can always eat again." He led Alanar into the kitchen and looked around. "I'm guessing no one went for today's allotment?"

"I'm guessing not," Alanar agreed as he sat down at the worktable. "I don't know."

"Right. Let me see what I can come up with." Owyn started rummaging through cupboards, pulling out staples. The stove was cold, and he rolled his eyes. "It's going to take forever to get a pot of water to a boil."

"Then come and eat with me?"

Owyn jumped, turning toward the door. Rhexa stood in the doorway. She wasn't smiling.

"I knocked, but I don't think anyone heard me," she said. "I heard you were back. And Jehan told me—"

"Did you know?" Owyn asked. "Did everyone know before I did?"

Rhexa shook her head. "No, I didn't know. Not until the tunnel guides came and told me, after they got back from taking Aria and Treesi through. I gave Jehan several pieces of my mind, and he said he'd explain once he spoke to you. I haven't seen him yet."

Owyn took a long breath. "Aria is pregnant. Risha didn't set the block like she said she was going to. She screwed around with Aria's body, and now Aria is pregnant. And scared. And not thinking. And...yeah, not thinking." He turned and looked at the stove. "And she's running away. She's gone. Treesi's gone. Aven is gone. Mem is gone. Everyone I have ever loved and trusted is gone, except for you two." He didn't turn. He *couldn't* turn.

They might not be there when he turned around.

He heard movement from behind him, and arms encircled him, holding him tight. "Oh, Owyn," Rhexa breathed into his hair. She didn't say anything else.

Really, what else was there to say, though?

"I don't know what to do anymore, Auntie," he murmured. "I can't...they're all gone. They didn't want me. No one wanted me. They needed me, but they didn't want me."

"That's not true."

"Then why didn't they take me with them?" he demanded. He turned, pulling out of Rhexa's arms. "Aria, she needs me. I'm her Fire. The Mother says I am part of this, and Aria doesn't get to say no. But she left me! She told me she loved me, and she left me! Aven said the same thing. He loved me. Where is he now? And Mem..." He shook his head. "I don't even know. Everything he told me about how much he loved me and how proud of me he was...and he thought I wasn't anything but a whore. And then he was gone, too." He snorted.

"About the only comfort there was that I know he didn't leave me willingly. He was took." He grimaced. "Taken. He was taken. But it's the same thing. They needed me. But none of them wanted me. If they wanted me, I wouldn't be alone now."

Rhexa sighed and folded her hands in front of her. "They'll come back, Owyn," she said. "Aria and Aven and Treesi. They'll come back. They do love you—"

"Really?" Owyn interrupted. "So this is how you're supposed to show you love someone? By abandoning them? I don't know a lot about how regular people show love, but I'm pretty sure that isn't it."

Rhexa shook her head. "I don't have any good answers for you, Owyn. I wish I did. Come and eat something, the both of you. Maybe we'll be able to find an answer or two after."

Owyn closed his eyes and rubbed his hand over his face. Then he shook his head. "Allie, you go. You haven't eaten today."

"What about you?" Alanar asked.

"I'm not hungry," Owyn answered. He looked over at the tall healer. "And I'm not really good company right now. Go on and get some food. I'll be here when you get back."

Alanar got out of his chair. "Will you?" he asked. "Because if you try to run off, Owyn, I'm going to follow you."

Owyn couldn't help it — he smiled. "I've heard about your temper. I'm not going to get you mad at me. You'll break both my arms."

Alanar's jaw dropped. "Who told you about that?"

"Marik," Owyn answered. "You scare the piss out of him."

Alanar started laughing. "He's funny. No, I won't break your arms." He grinned. "I'll break your legs. So you can't run away from me. So be here when I get back."

"Alanar!" Rhexa scolded. But she was laughing as she took his arm and led him out of the kitchen. Owyn took a deep breath, then looked at the stove.

"Well, we'll need a fire for later," he muttered, and knelt down in front of the firebox.

"OWYN?"

Owyn looked over his shoulder at the kitchen door. What was the Senior Healer doing here? "In here!" he called. He heard footsteps, and Jehan came into the kitchen. He stopped and smiled.

"Fresh bread?"

"Beaten biscuits. It's too late in the day for a real bake," Owyn answered. "They're just out of the oven, if you want one."

Jehan smiled and picked one up off the tray. "And making beaten biscuits lets you work out some of your frustrations?" he asked as he broke the biscuit in half. He took a bite and nodded. "Very good!"

"Thank you," Owyn answered. "And...yeah. I'm still mixed up about this. I don't understand how she can say she loves me and turn her back on me. I'm supposed to help her and support her, right? I mean, you're the one with experience here. You were a Companion."

"Under very different circumstances," Jehan said. He gestured to a chair, and when Owyn nodded, sat down. He finished his biscuit, then shook his head. "I can't see Milon ever turning his back on any of us. Unless you count that he died." He looked at the table top for a moment, then shook his head again. "No, don't try to compare Aria to her father. Milon never had to face the challenges she's facing. He never had the chance. If he'd survived? If we'd gotten him out of the Palace that night? Who knows? But for now, Aria is Heir, and she has to face, or not face, her own challenges."

Owyn nodded. He picked up a biscuit and joined Jehan at the table. "So what would you do?" he asked. "If it was your Heir?"

Jehan chuckled. "That sort of question calls for another biscuit." He got up, picked up another, then came back to the table.

"There's honey in the pot there," Owyn said, pointing with a piece of biscuit. "So? What do you think?"

Jehan dolloped some honey onto his biscuit and ate it slowly. He licked some honey off his thumb, then sat back in his chair. "I honestly have no idea," he finally answered. "I can't imagine Milon ever doing what Aria has done. I can't imagine Milon ever pushing us away the way Aria has done to you."

"Was Milon the Heart, too?" Owyn asked. "Or was there someone else?"

"You know about that?" Jehan asked. "Milon was our Heart. Aria isn't?"

"No," Owyn answered. "Aven is."

Jehan looked startled. "He is?" He frowned slightly. "I see why you're so intent on getting him back here, then. Yes, that's the right decision. And I wish I'd known that sooner. I'd have worked harder to convince him to stay." He nodded. "I think you're doing the right things in trying to get the message to him."

Owyn finished his own biscuit, tossing the last crumb to Trinket, who had come out from underneath the stove. "There has to be something else I can do," he said. "Something I haven't thought of, or tried. Something to fix this before it's too badly broken. Any ideas?"

"You're not giving up on her?" Jehan asked.

Owyn just stared at him. "If you think I'm giving up, even after everything, then you are out of your fucking mind. If you don't mind me saying so."

Jehan laughed. "I thought you'd say that. But I had to ask."

Owyn nodded. "I know. And...you understand. You get it. You've been there. And you had to walk away, because your Heir died." He licked his lips. "She's not dead. She's just...hurting. We're all hurting. Marik said it right. We've all been through a lot. But we have a lot more to go through before she's on the throne. We're...She's testing our temper."

"Aria?" Jehan asked.

"No," Owyn answered. The realization sat solidly in his bones. "The Mother. She's testing us, to make sure we're strong enough. She's testing our temper. Refining what She has to work with. Do you understand?" When Jehan shook his head, Owyn laughed. "Course not. You're not a smith. Look, you start with raw material. Full of impurities and all sorts of crap. You have to melt it down and refine it. Get all the garbage out. Melt it, work it, beat the shit out of it, and I do mean that literally." He paused, leaning back in his chair. "It's hard work, and sometimes it don't work at all, and you have to start again. Sometimes, you end up with something that shatters the first time you use it. Sometimes, though, it works. You end up with a tool that's stronger than when you started." He cocked his head to the side. "A tool...or a weapon."

"So you're being refined," Jehan said. Owyn nodded.

"We were the ore She had to work with," he agreed. "And we're still in the forge. She's making us into what She needs, but we're not there yet." He sniffed. "And She may have gone too fast. Same as I went too fast the first time I started Aria's rose—" He stopped. Jumped out of his chair and ran out of the kitchen and down the hall to Aria's bedroom. The door was open, and he looked inside to see that there was nothing on the nightstand but a vase, and the vase was empty. No gem. No pearl. And no rose.

"She took it with her!" he crowed, and turned to see that Jehan had followed him. "She took the rose with her." He grinned. "She does still love me. But right now, the Mother is working on her. So I have to do what I can to help."

"And that would be?" Jehan asked.

"Find Aven." Owyn frowned slightly. "Do you have a good map of the coast? A recent good map?"

Jehan looked almost perplexed by the question. "Yes," he said, drawing the word out. "Why?"

"Because I'm going to need to make a fair copy. And I'll need supplies. I'm leaving."

"You're what?" Jehan gasped. "Owyn—"

"I have to find Aven," Owyn repeated. "That's the only thing I can do to help, right? We both think so?"

"Yes, but—"

"But nothing!" Owyn insisted. "The only thing I can do is find Aven. And I can't do that here. All I'm doing is helping Rhexa take care of people. And that's a good job, but they're not the people I need to be taking care of. I need to be doing more to help Aria. Which means I need to find Aven."

Jehan sighed. Then he nodded. "Come to my office. We'll make a plan."

CHAPTER SIX

Owyn wasn't sure how he'd managed to acquire quite so many things in so short a period of time. They'd only been in Terraces a few months. How had he ended up with so many shirts? Then again, in the first few weeks here, he had gone through a lot of shirts. He sorted through them, putting the ones that would wear well on the road onto the bed, and putting the rest back into the chest of drawers. The same with trousers. He was sorting through socks when he heard Alanar shouting his name.

"I'm in our room!" Owyn called back.

Alanar appeared in the doorway, looking windblown and wild. "What do you mean you're leaving?"

Owyn stared at him in shock, then laughed. "I hadn't expected gossip to spread that fast. I only just made up my mind a couple of hours ago."

"Hadn't expected...the entire healing complex is talking about it!" Alanar exclaimed. "Malani told me when I finished my night rounds!"

"Is it that late?" Owyn asked, glancing at the windows. It still got dark early in the day, so he hadn't noticed how much time had passed.

"Owyn!"

"Right, sorry," Owyn said. He frowned, trying to get his thoughts in order. "Aria's gone, and there's nothing I can do to help her here. I can't follow her. If I did, knowing she didn't want me with her, I might break things even more than they are. Break them past mending. So I'm going north. I'll be carrying news from the Senior Healer to the Earth tribes along the coast, and I'll be visiting the blended villages and sending messages out to the deep. We need Aven back here. I can't fix things. He can."

Alanar leaned against the doorframe and folded his arms over his chest. "Going north takes you past the Palace. You'll be caught."

"Jehan and me, we planned out a route. After Shadow Cove, I head for the ruins of the old healing center, then swing east for a day. Then I head north past the Palace and go back to the coast."

Alanar scowled. "It's dangerous. You'll get caught." His frown deepened. "You can't go alone. I'm coming with you."

"What?" Owyn gasped. He stared at Alanar. "No! No, you're needed here. You're the only other full healer they have left."

Alanar sniffed. "They should have thought of that before they sent Treesi off. No, there's Pirit. And we have three new healers-in-training. They'll be fine without me for a little while."

"This might not take a little while, Allie," Owyn said. "It might take me months."

"And I'm not letting you go out there, alone, for months," Alanar replied. His lips twitched. "To quote someone who was threatening to drag me by the hair, you're all I have left."

"Oh," Owyn breathed. "Oh, Allie."

"She's gone," Alanar added. "They're all gone. You are all I have left here. If you leave too...I don't want to be alone, Owyn. I can't be alone. Not again."

"I don't want to take you into danger."

"Then don't go?" Alanar suggested. He smiled. "I know it's not that easy."

Owyn chuckled. "It's not. Can I touch you?"

"Do I ever say no?" Alanar answered. Owyn smiled and rested his hands on Alanar's waist.

"My plan—"

"You had one?"

"Hush, you," Owyn grumbled. "My plan was to go alone and fast. If you come with me, we'll need at least one guard to ride with us, just in case."

Alanar frowned slightly. "Why?"

"Because the last time I had someone I cared about alone out on the road, we both almost died," Owyn answered. "I'd like to avoid repeating that. If that's all right with you?"

"I am completely in agreement on not dying," Alanar answered. "I am still coming with you. We can ask Marik to come with us."

"Marik isn't cleared for guard duty yet," Owyn said. "And when he rode out to meet me today, he understood why. He's not ready to be a guard."

"So we'll get someone else, too," Alanar said. "It'll be good for him to get out—"

"No," Owyn interrupted. "Too large a group will be noticed. One guard. Not Marik. As much as I'd like him to come with us, he's not ready."

"So I am coming with you?" Alanar brightened. "What do I need to do?"

Owyn scratched the back of his head. "We need to get some appropriate clothes for you. Boots. Do you even own shoes, Allie? I've never seen you wear any, even when it's cold."

"I don't like shoes," Alanar admitted. "I can't find my way wearing them. I've tried."

"Ah. Well, you need boots if you're going to ride," Owyn said. He stopped. "You...can ride, can't you?"

Alanar grinned. "It's been a few years since I last had to, but yes. I'm not going to have a good first few days, I know that."

Owyn nodded and looked around. "All right. Let's see what you have in clothes, and we can go to the dispensary and get what you need. Then we'll sit down with Jehan and see what needs to be adjusted in my plans."

They went through the drawers again, with little to show for it. Alanar didn't keep much other than his healer uniforms, and had next to no clothing that Owyn thought would wear well on the road. He owned no socks and no shoes. Finally, Owyn took Alanar's arm and led him toward the door.

"We'll need to get everything new for you," he said as they headed out of the house.

THEY REACHED THE DISPENSARY just before they closed for the night. By the time they returned to the house, carrying two packed rucksacks, Rhexa was waiting for them on the front steps of the house. She got up as they came toward her.

"You're leaving?" she asked softly. "And you didn't tell me?"

"I haven't had a chance to yet," Owyn said. "Come inside." He led Alanar into the house, hearing Rhexa behind them. She closed the door as Owyn lit the lamps, then went to sit down on the couch closest to the fireplace, reaching into her pocket as she sat down. Almost instantly, Trinket appeared from out of the embers — the fire-mouse ran to Rhexa and took one of the tear-nuts that the woman held out to her.

"Auntie, you're going to make her fat," Owyn protested.

"I'm making her happy," Rhexa replied. She gave another nut to Trinket, then looked up. "Well?"

"Well, in a nutshell, there's nothing I can do here to help Aria. And about the only thing I can do is try to get word to Aven as soon as I can. So I'm going to go north, visit some of the blended villages."

"Alone?" Rhexa asked.

"No," Alanar answered, coming to sit down across from Rhexa. "I'm going with him. And we'll have a guard."

"You're going, too?" Rhexa looked at Alanar. "And here I was going to offer you a place to stay so you wouldn't have to be alone until someone came back. What did Jehan say about that?"

Owyn glanced at Alanar, then cleared his throat. "We...haven't told him about that part yet," he admitted. "I'm thinking he won't like it. We'll tell him in the morning, so he can figure out a guard for us."

"But it's not up to him," Alanar added. "I can stay or go as I want. And I want to go with Owyn."

Rhexa sighed. "I don't like the idea of you two riding off into danger. Even with a guard."

"Everything outside of Terraces is dangerous," Owyn pointed out. "Any time someone goes to Cliffside for supplies, or up to Sanctuary to trade, we run the risk of them not coming back." In the silence that followed his words, he realized the implications. Would Aria and Treesi even get to Forge? Or would Mannon's men find them? He swallowed and shook his head. "I can't just stay and do nothing!"

"I understand," Rhexa said. "What can I do to help?"

Owyn frowned, thinking. "We have everything we need for Alanar, except boots. Those will be ready tomorrow. I have to pack. Supplies and things are coming from the dispensary, and will be ready in the stables when we leave—"

"Which is when?"

"The day after tomorrow," Owyn answered. "I...can you take Trinket? Take care of her while I'm gone? She won't be a bother."

Rhexa looked startled, then looked down at the mouse on the floor. "Of course. And I know she won't be a bother, but will she stay with me? I don't want her to run off looking for you and get hurt."

Owyn considered the question, then went and sat down on the floor. Trinket ran to him and climbed up his trousers to sit on his knee. He gathered her up in his hands and ran one finger down her spine.

"Trinket, I want you to go with Auntie Rhexa," he said. "I'm going to be going away for a while, and you can't come with me. Not this time. You have to stay. You like Auntie Rhexa. She has a nice fireplace, and she feeds you tear-nuts. And it's just until I come back." He held his palm up so that he could see the mouse's obsidian black eyes. "Understand?"

Trinket stood on her hind feet, chittered at him, then jumped from his hand to his knee, and from his knee to the ground. She ran over to Rhexa, and jumped up onto Rhexa's trouser leg, climbing up to sit on her knee.

"I think she understands," Rhexa said, laughing. She offered Trinket another tear-nut. "Is there anything else I can do?"

"Keep an eye on Jehan?" Alanar asked. "He works too hard."

"That I will do gladly," Rhexa agreed. "And...what about the report you were working on, Owyn?"

"I'll give you all of my notes," Owyn said. "I was almost done. I should be able to finish the initial report tomorrow — there isn't much else to do since the supplies are coming from the dispensary. Then Marik can help you with determining which need to be repaired and which need to be replaced. He's already been helping me, when Pirit hasn't had him running errands for her. I'll talk to him tomorrow."

"And you should get some sleep," Rhexa added. "Never mind that the dispensary is handling your supplies, there's always a million things to do before you leave. Have you eaten anything since midday?"

"A couple of biscuits—"

Alanar turned to him. "You made biscuits?"

"Yes, and I can put something together for us. Auntie, stay?" Owyn got up off the floor. "It won't be much—"

"You'll be here," Rhexa said. She put Trinket down on the floor and rose to stand in front of Owyn. She hugged him, then stepped back, keeping her hands on his shoulders. "That's enough."

OWYN PUT THE LAST SHIRT into his pack, closed it, and cinched it tight. "That's it," he said. "Except for what I need for tomorrow and for when we leave, I'm packed."

"And we're definitely going?" Alanar asked. Owyn looked over to where the healer was sitting in the center of the bed, his long legs folded underneath him.

"How many times have you tried to talk yourself out of it?" he asked.

Alanar laughed. "How did you know?"

"Because I've been trying to talk myself out of going," Owyn admitted. "I mean, before I came here, I'd never left Forge before. And before yesterday, the furthest I've been by myself was Sanctuary. So yeah, the idea of leaving here is scary. I keep thinking I don't know enough." He took the pack and set it into the floor. "But there's no way for me to learn without actually doing it."

"If you only know the theory, you don't really know. You're guessing," Alanar said. "That's all a theory is, really. It's someone's best guess about how things work."

Owyn nodded, looking at the wall where his smoke blades hung from hooks. Should he bring them? Or would his whip chain be enough?

"Can you use a weapon?" he asked idly.

"I can use a staff," Alanar answered. "But it's been a while since I last practiced. Treesi used to work with me."

"She fights, too?" Owyn nodded. "That's good to know. All right. Do you have one, and I just don't know about it? I missed it somehow in the move?"

Alanar laughed. "No, I don't have one at the moment. My last one was...ah, let me see. About six inches ago. Maybe eight. I had my last growth spurt, and I never got a longer staff. I'll need to get used to having a longer reach." He shrugged. "I'm tired. Bed?"

"I need to wash up," Owyn answered. "Go ahead, and I'll be there in a bit." He walked out of the bedroom and down to the bathing room, where he stood at the basin and stared at himself in the mirror.

"I am not insane," he told his reflection. "I just need to do something. And going is doing something." He frowned. "I should dance. Tomorrow. See if there's anything I need to know before I leave." He washed his face, ran a comb through his hair, wincing as it snagged on knots. He'd let it grow longer than he'd ever had it before. Alanar liked it, but it would be harder to care for on the road. He should cut it short before they left.

Alanar's hair was going to be all kinds of fun on the trail. They'd have to braid it and keep it braided. Cutting his hair was not an option. Owyn looked at the mirror again, took a deep breath, and headed back to the bedroom. Alanar had turned down the bed and was lying on his stomach on his side, his head pillowed on his arms. His hair was spread out over his back and arse like a silken cape.

"I was thinking," Owyn started.

"Oh, no," Alanar intoned, and Owyn laughed.

"We're going to have to braid your hair and keep it braided while we're on the road," he finished.

Alanar lifted his head. "We could cut it—"

"No."

"It'll be easier to—"

"No."

"Owyn, be reasonable—"

"No," Owyn repeated. He climbed onto the bed and ran his hand over the long length of Alanar's hair, enjoying the feeling of the long length of Alanar beneath it. "I like your hair. We're not cutting it."

"It is my head, you know. My hair," Alanar pointed out. "Why do you think you get a say?"

"Oh, I know I don't have a say. I do, however, have an opinion," Owyn answered. "Your hair is beautiful, and I really don't want you to cut it." He ran his hand down Alanar's back again, trying to imagine the healer with short hair. The image just wouldn't come. "I can't think of what you'd look like without it."

"That's easily fixed, you know," Alanar said. He rolled onto his side.

"Only if you want me to cry." Owyn stretched out next to Alanar, resting his hand on Alanar's hip.

Alanar smiled. "No crying," he said. "Come here."

Owyn turned down the lamp, and they shifted around so that Owyn was lying with his back pressed against Alanar's chest. Alanar pulled the blankets up over them, then wrapped his arms around Owyn. Owyn sighed and tried to relax, but in the dark quiet of the room, broken only by Alanar's breathing, his thoughts wouldn't leave him alone.

"What is it?" Alanar murmured, his breath warm on Owyn's ear.

"Wondering if they found a good place to camp. If they're warm. If they're safe." Owyn sighed. "Thinking too much."

Alanar started to stroke Owyn's chest. "Do you want help with that? You need to sleep."

Owyn twisted to look over his shoulder, and was unsurprised when Alanar leaned over him and kissed him.

"Is that an official recommendation from my healer?" Owyn asked. Alanar chuckled.

"It can be, if necessary," he answered.

"Well, I always listen to my healer," Owyn said. Alanar burst out laughing, moving so that Owyn tipped over onto his back.

"I'll make sure to remind you of that the next time you argue with me," Alanar said as he leaned over to kiss Owyn once more.

OWYN WOKE UP WITH THE sun as usual, and gently slipped out of Alanar's arms and out of the warm bed. He shivered in the cold morning air and dressed quickly, heading out to the kitchen to start the day. He cleaned the fire box, raked out the ashes, and started the oven heating. Once the fire was burning, he went off and washed up so he could cook. He set a pot of water onto the stove to start heating, and pulled out his big bread bowl.

As he measured out his flour, Owyn stopped. This was the last time he'd be doing this for a while. He glanced at the crock that held his bread starter. If he let it die, it would be a waste of work and time. He'd give it to Rhexa. She liked his bread, and the starter was an important part of that. Rhexa would take care of it, and he'd have it back from her when he came back.

That settled, he turned his attention to mixing and kneading. He covered the bowl with a towel and put it onto the shelf over the stove to rise. He'd learned through trial and error with this oven that by the time the bread had been shaped and had risen the second time, the oven would be the perfect temperature to bake. And in the meantime, the water was hot enough to make tea. He set a pot to brewing, and walked out to the front room and opened the door to look outside. The skies were gray and heavy, and he smelled rain.

He looked up at the sky. "Well, I know You're in charge," he said to the clouds. "And we're all working to Your will, but if You wouldn't mind keeping an eye on them? Aria isn't all that fond of cold rain, so maybe keep it here, and not send it south? I'd appreciate it." He took a deep breath, then chuckled and shook his head. "I really hope You're listening."

He sighed, shook his head again, and stepped down off the porch. He needed to go get supplies for the day.

CHAPTER SEVEN

Owyn was just taking the bread out of the oven when Alanar came into the kitchen. To Owyn's surprise, he wasn't alone. Jehan was with him and looked furious.

"What am I hearing?" he demanded. "You're not seriously thinking of dragging Alanar along with you!"

Owyn put the baking tray down and tossed the towel he'd been using to protect his hands over his shoulder. "Why are you yelling at me?" he asked. "I'm not dragging him anywhere."

"I told you," Alanar added. "Going with Owyn is my own idea. He didn't want me to come with him. He didn't ask me. I told him I'm not letting him go alone." He folded his arms. "You can't stop me from leaving with him."

"I can stop the both of you from leaving, if I have to," Jehan replied. Then he sighed. "But I won't. Alanar, are you sure?"

Alanar's mouth quirked. "You know, for someone who can't see, I'm really good at seeing through people. You think I can't manage on the road, because I'm blind."

Jehan sighed. "I didn't say that. But it's a risk I don't think you should take."

"We'll be taking a guard," Owyn said. "And Alanar says that he can fight."

Jehan turned and looked at Alanar. "You can?"

"Staff," Alanar answered. "Pirit insisted we learn. I'm out of practice, but I was good enough to defend myself."

Jehan's brows rose, and Owyn bit down on a laugh. He looked as shocked as Owyn himself had been, and it was satisfying to know that he wasn't the only one who'd underestimated Alanar. He turned back to his bread, and to the pot of porridge that he'd set up to cook when he had put the bread in to bake. "Breakfast?" he asked, talking to no one in particular. "There's tea on the table. Porridge, and fresh bread. And Katrin had a fruit compote this morning when I went for supplies. That'll be nice in the porridge."

"Katrin makes good compote," Alanar said. He came up behind Owyn and slipped his arms around him, pinning Owyn's arms to his sides. "It all smells wonderful. Thank you."

Owyn tipped his head back and smiled up at Alanar, then nudged him gently with one elbow. "You need to move, Allie. I can't serve like this."

Alanar chuckled and leaned down. "Can't you?"

Owyn laughed. "You're insane. Food. Serve food. Go sit down."

Alanar leaned down and kissed Owyn on the tip of the nose, then let him go. "In here or the big table?"

"Since it's the three of us, the big table," Owyn answered. "If you're staying, Jehan?"

"Thank you," Jehan said. "I'll stay. Try to talk some sense into you both. What can I help with, Owyn?"

Bread was sliced, and porridge measured into bowls, and they all sat around the table in the front room to eat. Between bites, Alanar explained his reasoning — he wasn't going to be left alone again, not when the only person he had left was Owyn.

"I don't think I could bear it to not know what happened to him, if he didn't come back," Alanar finished. "I can't lose someone else, the way I lost Virrik."

"Oh," Owyn breathed. "I forgot. Allie, I met Virrik's aunt in Shadow Cove. The canoe that was there wasn't from Arana's line. It was from Tersera's. I told her, and she said she'd let the rest of her canoe know he was gone."

Alanar put down the piece of bread that he was about to eat. "I hadn't even thought about that, about making sure they knew. Was it Ketti? I've met her. I doubt she'd remember me, though. It was when they brought Virrik to start his training."

"Yeah," Owyn said. "I liked her. She's a bit bloodthirsty, though. Said that she understood that Aria wants Risha's head, but she wants whatever's left. I didn't ask why. I don't know if I want to know."

"To feed the sharks," Jehan said. "It's a Water thing. If you're given back to the deep properly, the Mother will find you. If you're fed to the sharks...well, the only thing She'll find is shark shit."

Owyn stared at Jehan for a moment, hearing Alanar hooting with laughter. "Really?" he gasped. "That's really what they do?" He started giggling. "That...that's perfect! That's the best thing I have ever heard. And no one deserves it more!"

Jehan smiled. "I thought you'd like it." He picked up his teacup and drained it. "Now, are you certain about this, Alanar? I really could use you here."

"I'm certain, yes." He reached over and rested his hand on Owyn's arm. "I'm going with Owyn."

Jehan sighed. "Then you probably have a lot to do before you leave. I'll leave you to it." He stood up and smiled. "Thank you for breakfast."

Owyn smiled in return. "When we get back, we can do it again."

Jehan touched his lips, then opened his hand to the sky. "Your words to Her ears," he said. "I'll see you before you leave. I'll have a map for you."

He turned and left, closing the door behind him. Owyn leaned back in his chair. "More porridge," he asked. "Another piece of bread?"

"No, I'm full," Alanar answered. "You wanted to dance this morning. Are you still going to?"

"Yes. I'll wash up, then get my blades and my book."

"Here, or the lowest terrace?" Alanar asked as Owyn got up.

"Down in the lowest terrace," Owyn answered. "We'll be less likely to be interrupted."

Cleaning up took no time at all. It was still quiet in the streets as they made their way down the stairs to the lowest terrace. The ground was cold and wet when Owyn took off his boots, and he tried to control his shivering as he walked out to the middle of an open grassy area. He looked over to where Alanar had taken a seat on one of the covered benches.

"I'm starting," he called.

"I'll be here when you come back," Alanar answered. Owyn smiled. He closed his eyes and started to breathe. Once. Twice. Thrice, and he began to move, the cold forgotten as his movements began to build up heat. He felt the stillness building...and then it dropped him, abruptly enough that he gasped and fell.

"Owyn?" Alanar called. "What is it?"

"I..." Owyn sputtered. He slowly got up off the ground and picked up his blades. "It didn't work. Let me try again." He shook his head, closed his eyes, and started to breathe—

This time, before he'd even let the full third breath out of his lungs, he felt himself being shoved. He staggered, then looked around.

There was no one else on the terrace. No one who could have touched him. He looked up.

"Really? I'm supposed to go in blind?"

"Hey!"

"Sorry," he called to Alanar.

"What's happening?" Alanar asked. He came over to Owyn. "Who are you talking to?"

"The Mother. Who apparently doesn't want me to see anything. She pushed me!"

Alanar blinked. "What?"

"You heard me. She *pushed* me!" Owyn looked up again. "There's something She doesn't want me to know. Not yet."

"Does that mean we shouldn't go?" Alanar asked. "If it's not safe for you to see—"

"I didn't say it wasn't safe," Owyn said. "I said She doesn't want me to know. Which means it's something that will change what I've decided to do." He frowned and scratched the back of his neck. "Mem told me that sometimes, if you're on the right path, you can't catch a vision. Because you're doing what you're supposed to be doing, and a vision might fuck it all up. I think I just ran into that."

"You think so?" Alanar asked. He touched Owyn's arm. "Are you sure you're all right?"

"Funny question, coming from you," Owyn teased. "Am I all right?"

"Your heart is racing," Alanar answered. "I think you're fine otherwise."

"I'm fine," Owyn said. "Not even a headache. Come on. Let's go to the dispensary and get your boots. We've got a lot to do today."

IT WAS ODD. NOT BEING able to find visions somehow made the decisions Owyn had made over the past few days feel more right. He tried to explain to Alanar as they walked to the dispensary.

"Now I know I'm doing the right thing," he said. "Because the Mother doesn't want me to change what I'm doing. It's just now I know it's not going to be easy. But I wasn't expecting easy. Nothing ever is."

"So, you're doing the right thing, and that's why you can't see anything when you dance?" Alanar asked. "That...I don't understand."

Owyn nodded. "Look, if I know what the hard part is that's coming, I might change what I'm doing, right?" He waited for Alanar to nod. "And if I change what I'm doing—"

"You're not going to be doing the right thing anymore," Alanar finished. "I understand. I think. That seems...petty. A warning of what's coming might be nice. Trusting you might be better."

Owyn shrugged. "I'm fine with this, Alanar. I know I'm doing the right thing. It's just...She doesn't want me to change what I'm doing. Which means that there's probably deep water in my future." He shivered. "Which...I know there's deep water in my future. Just not when. But if it's soon, then it's better that I don't know, so I don't fuck things up."

"You know you're not making any sense right now?" Alanar asked. "What does deep water have to do with anything?"

Owyn bit his lip. The only ones who knew about his waking vision were Memfis, Aria and Aven. "It's a Smoke Dancer thing," he answered. "If you really want to know?"

"You can tell me later," Alanar said. "Now, what are we here for?"

"Boots for you, and to make sure the supplies will be ready for when we leave tomorrow." Owyn led them into the dispensary. Katrin was behind the counter, and smiled when they came inside.

"Owyn! Healer Alanar! Good morning!" she called cheerfully. "The boots are ready. Healer Alanar, if you'll have a seat?" She disappeared through the door behind the counter, and Owyn and Alanar both sat down on a bench next to the wall.

"I just hope you're ready for me to be tripping over my own feet and walking into walls while I'm wearing these," Alanar said. "I can't tell where I am when I'm wearing shoes."

Owyn looked at him. "Is that just you, or all Air? I didn't think Aria had an issue with shoes, but she might not have told me."

"I think it's just me," Alanar answered. "I'm not sure. I've never met another blind Airborn. I don't have anyone else to whom I can compare my experiences. All I know is that if I'm barefoot, I can find my way around. If I wear shoes, I can't. I imagine it's very much how you would feel if you were blindfolded." He smiled. "We had a winter a few years back where we didn't have a lot of snow. We had freezing rain, and the streets were covered in ice. So, Virrik made me wear a pair of his boots. And then he had to lead me around because I kept getting lost. So we compromised. I wore the boots until we got to wherever we were going. Then I took them off." He shrugged. "We didn't go many places that winter. We were studying, so we stayed in a lot."

Owyn laughed. "Because between having to go out in the cold, and staying in with a book and a nice warm fire, I know what I'd choose."

Alanar smiled. "Nice warm fire. Nice warm someone to curl up with and read. Or not read. That was the winter before Treesi joined us and right after Virrik and I became a pair. So it was just me and Virrik. It was...nice. He had a good reading voice. Like you."

Owyn took a deep breath and laced his fingers into Alanar's. "I wish I'd had a chance to know him. Whenever you talk about him, he sounds pretty wonderful."

"Aven reminds me a lot of Virrik," Alanar said. "So you have a bit of an idea how wonderful he was."

Owyn nodded. "Yeah, he is pretty wonderful," he agreed. Then he sniffed. "He'd be more wonderful if he was actually here. Since we need him and all."

Katrin came back to the counter, then came around. She was carrying a pair of boots in one hand, and a pair of thick socks in the other. "Here we are. Alanar, they'll be a little stiff until you break them in."

Alanar smiled. "I'll manage. Thank you, Katrin." He held one hand out, and took the socks that Katrin handed him. He scowled for a moment, then sighed. "All right. Time for me to be clumsy." He tugged the socks on, then took the boots one at a time and put them on. He stood up, and visibly shivered. Owyn jumped to his feet.

"Hey, it's all right," he said. "I'm right here." He took Alanar's arm. "Katrin, do you have a staff? A good one for Alanar?"

Katrin looked thoughtful. "For walking or fighting?" she asked. "Or both?"

"Both," Alanar and Owyn said at the same time. Katrin laughed and went back through the door behind the counter. Owyn chuckled, and Alanar draped his arm over Owyn's shoulders.

"I'll get used to this," he said. "While we're on the road. I'll need some help, but I'll get used to it."

"Whatever you need, Allie," Owyn said. He leaned into Alanar's side. "We'll make it work."

He squeezed Owyn gently. "I won't slow us down."

Owyn reached up and took his hand. "I never thought you would."

KATRIN RETURNED WITH a heavy staff that Alanar pronounced to be more than adequate. She promised that all of their supplies would be ready for them in the stables at dawn the next morning, and wished them well. Owyn led Alanar back out of the dispensary, and they started for home. They went slowly, their pace set by Alanar, who used the staff to test where he was going to put his feet before he took a step.

"As soon as we're back to the house, I am taking these off," Alanar grumbled before they were halfway to the marker for Northwest.

"You might want to leave them on, so you can get used to them," Owyn suggested. Alanar growled at him, and Owyn coughed and fell silent.

"I'm sorry," Alanar murmured. "It's just...I can't tell where I am or what's around me. I don't like it."

Owyn stopped. "All right. You take them off when we get home. And you can take them off when we're on the road, when we stop to rest for the night. But you have to have them on when you're riding."

Alanar nodded. He leaned heavily on his staff, then sighed. "Maybe I shouldn't go with you. I'm not going to be much help."

Owyn rested his hand on Alanar's arm. "You have until tomorrow morning to change your mind. And if you change your mind, I won't blame you. You can stay with Rhexa while I'm gone. She'll love having you."

Alanar smiled slightly. "I don't want to stay behind," he said as they started walking once more. "But I don't know how I can help you."

"You'll keep me grounded," Owyn answered. "You'll keep me from getting so wound up I can't think. You'll listen to me and tell me when I'm making sense and when I've lost my mind—"

"Which is most of the time."

"Fuck you very much, thank you," Owyn answered cheerfully. "And having you with me will keep me from pushing too hard or doing anything stupid. I take care of other people. You and Treesi both told me that. I'm not very good at taking care of myself. If you're with me, it won't be just me. It'll be us, and I'll have to think about what I'm doing."

Alanar was quiet as they turned onto Northwest. He didn't speak again until they were near their own house. "So you need me to come with you so you have someone to take care of?" he asked slowly. "And so that someone can take care of you?"

Owyn considered it, then nodded. "Yeah, that's what I'm saying. If I can take care of you, then I'm not going to push myself until I fall over. Because if I fall over—"

"You can't take care of me. And if you do push, then I can take care of you." Alanar chuckled. "That's really weird logic. Owyn logic. But I can't argue with it. All right. We're going. We have to get the map from Jehan. What else?"

"You should go say goodbye to the children, and to the healing assistants. They're probably hearing all kinds of rumors." Owyn frowned. "I'll finish that report I promised Rhexa. I should spend some time with her."

"When are we going to practice?" Alanar asked.

"After we're done with our errands? That way, you have time to put me back together once you take me apart," Owyn answered. Alanar laughed.

"You have a lot of faith in me," he said. "Are we home? I want to take these blasted things off."

CHAPTER EIGHT

Owyn spent the rest of the morning with Marik, finishing his assessment of which houses were unlivable. Marik seemed quieter than usual, taking notes but offering little in the way of opinion or advice. Before they were an hour in, he was starting to suspect that Marik was angry at him. By the time they settled into one of the covered benches in the lower terrace to go over their notes, he was certain. Owyn looked down at his ink-stained fingers and his book of notes before turning to Marik. He was on Marik's left, on the side where Marik now wore a patch. He couldn't tell what Marik was thinking. He bit his lip and decided it was better to clear the air.

"So...you've heard?" he said. "And you're pissed at me?"

"I understand why you're going," Marik said softly. "And...I know Alanar well enough to know he won't stay behind. No, I'm not angry at you, Owyn. I...I'm angry at me. At the Mother. At everything else. Because I want to go with you and I can't."

"Alanar wanted you to come with us," Owyn said. "You were his first choice for a guard. But you said you weren't ready."

"And I'm not. That's why I'm angry. I should be out there with you. I should be doing something to help the Heir...and I can't." Marik reached up and touched the patch over his left eye. "I loved him, Owyn."

"Teva?"

"Yeah. He knew it, too. He knew I'd drop anything to spend time with him, that I'd spend the night under his roof if he asked it, even though I hate being inside. He knew that I'd let him do just about anything to me." He turned and looked out over the sea. "He used that against me. He used me. And I failed my Heir because of it."

"You didn't," Owyn said gently. He rested his hand on Marik's arm. "You didn't fail. It wasn't your fault. I don't think anyone knew the real Teva. Not you, not Treesi, not anyone. We all trusted him. He betrayed everyone."

Marik nodded. "I know that. I know it...but it doesn't sit well. Because it means...." He shook his head. "It means I was a fool. And that really doesn't sit well."

"Oh, I know that feeling," Owyn murmured. "I know what it's like. When it happened to me, I ended up a slave." He snorted. "And then he tried to kill me, too. So I do understand where you're at right now."

Marik twisted in his seat. "What?"

Owyn smiled. "It's a long story. Short version? I was a whore. One of my regulars decided he wanted me all to himself. He got me arrested. I was sold as a slave, but not to him. Mem bought me. And Fandor kidnapped me. He tried to kill me. I killed him first."

Marik looked thoughtful. Then he nodded. "All right. So you're ahead of me on that last part. "

"By killing the man who tried to kill me? Yeah, but you'll catch up." He grinned. "I mean, if you want to. I'd be happy to do it for you, if you wanted. Or we could give him to Virrik's people. They'll feed him to the sharks."

Marik coughed. "You know about that? How...never mind. Aven, I guess?"

"Jehan," Owyn answered. "We were talking about Risha. Do you think that feeding sharks that much poison will hurt the sharks?"

Marik opened his mouth, then he chuckled and shook his head. "There isn't much in the deep that can hurt a shark," he answered. "They're not even afraid of water cats. Maybe the big wolf-singers—"

"The what?" Owyn asked.

"You...no, of course you wouldn't know. They live really far out in the deep. We don't see them much this close to land, except for further up north. They're big, really big." Marik held his arms wide. "Black and white, my father used to tell me. And they have rows and rows of teeth like razors. They hunt like wolves, and they sing to each other underwater."

Owyn frowned. "You sure he wasn't telling you stories to make you go to sleep?"

Marik grinned. "I don't think so. Maybe. My father was a joker. You can ask Aven when you get him back. He'll know. And then we'll both know."

"I'll put it on the list of things to ask him."

"Before or after you fuck him senseless?" Marik asked, his voice low. Owyn burst out laughing.

"Well, I'm not asking him during!" he wheezed. "If you're doing it right, you shouldn't be able to think straight, let alone have a conversation about singing fish!"

Marik started to giggle. "Is that what I was doing wrong?" he asked.

Owyn shook his head. "You're insane."

"So are you," Marik answered. He looked back out over the water. "I wish I could go with you. But I'll do what I can here. Take care of people while you're gone." He turned and tapped the book Owyn held. "I'll finish this, too."

"Thank you," Owyn said. "I was hoping you would. I was going to ask."

"It's important. It'll keep me busy. And...it'll help me not think." He took the book from Owyn. "I need to work on learning to fight again. Learning...how to do everything again."

"Did you ask Alanar?"

Marik shook his head. "I thought about it, but it felt odd, asking him how to handle losing one eye when he lost both." He shrugged. "I'll manage. I'll learn. Maybe by the time you get back, I'll be more comfortable with leaving." He grinned. "Which makes no sense. Once you get back, why would I leave?"

"You know we're not going to stay, right?" Owyn asked. "Once we have Aven back, and Aria and Treesi. And Del. Once we're all here, we have to move on to our next step. Whatever that is." He scratched the back of his neck.

"Once everyone is here and we know what the next step is, I'll take it with you. I'll be ready then," Marik said. His voice was very firm. "It gives me a goal. Something to work toward." He stood up, taking the book from Owyn. "Come on. Let's go see Rhexa."

Owyn nodded, then asked, "Do you know how to use a staff, Marik?"

"Yeah, why?"

"Then you should come by the house," Owyn said, following Marik back toward the stairs. "Alanar needs to practice with his staff. You could help."

"And maybe get a feel for fighting again?" Marik asked. "That's...not a bad idea. All right." He looked quizzically at Owyn. "Do you fight staff?"

"I know how to fight with my smoke blades, and I can use a whip chain. But that's not the same, and the last time I used the whip chain against someone with a polearm, I ended up almost getting beheaded."

"I remember that," Marik said. "Is that how they got you?"

"Yeah." Owyn sighed. "Here's hoping I never have to do that again."

"Don't hope. Prepare for it. Know how to counter it," Marik said. He frowned. "I don't fight polearm — it's different from staff. I don't know who does. But you should find someone and practice."

"That's not happening before tomorrow," Owyn said. "I'll just be careful, now that I know it's an issue." He frowned. "Maybe I should bring a crossbow?"

"Can you use a crossbow?" Marik asked.

Owyn frowned. "It's...you aim and fire, right? How is that hard?"

"You really have no idea," Marik said with a grin. "Right. We'll go down to the training ground and I'll show you."

THEY DELIVERED THE notes to Rhexa, and Owyn invited her and Marik to eat with them that night. Then they went and found Alanar, who had already returned to the house.

"What are we doing?" Alanar asked when Marik told him to get his staff.

"Marik is showing me why using a crossbow is harder than I think it is," Owyn answered. "And he wants to try fighting again. I thought maybe practicing with you would help you both."

Alanar nodded. "All right. As long as I don't have to wear boots. Let me get my staff."

"Boots?" Marik asked. "You've got him wearing boots?"

"Only when we're riding," Owyn answered.

"I didn't think anyone would ever get Alanar to wear shoes or boots. He hates them." Marik looked around the front room. "I'm stepping outside, if that's okay?"

"I'm surprised you came inside," Owyn admitted. "We'll be right out."

Once Marik had gone outside, Owyn headed to the bedroom to collect his own weapons. Alanar was standing in the middle of the room, holding his staff. He turned as Owyn came in.

"So I'm practicing against Marik?" he said softly. "Why?"

"Just what I said," Owyn answered. "You need to practice, and he needs to see that he can still fight. He'll be better than me to go against, because he knows staff and I don't. Not really. Smoke blades aren't a staff, and I don't want to try whip chain against you. I might hurt you."

Alanar smiled. "So it's not just for my benefit?"

"Only half for your benefit."

Owyn's answer made Alanar laugh. "You sure you didn't get any healing?" he asked. "You're good at it. The talking part, anyway."

"You were there when Pirit tested me," Owyn countered. "Not a drop. But talking, I'm good at that. And caring for people—"

"Is just something you do. I know." Alanar smiled. "All right. Let's go."

They walked out to find Marik sitting on the ground in front of the house, his hands folded. There was a large, black bird sitting on his knee — a larger one than Owyn was used to seeing. The bird's thick beak looked sharp, and was as long as Owyn's thumb.

"Who's your friend?" Owyn asked. "Can we come closer?"

"He's a northern bird, and yes, you can come closer," Marik answered. "He's a long way from home. He belongs up in the foothills, where it's colder." He looked up. "Aria would have known him — her folks train them and keep them as hunting animals the way we would keep dogs."

"A shadow hawk? I've heard of them. He is a long way from home, then," Alanar said. "Can he live here?"

Marik shrugged one shoulder. "It'll be warmer than he's used to in the summer, but I think so. He'll be able to hunt, and he's told me he likes fish. He should get on all right."

"Just tell him to leave Trinket alone, all right?" Owyn asked. Marik grinned. Then he nodded.

"He won't eat the brightly colored thing," he said. Then he laughed. "He wants to know if it would taste good, though."

"No," Owyn answered. "Absolutely not. Trinket tastes terrible. Tell him that."

Marik laughed harder, nodding to show that he understood. The bird fluffed its feathers and made a harsh noise, then flapped its wings and flew off. Owyn turned to track the bird as it flew up to the roof.

"He said something rude, didn't he?" he asked. Marik dusted his hands off and got up, still giggling.

"Umm...yes. He's smart. Smarter than I'm used to in a bird." He looked up at the bird and grinned. "I like him. I told him how to get home, if he wants to leave. But I hope he stays." He turned to look at them. "Ready to go practice?"

They headed into the caverns below Terraces, down to where Pirit had hidden her army. There were still people living down in the caves, and it was still the best place to store weapons and extra supplies. And the best place to train — there was no need to worry about wind or weather when you were inside a bubble cave. He and Alanar waited at the practice field while Marik went to the armory.

"Are you ready for this?"

"I should see if I still remember how," Alanar answered. He hefted the staff and walked out onto the field. Owyn stayed by the gate and watched as Alanar picked the staff up. He didn't hold it the way that Owyn had seen other staff fighters do — instead of holding the staff in the middle, Alanar held it near one end, angled down across his body. He stood still for a moment. Then, with no warning, he lunged, stabbing the staff forward like a spear. Owyn caught his breath — a lunge for someone as tall as Alanar, and with a staff that was equally as tall, meant that he could strike someone at a greater distance than Owyn could reach with his whip chain. Alanar recovered, twisting slightly, the staff moving in front of him. Blocking, Owyn realized. Holding the staff that way meant that all Alanar needed to do was move slightly, and he could block a blow from any height.

"Oh, he's practicing?" Marik said from behind Owyn. "Oh...he hasn't forgotten much."

"I've never seen anyone use a staff like that," Owyn said without turning. He couldn't look away — Alanar was just too interesting to watch. "I'm used to people holding it in the middle. This is a lot more flexible."

"I've seen people fight your way," Marik said. "Most of them learned it from someone Fire, or lived in one of the Fire and Earth villages in the eastern mountains. Further east, they fight that way, too. But this is how we learn it here. It might have some Air influence. I don't know."

Owyn finally made himself look over his shoulder at Marik. Marik was holding a staff in his right hand, and had a crossbow in his left. He set the crossbow down to lean against the fence, and stepped through the gate. "Alanar?"

"I thought I heard you," Alanar called. He stopped, leaning on his staff. He wasn't even breathing hard.

"I thought you said you were out of practice!" Owyn called. Alanar laughed.

"I'm alone in here," he said. "Against an opponent?"

"You're going to leave me all over the sand," Marik said. He moved to the middle of the ring and picked up his staff. Then he frowned. "This is going to be interesting."

"Why...oh." Alanar nodded. "You're right handed. So you'll be putting your left side forward."

"And that's the side I can't see on," Marik agreed. "Take it easy on me, will you?"

Alanar nodded. "Of course. I'm not going to make more work for myself."

"Oh, fuck you!" Marik laughed.

"Promises, promises." Alanar raised his staff. "Any time you're ready. I'll defend."

Owyn leaned on the fence and watched them. Alanar moved slowly, smoothly, countering Marik's hesitant attacks, slowly gaining speed as Marik grew more sure of himself.

"There you are."

Owyn turned and smiled as Jehan walked over to him. "We didn't sneak out, if that's what you were thinking."

"I wasn't thinking it," Jehan said. "I was wondering where you'd gone to practice. I thought you might be on the low terrace."

"Marik said here was better, and he wants to show me how to use a crossbow." Owyn nodded toward the fighters. "He's getting more comfortable."

Jehan studied Marik and Alanar for a moment. Then he nodded. "I'll work with him. I'm out of practice myself." He snorted. "Twenty-five years out of practice. I don't even know if I remember how to hold the staff!"

Owyn heard the crunch of a footstep on gravel, and glanced over his shoulder to see that Pirit had come to join them. She stayed in the caverns most of the time, despite Jehan making sure that she had a house of her own. She told them that after so many years living below ground, she couldn't get used to living in a house again. It was too noisy. Owyn rarely saw her, except for when she helped in the healing complex. He smiled at her. She returned the smile and came closer, resting her hand on his shoulder.

"I hear you're leaving us," she said. "And taking Alanar with you."

Owyn nodded. "I need to find Aven. I made up my mind to go. Then I went vision hunting, and got shoved out—"

"Oh," Pirit breathed. "So you're on the right trail, then. And I was going to try and talk you into staying."

"Wait, what does that mean?" Jehan asked.

Pirit looked up at her son. "It means that the Mother doesn't want him changing his mind, so She's not showing him what he'll be facing. He's going to do the right thing, but it won't be easy."

"It's never easy," Jehan grumbled. "Mother, once Alanar leaves, I'm going to need more help—"

"What about Treesi?" Pirit asked. Owyn blinked, then looked at Jehan.

"You didn't tell her?"

Jehan glared at him, then turned back to his mother. "Treesi has gone to Forge with Aria. Aria needs time to recover, and she can't do it here."

Pirit's brows rose. "I...see. And this has what to do with her pregnancy?"

"Everybody knew about *that* but me," Owyn grumbled.

"She didn't tell you?" Pirit looked at Jehan. "Did you know that Aria was keeping secrets?"

"Not that one, no," Jehan admitted. "She told all of us that she'd tell Owyn herself."

"You're saying she has other secrets?" Owyn asked. Jehan shook his head.

"I'm saying, right now, that Aria is breaking under the strain. I'm hoping that by letting her do what she feels she needs to do, and by having Treesi with her to support her, that she'll recover."

Pirit sighed. "I wish you'd told me. I'd have gone with her. She should have someone...more experienced with her."

"Treesi will do just fine," Owyn protested. "And Aria's more inclined to trust her Earth."

Jehan looked at Owyn, then back at Pirit. "He has a point. But now...now we're going to be short-handed."

"Because Alanar won't stay behind if I leave. He's insisting on coming with me," Owyn said. "Which is why we're doing this." He gestured at the practice field, where Marik had stepped back to readjust his grip on his staff. "Marik is helping Alanar get back into practice."

"And Alanar is helping Marik understand how to function with one eye," Pirit added. "This is a good thing. Is that what you're out of practice with, Jehan? Staff?"

"Yes," Jehan answered. "Not much call for it on a canoe."

"You'll remember," Pirit said. "And he'll be fine."

Owyn glanced at her. "Which he?" he asked.

She smiled. "All three of you. You will all be fine." She squeezed his shoulder. "If I don't see you before you leave, good hunting."

CHAPTER NINE

"There isn't nearly enough sleep in the world to justify being awake this early in the morning," Alanar grumbled.

Owyn yawned. "We could have gone right to sleep, you know," he answered.

"Our last night in a real bed?" Alanar asked. He took Owyn's hand as they walked toward the caverns that led to the stables, where Marik had promised to meet them. "I wasn't letting that go to waste."

Owyn laughed. He was tired, and after last night, he wasn't looking forward to being in the saddle for most of the day. But since Alanar hadn't ridden in years, they'd have an excuse to stop early. At least, that was the excuse he'd use when he said they were stopping early. His goal for today was to reach Shadow Cove. That was far enough, and would give him an idea of how well Alanar could ride. If all went well, then tomorrow, he'd push. The map showed only one coastal village between Shadow Cove and the ruins, so maybe they could make the ruins to camp tomorrow night. But if they weren't up for that much riding tomorrow, then tomorrow night their goal would be that coastal village, and they'd make the ruins the day after.

"You're not even listening to me, are you?" Alanar asked, poking Owyn in the arm and bringing his attention back.

"No, sorry," Owyn admitted. "I was thinking of where we might be spending the night tonight and tomorrow. Just thinking of the next step. Mem was always after me to pay attention to the next step."

"You're paying attention to about six steps on," Alanar pointed out. "We have to leave first. Let's worry about getting on the road." He squeezed Owyn's hand, then stopped walking, letting Owyn's hand fall as he changed his staff from his left hand to his right. He resettled his bag on his shoulder and grimaced. "I'll have to put these on soon, won't I?"

"You have to wear boots to ride," Owyn reminded him.

"I know," Alanar agreed. He shifted his staff back to his left hand, and took Owyn's hand in his right. "I just don't have to like it."

Owyn sighed. "I know. We're going to stop at Shadow Cove today, so you have a chance to get the feel for riding."

"That's not far," Alanar said. "It's...what? Only three hours past Serenity?"

"The coast road was out when I rode that way, so we're going inland. So it'll take a few hours more than you think. Going from Serenity over the coast road, I didn't get there until sunset, and you know about when I left here."

Alanar nodded. "All right. You know where we're going. I'm clearly not the one navigating."

Owyn chuckled. Then he waved. "Marik!"

"You two seem awake," Marik called as they walked toward him. "Are you ready?"

"No," Alanar answered. "But we're going. Who is riding with us? Do you know?"

"Not me," Marik answered. They started walking through the caverns. "Garrity and Evarra, I think."

Owyn nodded. He knew them both — they were two of Pirit's hand-picked fighters. "All right. And what did you decide about giving me a crossbow?"

"Well, Garrity and Evarra will both have theirs, so you really don't need a third one. But I decided that you're not likely to kill yourself with it," Marik answered. "Or kill anyone else, for that matter. Not without a lot more practice. However, I did put one in with your supplies, and extra quarrels. Don't use it unless you absolutely have to, make sure that anyone you care about is behind you before you fire, and try to control the recoil."

Owyn nodded. "Right. Here's hoping I don't have to use it."

They entered the stables, and Owyn saw Garrity and Evarra talking with Jehan, who had his back to them. Garrity nodded, and Jehan turned. He frowned.

"Where are your smoke blades?" he asked.

Owyn shook his head. "I'm not bringing them," he answered. "I thought about it, and they make me stand out. The only person who uses smoke blades is a Smoke Dancer. It's been outlawed for...I dunno. Longer than I've been alive. I don't want people looking too closely, or deciding that it might be worth turning me in as an outlaw. I have my whip chain."

Jehan frowned. "That's your only weapon?"

"I have a crossbow!" Owyn answered.

"Which he's not really all that good at using yet," Marik added. Jehan rolled his eyes.

"You're going into dangerous territory," he growled.

"I know that," Owyn replied. "And I know that if I make a target of myself, it'll be that much more dangerous for all of us. So I'm not doing that." He tugged down his scarf to reveal his bare throat. "I left my gem here, too."

Jehan's jaw dropped. "I...you shouldn't—"

"Why shouldn't I?" Owyn countered. "I'm not going to lie to myself and say everything is going to be fine and wonderful. I know I'm walking out of the only safe place left in the world. And I know there's something out there that would make me change my mind and not go, if I knew what it was. That's why the Mother won't let me see what's coming. So I know I have to go, but I'm going to take every precaution I can. Like leaving behind things that make me stand out too much."

"And I won't?" Alanar asked.

"Nope," Owyn answered. "Because we're going to tell people who get nosy that you're my husband, that we just got married, and that we're going north to visit your family in the Solstice village and bring them the news."

Alanar looked startled. "When did you think of that?" he asked.

"Last night," Owyn answered.

Alanar coughed. "Last night. Really," he repeated. "Then I clearly was doing something wrong."

Marik burst into laughter. "More information than we needed, Alanar!"

Owyn reached over and took Alanar's hand. "I woke up in the middle of the night and couldn't get back to sleep," he explained. "I didn't want to wake you up, so I thought about ways to cover what we were doing to anyone outside the Water villages. Any objections? I mean, if you don't want to be married to me—"

Alanar shook his head. "Stop that. You're a perfectly fine husband, even if I only get to borrow you for a while." He smiled, raising Owyn's hand to kiss his knuckles. "Maybe I can ask Aria if it can be more than a while."

Everything stopped. The entire world stopped. Owyn's breathing stopped. His heart stopped. Everything just...froze. Then it all lurched into motion again, like it had been kicked by a mule. "I...what? What?"

Alanar's smile faltered. "I...I'm sorry. Was that...too...I don't know. Owyn?"

"No, no, no," Owyn sputtered. "Stop. Just...stop." He swallowed. "You...just asked me to marry you. Did you mean to do that?"

"Yes, I did, Owyn."

"Me. Marry me. Can you do that? I mean...me?" He looked at Jehan. "Can he do that?"

"Alanar, you broke him," Marik murmured. Owyn scowled at him, then looked at Jehan, who looked completely bemused.

"I don't see any reason he can't, Owyn," he answered. "Is there something I'm missing?" He frowned. "Oh, I see where the problem is. Yes, Companions can marry. And no, you don't need Aria's permission."

Owyn looked up at Alanar. "Did you know that?" he asked.

"I didn't," Alanar admitted. "But it's nice to have confirmation. And...do you think you can answer? Because I'm terrified that now that I got up the stones to ask you, you're going to say no."

"You've been planning this?" Owyn squeaked.

Alanar's face turned red, and he idly reached down and picked up the end of his braid. He started playing with it as he answered, "Ummm...yes? I was going to do it for Turning, but I got scared and didn't. I have a pledge bracelet, even. Trees picked it out for me. I put it in my pack, so I have it with me. I thought...maybe I'd be brave enough..."

"Treesi knows? And she doesn't mind?"

"She told me that she expects me to share, that you're a Companion and you need to be there for the others, too. And honestly, I'm fine with that. I knew it before she said anything. You have your responsibilities as a Companion," Alanar answered. "I just want...permanent. I want to belong to you. With you. Because I love you."

Owyn stepped back and covered his face with his hands. Married? Him? He couldn't...could he? Could he? "Yes. Yes, I'll marry you." He looked up over his fingers. "I said that out loud, right?"

The pure joy in Alanar's face was all the answer he needed.

Their departure was delayed slightly by celebration — Marik ran off to get Rhexa, so she could hear the news directly from Owyn. She surprised them all by bursting into tears and throwing her arms around Owyn. He patted her on the back and looked around for help until Jehan took pity on him and took charge of Rhexa.

"You can't be gone too long now," she said, smiling through her tears. "We have a wedding to plan. Oh, Owyn! I'm so happy for you!"

Finally, Owyn helped Alanar to put on his boots and to mount his horse, a gentle gelding named Meadowfoam. Meadowfoam was connected by a leading rein to Freckles, who danced underneath Owyn, more than ready to be off. Garrity and Evarra mounted their own horses. Their packhorse, Owyn was amused to see, was Anvil, the packhorse that had accompanied them from Forge.

"Are we ready?" he asked.

"No," Alanar answered. "But we're going anyway. You have the map?"

"I have the map." Owyn looked down at the hammered silver bracelet that Alanar had given to him and insisted that he wear. "I need to find one for you," he said.

"A map? It won't do me any good," Alanar said.

"No!" Owyn laughed. "A pledge bracelet. When we get to Shadow Cove, we'll see what we can find. It'll be temporary, though. I'll make you a real one when we get back."

Alanar's face turned pink. "You'll make it? Really?" He smiled. "I don't need a temporary one. I can wait for one you make for me."

"I want you to have one now. And one later." Owyn reached over and took Alanar's hand. "I am going to spoil you rotten. I just want you to know that."

Alanar smiled. "You already do, love. You already do."

Owyn laughed and turned around, looking back at Garrity and Evarra. "You two ready?"

"We've been ready," Garrity answered. "Let's go."

Owyn nodded, and they rode out through the caves and into the sunshine.

THE RIDE WAS QUIET, and Owyn spent a good portion of it bemused. Marriage was the last thing he'd ever expected would happen to him! He wasn't exactly the sort of man anyone — man or woman — looked for in a husband. After all, who would want someone who was a failed thief, a former whore and a freed slave?

But he wasn't only that. He was a Smoke Dancer, too. And a smith. And he was a Companion. And...Alanar wanted him. Even knowing about Owyn's time on the streets, Alanar loved him and wanted something permanent with him. Loved him enough to ignore his past. No, that wasn't right. Alanar loved him enough to accept his past, the way that Aven and Aria and Treesi did. But there was no Mother Goddess forcing Alanar to that choice. Alanar had made that decision all on his own.

And he understood that Owyn still needed to be there for Aria and Aven and Treesi. That any promises they made to each other included supporting their Heir and the other Companions, included Owyn's love for the others, included Alanar's responsibilities as a Healer.

"You're very quiet," Alanar said. "And your pulse is racing. Second thoughts?"

"No," Owyn answered. "Not a single one. Which is sort of strange for me. No, I'm just wondering why you're so calm. You know I'm going to be in Aria's bed at some point. Or Aven's. You already know I've been in Treesi's—"

"Because Treesi's bed is our bed," Alanar pointed out. "Owyn, why shouldn't I be calm? I knew all of this before I asked you. I knew all of this when I bought that bracelet." He smiled. "I know

I'm technically marrying a married man, for all that the Companion bond isn't the same as marriage. I know that Aria has to come first, and I'm fine with that. You have so much love for all of us. I'm not worried you're going to run out." He shrugged. "There will be times when my patients come first. You know that."

"Yeah, I know," Owyn agreed. There had already been nights when Alanar had been called away for some medical emergency or another. He was a healer, so his patients came first — they had to. And someday, Alanar might even be Senior Healer. Jehan certainly thought of Alanar as his successor, and treated him accordingly. If that happened, then the entire Earth tribe would come first. Owyn looked at Alanar, and realized why he wasn't worried. Why Alanar wasn't worried. Because the both of them knew that when they stood in front of all their friends and family, and swore to each other, they would be promising to support each other in their responsibilities, no matter what.

"I understand. We're going into this knowing we both have other people who need us," Owyn said. "That sometimes, we're going to be busier with other things. We know that there are going to be times when we're sleeping alone. Or with other people. And we're both all right with that. I think we'll do just fine."

Alanar nodded. "Exactly. We're not saying marriage instead of. We're saying marriage in addition to. Each of us needs...a focal point. Someone to lean on, and we're promising to be that to each other."

Owyn smiled and reached across to take Alanar's hand. "Focusing on. Leaning on. Loving—"

"In all meanings of the word," Alanar interjected, and Owyn laughed.

"Yes, in all meanings," he agreed. "Do you need to stop? We'll be halfway fairly soon."

"I could stretch, yes." Alanar turned his head. "And eat. I'm hungry."

Owyn nodded and turned to look over his shoulder. "Stopping up ahead!" he called.

They dismounted at the fork in the road where the rider from Shadow Cove had left Owyn, and Owyn helped Alanar over to a rock where he could sit and take off his boots. Owyn sat on the ground at his feet and unfolded the map, studying the road, judging how far they had come, how far they still had to go.

"How are you feeling, Allie?"

"A little stiff, but not bad," Alanar answered. "Surprising, actually. I wonder if I'll be able to move tomorrow?"

Owyn chuckled. "I'll rub your legs tonight."

"And the rest of me, I hope?"

"And the rest of you," Owyn agreed. He leaned back against Alanar's legs. "We're making very good time. We'll be at Shadow Cove long before dark at this rate." He tipped his head back. "Do you want to eat now?"

"Please. What do we have?"

Owyn got up and went to help Evarra unpack their meal, bringing back a water-skin and two heavy rolls. "Stuffed rolls, I think. Not sure what they're stuffed with." He resumed his seat at Alanar's feet and handed one of the rolls to him. "And I have a water-skin. There are late apples if you want anything else."

Alanar grinned. "I think I know," he said. "Katrin makes these amazing travel rolls — minced meat and dried fruit. They're wonderful, and they keep well on long journeys." He took a bite and smiled as he chewed.

Owyn examined his roll and took a cautious bite. The filling was a savory mix, held together with a thick paste that might be considered gravy if it was thinner. "I want this recipe," he mumbled around a mouthful.

"She won't share," Alanar said. "People have been asking for years."

Owyn chuckled. "It never hurts to ask." He leaned back against Alanar's legs, then looked up. "You've had these before," he said. "When did you go on a long journey?"

Alanar tipped his head back, closing his eyes as the sun shone on his face. "After my mother died. My father took me north, to the Solstice village. I met my mother's flock for the first time, and we stayed there for a year. Fa thought it would help me. And I went back after the fire, after Fa died. They're the ones who taught me to use my air sense to tell where I am."

Owyn nodded. He leaned his head back against Alanar's knee, and closed his eyes as Alanar started finger combing his hair. "We can go," he said. "When this is all done. When it's time for me to take my season, we'll go and visit your family."

"I was actually hoping we could go to Forge," Alanar said.

"Nothing that says we can't do both," Owyn answered, sitting back up. "Go north, visit with your family. Go south, and you can meet my grandmother. Well, my sort of grandmother. We're not really related at all." He finished his roll, picked up an apple and put it into his coat pocket. He'd feed half to Freckles before they got moving again. The other half would go to Meadowfoam.

"Your grandmother. That would be Meris?" Alanar asked. "I'd like to meet her. She sounds wonderful."

Owyn nodded. He took a deep breath, tipping his head back again. Alanar started petting his hair again, and Owyn sighed, letting Alanar's touch relax him.

"You're going to fall asleep if I keep this up," Alanar said softly.

"You're right," Owyn agreed. "I am. We should get back on the road." He got back to his feet and stretched, then stood in front of Alanar, close enough that their knees touched. He cupped Alanar's cheek with one hand, then kissed him. Alanar smiled, running his hands up Owyn's sides. Then he sighed.

"Help me with my boots?" he asked.

CHAPTER TEN

They cleaned up their resting place, and got back on the road, riding into Shadow Cove long before the sun was touching the sea. Owyn slid down from Freckles' back and smiled as Barsis came toward them.

"Well, hello there!" Barsis called. "And what brings you back so soon, Fireborn?"

Owyn laughed and clasped his hand. "This time, it's a personal trip," he answered. He held his wrist up, showing off the bracelet. Barsis' eyes widened.

"Well, congratulations!" he gasped. "That's a blessing in dark times. Who's the lucky one?"

"That would be me," Alanar called. "Wyn, help me down?"

Owyn went to help Alanar dismount, then held his arm and escorted him over to Barsis. "Headman Barsis, may I introduce my pledge, Healer Alanar of Terraces? We're heading north to break the news to his family."

"Break the news? Really?" Barsis blinked. "Alanar. The blind healer?"

Alanar arched a brow. "I'm known?"

"We've heard your name, Healer. It's an honor. Ah...will you be—?"

"Give me an hour to settle, and I'll see to your village," Alanar answered with a smile. "Of course. You needn't have asked."

"You never know, Healer," Barsis said with a shrug. "There's some that claim to be, and don't follow the old ways."

Owyn glanced at Alanar. "You've had a healer through here?" he asked slowly. "You didn't mention that."

"Didn't think of it. Back before the winter, it was," Barsis answered. "She and her man came through, stayed a night, then went on." He shook his head. "I can't remember her name, but she claimed the healer's right to shelter, then didn't see to the village."

"Risha," Alanar whispered. "She was here."

"Risha?" Barsis repeated. "The Senior Healer? The one that you told Ketti did for her boy?" He spat, swore violently, then spat again. "That wasn't the name she gave us. But it must have been her. And I harbored her here? Gah, I should have told you!"

"There wasn't any way you could know," Owyn said. "Do you know where she went?"

Barsis shook his head. "North. I heard her say they were going north. Other than that, she didn't say nothing. They stayed in the guest house, didn't come to the evening meal. Left at first light. Weren't what you call friendly, you know? And like I said, she didn't honor her end of the bargain. Now I understand why."

"They stayed in the guest house?" Alanar grimaced. "We're going to sleep in the same bed?"

Owyn looked at him. "I already slept in that bed," he said. "Might want to dip me in whatever you use to clean the surgical instruments."

Barsis chuckled. "It's not the same bed, nor the same guest house," he said. "The roof of the old guest house caved in under the snow. Until we repair and rethatch the roof and make a new bed, we've moved any guests to stay where you stayed the other night. Not that we have many guests." He smiled. "That is my house. So you're in my bed."

Owyn blinked. "Then...where are you sleeping?" he asked. "Barsis, we can't put you out of your own bed!"

Barsis chuckled. "It's no hardship, Fireborn, but I do thank you for your concern. I'm bedding down with my sister and her family. It's only for a night or two, and it's good to spend time with my nieces and nephews." He scrubbed his hand over the back of his neck. "I'm usually too busy during the day. Now, who are your friends?"

"Garrity and Evarra," Owyn said. He turned and gestured them closer. "Our guards."

"Well met, then," Barsis said. "We'll find beds for you both. And there's a stable if you want to see to your beasts."

"Thank you, Headman," Evarra said. "I've been here before. But you weren't headman the last time I came through. May I ask what happened to Zaric?"

"Zaric was my father," Barsis answered. "He went to the deep this past winter."

"I'm sorry," Evarra murmured. "He was a good man."

"He was that. Now come along," Barsis said, waving one arm wide. "Come let's get you settled. I'll spread the word that Healer Alanar will be seeing to people before the evening meal."

ALANAR WAS BUSY FROM the moment they walked out of the guest house until well after the evening meal. He finally joined them and sat down next to Owyn; Owyn wrapped the blanket he had around his own shoulders around Alanar, who sighed.

"When we get back, I'm going to talk to the Senior Healer about setting up a regular circuit of healers for the surrounding villages. Any place we can reach in a day's travel, at least until we have more healers to send out further. These folks have been neglected, and they shouldn't have been," he said, leaning against Owyn's side. "Mother of us all, I'm tired!"

"I'll put you to bed once you eat something," Owyn said. He picked up the bowl that he'd had tucked next to him. "Here. It's still warm."

"I'm too tired, Wyn," Alanar grumbled.

"Eat or I'm feeding you," Owyn warned. He scooped up a spoonful of stew. "It's fish stew, and it's good. Open."

Alanar rolled his eyes. Then he opened his mouth and let Owyn feed him the first bite. He chewed and swallowed, then held out his hand. "Let me have the rest."

"I can keep feeding you," Owyn offered. Alanar laughed.

"No. I can feed myself." He took the bowl and took another bite. "This is good. Is there bread?"

"Flatbread, yes. I've got some. And there's tea, but I figured you'd want that hot. I'll get it."

Alanar leaned more heavily into Owyn's side. "I don't want you to move. You're warm and I'm tired."

Owyn put his arm around Alanar. "Then eat so I can put you to bed. I promised to rub your legs."

Barsis came over and sat down in the sand facing them. "Thank you, Healer. I appreciate what you've done for my people."

Alanar smiled. "You're welcome, Barsis. I'll speak to the Senior Healer when we get back about sending someone out here to see to you. It's not right that you go without a healer's care."

Barsis looked at Owyn. "You said you're heading north?" he asked. "Isn't that dangerous?"

Owyn snorted. "Breathing is dangerous these days, Barsis," he said. "I'm doing whatever I can to keep us from being noticed. I left anything that can identify me back in Terraces—"

"I noticed you weren't wearing your gem," Barsis said. "I'd wondered. That makes sense."

Owyn nodded. "We're going to ride north tomorrow. Hopefully as far as the ruins, but we can stop at...what was that village?"

"Half Moon Bay?" Alanar asked.

"That's the one. If we stop there, we'll make the ruins the day after, and then head east. I'm hoping to make it to the Solstice village in a month."

"We'll prepare some supplies for you for a few days," Barsis said. "It'll be a long while before you see another village going east. And I wouldn't bother with Half Moon."

"Why?" Alanar asked, and yawned. He laughed. "Sorry."

Owyn kissed Alanar on the forehead. "Bedtime."

"No, information first," Alanar insisted. "Why won't we find any villages going east?"

"Because there aren't any," Barsis answered. "Land dried up, folks moved on. East of here used to be prime farmland for days. Now? Nothing out there but his soldiers." He scowled. "Half Moon was wiped out by the storms. We have their survivors. So between here and the ruins is nothing but rocks. So you sure you want to go north overland? We can take you well north of the palace by ship. It'll be safer, and will cut your journey in half. I know you're not a sailor, Fireborn, but think of your man."

Owyn considered it. Going by ship would be a lot easier on Alanar than riding. And, as Barsis said, it would be safer. Maybe that was what the Mother didn't want him to know? That to do whatever he needed to do, he needed to go by ship? For a moment, he regretted not bringing his smoke blades. But would he see anything?

"You're thinking deep thoughts," Alanar murmured, sounding sleepy.

Maybe he didn't need smoke blades, Owyn realized. "Are you awake enough to talk?" he asked Alanar.

"Depends," Alanar answered. "I think so, if we keep it short."

Owyn turned to Barsis. "I'll have an answer for you once we have a chance to talk," he said. He slid out of the blanket and got to his feet, then helped Alanar up. He slid one arm around Alanar's back as they walked back to the guest house, and wasn't sure if it was to support Alanar, or comfort himself.

"What is it?" Alanar asked. "Your heart is racing, and not in a fun way."

That answered that question. "We need to talk. I need to tell you some things, and we need to decide if it's worth it."

"You're being cryptic again," Alanar said. "I'm awake."

"We'll talk in private," Owyn answered. He led Alanar into the guest house and closed the door, turning up the flame on the little oil lamp that hung from the ceiling. He turned to see Alanar had put his back against the door, and folded his arms over his chest.

"Why do I have a feeling I'm not going to like this?" he asked.

"Probably because you're not," Owyn answered. "What do you know about Smoke Dancers?"

"Next to nothing, really," Alanar answered. "You don't talk about it. I assumed you couldn't talk about it to someone who wasn't a Smoke Dancer."

Owyn shrugged. "That's part of it. But I told Aven and Aria this. And you should know, too. Especially since we're getting married. A Smoke Dancer, the first thing they ever see? Is how they're going to die."

"What?" Alanar yelped. "You...I mean, you *know* that?"

"Just how. Not when," Owyn added. "But mine? Is out there," he gestured, then laughed. "Sorry. I drown, Allie. In salt water."

Alanar paled. "That's what you meant by deep water, yesterday. When you said there was deep water in your future."

"And that's what I think the Mother wasn't letting me see. That I'd have to face that. That I'd have to go out in a ship to do this."

Alanar shook his head. "No," he said. "No, we are not. I'm not risking you like that. Not unless we have no choice."

"But he's right," Owyn said. "It'll be safer. And easier on you—"

"No," Alanar repeated. "I can ride. I'm fine." He smiled. "I have a brand new husband. Almost. I'd like to still have him for the ceremony. And for a long time after. We'll stay away from the sea."

"Are you sure?" Owyn asked. "I'm willing to take the risk—"

"And I'm not willing to let you take the risk," Alanar interrupted. "I'm sure. We're staying with the plan." He smiled. "Go tell Barsis. I'll warm the bed."

"ARE YOU SURE?" BARSIS asked as they walked to the stables. "Your guard are readying your horses, but I can have the skiff ready to sail in under an hour."

"I'm sure, Barsis," Owyn repeated. "And thank you. But we're going to ride. Alanar is pretty insistent."

Alanar smiled. "I can't make healing rounds when we stop if we're on the water, Barsis. There are people out here that have been neglected for too long."

"But the risk—"

"We'll be fine," Alanar said. "Wyn, help me with my boots?"

By the time Owyn had helped Alanar put his boots on, and taken his arm to lead him to the stables, Garrity and Evarra had led the horses out. Barsis was talking intently with Garrity, and Owyn laughed softly.

"I think Barsis is trying to convince Garrity to talk to us about going by ship," he said softly.

"The answer is still no," Alanar said.

"I like the reason you gave him," Owyn said. "It's a good one. We'll be stopping in places, and you can take care of people while I send messages."

Alanar nodded. "I thought of it this morning, while I was dressing," he replied. "I'm not a good liar, so I thought if we had a reason that we had to go overland, and it involved something only I could do—"

"No, it's a good reason," Owyn said. "It makes perfect sense." He tied the laces of Alanar's boot and stood up. "All right. Give me your hand."

They reached the group, and Owyn helped Alanar mount Meadowfoam. Then he went to Freckles and took his map out of his saddlebag. As he unfolded it, he felt a presence at his elbow, and looked over his shoulder to see Barsis was looking over his shoulder at the map.

"That's a nice map," the headman said. "Look much more accurate than anything I have."

"It's as accurate as we could make it, given the information we had two days ago," Owyn answered. "I'll be updating it as we go, though. Because we know that what we knew two days ago may not be what's out there now." He smiled as he realized he now had another, perfectly reasonable excuse to go overland. "I mean, the Heir needs to know what she's holding, right?"

"Truth," Barsis agreed. He looked thoughtful. "I wonder...would you stay another day, at least? Let me copy this?"

Owyn sighed. "And give you more time to try and convince me to go by ship?" he asked, and Barsis grinned.

"Am I that obvious?" he asked. "You're a good man, Owyn Fireborn. So is your Alanar. And I've lived long enough to see that the good men, they're the ones who tend to fall first. I'd like to avoid that with you two."

"And I appreciate that," Owyn said. "Since I want to avoid it, too. But if we take the safe route, we can't do our jobs. Barsis, I appreciate what you're trying to do. We just can't accept the help. We'll be all right."

Barsis nodded. "I understand. I don't like it, but I understand. Can I at least send another guard with you?"

"Too large of a group will attract attention," Garrity said as he came to stand with them. "Owyn, we're ready. We've loaded all the supplies that Barsis was kind enough to give us." He grinned. "You're very generous, headman. You're sure your folk won't need this?"

Barsis shook his head. "We've more than enough to share, Garrity. You are welcome to what we have."

Owyn nodded and turned to Barsis, holding out his hand. "We'll see you on the return trip."

Barsis clasped his wrist tightly. "I'm holding that as a promise, Fireborn."

"Good," Owyn answered. "It was meant to be."

Barsis squeezed his forearm, then let go. "Go well, Fireborn. Take care of that healer of yours."

"I thought I was supposed to take care of him," Alanar called.

"You do that, too," Barsis called back. "I'll see you come summer."

Owyn nodded and swung himself up onto Freckles' back. He glanced over his shoulder — Evarra was already mounted, and Garrity reached his own horse and climbed into the saddle.

"Are we ready?" Garrity called. When Owyn nodded, he turned his horse toward the trail. "Let's go!"

THE DAY REMAINED OVERCAST and cold, and Owyn kept an eye on the skies. They were close to the ruins, he thought, but it was harder to track the passage of time when everything was uniformly gray.

"Will it rain, do you think?" he asked. The idea of riding through the rain to the ruins, then camping rough was not appealing.

"It doesn't smell like rain," Alanar answered. He tipped his head back, closed his eyes, and sniffed again. "No. It just smells gray."

Owyn looked quizzically at Alanar. "Smells gray? What does gray smell like?"

Alanar looked thoughtful. "A little damp. Mold. Mud. Old leaves and dried grass. Woodsmoke. A bit of frost, but not much." He took another sniff. "Sea salt. But that will change as we go inland."

Owyn frowned and sniffed. He did it again, then shook his head. "I can't smell any of that," he admitted.

"It's something you learn, when you can't see," Alanar said. "It..." His voice trailed off, and he turned his head slightly. "That's odd. The woodsmoke is a lot stronger than it should be, if we're nowhere near anything.

Owyn frowned. He looked over his shoulder at Garrity, who was riding close enough that he could hear them. The guard nodded.

"I can smell it." He rode up next to Owyn and turned his head from side to side, scanning the horizon. "I don't see anything, but it's there. And the wind is coming from the ruins."

"So...someone else is camping there?" Owyn suggested, hoping that he was right. "And...we'll just go camp in another part of the ruins?"

"Owyn, is there anything past the ruins?" Evarra asked, coming up on Alanar's other side. "Another village? Something between the ruins and the Palace. I thought there was. That might be what we're smelling."

Owyn took the map from his saddlebag and unfolded it, studying the coastline. "No. Nothing between the ruins and the Palace. So maybe just someone else camping?"

"I doubt it," Garrity said. "Let's not take the chance. We should start heading east now. We can find a sheltered spot and camp. Cold camp, I think."

'If we can do that without freezing to death." Owyn said.

They started east, and Owyn kept looking to his left, toward the ruins. He could see the trail of smoke now, a slender thread rising toward the sky.

"We're that close?" he asked. Garrity glanced to his left and nodded.

"We made really good time," he said. "And you two are much better riders than I thought you'd be. We'd have been at the ruins long before sunset. Now, we'll put some distance between us and that fire. We'll camp at sunset. We can see when we stop if we're far enough to risk a fire."

"Out here, as flat as it is?" Evarra said. "A fire will stand out like a beacon."

They rode in silence as the skies grew darker. Owyn looked back several times, but saw nothing. Eventually, he couldn't even see the smoke anymore. He turned to Alanar, who had an odd expression on his face.

"What is it?" Owyn asked.

"I..." Alanar said slowly. He turned his head and frowned. "There are people out there. Horses. Garrity??"

Garrity rose up in his stirrups and looked around, then coughed. "There's a rider ahead of us!"

"One rider?" Owyn said. "That's not a threat. We can handle one rider, can't we?"

"It's not just one rider," Alanar said. "There are more that way." He waved one arm northward.

Garrity looked at Evarra, who reached back and unhooked her crossbow from her saddle.

"I'll take point," she said. "You watch the backtrail."

They rode on, following Evarra, with Garrity riding behind them. Owyn considered taking his whip chain out, but he'd never used it from horseback. He might take Freckles' ears off. Instead, he reached to his right, taking Alanar's hand.

"Feel anything else?" he asked softly.

"More horses, more people," Alanar answered. "Owyn, I think we're surrounded."

Evarra swore softly at Alanar's words. "And there's the rider."

Owyn looked past him to see a man on horseback, coming toward them. As the rider drew closer, he tugged down the scarf that covered his face, and Owyn swore.

"Fuck!"

Mannon smiled. "I've been expecting you," he said. "And I mean you no harm. I've a camp, and there's a hot meal waiting. In the Mother's name, I offer you welcome. Will you join me?"

CHAPTER ELEVEN

Owyn blinked in shock. He knew those words, from his reading with Aria. "Evarra, wait," he called. He urged Freckles forward a little. "Did you just offer us the Mother's Peace?"

Mannon smiled broadly. "I did. I'm glad you recognized it. You're Owyn, the Fireborn. Correct?"

"Yes," Owyn answered. "Doesn't make any sense to hide it now, does it? For how long will you honor Her Peace?"

"Normally, it's from sunset to sunset," Mannon answered. "Which I'm guessing you know. However, since it's fairly close to sunset now, that would hardly be fitting. Nor enough time for us to talk. So from now until sunset the day after tomorrow?"

Owyn licked his lips. He turned to Alanar. "Are you following?"

"Not a blasted word! Owyn, I don't have any idea who you're talking to!" Alanar whispered back. "Are we in trouble?"

Owyn glanced at Mannon and considered the question. "No," he answered slowly. "No, I don't think so. Healer Alanar, may I present Mannon?" He looked at Mannon. "I have no idea what to call you, you know," he added. "You're not the Firstborn. You're not the Heir. Far as I know, you don't really have a title."

"Just Mannon is fine," Mannon answered.

Alanar's eyes widened. "And we're not in danger?"

"He's offered us the Mother's Peace," Owyn said. "That's a sacred bond." He closed his eyes, took a deep breath, and wondered if he had completely lost his mind. The Mother's Peace was a sacred bond...but so was the anointing of the Firstborn. Mannon had shown no issues with violating *that* bond. Would he honor this one?

Did they have a choice?

Cold rain started falling, icy drops splashing against Owyn's hands. That made the decision for him. He wasn't going to let Alanar stay out in cold rain.

"We accept," Owyn said. "Tell me you have a shelter?"

"Follow me," Mannon said. He turned his horse and headed north. Garrity drew his horse up next to Owyn.

"Are you insane?" he hissed. "We're all dead!"

"We've been dead ever since we saw the smoke," Owyn answered. "We're surrounded. Alanar said so." He looked at Mannon. "I've no doubt you could kill him from here. He knows it. He knows we're armed. Even if we kill him, we're dead. And I don't want to throw our lives away. Not when he wants something from us. Let's see what he wants. And get out of the rain while we're doing it."

"You're fucking insane," Garrity growled.

"Granted," Owyn agreed. "And terrified I'm wrong. But we're in this now, and there's only one way to go." He pointed north, after Mannon. "That way. Put your hood up, love." He tugged his own scarf up around his ears, and urged Freckles forward. As they rode after Mannon, guards started appearing, falling in around them. Not guarding, Owyn realized. They were too relaxed. None of them had their weapons ready.

It took him a moment to realize why. They were escorts.

"Do you mind if I ride up ahead?" Owyn asked.

"Not without me, you don't!" Alanar answered. "Besides, you've got the leading rein. You can't go without me."

"I wasn't planning on it." He urged Freckles to move a little faster, closing the distance between them and Mannon. Who slowed his horse and looked over his shoulder when he heard them approach.

"Mind the company?" Owyn asked, slowing Freckles to match Mannon's pace.

"Not at all," Mannon answered. "May I ask a question?"

Owyn nodded. "Of course."

"How's Del?"

Owyn took a deep breath. It wasn't the question he'd been expecting. "I can't answer," he said. "I don't know. Aven is out on his season, and Del went with him."

Mannon looked at him, and there was something very like relief in his face. "He survived? Aven survived?" He let out a breath. "I wasn't sure he would. That woman..." He sniffed. "I want you to know this, and to tell Aria. That...abomination was none of my doing. And Risha will burn for it, once I catch her. There's a hefty price on her head, so it's only a matter of time." He frowned. "She's unhurt? Aria?"

"She's fine," Owyn answered. "My turn for a question. How did you know to meet us here? How did you know my name?" He paused. "Two questions."

"I asked more than two," Mannon replied. "It's only fair. And I'll answer that once we get out of the rain." He gestured. "Camp is in a hollow up ahead and...is that a pledge bracelet?" He reached out and tapped Owyn's wrist, where his bracelet was just visible past the cuff of his coat.

"Yes," Owyn answered. "That's why we're out here." He looked over at Alanar. "We were heading to the Solstice village."

"I have family there," Alanar added. "And we can send a message to my mother's flock."

"I thought you might have a touch of Air to you," Mannon said. His gaze shifted, moving from Alanar's face to his shoulders, then back. He didn't say anything, though. "Why do I have the feeling that if I called you cousin, you'd spit in my eye?"

Alanar smiled. "My aim isn't that good. And I'd forgotten you were part Air."

Mannon chuckled. "I appreciate the candor," he said. "Congratulations to you both."

"Thank you," Owyn said.

Mannon nodded. "Tonight, we'll camp here. Tomorrow morning, I'll take you to the Palace."

"Why?" Alanar asked.

"Because we need to talk," Mannon answered. "And this sort of discussion needs to be done while warm and dry. You and your guards are my guests, and under the Peace until sunset of the day after tomorrow. I'll even extend it to midday the day after that, so you can sleep well and have a good meal. Then ride out at a reasonable time after we talk." He shook his head and grimaced. "I hate being wet."

Owyn snorted. "Never thought I'd say it, but I agree with you." He looked down at his reins. "Can you give me an idea as to what we're talking about? It might not be anything I can help you with."

"To put it bluntly," Mannon answered. "I need you to carry a message for me. To Aria. Because she'll do worse than spit in my eye if I try to speak to her myself." He sighed. "And I wanted news of my son. I miss him." He shook his head again. "Enough. We'll talk more in the Palace. You have a tent to yourselves, and there will be a meal waiting for us. I'll leave you in peace tonight, and we'll ride on tomorrow."

True to his word, there was a tent waiting for them, warmed by a brazier, along with a hot meal, and dry clothes. Garrity and Evarra were given a tent next to Owyn and Alanar, and they were bid goodnight by Mannon, who disappeared into his own tent.

"How could he have known we were coming?" Alanar asked softly as he rested his head on Owyn's shoulder in the darkness. "He knew your name, even."

"But he didn't know yours," Owyn pointed out. "Or Garrity and Evarra. At least, I don't think he knew."

"He could be manipulating us," Alanar said. He shifted. "Is he a Smoke Dancer?"

"Mem never said, and he knew Mannon," Owyn answered. "And that wouldn't have told him my name. At least, I never got a name through a vision." He snorted. "I think we know why I couldn't see now."

"Are you sure?"

"Well, no," Owyn said with a laugh. He kissed Alanar's forehead. "Go to sleep, love."

Alanar cuddled closer, and grew heavier in Owyn's arms as he relaxed into sleep. Owyn lay awake late into the night, staring at the dark ceiling and asking questions that had no answers.

At least, no answers yet.

THE NEXT MORNING, OWYN was surprised to see only three horses saddled — his, Alanar's, and the big gray gelding that Mannon had been riding. He frowned.

"Why only three?" he asked. He wasn't expecting an answer — the guards had ignored him as he came across the camp. So he jumped in surprise when someone did answer him.

"The guards will be staying behind to clean up the camp," Mannon said. He came around the gray, who nudged his arm. Mannon chuckled. "Behave, Alabaster. You'll get your apple later."

Owyn grinned. "He's as bad as my Freckles, it sounds like. So you're all right with just the three of us riding out?"

Mannon nodded. "You're not going to risk your Alanar. And you're curious. You want to know why."

Owyn looked at him. "It's not fair. You shouldn't know me that well yet."

"I don't," Mannon said. He scratched Alabaster on the forehead, then gestured back toward the tents. "I know how I'd react in your position. Where's Alanar?"

"Putting off putting on his boots," Owyn answered. "He can't tell where he is when he's wearing them."

Mannon looked startled. "He's got the air sense? But—"

Owyn lowered his voice. "You've got a price on Risha's head for what she did to Aven, and what she tried with Aria. And I know what she did to Del. He told us. You should know...Alanar was where she got the idea."

Mannon's jaw dropped. "At his age...you're telling me he was her *first victim*?"

"He'd argue about the victim part. He was injured in a fire. The healers said that he had to lose his wings to save his life."

Mannon closed his eyes and let out a long breath. "I'd wondered."

"I know. I saw you look, yesterday," Owyn said. "I thought...if you knew, you wouldn't make the mistake of asking or assuming..."

Mannon looked at him, then nodded. "Thank you," he said. "That would have been very awkward, indeed. Is that what blinded him?"

Owyn nodded. "Yes."

They walked back toward the tents, and Mannon looked up at the sky. "It'll rain again," he said. "But hopefully, not until we're back at the Palace." He took a deep breath, then looked at Owyn. "Why are you telling me this?"

"Why am I trusting you, you mean?" Owyn asked in response. "I'm not sure I do. But you could have killed all of us last night, without even trying. You didn't. You want something from us. From me, I think. And I think it's something I need to hear." He paused, looking up at the taller man. "And having you get uncomfortable when you find out that Alanar used to have wings is going to put a damper on whatever you want to tell me, on account you'll be all embarrassed and you won't want to show it. So I'm telling you."

Mannon snorted with amusement. "You're impressive, Fireborn. And yes, I do want something from you. I want you to carry a message to Aria."

"You said something about spitting in your eye," Owyn said. "She'll spit in mine if I bring her a message from you. And her aim is better than Alanar's."

"I'm hoping that by sending the message with you, you'll be able to help her to see reason."

Owyn sniffed. "Here's the thing, though. She's not exactly what you'd call reasonable where you're concerned," he said. "And why should she be? You're the man who threatened to rape her the first time he laid eyes on her."

Mannon winced. "It's...not exactly what I said, but I can understand why she heard it that way. I phrased it...horribly." He sighed. "I said I'd have her make me a new heir. Del can't follow me to the throne—"

"Because he's not the Heir," Owyn supplied.

"Because that bitch broke him, and he's afraid of his own shadow now," Mannon corrected. "I had hopes that Aven might be convinced, but he follows Aria. I said that thinking that I could pair Aria with Del—"

Owyn couldn't help it — he burst out laughing. Mannon looked sourly at him.

"If Del could speak, my ears would still be ringing," he grumbled. "He was there, by the by. He heard the entire thing." He shook his head. "I'd hoped that if she could pair with him, it might help him to heal."

"She won't have him," Owyn blurted. He stopped, closing his eyes and mentally kicking himself. He shouldn't have said that. Because now...

"What does that mean?" Mannon asked. Owyn sighed and looked at him.

"It means that he's our Air. And she won't have him. Because he's your son."

Mannon's eyes widened. "My Del? Is your Airborn? *My* Del?"

"Unless you know another Del who's fucking gorgeous, doesn't talk, used to have wings, and wants Risha's head on a plate?" Owyn asked. Mannon's smile in response was both delighted and startling.

"Owyn, you have just made me a very happy man. And I think you'll find Aria very reasonable when she hears the message I want you to carry. Which I cannot tell you here. I need to tell this to you someplace where I know we can be absolutely safe. So let's go and convince your man to put his boots on, and we'll set out. We should be at the Palace by midday."

THEY RODE OUT, AND no one spoke much as the sun crept higher and higher overhead. Owyn could see the Palace growing larger in the distance. And he could feel Alanar growing more and more nervous.

"You're both very quiet," Mannon said. "I promise you, you are both completely safe."

"Is there a reason you expect us to believe you?" Alanar asked softly. "Why are you drawing this out like this?"

"Healer, I have no intentions of killing you. You are my guests, the both of you. And your guard, when they catch us up," Mannon answered. He hesitated. "I'm not speaking of things in the open air. You never know who is listening."

"There's no one around here," Alanar said. "Us and the horses. Rabbits." He gestured. "Over there. But not a single person to hear you."

Mannon's brows rose. "You're that sensitive?"

"Level five healer," Alanar replied.

"Can you truth-tell?" Mannon asked. "Do you know that one?"

Alanar looked startled. "I...I've read about it. Well, had it read to me. I know the theory."

Mannon chuckled. "Hold your hand out."

Alanar held one hand out, and Mannon rested his hand lightly on Alanar's palm. "I have no intentions of killing you," he repeated. "You are my guests, until midday the day after tomorrow. I have a message to send to the Heir, one that I cannot risk being overheard. I hope it will be enough to end this." He took his hand back and smiled. "Well?"

Alanar lowered his hand to his saddle horn. "And now I'm even more confused," he said.

"Why?" Owyn asked. "What was that supposed to do?"

Alanar tipped his head to the side, a position that Owyn recognized as one he took when he was thinking of how to explain something. Then he nodded. "When someone lies, there are signs a healer can read. Their heart rate increases. They start to sweat, just a little. Just enough. Basically, you can lie with your voice, but not your body. Your body shows the lie."

"And was I telling the truth?" Mannon asked.

Alanar smiled. "You aren't lying," he admitted. "But I'm not sure you're telling the truth, either."

"Now wait a minute, Allie—"

Mannon laughed. "He means that I believe what I'm saying, and therefore, to me, it is the truth. But it might not be the actual truth."

Alanar nodded. "That's it. That's exactly it. Owyn, you know about the incurables in the green level, right? The delusional ones believe their madness so completely that it's the truth to them."

"So I'm either telling the truth, or I'm completely, irrevocably insane," Mannon agreed. "Which is it, Healer?"

"I have no idea," Alanar answered. Mannon whooped with laughter, and Owyn reached out to grab Meadowfoam's halter as the startled gelding danced away from Mannon.

"Gently," Owyn crooned. "Easy." He calmed the horse, then looked at Alanar. "Allie?"

"I'm fine. Startled, but fine. I knew you were there."

"I apologize," Mannon said, and he did sound contrite. "All of the horses in my stables know me. I forgot that yours don't."

"They know to stay calm when you bray like that?" Owyn snapped. Then he winced. "Fuck. Sorry. Sorry, that was—"

"Entirely accurate," Mannon interrupted. "I do bray like a donkey. Yana used to say the same—" His voice trailed off. He cleared his throat and looked forward. "We're almost there."

They rode in silence the rest of the way to the Palace, and in the courtyard, Mannon gave the servants who met them orders that Owyn and Alanar be taken to the suite that was waiting for them.

"Wyn, how did he know?" Alanar asked as they followed the servants through the halls. "I don't think he ever answered us. Did he?"

"No," Owyn answered. "He never did. But he's been nothing but nice to us since we met him."

Alanar nodded. "That is true," he said. "But I keep waiting for something to jump out at us."

"You and me both," Owyn said. "For now, let's make the best of it."

The best of it turned out to be a suite larger than their house — an enormous sitting room, two bedrooms, and a bathing room that reminded Owyn of the bath house in Forge. There were fresh clothes on the bed, and wine and small plates in the bath.

"Well, he definitely wants us comfortable," Owyn said, lounging in the hot water and sipping from a glass of wine. "Or off guard."

"I'd say off guard, but there are no guards," Alanar said, sitting opposite Owyn in the large bathing pool. He unwound his long braid and started combing out his hair, then closed his eyes. "Owyn, I'm not sure what to believe anymore."

"I know," Owyn agreed. He finished his wine and sat up. "I'm more shocked that he didn't disarm me. I still have my whip chain. Do you want help with that?"

"No," Alanar answered. He smiled. "I know you. If you get your hands in my hair, then we're not getting out of this bath for another hour."

"Because I like your hair," Owyn said. He slipped through the water to the other side of the bathing pool, and straddled Alanar's legs. "And I love you."

"And if we spend an hour in here, then it's an hour where we have no idea what is happening," Alanar pointed out, resting one hand on Owyn's waist. "Go dry off. I'll be out soon, and we'll see what we can learn."

"Not just yet," Owyn said. He kissed Alanar, as deep as he could without setting other things in motion. "Have to do that first," he added as he moved away and climbed out of the bath. He wrapped a drying sheet around himself, then took a deep breath. "Right. Let's see what we see."

He walked out into the bedroom, going through the clothes until he found things that would fit him. Barefoot, he walked out into the sitting room and started looking for a bell. If this was like Granna Meris' house, there'd be a bell. At least, he thought there'd be a bell. Best to get this started. Before he found it, there was a knock on the door.

"Come in?" Owyn called.

A servant entered, standing by the door with his hands tucked behind his back. "Your pardon, Fireborn, but the master asks if you're ready to meet?"

"Just about, yes," Owyn answered. "Where's the bell? I was looking for it."

The servant came further into the room and showed Owyn a row of braided cords hanging against the far wall. "Blue is for service. That will call me," he said. "Green is for the kitchens. Red is for the guard. You shouldn't need that one."

"Right. And if I'm calling you, what do I call you?" Owyn asked.

The servant smiled. "Denis, Fireborn."

"Thank you, Denis. If you'll let Mannon know we're just about ready?"

"Of course, Fireborn. There's supper, when you're ready for it. Shall I bring it?" When Owyn nodded, Denis bowed and left the room. Owyn went back to the bedroom. Alanar was out of the bath, and drying off.

"We've got our own servant," Owyn told him. "His name is Denis. And he's gone off to tell Mannon we're ready and to get us something to eat."

"Help me dress, then?" Alanar asked. "I'm not sure what we've got."

"We could distract him," Owyn said. "You could go out in your hair and nothing else."

Alanar grinned. "Distract who?"

"All right. Distract me. Here. These look long enough for your legs." Owyn handed Alanar a pair of loose dark-gray trousers. Through the partially-open bedroom door, he heard a knock. Then Mannon's voice, calling, "Fireborn?"

"Just a moment!" Owyn called back. He helped Alanar into a wrapped shirt made from a deep blue silk, and stepped back to admire him. "That's a good color on you. We'll have to get more of it."

"What color is it?" Alanar asked.

"Dark blue. Like right before the stars come out." He smiled and took Alanar's hand. "Come on."

They walked out into the sitting room, where Mannon was waiting for them.

He wasn't alone.

Owyn stared for a moment, not sure he was really seeing what was in front of him. Who was in front of him. His voice cracked when he finally gasped, "Mem?"

CHAPTER TWELVE

It had only been a few months. But Memfis looked older, thinner. His hair was longer than he usually kept it, and there was more gray than Owyn remembered. But it was him.

It was *him*.

"Mem," he repeated, and heard his voice crack. It didn't sound right. The name...just didn't *sound* right. Then he realized what was wrong. "Fa."

It wasn't until he was throwing himself into Memfis' arms that he even registered that he had dropped Alanar's hand, that he was even moving. Then Memfis was hugging him tightly, an embrace he hadn't realized that he desperately missed. And he didn't realize that he was crying until Memfis wiped the tears from his cheeks.

"Mouse. I'm so sorry," Memfis said, his breath ruffling Owyn's hair. "I was wrong. I was wrong and I'm sorry. I should have trusted you."

Owyn nodded, sniffing. "Yeah," he mumbled. "Yeah, you should have. But it's over now. It's done." He wiped his nose on the back of his hand and stepped back. "You been here? The whole time?" He frowned, then looked at Mannon. "That's how you knew we were coming? Mem told you? You were looking in the smoke, Mem? For *him*?"

Memfis nodded. "I did. And yes, I did."

"How? I have your blades," Owyn demanded. "They found them in the tunnels."

Memfis smiled. "Good. I thought I'd lost them. Mannon provided me with another set. They're good, but they're not mine."

Owyn studied Memfis. "When I looked into the smoke, I saw you. And you were chained up, in a fancy room—"

"Must have been from right after you got here," Mannon offered.

"And there was wine," Owyn finished.

"Definitely right after you got here, then," Mannon confirmed. "You tell him, Memfis. He's still not sure if he can believe me."

Memfis nodded. "Let's sit. Have you boys eaten?"

"Not yet," Alanar said. "Denis is bringing something. It's good to hear your voice again, Memfis."

"It's good to see you, too," Memfis said. He rested his hand on Owyn's shoulder and they made their way to the couches — a pair of overstuffed ones that faced each other over a low table. Owyn stepped away from Memfis and took Alanar's hand, leading him to one. Memfis sat on the one facing them, and Mannon took a chair set slightly away from them.

"All right," Memfis said. "I'll start at the beginning. I went hunting visions, and was misdirected in the tunnels by Risha's people. And I was waylaid by guards while trying to find my way out." He rubbed his hands on his trousers. "I woke up in a cell. I'm not sure how long I was there. I couldn't see out. A few days, at least. Then guards came and brought me here."

"It was when the guards I had assigned to Risha rotated out of the Terrace tunnels, and I found out that Risha had taken a prisoner and not told me," Mannon offered. "I sent a cart, and told her that I wanted him here."

"You had guards assigned there?" Alanar asked. "And you still had no idea what she was doing?"

Mannon took a deep breath. "None. Once I came back here after Terraces fell and Risha ran, I had a long talk with the guards who'd been assigned there. There were several I found who helped her, and kept information from me. They were all charged as accessories to her crimes, and they're all down in the dungeons, waiting to be sentenced with her."

Alanar nodded. Then he asked, "Did any of them mention Virrik?"

Mannon closed his eyes. "One of them. Graphically."

Owyn squeezed Alanar's hand. "Either we'll find her, or Mannon will. She'll pay, Allie."

Mannon leaned forward in his chair, a look of concern on his face. "This Virrik, he was someone important to you?" he asked. "They told me he was a student healer."

"He was one of my training partners, and he was my lover," Alanar answered. "I didn't know why he'd left me. I couldn't even imagine the idea that Risha was removing students she thought could challenge her as Senior Healer." He turned to Owyn. "Wyn, that means I was next, doesn't it? I don't know why I didn't think of this before, but she would have killed me next."

"She can't hurt you anymore, Allie," Owyn said. He smiled and raised Alanar's hand to kiss his knuckles. "She'll have to go through me."

"Owyn, what are you wearing?" Memfis asked. Owyn looked down to see that his shirt cuff had slid back to reveal his pledge bracelet.

"Oh, I..." Owyn sputtered, looked at Alanar, and laughed. He sat up straighter and looked across at his adoptive father. "Mem, Alanar and I are getting married."

"And Aria gave her permission?" Memfis asked, sounding stunned.

Owyn looked at Alanar, and told the truth. Half the truth. "She didn't say no."

"Well," Memfis breathed. "That's...I don't even know. I'm...I don't know what I am." He looked at Mannon. "My boy is getting married."

"I did know that, Memfis," Mannon said with a smile. "I knew it first. Now, back to the story. My turn?"

"Go ahead."

Mannon nodded. "Del and I were in Forge when Memfis arrived at the Palace. That city is in a constant state of chaos, and it's been getting worse these past few months." He paused, looking at Owyn. "Remind me to ask you about what happened to Fandor."

"He's dead," Owyn answered. "I'm not. Is there anything else you need to know?"

Mannon snickered, looking at Memfis. "I know he's not your blood, but he reminds me so blasted much of you when you were his age!" Memfis shrugged, and Mannon turned back to Owyn and Alanar. "I'd left orders that Memfis was to be treated as an honored guest, but the guards decided that honored prisoner was the safer path. So they kept him in chains, and made sure his every need was seen to. Including, to my regret, wine. Thankfully, that only lasted a few days."

Memfis snorted. "And it took me almost a month to stop craving it again. It's harder to crawl out of the bottle a second time."

"Oh, no!" Owyn groaned. "Mem!"

"I thought I'd lost everything, Mouse," Memfis said. He shrugged. "I crawled back into the bottle that first night and was waiting to die."

"And I didn't let him." Mannon grinned when Memfis looked at him. "Ordered him not to. And he listened. First time for everything."

Owyn nodded slowly. "Why?" he asked Mannon. "Why keep him alive? Us alive? We're a threat to you. Aren't we?"

"I thought everyone was a threat to me, once," Mannon said, leaning back in his chair. "It took me a long time, and some outside influence, to learn I was wrong. About many things." He looked over his shoulder. "Sounds like the servants with your meal. Shall we wait to continue?"

"Can we talk and eat?" Owyn asked. "Because I'm trying to figure times, and nothing is adding up. Mem was only gone about a week before things went bad and Risha tried to kill Aven and Aria. And she only had them for a day and a half, roughly. She sent for you, and...look, here's the question. How'd you get word, and then get to Terraces so fast?"

"There was a guard station halfway between Terraces and the Palace, near a place called Half Moon Bay," Mannon answered. "Half Moon was leveled during the winter storms. But before that, there was a posting station there. I'm guessing no one told you because there's no one there, currently." He smiled. "You look confused. A posting station is a place to change horses, for guards or messengers on the move. There used to be guard stations every ten or fifteen miles or so, all along the coast road. But given the shortages, I haven't been able to keep them up." He looked thoughtful, then asked, "It took you how long to reach the ruins from Terraces?"

"Two days," Owyn answered. "We stopped last night."

"And from Forge to Terraces?"

"Twelve days," Owyn answered. "Why?"

"Because it gives me an idea of how fast you travel. And it tells me that neither of you are experienced riders," Mannon said. Owyn nodded, and Mannon continued. "You're going slower than I would, and making more stops to rest your horses and to rest yourselves. For me, or for my guard, we can make it from the Palace to Terraces in just under half a day. And that's with stopping at the posting station and keeping minimal breaks for comfort stops. Del was trained the same way, for all that he looks like he'll wilt with a harsh word.

So, how did I get there so fast? Risha sent her guard out to tell me at dawn. He reached the Palace just after midday, and we were on the road in under an hour. And rode right into that storm. That's the only thing that slowed us down — it took us longer than it should have to make the trip." He fell silent as the servants filed into the room, carrying trays and covered dishes, plates and glasses and pitchers. They set everything up on the low table, then withdrew, and Mannon waited until they were gone to continue. "To go to Forge, I go by ship. It takes about a day in a good wind."

Owyn nodded. "Right." He paused, reached out and picked up a cover to see what was underneath. "There's food, love. I'm not sure what it is, but it's food."

"It smells good," Alanar said. "Just fill a plate for me?"

"I'll do it," Memfis said. "Go on and keep talking." He leaned forward and started uncovering dishes. Owyn turned back to Mannon.

"All right. Got another question. You kept Memfis as a guest, not a prisoner. Why?"

"Because I hoped he'd be receptive to talking," Mannon answered. "If everything had gone the way I'd hoped, I'd have brought him back to Terraces months ago to sit down with Aria. But because of bad timing, Del and I came back from Forge in enough time to pull Memfis out of a bottle. I gave orders to not allow him any more alcohol, but before he was completely sober, Risha's guard arrived with the message that I was urgently needed in Terraces. So Del and I were off again, and you know where Del is now. When I came back to the Palace, Memfis was sober enough that I could tell him what I am going to tell you. He agreed to act as a counselor—"

"You what?" Owyn gasped.

"Let him tell it, Mouse," Memfis said. "Here. This is for Alanar."

Owyn took the plate and handed it to Alanar. "Ah...let's see. You have...green stuff north. Some kind of meat in sauce west. Brown stuff south east, and a roll north east."

"You make it sound so appetizing," Alanar grumbled, and Mannon snorted with laughter.

"The green stuff is cooked broadleaf with garlic," he said. "The meat is venison, and the sauce has cherries and wild mushrooms. The brown stuff is stewed fruit. Apples and pears, from the smell."

Owyn took a plate from Memfis and sniffed the stewed fruit. "Stewed in what?" he asked.

"Cider, usually," Mannon answered. "That's how I like it." He got up and came over to the table, looking over the bowls.

"Your usual?" Memfis asked.

"If you don't mind?"

"Then sit over here," Memfis said as he started to fill another plate. "I'm not carrying this around the room." Mannon laughed and sat down next to him, smiling at Memfis as he handed the plate to him. Owyn studied them for a moment, and the mouthful of food turned to sawdust in his mouth.

"What?" Alanar asked. "What's wrong?"

Owyn swallowed, coughed, grabbed for one of the glasses and a pitcher. He filled the glass, took a gulp of what proved to be cider, then coughed again. Only then did he look at Memfis and croak, "*Really?*"

Memfis looked at him. He frowned. Then he looked at Mannon. "Oh," he breathed. He looked back at Owyn. "No."

"Could have fooled me," Owyn said. He paused, thought about what he'd said, then realized something. "Well, fuck. I just did to you—"

"What I did to you months ago. Yes." Memfis took a deep breath. "And now I see why it bothered you so much. Again, I apologize. I should have trusted you. And you should trust me. No, Mouse. I'm not sleeping with him."

Mannon sputtered, caught with a mouthful of cider. He coughed, wiped his mouth, then glared at Memfis. "You waited until I had a full mouth to do that!"

Memfis looked at him. "I didn't, but you can think what you like." He picked a napkin up off the table and handed it to Mannon before turning back to Owyn. "I'm not sharing his bed. But I am supporting him in this plan. He's convinced me."

"And since my best counselor is currently learning to be a fish, I'm glad of it," Mannon added. "The truth of the matter is that I am holding the throne without the benefit of Companions. Memfis has been a great help to me over the past few months."

"But why?" Alanar asked. He set his plate down on the couch next to him. "I still don't understand how you convinced Memfis to help you. What are we missing?"

Mannon looked at Memfis, then around the room. He narrowed his eyes for a moment, then asked, "Alanar, is there anyone in earshot?"

Alanar looked startled. Then he cocked his head to the side and closed his eyes. "No. No one close."

"This is why," Mannon said. "Hold out your hand." He took something from his pocket and reached across the table to drop it into Alanar's outstretched hand. Owyn stared in disbelief at the ornately carved gem — it was clear, with what looked like clouds swirled deep in the heart of it.

"Fuck me sideways," he breathed. "That...that's *yours*?"

"Is this what I think it is?" Alanar asked. He picked the gem up and held it between his fingers. "Is it Fire or Air?"

"Air," Owyn answered. He looked closer, then looked at Mannon. "You were Yana's Air? We were told that she never had her Companions."

"She had two," Mannon answered. "Her Fire was a young man who followed her out of Forge." He frowned, then shook his head. "I never knew him. He died in that last battle, and his ashes were interred at the Temple with the other Companions." He paused. "Delandri. That was his name. Del was named for him. And there was me. She gave me this when she woke after the battle." Mannon reached out and took the stone from Alanar, studying it for a moment. His expression grew somber, then sad. "The moment she laughed and put this in my hand, and called me hers, I knew that I'd been wrong. That everything I'd done was wrong. That if I'd waited, as my father told me, that I'd have found my purpose. Everything I'd done since then has been an attempt to right those wrongs."

Owyn frowned. "Kidnapping Aria. Murdering her mother. Maybe killing Aven's mother, too. Trying to burn Forge. All that was to right wrongs?"

Mannon closed his eyes. "Liara's death was a mistake, one that I didn't know about until the survivors of the shipwreck limped back into harbor and they told me that they'd taken a prisoner at the ruins of the Temple—"

"That's another one!" Owyn interjected.

"Mouse," Memfis said softly.

"No, it's a fair question," Mannon said. "Destroying the temple came about a year before that battle, once I knew there was an Heir in the world again. I hadn't yet met Yana. So that was one of my wrongs." He shook his head. "One of my greatest wrongs."

Owyn nodded, looking at Alanar. "What do you think?"

"Why didn't you just step down when Yana chose you?" Alanar asked. "If you understood that what you had done was wrong?"

Mannon took a deep breath. "There...were reasons—"

"Tell them the whole truth," Memfis growled softly. "That was the deal. I would tell you how to reach them if you told them the whole truth."

Mannon nodded. "It was." He looked across at Owyn and Alanar. "Yana was injured in the last battle. A blow to the head. When she was brought to me, we weren't certain that she'd ever wake. And when she did wake, her mind was gone. She was like a child. I wasn't so much her Companion as I was her caretaker. She could never have taken the throne." He leaned back in his chair. "If there'd been more than just me, perhaps. But Delandri was dead. He never knew his son—"

"Del isn't yours?" Owyn blurted.

"Oh, he's my son, as much as you are Memfis' son," Mannon answered. "I'm the one who rocked him at night when he cried. I soothed his nightmares and steadied his first steps. I raised him. I love him." He stopped and closed his eyes. "And when he needed me the most, I wasn't there. I came back from Forge to find my Yana dead, and my son broken. I didn't know for years the truth of what Risha had done to him, and by then she was Senior Healer and I had no one to replace her. I think she knew I was going to. I think that's why she was targeting her potential replacements." He looked down at the gem, then put it back into his pocket. "I've been waiting since Yana died for this moment. The message that I want you to carry to Aria is that I am ready to stand down. I will hold the throne in her name until she makes the journey to the Temple ruins to claim Axia's Crown."

CHAPTER THIRTEEN

Owyn stared at him for a moment. "You...you're abdicating," he said. "Now. Why not when you knew Aria was Heir?"

Mannon took a deep breath. He picked up his cup of cider and took a sip. "I'm assuming that you're learning about governance? Tribal laws and customs and all of that?"

Owyn nodded. "Yeah. We all are. Well, all of us that are here."

"Del probably knows more than any of you," Mannon said. "He's been learning about governance since he was tall enough to see over my desk. What do you think would have happened if I'd stepped down when I first learned about Aria? Before she found you or her other Companions. Before any of you knew what you were doing?"

Owyn picked up his own cup. He drank some of the cider and considered the question. What would have happened?

"Oh," he murmured. He nodded slowly. "All right. I think I get it."

"Good," Alanar said. "Explain it to those of us who have no idea about governance."

Owyn smiled at him. "To put it bluntly? Aria wasn't ready to take the throne. Not then, and I don't think she is yet. We're none of us ready. So if Mannon stepped down when he first met Aria, well...she would have been run roughshod over, by people like Fandor and Risha."

"None of you have the training you should have had. Which is my fault," Mannon said. "I will make it very public that I stand as regent, and that when Aria goes to the Temple and receives the Crown, that I will stand down. And...I will face whatever judgment she offers." He set his cup down. "I didn't stand down for Yana because she couldn't rule. I told her that I would hold the throne for her, and for our son. I honestly thought that I would standing down for Del. I thought that because he was the child of the Heir, that he would be the one to follow her. That's usually the line of succession." He spread his hands. "Then Risha...well, you know what happened. I didn't think he could take the throne either. So I had no viable heir, and the actual Heir was dead." He shrugged. "I kept moving forward. I kept on. I trained Del as if he were going to follow me in case he had to. And then Aria appeared. When I first met her, she was with my brother Jehan, Aleia and Aven. And she swore that she did not have the Diadem. That it and the Companion gems had been taken from her, and she didn't know where they were or what had happened to them." He paused, and sat up straight. "But Aven had his Water gem. I saw it on him when we pulled him out of that torture chamber. Did she lie to me?"

Owyn shook his head. "Before they found me. I don't know."

"No," Memfis answered. "She wasn't lying. Aven told me that Aria didn't know he was carrying the Diadem and the gems."

Mannon nodded. "I was wondering if she was that good a liar. Usually, I can tell. No matter. She holds the Diadem. She'll hold the Crown. I will hold the throne in her name until she is ready."

Owyn closed his eyes, trying to think. What would Aven say? How would he react to the story that Mannon had told them?

Aven wouldn't believe him. Not for a minute.

"Alanar?" Owyn said. "Has he been telling the truth?" He looked at Alanar, who frowned slightly.

"As far as I can determine? Yes."

Owyn nodded. "Fair enough," he said. "All right. I'll carry your message. But I want it in writing, in your own hand. Including the bit about abiding by whatever judgment she sees fit. You were responsible for killing her parents, after all."

"Milon didn't die at my hand. He died from his injuries, but I shouldn't argue the point. He died because of my actions, therefore I was responsible for his death, and Liara's, and a great many other deaths." Mannon sighed. "Done. I'll have it for you in the morning. You are still welcome to stay another day." He glanced at Memfis. "Especially since you have news to share."

Owyn considered, then shook his head. "No, the only way we'll be able to manage this is to go back, deliver the message, and then set back out for the Solstice Village—"

"I could send you back by ship," Mannon offered. "You'll be in Terraces in a few hours. Then you can go north in comfort, at least until you reach Featherfall. It'll be rough from there — the roads east into the mountains are hard going, even in the spring. There's still snow on the ground, up high, and will be until high summer." He paused, then added, "Or I could send a messenger for you. If all you were doing was going to the Solstice village to send a message to Alanar's mother's flock, I can send a messenger. Unless you think they'd want to see you, to confirm that I'm not trying to delude them into anything?"

Alanar hummed softly. "I don't know, to be honest. My grandfather was old when I was there last. I don't even know if he's still alive. They're not exactly communicative."

Owyn picked up his cup again, sipping slowly. If they sent a messenger to the Solstice village, that would be the end of their trip. They'd head back to Terraces tomorrow or the next day. Which meant that there would be no other messages sent out to the deep. He wasn't going to tell Mannon that the Companion bond was fractured, or that they had no idea if Aven and Del were going to come back. He couldn't — not when they were so close to fulfilling the prophecy and the Mother's bidding. Aria on the throne...

With two of her four Companions. Would that be legitimate? He had no idea. Probably no worse than Mannon's rule, but they needed to do this right.

Which means that they needed to get Aven and Del back.

"I think we'll ride on," he said slowly. "But I'll let you know definitely one way or the other tomorrow. Regardless, we'll leave the day after. I want to have a look at your records, if I may?"

To his surprise, Mannon smiled broadly. "Of course! I was hoping you'd say that. I want Aria to know her future house is in order." He glanced at Memfis, then stood up. "I'll let you have your privacy now. Thank you, Fireborn, for being willing to listen. Healer Alanar, it was a pleasure to meet you."

"If we're staying a day, I'd be happy to make my rounds in the Palace, if you have need?" Alanar offered.

"Yes, yes, of course. I'll have my steward make the arrangements. Owyn, we'll meet with him tomorrow over the records," Manon said. "I'll leave you in peace now. And if you decide not to dine with me tonight, I will see you in the morning." Then he turned and left.

Owyn said nothing for several minutes. Not until Alanar murmured, "He's out of earshot now."

"Fuck me," Owyn breathed, slumping back in the couch. "That...that was not what I was expecting." He looked across at Memfis. "You couldn't send one message?"

Memfis spread his hands. "I would have, if I could. He considers me a counselor, but I have no freedom. If you'd asked for me to leave with you, he'd have refused. I'm a very pampered prisoner, Mouse. I haven't seen the outside of the walls since I was brought here."

"You seem to be getting along very well with him," Alanar said.

Memfis scowled in response. "I'm not entirely sure of him," he said. "But based on what I've learned and what I've seen, I'm willing to follow him. For now. Mother of us all, Mouse, it's good to see you." He paused, and Owyn got the message — drop it. He rested his hand on Alanar's arm, and Memfis smiled. "Tell me, how is everyone?"

Owyn answered without hesitation, and lied his head off. "Aria is good. Working too hard, not sleeping enough. Pushing back when I try to take care of her. She's still mad at me, I think. Aven is taking his season. Recovering from what Risha did to him. He'll be back soon, we think. Del went with him, to help him. And because Aria didn't want him around. Treesi is a full healer now." He frowned. "Wait, did you know that she's our Earth? I forget."

"It's only been a few months, Mouse," Memfis replied. "Yes, I did know. Now you just need your Air—"

"That's Del," Owyn interrupted. "We all recognized him. Once he and Aven come back, we'll be whole. Once Aria calms down about him, that is. She's pushing back on him, because he's Mannon's blood. Because we thought he was Mannon's blood."

"Del?" Memfis looked stunned. "That means you have two Companions taking a season at the same time?"

"It's not like we're ruling yet, Mem," Owyn pointed out. "We've been focused on rebuilding Terraces. It was hit hard. And that's been giving Aria some good practice in administration. Me, too. And, honestly, it was better that Aven not go alone. He...wasn't in a good place." He glanced at Alanar, then sighed. "He wasn't sure he was going to be able to change again."

Memfis' jaw dropped. "I...Mannon didn't give me all the details. Do I want to know?"

"Just know that what Risha did to him is what killed my Virrik," Alanar said.

"And Virrik is who we found in the cove," Owyn added.

Memfis swore softly. "I...I understand now why you didn't let him go alone. And...can he? Do you know?"

Owyn nodded. "I went out into the water with him, Mem. Waist deep. And I held his hand while he changed."

"You? You went into salt water?" Memfis shook his head. "I'm dreaming."

"Fuck you very much," Owyn growled.

Memfis grinned. "I have missed you so much, Mouse." He shook his head. "What else?"

"Umm...Rhexa was right," Owyn said after a moment. "Jehan confirmed it—"

"Jehan? Aven's father? Where did he come from?" Memfis demanded.

Owyn coughed. "Jehan was locked up in the green levels. I saw him when I went hunting visions, and we found him when we went after Aven. Mannon didn't tell you?"

"Jehan is Senior Healer now," Alanar added.

Memfis stared at them for a moment, then cleared his throat. "And Aleia?"

Owyn shook his head. "She wasn't there. We don't know. I...Jehan thinks that if she was ever in Terraces, that Risha would have killed her, the way she killed Virrik."

Memfis closed his eyes. "Mother hold her. I hope not," he murmured. Then he opened his eyes. "Rhexa was right. You're her nephew?"

Owyn nodded. "I can't get my mind around the new name, though. She tried calling me Jaxis, and I never answered. I'm Owyn, and I always will be. But I'm in the rolls at Terraces as Owyn Jaxis, son of Dyneh, Huris, and Memfis."

Memfis blinked. "Crowded bed, that."

Alanar giggled. "You just need a bigger bed," he said with a laugh. "A nice wide one, like we have."

Owyn grinned and leaned into Alanar's arm. "What else? Ah...we moved. After everything that happened, Aria couldn't stay in the same house. We're across from Auntie, now, and closer to the healing complex. Umm—" He looked at Alanar. "What else?"

"Pirit is alive," Alanar added. "Teva betrayed us, threw his lot in with Risha. Hurt Marik badly enough that he lost his eye."

"Pirit? Jehan's mother? Is alive?" Memfis shook his head. "I've missed a lot. Is she still intimidating?"

Owyn answered, "No," at the same time as Alanar answered, "Yes." They both burst into laughter. Memfis smiled at them.

"And you're getting married," he said. "I never expected to see that. When?"

"Well, Alanar asked me...what, all of two days ago?" Owyn asked. Alanar nodded. "So we haven't thought that far ahead."

Memfis looked startled. "You planned this entire trip in two days?" he asked. He looked around, then lowered his voice. "Alanar?"

"Still no one close enough to hear," Alanar answered.

"Then what the fuck is really going on?" Memfis demanded.

"Well, we are really getting married," Owyn answered. "But we planned this trip to hit as many Water villages as possible, because we aren't sure Aven is coming back. Aria...well, she fucked up. Badly. She said that she wouldn't have Mannon's blood at her side or in her bed." Memfis winced, and Owyn nodded. "Right. Especially since now we know that Del isn't, but Aven is. And it was right after he woke up, and we weren't even sure he was going to walk again, let alone change. We made the mistake of leaving him alone, and he snuck out, with Del helping him. And he left his gem behind." He looked at Alanar. Tell Memfis that Aria was pregnant? No. Better to keep that secret. "We need him back, because things are falling apart. I've been trying, but it's just me, and I can't. Aria isn't in Terraces. She went back to Forge. Without telling me she was going. She closed me out, she took Treesi and she left. So...I can't fix it. I need Aven back." He sighed and looked down at his hands. "I don't have to tell you not to tell him that, right?"

"No, you don't," Memfis said. "Mouse—"

"I don't think there's anything in any of the histories that says that being a Companion would be easy," Owyn said. "I just didn't think it would be so fucking lonely."

"You're not alone anymore," Alanar said. He slid his arm around Owyn's shoulders. "I'm here."

Owyn nodded. He closed his eyes. "So, that's why we're riding. We have to hit all the Water villages. I've already sent messages from Sanctuary and from Shadow Cove. Half Moon was our next stop, but they're gone. The plan was overnight at the ruins, then head east, for the Solstice village."

"And hopefully, by the time we get back to Terraces, Aven and Del will be back, and we can figure out the next step." Alanar started rubbing the back of Owyn's neck. "Wyn, you're doing fine."

"I don't feel fine," Owyn muttered. "I feel like I'm missing something." He frowned. "How are we supposed to go north if we're supposed to go back to Terraces with the message for Aria? I may have backed us into a corner. We might have to go back."

"Or we can ask if stopping back in the Palace on our way back is an option, and we can get the message to deliver then," Alanar suggested. Owyn nodded. Then he tipped his head onto Alanar's shoulder.

"Maybe we should just go back," he murmured. "If he's going to stand down for Aria...maybe I sent enough messages. Maybe he'll be there when we get back?"

"And maybe my wings will grow back in and I can fly out to meet him," Alanar offered, and Owyn scowled at him. "You're making that face, aren't you?" Alanar asked. "The one you make when you know I'm right."

"I don't have a face like that," Owyn protested. "And anyway, how do you even know I have that face?"

Alanar grinned. "I know you, love. And we can talk about it. We don't have to decide right now. You told Mannon that you'd tell him in the morning."

Owyn nodded, looking across to Memfis, who was sitting and looked to be paying rapt attention to Owyn and Alanar. Except that he was frowning — a slight wrinkle between his brows told Owyn that, while Memfis' body was here, his mind was ranging.

"What are you thinking, Fa?"

Memfis smiled. "I'm thinking I'm still not used to hearing you call me that," he answered. "And wondering if Mannon knew any of that."

"He didn't know about Del," Alanar said. "He didn't know that Aven survived. You can't hide that much surprise. Not from a healer."

"I think his source of information from Terraces dried up and blew away when Risha and Teva ran for it." Owyn offered. "How bad were the storms here, Mem?"

"Half the lower Palace flooded," Memfis answered. "There are parts of the lower levels that are still unusable. One of the towers was undermined, and is completely off limits." He leaned back and rubbed his forehead. "Repairs have started. I'm overseeing those." He smiled. "I want to hand a well-kept Palace over to Heir."

"I'm sure she'll appreciate it, once she gets her head back on straight," Owyn said, and winced at the tart tone to his voice. Alanar's arm tightened around him.

"She'll figure out her way, Owyn," he said. "She just needed to get out of sight for a while. She's under so much pressure."

Owyn sighed and nodded. "I know. I just wish she'd trusted me to help her." He shrugged. "But then, I did lay into her pretty hard about what she did to Aven and Del. Maybe she thinks she can't trust me anymore. Maybe we really are broken beyond repair."

"Don't say that," Memfis said. "You said it yourself, Owyn. No one ever said that this would be easy."

"And I said that the Mother is still working on us," Owyn added. "Remember that? We weren't ready when we got to Terraces. We're still not ready. She's got us on her anvil and She's working us hard — fuck, Mem. If this is what ore feels like, I'm going to have a hard time going back to working a forge!"

Alanar moved, taking his arm from around Owyn's shoulders. He mimed hammering something on an imaginary anvil, saying "Ow!" with every stroke. He stopped and shrugged. "You know, there are some that like that sort of treatment."

"Not me," Owyn said. "But yeah, we're on the anvil. We'll either come away as finished, or we'll shatter from too much working. And I don't think I can tell which it will be from here. Not from inside."

"I doubt the ore can ever tell what it will be when it's finished. It's all up to the smith," Memfis said.

Owyn shook his head. "I don't know. If you want a good tool, you have to start with good ore. But sometimes, all you have is pot metal, and you have to make the best of it. You taught me that, Mem. So, did the Mother pick us because we were good ore, or because we were all she had to work with?" He ran his nails over his chin, feeling the scratch of whiskers. "I forgot to shave."

"You're not pot metal, Wyn," Alanar said. "Even when you're scratchy. The Mother chose you because you were what she needed." He poked Owyn in the ribs. "Do you really think that the Mother is willing to settle for pot metal? She had the entire Fire tribe to choose from. She chose you. Because you were the right person."

Owyn sighed. "Sometimes, it doesn't feel that way," he grumbled. "It doesn't feel like I'm doing any good at all. I mean, really, who am I to be chosen by the Mother to stand for the whole tribe? Anyone else would have been better! I mean, literally anyone else!"

Alanar chuckled, leaned close, and kissed him on the cheek. "That's how we know you're the right person," he murmured.

Owyn snorted. "You know that don't make any sense?" he asked.

"It does," Alanar insisted. "Consider what happened when someone decided that they deserved the throne, no matter what the Mother said."

Owyn frowned, then looked toward the door. "Oh," he said. "So because I don't think I'm right for this—"

"It makes you perfect," Alanar finished.

Owyn thought about it, then shook his head. "Nope. Still don't make any sense," he said, laughing. "I told you. I can't tell from inside."

"You're too close," Memfis agreed. "Trust Alanar. He's right." He got up and brushed off his trousers. "I'll let you two have some privacy. The evening meal is the first bell after sunset. Denis can show you to the dining room." He left the room, and Owyn slumped against Alanar's side.

"I dunno why I thought I'd be good at this, Allie," he murmured. "I can't lie for shit."

"You did fine," Alanar said softly.

"I lied to Mem!"

"And he didn't notice. He can't share a truth he doesn't know." Alanar hugged Owyn tightly. "We'll be fine. Tomorrow, you'll check the records and I'll see to the servants. Maybe I'll learn something. And we'll decide if we're going north or south. For now...I think I want to explore the bed."

Owyn looked at him. "Explore the bed?"

Alanar smiled. "Let's go find all the places where the bed squeaks." His smile broadened. "Or all the places in the bed where I can make you squeak."

CHAPTER FOURTEEN

D enis led Owyn into a large room that was lined on both sides with floor to ceiling bookshelves. The far wall was entirely made of windows, and Owyn turned in a circle and whistled.

"I've never seen this many books in one place ever!" he breathed. "How many are there?"

He heard a laugh that seemed to come from a table positioned in front of the windows, which was piled high with books. "Thank you, Denis," Mannon said as he stood up. "And, to answer the question, according to the catalog, there are about three thousand books in the Palace, spread between this library and the smaller reading room in the Heir's Tower." He grimaced. "Which we will hopefully not lose if that tower decides to crumble."

"Is that the one that was undermined?" Owyn asked. "Mem mentioned something about it."

"Yes, and it's not safe to enter," Mannon replied. "So Memfis and the architects have the unenviable task of trying to figure out how to save a structure they can't safely inspect." He gestured to an empty chair at the table. "I missed you at the evening meal last night."

Owyn took a seat. "We went to bed early last night. It's been a long few days."

Mannon chuckled. "And a long few days without a real bed?" he said, and Owyn felt his face grow warm. Mannon just shook his head. "I apologize, Fireborn. But I was young once, too. I remember."

"You can call me Owyn," Owyn said. "And three thousand books? Really?" He turned in his seat to look around. "Is that all there are?"

"If you mean all the books that have ever been written?" Mannon asked. "No. There are books that were written ages ago, and the only way we know of them is that we have references to them in other books." He looked around. "Books are temporary treasures. But the knowledge in them? That lasts."

"Not if nobody knows it," Owyn countered. "How much of this stuff is still being taught? How many copies of these books exist outside this room? If that tower fell tomorrow, how much knowledge would be lost forever?"

"A very good point, and one I haven't had time to give more than a passing thought to." Mannon nodded. "So how do you save that knowledge?"

Owyn leaned back in his chair and frowned. "Spread it out. More copies of those books, in more places. True copies, not like what Risha tried to do."

"What did Risha try to do?" Mannon asked.

"She changed the textbooks that healers-in-training were given, so that they said that Water and Air were subhuman," Owyn answered. "It was Jehan's book she messed with. Do you know he's fucking terrifying when he's mad?"

Mannon snorted. "Having been on the receiving end of that anger? Yes, I do. She changed *Comparative Anatomy of the Tribes*? And expected no one to notice?"

"She'd already killed off any of the healers who would have, in the purges...hey." Owyn stopped and sat up. "You were supposed to be behind those!"

"I was?" Mannon looked startled. "Behind killing healers?" He frowned. Then he scowled. "I think I need to have a few more words with those traitors who used to be my guardsmen." He shook his head. "I had no idea that things had been subverted so badly in the Earth tribe. I knew there were problems with the healing centers—"

"There are no other healing centers," Owyn interjected. "None. Because you were supposed to have ordered them all destroyed when you found out the healers were working against you."

Mannon stared at him. "You seem to be making the assumption that what you know about me is the truth," he said. "As I said, I had no idea that things had been subverted so badly. I let Risha handle things there. Mostly, to keep her occupied and away from Del, but also because she became Senior Healer and she followed me. At least, I thought she followed me. Now...well, I'm regretting that choice. But I spent a great deal of time focusing on Fire, and on the rebellions that seemed to spring up there every time I looked away, so perhaps the fault is my own for not seeing." He looked at Owyn, then smiled. "Yes, I know. The fault is entirely mine, from beginning to end. I'm trying to make things right, and it only seems to get worse." He took a deep breath. "I'm just hoping that I'm standing down in time to let Aria do what needs to be done."

Owyn leaned back in his chair and studied Mannon. "You know, I don't understand you," he said. "You could have stood down years ago. You could have named yourself regent for Yana, the same way you're planning on doing for Aria—"

"Don't think that I haven't had those thoughts," Mannon interrupted. "Should I have taken her North, or out to the deep, to find her other two Companions so that I wouldn't be the only one? What happens when a Companion dies? I've checked the records, and I can't find anything that says — apparently, there's never been a Companion that died before their Firstborn. There might be something in the Companion lore, the information that only they're taught. Jehan would know. You can ask him when you get back. But, going back to Yana, her Fire was dead. Should I take her back to Forge, and risk riots in her name so that she could find a new Fire?"

he sighed and shook his head. "There are so many things that I could have done and didn't. And none of it matters because we're here now. We can only go forward."

Owyn nodded. "I understand that," he agreed. "So...show me your books?"

They spent the rest of the morning going over ledgers and accounts and record books. Mannon even brought out his personal journals of research, then ordered cider and light snacks to be served as they discussed his attempts to revitalize the farmlands in the eastern Earth Tribe lands.

"There are records that claim that burning the remains of the previous year's crops and then letting the field lie fallow for a year will enrich the land," Mannon said, gesturing with his pen at the bookshelves. "We have books and treatises on land management, and I've annotated them all over the years. Nothing seems to make a difference."

"Because as a farmer, you're a really good librarian?" Owyn asked. He sipped his cider. "Sounds about how I'd do at it."

Mannon chuckled. "I am that. A librarian. I can lay my hands on any book in this library in a matter of minutes — I know exactly where they all are. I know which ones are in the tower, too." He picked up his own cup and took a sip, then waved his hand over the books they had been examining. "And your thoughts, Owyn?"

"You mean besides thank you for remembering to call me by name?" Owyn asked. He leaned forward and looked at the closest book, at the neatly written information recorded on the pages. It was the same handwriting in most of the books. Mannon's own handwriting, he suspected. "You're a clerk at heart, aren't you?"

Mannon smiled. "I like things organized. I like to know exactly where everything is. I—"

"Make lists?" Owyn added. "Write everything down or you forget it, especially if you get excited? Forget it even if you did write it down, if you get excited enough? Put everything right back in the same spot, or you'll never find it again? Or...put things in neat piles, and you know exactly what is in each pile so nobody better move it or you lose things?"

Mannon started laughing. "Jehan told you that!"

"Nope," Owyn replied. He tapped his chest. "That's me. Every bit of it." He grinned. "The day I met Aven and Aria, I almost killed Aven. Mem told me that Waterborn can't have milk, and I was so fucking excited to finally meet them that I forgot. Mem left me to take care of them, and I fed him cheese."

"Oh, you didn't!" Mannon looked horrified. "How sick was he?"

Owyn snorted. "I'm amazed he let me come close to him ever again. Or cook for him, for that matter." He shook his head. "The mistakes we make, right?"

"And all we can do is try to do better," Mannon agreed. He touched the book in front of him. "I've been trying to do better for twenty years now."

They continued until someone knocked on the library door. An older man entered and approached the table.

"Apologies, my lord," he said. "I've been with the young healer this morning. He's working his way through the entire servants wing, and I lost track of time. I should have been here ages ago."

"If you're keeping him from working himself to a nub, I won't complain," Owyn said.

"Owyn, this is Nestor, my steward," Mannon said. "He's been in the Palace approximately forever."

Nestor smiled and bowed. "Not quite that long," he corrected. "But perhaps a good fraction of it."

"Nestor, I'll leave you to work with Owyn. Answer all of his questions. I've got some work to do, and I'll come back when I'm finished." Mannon rose from his place at the table and left the library. Nestor came around and took Mannon's abandoned chair.

"He's a good boy, your Alanar," Nestor said. "And I did assign a young maid to make certain he took breaks and ate."

"Thank you," Owyn said. "I appreciate you looking out for him."

"Of course, of course," Nestor said. "Now, I'm certain you have dozens of questions. Ask me anything."

"How long have you been here?" Owyn asked. "Really?"

Nestor looked thoughtful. "When I entered service here, my great uncle was the steward, and Riga was still Heir. I started as a page, and worked my way up. Riga became Firstborn when I was a footman."

"So you've served the Firstborn — several of them, it sounds like — and Mannon," Owyn said. "So how does he compare?"

Nestor chuckled. "You, young man, have just lost me a wager. I was certain that you were far too polite to jump right into the personal questions. I told Mannon that you'd at least wait until we'd discussed one completely unrelated topic before you asked me about him."

Owyn grinned. "Sorry. But not much. I've got limited time, and no patience. So?"

"Well, to be honest, we resisted at first," Nestor said. "Of course we did. Who would not have? But the servants here...this is our Palace. I've seen four Firstborns with my own eyes. The Palace truly belongs to the servants — it doesn't matter to us who sits on the throne or if they're wearing the Crown or the Diadem. There's still dishes to do and privies to clean. Some left. Some couldn't stomach the idea of staying. But most stayed. Really, where could we go? Some of us were born in the Palace, born into service. We are, perhaps, our own tribe. The Palace tribe, and there's no place else for us in the world. So we stayed." He shrugged. "And then she came. Our Broken Lady. And he changed." He looked around, almost as if he were looking to see who might be listening. Then he turned back to Owyn. "Now, I've been here a long time. I've known Mannon since he was a boy. And he was Elcam's treasure — his first born son. Elcam was still Heir when Mannon was born, and he was certain his boy would be chosen to wear the Diadem after him, so he treated Mannon accordingly."

Owyn nodded. "He prepared Mannon."

"Exactly. He trained Mannon the way that he'd been trained, made him believe that he would be the one to receive the Diadem when they went north to the Temple. And when the time came, and when Elcam received the Crown...well, no one was expecting Tirine to receive the Diadem. And then Elcam died, and Tirine received the Crown...and Mannon was passed over again."

Owyn sniffed. "That doesn't excuse what he did. Anything he did."

To his surprise, Nestor nodded. "I never said it did. And I will admit that the first few years, there was more than one occasion when I was more than a little tempted to slip poison into his soup."

"What stopped you?" Owyn asked.

"Killing him would have set off even worse levels of chaos. We — the servants — decided to wait until we had a clearer path. Unfortunately, what we hoped for never came to pass."

"And then Yana came," Owyn said.

Nestor sighed. "Our Broken Lady. By the time we heard that there was an Heir, she was already marching north from Forge, gaining followers and momentum as she went. We did everything we could to prevent Mannon's march, but all we managed was to delay him." He paused. "It was a week later that he returned, with Yana. He ordered us to tend to her, to care for her. To make her comfortable, until she either woke or passed." He met Owyn's eyes. "I was there when she woke. I was there when she saw Mannon for the first time and called him hers. I've never seen a man so stunned. And then he cried."

"He did?" Owyn stared at Nestor. "You're not joking?"

"Not at all." Nestor took a deep breath. "And after that, things changed. He stopped raging and started ruling. But by that time, there were so many things that he'd already set into motion, it was as if he was trying to stop an avalanche." Nestor sighed. Then he pointed to a row of identical blue-bound books on a nearby bookcase. "The records from those years are there. In order, because otherwise Mannon gets upset. If you decide to read through them once we're finished, leave them on that table in the corner to be put back properly."

Owyn nodded. He looked out the window and considered his next question. "Nestor," he said slowly. "How did Yana die?"

Nestor closed his eyes. "Now that's a question I both expected you to ask, and hoped you would not," he murmured. "We don't know why she was in the Heir's Tower or why she took Del with her. All we really know is that she fell."

"Fell?" Owyn repeated. "She fell. But she was Air—"

"She didn't fly, Owyn," Nestor said. "Mannon said that he thought the head wound made her forget how. She never flew, once she was here. And Del...he didn't know how. He was so young, and he had no one to teach him. Mannon was going to bring in someone, but he had to go off to deal with something, some unrest or other. I don't even remember anymore. The records will have it." Nestor paused. "She fell, and took Del with her. That he survived...well, it was the hand of the Mother. And Risha, who was our Palace healer at the time."

"Yeah, I know the rest of that one," Owyn said. "Thank you."

"What else can I tell you?" Nestor asked. Owyn frowned as he thought.

"How are we going to transition from Mannon's rule to Aria's?" he asked. "What's the procedure? How did it work from Firstborn to Firstborn? And how do we get people to accept her?" He gestured to the window. "Mannon put people in place who supported him. And you said that he couldn't make changes because it was like stopping an avalanche. So how do we stop the avalanche when it's Aria on the throne?"

Nestor studied him for a moment. Then he smiled. "If you're an example of the Companions that she has called to her side, I think that your Aria will be quite the Firstborn. We'll lay plans, and we'll look into who holds power where, and if they can be swayed, or if they need to be removed from power. Aria must first make the Heir's Progress, and follow Axia's path through Adavar. When she does, the people will see her, and they'll know that there is once more a Firstborn in the Palace."

"She's not that yet," Owyn said. "She's not got the Crown yet."

"Well, that's just a matter of going north, then, isn't it?" Nestor asked. "Tell me about her other Companions?"

Owyn smiled. "Let's see. Aven is our Water, and you know his parents if you been here forever. Milon's Companions Jehan and Aleia?"

Nestor laughed, clapping his hands like a child. "Oh, really?" he crowed. "How wonderful! Who else?"

"Our Earth is a Healer, and her name is Treesi. She's from someplace east of here. And you know our Air."

Nestor looked puzzled. "Your Alanar? Is he Aria's Air?"

"No," Owyn laughed. "No, our Air is Del."

Nestor's face paled. "Del? Our Del? Our poor broken child?"

Owyn nodded. "He's it. We all knew it the minute we saw him."

"But...but..."

"He's smart as anything, too," Owyn continued. "He's going to be a great part of us."

"But he doesn't speak!" Nestor protested.

"So?" Owyn looked curiously at Nestor. "You called him broken. I'm betting you never called him that to his face?"

Nestor reared back in shock. "Of course not! That would have been rude!"

"And he'd probably have taken your head off. He's tough as steel, that one. He's out at sea with Aven at the moment, and I've heard tell that he's a fantastic trader."

"A trader?" Nestor echoed. "Our Del? He was always so fragile. Afraid of his own shadow. I'd never have believed it."

"Do you blame him? After what he went through?" Owyn asked. "But he survived it. That shows his strength. And...you not believing he could? Maybe that's part of the problem. If the people around him didn't believe he could, why should he even try?" He met Nestor's eyes. "Mannon believed in him, didn't he?"

"Mannon thinks that boy hung the stars in the sky," Nestor answered.

"There you go, then. If you've got the right people behind you, you can do pretty much anything." He grinned. "Now, why don't we just get the rest of this out of the way. What else are you not supposed to tell me?"

CHAPTER FIFTEEN

There was no sign of Alanar when Owyn arrived in the dining room for the midday meal. Nestor hurried off when Owyn asked about him, and came back with the news that Alanar was dining with the servants, that Memfis was with him, and that Owyn was not to worry about him.

Owyn scowled at that. "He knows that only makes me worry more." He heard someone laugh behind him, and turned in his chair to see Mannon had come into the dining room.

"Healer Alanar is making great friends below stairs," Mannon said as he sat down at the table. "And the housekeeper is treating him like gold. I daresay he's eating better than we are today." He picked up his cup and asked, "Do you think you've accomplished anything?"

"Maybe," Owyn answered "We've got something that might be a plan. But I want you to look at it."

Mannon nodded. "Tell me about it."

Owyn took a bite of bread, chewed and swallowed it. "A census, first. We need to know who is out there."

Mannon looked shocked. "That's a massive undertaking," he said.

"Oh, it's huge," Owyn agreed. "Which is why it needs to start as soon as possible. And the people who go out to count noses need to do two things. First, they need to spread the word that you're standing down for Aria. People need to know why we're counting noses, so maybe they won't hide from the people counting. But we're going to miss a lot of people who don't want anything to do with you. Can't be helped, really." He shrugged and took a sip of tea. "And second, they need to see how folks react to the news. We need to know which leaders and which communities are going to be the troublemakers." He frowned. "I'm not sure how we're going to get to the Air tribes in the mountains, or out to the Water tribes in the deep. Haven't come up with that one yet. Maybe if we contact Alanar's flock...Nestor?" He turned in his seat, and saw that the older man was already writing it down. "Thanks. And we can get Aven's help once he's back, assuming his grandmother's canoe will even speak to us." He turned back to Mannon. "That's the first bit. While you're doing that, we're going to head to the Temple."

Mannon nodded. "That makes sense. And once she has the Crown?"

"Then we have a very public ceremony transferring power," Owyn answered. "And then, whatever happens next depends on Aria. Nestor told me that we have to have a progress? That it's the law?"

"The Heir's Progress is a mandatory part of the ritual of succession," Nestor said. "The lore dictates that the Heir must follow Axia's path through Adavar. To not complete the progress is to court disaster."

'Right," Owyn said. "I never heard of that before, and I'm assuming you didn't do it?" He turned toward Mannon, who grimaced. "Didn't think so. Aria has to go, so she can start putting things right, and so that everyone knows her. Oh, and part of that census is going to be finding everyone we can under the age of sixteen who might be related to a former Firstborn. We need a pool of young people to take to the Temple to find our Heir." Privately, he thought he knew who their Heir would be — the baby Aria carried. But he wasn't telling Mannon that!

Mannon nodded slowly. "You've put a lot of thought into this, I think."

"I'm not sure we've put enough," Owyn countered. "But it gets us started and moving forward." He looked up as the dining room door opened again, and smiled to see Memfis leading Alanar into the room. "There you are!" he called, and got out of his chair. He hurried over to Alanar and took his hand. "I was worrying about you."

"I'm fine," Alanar said, squeezing Owyn's hand. "I'm done taking care of the servants. There's an ague running through the children, or I'd have been done sooner. I've taken care of them, and they'll be fine in a day or two. The adults are remarkably healthy."

"I do take care of my people," Mannon called. "Thank you, Healer."

Alanar bowed his head in response, then smiled. "So what have you been up to?" he asked.

"Come sit, and we'll tell you. Mem, I want your opinion, too." He led Alanar to sit in the chair next to his, then sat back down. He kept Alanar's hand in his as he repeated the plans to him and Memfis. When he finished, he looked at Alanar. "All right. Poke holes in it."

"Where are you getting the manpower for the census?" Alanar asked. "You're going to need a lot of people and a lot of time."

"We can move people by ship," Mannon said. "And reestablish the posting stations so that we can have more ready movement. And I'm thinking we'll find at least half the people we need in the guard."

"You have that many guards?" Alanar asked. He whistled. "How do you feed them all?"

Mannon snorted. "We eat a lot of fish. That seems to be in good supply, at least. Now, I do agree with Owyn's assessment that Air and Water will be harder to reach. I don't think we'll have a completely accurate count."

"Probably not," Owyn said slowly. "But will the troublemakers we have to watch for be among them, or will they be down here, in the Earth tribes and south in Fire?" He frowned. "Where was Risha from?"

"South, on the Fire and Earth border," Alanar answered.

"That's going to be our area to watch, then," Owyn mused. "Pirit said that she thought Risha learned her poison there. There'll be some there that won't want an Air Firstborn."

"Like it or not, that's what they're getting," Memfis said.

"They won't like it," Owyn replied. "And they might try to do something about it." He frowned. "I'm going to have to convince Aria that she needs to keep you around."

"Me?" Mannon asked. "I assume you do mean me. Why?"

"Because if you're here, working with her, no one is going to raise a rebellion in your name. It won't work. At least, it won't work once the morons who get duped into it see that you're not playing those games."

Mannon chuckled. "Memfis, I do like your boy. He thinks faster than a racehorse."

"He does that," Memfis agrees. "He's a fine smith, too."

"I'm not surprised," Mannon said, nodding. "Is he a Smoke Dancer, too?"

Owyn nearly bit his tongue to keep from answering. Memfis blinked, but before he could say anything, Mannon laughed.

"The panicked look on all your faces!" he said. "That's priceless. I'll take that as a yes, then." He looked around the table. "Honestly, there's been a Smoke Dancer who stood with every Firstborn since Axia came down from the mountains with the Mother. Even when the Firstborn themselves was a Smoke Dancer, there was another one as their Companion. Now, I know Del doesn't have the gift. Aven is part Fire, but I don't think he does, either. Which means you have to be, or the cycle is broken."

"That's very logical," Alanar said. "You make it sound so easy to figure out."

Owyn snorted. "So now what?" he asked

"Now what indeed?" Mannon echoed. He picked up his cup and took a drink. "I understand keeping your secrets safe so that no one can use them against you, but some things just aren't as secret as you think." Then he shook his head, chuckling. "Really, what do you expect me or anyone to do with this information? How exactly can it be used against you?"

Owyn shrugged. "I really don't know," he admitted. "But I do know that anything can be a weapon. So tell me – why am I going to hand one to you?"

Mannon nodded. "Good point. Anything can be a weapon, and we should not be careless. Now, we should eat."

Owyn turned toward Alanar. "Have you eaten?"

Alanar nodded. "With the servants. Something warm to drink would be nice, though. I'm chilled."

Owyn blinked. "Chilled?" He saw a maid nearby. "A pot of tea?" he asked. The maid nodded and hurried out.

"Tea would be good," Alanar said. He slipped his cold hand into Owyn's. "And then I think I might go and lay down."

"Allie?" Owyn turned in his seat. "Allie, are you getting sick?"

"He said there was an ague—" Memfis started to say.

Alanar shook his head. "Something I was just exposed to today isn't going to catch me that quickly," he said. "I'm fine. Just tired. I'll go take a nap while you work." He laced his fingers into Owyn's. "I overextended, working with the children—"

"Which lowers your own defenses, no?" Mannon asked.

Owyn looked at him, then back at Alanar. "Allie?" he said slowly. "Is that right?"

Alanar sighed. "It can be. I've never had it happen before—"

"And you also haven't pushed yourself the way you have over the past few days. You overextended when we stopped in Shadow Cove, too." Owyn reached across with his other hand and touched the backs of his fingers to Alanar's forehead. The skin was hot. "Well, that decides that," he said. "Mannon, we're going to be going back to Terraces."

"Owyn!" Alanar protested.

"No. You're sick," Owyn answered. "And you need a healer. We're going home. We can go north later, once you're well."

"I can send you back to Terraces by ship," Mannon said. "And send a messenger to the Solstice village."

Owyn felt his stomach clench. By ship?

"I don't want to go by ship," Alanar said softly. "We'll go back by horse, the same way we got here."

Owyn realized why Alanar was refusing. "No, Allie," he said. "We should go back by ship. I don't want you getting worse." He looked across the table at Memfis. "Tell him. We should go back by ship. Then he'll be well in a few hours. Right?"

"No, Owyn," Alanar said, his voice firm. "This is between us. There's no trying to get someone else to convince me. I do not want to go back by ship. We'll go back overland."

"If you won't go by ship, then what about a coach?" Mannon asked. "It would be more comfortable than riding."

Owyn looked at Mannon, nodded his thanks, then turned back to Alanar. "Allie? Would that be good?"

Alanar closed his eyes and frowned. "A coach...won't that be slower than riding?"

"It can be," Mannon answered. "If there's no place to change horses. But given the pace you made getting here, I'd say you'd reach Terraces faster than if you ride, even without being able to change horses. If you won't go by ship, then go by coach. You won't have to stop as often. By coach, you can rest, and I'll send you off with extra guards to make sure that you're safe." He snorted. "Riding while sick is wretched. I know. I've done it."

"Thank you," Owyn said. He stood up. "Now, if you'll excuse me? I'm putting my healer to bed."

Back in their suite, Owyn settled Alanar on the edge of the bed, then went and closed the door. When he turned back, Alanar's head was bowed.

"Allie, you didn't need to do that," Owyn said gently. "I would have gotten on the ship."

"I'm not asking you to do that," Alanar replied. "Not for me. Not over just because I've got the sniffles. I'll be fine. I'll sleep, and I'll be fine."

Owyn sighed and crossed back to the bed. "I'm still going to fuss over you. So...can I help you into bed?"

Alanar tipped his head back. "I thought you'd never ask."

ALANAR FELL ASLEEP almost immediately after Owyn got him into bed. Owyn sat for a while and just him, listening to him breathe. His breathing sounded raspy. Congested.

Alanar was sicker than he was admitting. Owyn needed to take care of him. What could he do here? He looked around the bedroom – there wasn't a fireplace in here. Maybe he could arrange for a brazier, so he could get a kettle going for steam? That usually helped with congestion. He headed out into the sitting room, and was just reaching for the bell when someone knocked on the door.

"Come in!" he called. He laughed as Denis walked in. "You're good! I was just about to ring for you!"

"I'm told that Healer Alanar is feeling poorly," Denis said. "I came to see if you needed anything."

"Can we get a brazier and a kettle?" Owyn asked. "There's no fireplace in the bedroom, and I wanted to get some steam in there. He's breathing rough."

"Of course," Denis said. "I'll bring one immediately. What about tea? Broth?"

"Yes. To both. Thank you." Owyn looked around. He frowned. "What else? Anything else you can think of? I...I never had to do this before."

Denis smiled. "It will be all right, Fireborn," he said gently. "I'll go fetch our housekeeper. Since we don't have a palace healer, Ambaryl takes care of our ails. She's had some healing training, and she'll know what to do."

"I'd appreciate that," Owyn said. "If she could come up and listen to him breathe? I don't like the sound of it."

"I'll go send for her now, and bring the brazier and kettle right back." Denis left the room, and Owyn slumped down onto one of the couches. They needed a healer, and there was no way Jehan would send one to the palace. Which meant that Owyn needed to get Alanar home. Maybe he could convince the healer to get on a ship?

And probably destroy any hope of a future for them. Alanar wasn't going to willingly go onboard a ship, not knowing about Owyn's waking vision. Owyn couldn't force him without destroying what they'd built between them, something he wasn't willing to do. So the coach was going to be their best option to get back to Terraces. If they left in the morning, they'd make the ruins and camp there tomorrow, and go to Shadow Cove the next day. Or maybe they could push and make it all the way to Terraces by the second day. He didn't know enough about coaches or how fast they could travel to know for sure. Maybe Denis could tell him?

Denis returned, carrying a large brazier, and with a kettle hanging from one arm. Owyn jumped up and hurried over to him, taking the brazier and grunting at the weight of it.

"You're stronger than you look," he told Denis.

"I'm in service," Denis replied with a laugh. "I have to be. Put that in the bedroom. I'll fill this, and then go fetch the coals. Ambaryl will be bringing tea and soup, and she'll take a look at Healer Alanar."

Owyn carried the heavy brazier into the bedroom and set it down so that he could look for a good place to put it. There was no hearth, and the floors were wood covered with carpets. He frowned. Where to put it? Was there a stand? The braziers he'd helped Memfis make had stands, so that they didn't burn the floor. He hunted around the room for a moment, then went back out into the sitting room. Denis had just come back into the room, carrying a coal bucket.

"Is there a stand?" Owyn asked.

Denis winced. "I forgot that? Ah...there's a cupboard, in the corner of the bathing room. There should be a stand in there. We mostly use braziers in there during the winter."

Owyn nodded and hurried off. Inside the cupboard, he found the folded tripod, and a stone basin. He brought them both out. "Brazier goes in the bowl?" he asked.

"Yes," Denis answered. "Do you not know how?"

"It's just different from the way we set up the ones we used to make," Owyn answered. "Let me get it set, and you can bring in the coal." He went into the bedroom and set the brazier up. When he straightened, he noticed Alanar's eyes were open.

"What are you doing?" Alanar asked.

"Getting some steam in here to help you breathe," Owyn answered. "And the housekeeper is coming up with tea and soup, and to listen to you breathe."

Alanar nodded. Then he winced. "My head feels like it's two sizes too big."

"Just lie still," Owyn said. "We'll get this set up, and we'll get some tea into you. Denis is here to help."

Owyn and Denis quickly got the brazier set up, the coals poured in, and the kettle in place. Once he set the full kettle on the brazier, Owyn sat on the side of the bed. "Any ideas what this is?"

Alanar grimaced. "Winter ague, I think," he answered, and Owyn went cold. He'd suspected that was going to be the answer. But Alanar surprised him by continuing, "I've had it before. Not this badly, though."

"Of course not," Owyn said. He touched Alanar's forehead, wincing at the heat radiating from him. "You live with other healers. They wouldn't let it get this bad." He made up his mind, then leaned down and kissed Alanar. "We'll be going home tomorrow."

"How?" Alanar demanded. "The only way we're getting home tomorrow if it's by ship. I'm not going on a ship."

"I didn't say we were going on ship. I didn't say that we'd be home tomorrow," Owyn corrected. "I said we'd be going home tomorrow. By coach. I'm not going to force you, Allie. I'm just worried."

"It's just winter ague!"

"And in Forge, winter ague kills!"

Alanar looked startled. "What?"

"You didn't know?" Owyn asked. "If there's no healer, what happens with winter ague? You didn't learn that?"

"I...I did, but I never thought..." Alanar stopped, closed his eyes. "You'd think I'd know by now that there are not enough healers. That there are people who die from simple things because there's no one to take care of them."

"Right now, you need to let me take care of you," Owyn said, smoothing Alanar's hair. "We'll leave first thing. We'll be home the day after tomorrow."

Alanar nodded. "I'm sorry I ruined our trip, Owyn."

"It's not your fault, love," Owyn said. "We'll try again when you're well. We'll go in the summer. It'll be nice."

"It'll be hot," Alanar grumbled.

"Until we get north, it'll be hot," Owyn agreed. He swallowed and forced himself to smile. Alanar said that he could hear it when Owyn smiled "But we'll be fine."

"I'm scaring you, aren't I?" Alanar asked.

"Oh, fuck yes!"

"I'm sorry, Owyn," Alanar repeated. He fumbled for Owyn's hand. "You do what's best. I'll abide."

There was a knock at the door, and Owyn turned to see Denis and a woman about his aunt's age.

"Fireborn, this is Ambaryl," Denis said. "She's brought the tea and the soup."

"Think you can drink, Allie?" Owyn asked.

"I'll try."

CHAPTER SIXTEEN

Owyn scrubbed his hand over his face and watched as horses were hitched to a large coach. He'd spent most of the night awake, listening to Alanar's labored breathing. This morning, Alanar seemed worse, and Owyn wasn't sure if leaving was the right answer.

"You look like you didn't sleep at all. Where's Alanar?"

Owyn turned at the voice and smiled weakly at Memfis. "I didn't. And he's still inside, where it's warm and Ambaryl can fuss over him. He doesn't sound good, Mem. I keep thinking that maybe we should stay? Or Alanar can stay with you, and I can go. I can bring a healer back here—"

"But do they have anyone they can send?" Memfis asked. "There didn't seem to be many healers there when I was there."

Owyn closed his eyes, then shook his head. "No. No, there's no one they can send. Right now for trained healers in Terraces? It's Jehan and Pirit. There are seven students, but they all just started training."

Memfis frowned. "And Treesi is off with Aria, you said."

Owyn nodded. "Right, and you don't know that. At all. But even if she wasn't, it doesn't matter. There aren't enough healers to send one here. Even if I thought Jehan would send one here. He won't. Better for us to go back."

Memfis nodded slowly, but there was an odd look on his face. Which vanished completely as he looked past Owyn. Owyn turned, and saw that Mannon had come out into the courtyard.

"How is Healer Alanar?" he asked as he joined them.

Owyn grimaced. "Not good. Worse than he was last night. His breathing is awful, and his fever keeps getting higher."

Mannon shuddered. "I wish you'd reconsider going by ship."

"I thought about it," Owyn said. He honestly had, somewhere in the darkness before dawn. "And the minute Alanar was well, he'd kick my arse from Terraces to Forge, and I'd only bounce twice."

Mannon looked stunned for a moment, then barked with laughter. "Only twice," he asked. "Is he that impressive in his anger?"

"I'm told so," Owyn answered. "I haven't gotten him mad yet. Don't want to. I intend to have a nice, long, married life. So we're going by coach." He glanced at the coach, then looked at Mannon. "How long will it take? You said it could be faster than going by horse. How much faster?"

Mannon looked thoughtful. "If you push, you could be back in Terraces late tomorrow, assuming the weather holds. If you need to stop, it'll be midday the day after. That's a long time to be out with winter ague. You'll end up sick."

"It'll be worth it. And we're heading for the healers," Owyn said. "Look, I appreciate your help. I do. We need to get on the road. But...ah...when should I expect that letter for Aria?"

Mannon held up a bundle. "This letter? I drafted it last night. Everything you said you wanted, all the assurances. It's not sealed, so you're welcome to read it. My seal is over my signature, so you can swear that I did write it." He handed it to Owyn. "If Aria agrees, have her send a messenger here, and I'll come to Terraces to meet with her."

Owyn nodded. "I'll tell her. Don't expect her to make up her mind right off, now."

Mannon smiled. "I don't. I don't imagine this will be an easy decision for her to make. I'm patient. I've waited this long, after all."

He looked at Memfis. "When the time comes to go to Terraces, you'll come with me?"

"You wouldn't be able to leave me behind," Memfis said. "I'd go now—"

"I need you here," Mannon interrupted.

"But you need me here," Memfis finished smoothly. He winked at Owyn. "We'll be all right."

Mannon scowled at Memfis. "You delight in making me want to pull my hair out, don't you?"

Memfis laughed. "It gives meaning to my life," he answered. "Now, it looks like the coach is loaded. And there's Alanar."

Owyn saw that Alanar was coming toward the coach, being led by Denis and leaning heavily on his arm. For the first time since Owyn had met him, the tall healer looked frail.

"I need to get him home," he whispered. "And soon." He looked at Mannon. "If we push, we'll be home tomorrow night?"

Mannon nodded. "If the weather holds." He looked up. "It looks like it might. But you won't get further than the ruins tonight, I don't think."

Owyn nodded. He looked up at the sky — clear blue, with thin, high clouds — then walked over to Alanar. "How are you feeling, Allie?"

Alanar scowled. "It's in my head, and it's fucking with my balance. I can't tell where I am, Wyn."

"Healer Alanar almost walked into a wall," Denis added. "I thought it best to help him."

"Thank you, Denis," Owyn said. He took Alanar's other hand. "Mannon says that we could be home tomorrow night, if we push it. Think you can make it?"

Alanar frowned. "What other options do we have? I'm not going by ship."

Owyn considered the only other option, then blurted, "No, but you could stay here and let Ambaryl and Denis fuss over you. And I'll go back by ship, and bring Jehan back with me tomorrow."

Alanar coughed, then coughed again, tugging his arm free from Denis' grasp so that he could wipe his mouth. "I...I don't want you going on a ship without me. And I'm not going on a ship at all."

"Allie, you need a healer," Owyn said, keeping his voice low. "I'm willing to take the risk to save your life, and our future."

"Will Jehan come?" Alanar asked. "To the Palace?"

"If we sent someone, probably not," Owyn answered. "If I go, and deliver Mannon's letter, and tell him he's needed? I think he'll come. Because it's you, and because I asked him to come." He looked at Denis, who was nodding.

"It'll be better for you to stay, I think," he said. "Being on the road will be hard when you're this sick, and if you take a turn for the worse, there's no one to help."

Alanar growled, low in his throat. His congestion made it sound like he was trying to imitate a spitting cat. "I'm not dying, you two!" he insisted. "I'd know the difference. I'm fine to travel. I just can't tell where my feet are. It's like wearing shoes."

"You're sure?" Owyn asked. Alanar growled at him again, and Owyn sighed. "You're sure. All right. Let's get you into the coach. Then we can both sleep, at least. Thank you, Denis." He led Alanar to the coach and helped him into the back. He could see blankets folded on one of the benches, and a small brazier on the floor.

"There's a basket coming from the kitchen," Denis said. "Flasks of tea and broth, and something more substantial if any of us feel like eating before we stop."

"Us?" Owyn asked. He turned to face the servant. "Are you coming with us?"

Denis nodded. "You need help looking after Alanar, and you need looking after yourself. I asked, and was given permission. I'm to make the trip there and back." He smiled. "You need looking after, too. Not as much as Healer Alanar, but you do. So I'm going to take care of you, so you can take care of him."

Owyn looked into the coach at Alanar, then over at Denis. "Thank you," he said. "And...do I thank Ambaryl or Nestor or Mannon for letting you come with us?"

"Ultimately, it was me, and you're welcome," Mannon said as he came over to them. "I'm just hoping that you're not sick as well by the time you get back."

"If I am, Jehan will put me to rights," Owyn said. He held his hand out. "Thank you. And...well, thank you."

Mannon smiled. "You're welcome. On all counts. Tell Aria I'm eager to work with her."

"The minute I see her," Owyn said. He turned to see Memfis was standing behind him. The older man smiled, then pulled Owyn into a tight embrace.

"Be careful," Memfis murmured. "I'll see you soon, I hope."

Owyn nodded. His throat felt tight, and he wasn't sure he could speak. He swallowed, then swallowed again. "You need to be there," he croaked. "You have to be there when I get married, Fa."

Memfis laughed. "I wouldn't miss it for anything. And we have some air to clear between us, and I don't think we can do it in the time we have. Let me just say this. I love you, my Mouse." He let go of Owyn and stepped back. "I never asked. How's Trinket?"

"Fine. Probably getting fat," Owyn answered. "Rhexa spoils her."

Memfis chuckled. "That's not a bad thing. Unless Rhexa has a cat?"

"No, and she's promised to take care of Trinket and keep her away from cats and shadow hawks."

"Shadow hawks?" Mannon asked. "In Terraces? That's a long way from their usual ranges."

Owyn nodded. "That's what Marik said. He talks to birds. He wasn't sure if the hawk was going to stay in Terraces."

"You have a friend who talks to birds?" Mannon asked slowly. "That's unusual."

Owyn grinned. "That's Marik." He looked around, seeing that Freckles and Meadowfoam had been brought out and were being put on leading reins. "Oh, thank you. I hadn't even thought about Freckles. Leaving him here would have been bad."

"Why?" Mannon asked.

"Not sure. But he's smart. He might have followed me, and taken Meadowfoam with him for good measure." Owyn turned back and smiled. "Thank you. Again. But we need to be going if we're going to get back to Terraces tomorrow."

"Go, then," Mannon said. "I'll see you when it's time."

Owyn nodded and headed for the coach. For the first time since they'd arrived, he saw Garrity and Evarra, and felt a momentary pang that he hadn't even given them a thought before now. Garrity waved at him.

"Heard you've been busy overthrowing the government," he said as Owyn came closer. "What in the Mother's name did you do?"

Owyn chuckled. "Wasn't my idea. It just seemed to happen. What do you know?"

"Pretty much all of it, I think," Evarra said. "That Mannon is stepping down in favor of Aria, and that you're to carry the message. We were below with the servants, and we bunked out with the guards. So we heard all the gossip. And we know that the all-fired rush to get back is because Alanar is sick."

Owyn nodded. "You do know all of it. Good. They've told me that if we push, we can be back in Terraces tomorrow night. Think you two can push harder, and be back before us? I think we need to give Jehan a warning about what's coming."

Garrity nodded. "Yeah, that's a good idea. We can do that." He looked at Evarra. "What do you think?"

She looked thoughtful. "We'll need our own supplies. Let me get them and we'll ride out." She headed toward a small group, where Owyn could see several packhorses.

Owyn turned back to Garrity. "Be careful, the two of you," he said.

Garrity smiled. "It's not the trip we thought we'd have, is it? But it might have turned out better than we hoped. You keep an eye on Alanar on the way back. We'll see you tomorrow." He clapped Owyn on the shoulder and went to join Evarra.

Owyn went back to the coach. Mannon and Memfis had both gone back into the Palace, so Owyn climbed in to see that Alanar was already bundled into blankets, and that Denis had taken the bench facing him. Owyn took his place beside Alanar, tugged a blanket over his legs, then reached for Alanar's hand.

"I'm ready," he said. "Let's go home."

Denis reached up and knocked on the wall of the coach. A moment later, they were moving.

THE WARMTH OF THE BLANKETS, the rocking of the coach, and Alanar's comforting presence against his side all combined to lull Owyn into a deep sleep almost immediately after they were on the road. He slept without dreaming until the coach hit something hard enough to jolt him awake.

"What?" he gasped, still closer to sleep than awareness. He scrubbed one hand over his face. "What was that?"

"A rock, I think," Denis answered. He set the book he'd been reading down and looked out the coach window. "The roads are getting worse and worse, I'm told."

Owyn blinked, trying to clear the sleep out of his eyes. He looked out the window and frowned, trying to judge from the light how long he'd slept. Where were they? "Yeah," he said absently. "Yeah, when we were on the road from Forge to Terraces, the roads were horrible. How long was I asleep? Where are we?"

"You slept most of the day," Denis answered. "Alanar woke about midday and ate something, but he thought you needed the rest, so we let you sleep."

"Really? I slept the whole day?" Owyn glanced to the side, where Alanar was leaning against the side of the coach, his eyes closed. Owyn couldn't tell if he was asleep, or just listening. "Did you leave me anything to eat?"

Alanar snorted, revealing that he was awake. Denis just looked appalled.

"Of course there's food left for you!" he declared. "I'm not sure if the tea is still warm, but there are flatbread rolls for you—"

"Flatbread...rolls?" Owyn repeated. "What's that?"

"They're tasty," Alanar murmured. His voice still sounded raspy and strained.

Owyn chuckled and reached for Alanar's hand. "Thought you might be awake. How do you feel?"

"My head feels like that rock we just hit," Alanar answered. "It's why my eyes are closed. It helps, I think. And my chest is congested. I'm surprised my coughing didn't wake you up."

"So am I," Owyn replied. "But we'll be home soon, and we'll get you fixed up. All right. What's a flatbread roll?"

Denis leaned down and took something out of a basket, handing it to Owyn. It was tube shaped, and wrapped in a cloth. Unwrapping it revealed what looked to Owyn like a round loaf of bread. He picked it up in both hands and turned it, and laughed when he saw the end.

"It's like a stew spiral?" he asked. Denis looked blank. "You don't have them here?" Owyn asked. "It's something I learned to cook in Forge, when I was learning to cook."

"What is it?"

Owyn took a bite from his roll, which proved to be filled with some kind of marinated vegetable mix, and slices of what tasted like bacon. He swallowed, then grinned. "I like this. Stew spiral. Okay, you take a cheap cut of meat. You pound it really, really thin. You fill it with thin slices of onions and garlic, maybe some sliced hard-cooked eggs, and herbs. Then you roll it up, tie it, and fry it. Then you let it cook on the hearth in a spicy pepper sauce all day, until the meat is tender and falling apart. You slice it, and you serve it with bread."

"When are you making this for me?" Alanar asked.

Owyn grinned. "If we can get the right cut of meat, I'll make it for you once you're well enough to taste it. You can't taste anything with a stuffed up head. Although the peppers might help."

"They might, but I'll wait." Alanar nodded. He cocked his head to the side. "The wheels sound different. Denis, are we slowing down?"

Denis looked out the window again. "Appears so. We might be at the ruins. And I was told to make sure you both stayed inside and warm while the guards set up camp."

"I can help set up camp," Owyn protested.

Denis smiled. "My orders were to take care of you, so that you didn't get sick before we reached Terraces and the healers. Now eat, Owyn, and I'll pour out some tea." Denis reached down again and pulled out a bundle that he unwrapped to reveal a flask. He filled a cup and handed it to Owyn. "Now, tell me more about this stew spiral," he added. "What's in the pepper sauce?"

Owyn ate his roll and drank his tea, and he talked about cooking with Denis and Alanar. Denis, it turned out, was married to one of the cooks in the Palace, and had three children, two of whom Alanar had treated for winter ague the day before.

Alanar smiled when he heard their names. "They're sweet girls, the pair of them. Neither one fussed at all when I was examining them."

Denis looked very pleased. "I'll tell them you said so, Healer," he said. "I'll admit, I wasn't sure how they'd react. They've never met a real healer before."

Alanar sighed. "That's so wrong. There are supposed to be healers everywhere. There are supposed to be more of us. And Risha stole that. From everyone. It'll take generations before there are enough healers again that every community has one."

Owyn bundled up the cloth that had been wrapped around his roll, and reached over to take Alanar's hand. "We'll find more. We'll find others, and we'll get them trained. That'll be something else for the census — finding people descended from healers so that they can be tested."

"How many of them will be like Risha, though?" Alanar asked.

"We'll root that out—" Owyn stopped and laughed. "I sound like Aunt Rhexa."

Alanar smiled slightly. "You do. And I know. We'll find untrained healers. We'll raise more. It's just an enormous undertaking, and...it'll be mine, won't it? I'm the strongest healer out there besides Jehan. Well, Aven might be stronger, but he can't stand as Senior Healer. He's a Companion."

"He'll help you," Owyn said. "And you know I will."

Alanar nodded. "I know. It's just...daunting. I never thought I'd be a leader."

"That'll make you good at it," Denis murmured. "You'll try harder. Think about it more."

Someone knocked on the door to the coach and called, "The tents are up, and the fire is lit!"

"Thank you," Denis called back. He turned to Owyn and smiled. "Let me show you to your tent. Then we'll get supper started while you rest."

"I've been resting," Owyn protested. "Why can't I help?"

"Because if you don't rest, Alanar won't rest?" Denis suggested.

Owyn scowled. He glanced at Alanar, then looked back at Denis. "Guess I'm resting, then."

CHAPTER
SEVENTEEN

O wyn helped Alanar out of the coach, and looked at the camp. There was a large blaze in a central fire-pit, and several tents had been erected. There were a lot more guards than he'd realized — he counted at least a dozen. Why so many?

"Denis, why'd Mannon send so many guards out with us?" he asked. "And which is our tent?"

One of the guards looked up when Owyn spoke. She walked toward them. "Yours is the tent in the middle, Fireborn. And we're all out here partly because we were just drilling and eating our heads off in the barracks, and getting out into the field is good for us. And partly because the only coaches in these parts are Lord Mannon's, and they've been attacked before. It's one of the reasons he doesn't use them much anymore — it's safer to go on horseback, light and fast." She looked around. "Now, your tent isn't quite ready — they buried the bed box in the baggage cart."

"The what?" Alanar asked, turning to face the guard. He winced and lowered his head, closing his eyes.

"Your head still bothering you?" Owyn asked.

"It's better, until I do something like that," Alanar said with a grimace. "Then the pressure in my head makes it feel like it's going to roll off my shoulders and across the floor. Denis, what's in that tonic that Ambaryl sent? It helped, but I don't want to take too much of it without knowing what's in it."

"I'm not exactly sure," Denis admitted. "It's good, though."

"It is," Alanar agreed. "I'll wait to take more, though. Now, what's a bed box? And what's your name?"

"I'm Esai, Healer." The guard smiled. "And the bed box is something Lord Mannon designed. It's more comfortable than a bedroll. I'll..." She stopped, and Alanar laughed.

"You were about to say you'd show me?" the healer asked.

Esai blushed. "I...yes. Sorry."

"It's fine. I'm used to it. Describe it, please?"

"It's..." Esai faltered. She turned toward Owyn. "Fireborn, you're a smith, I heard? Maybe you can help? I can't really describe it other than saying it's a bed in a box."

"You're going to have to show it to me," Owyn answered. "I have no idea what you're talking about."

Esai nodded. She looked, then nodded again. "They've found it. Come with me." She led them toward the middle tent, where Owyn saw two other guards carrying something between them — a wooden box that looked like the trunk he'd had in his bedroom back in Forge. As they got closer, he realized that the trunk was wider than the one he'd owned.

"Is that it?" he asked Esai.

"Yes. It's a very clever thing," she answered. They entered the tent, where the other guards had opened the trunk, and one of them was taking pegs out of the front corners. The front of the trunk was hinged, and fell forward to reveal that the box was filled with what looked like slats of wood.

"It's a box of wood. Wood slats, I mean," Owyn said slowly. "Looks like they've got hinges, though. Wait a minute..." His jaw dropped as one of the guards grabbed a rope handle on one of the slats of wood and pulled, dragging the slats out of the trunk. They unfolded into a frame, with a canvas sheet filling the interior space. "It's a bed-frame!" Owyn gasped.

"In a box?" Alanar asked.

"Yeah. They fold out, and there's a canvas in the middle, like a cot." As Owyn watched, the guard at the head of the bed took six horseshoe-shaped pieces of metal from the box. He reached down and slotted one into holes on either side of the hinge at the top of the bed, then handed three of the remaining to the other guard. There were, Owyn could see, identical holes around each hinge, and once the metal pieces were in place, the frame was forced open, and the canvas was stretched taut. "They're locking the hinges open," he added. "And it puts tension on the canvas. Esai, this is brilliant!"

She grinned. "It is, isn't it? You'll be comfortable, and it breaks down with almost no effort. We don't have many of them, so they're reserved for high-ranking officers and guests."

"Well, we appreciate it," Owyn told her. He looked up at Alanar. "Want to get some sleep, once they finish? Or are you hungry?"

Alanar frowned slightly. "I could eat, I think. I'm definitely thirsty."

"Someone should have started making supper," Esai said. "And there will be water heating for tea."

She led them out of the tent and toward the fire-pit. There were small camp chairs set up. Owyn led Alanar to one, then sat down at his feet and leaned against his knee. From where he was sitting, he could see a beach in the distance, and it reminded him of the cove. That night in the cove felt as if it had happened years ago, not months.

"You don't have to sit on the ground," Alanar murmured, running his fingers through Owyn's hair.

Owyn sighed and pressed closer. "If I didn't, you couldn't do that," he murmured. Alanar chuckled.

"Tea, sirs?" one of the guards asked. He picked up a kettle and filled two cups, passing them to Owyn. Owyn tipped his head back.

"Allie, I have a cup for you," he said. Alanar held his hand out, taking the cup that Owyn handed to him. He sipped his tea, then sighed. "I can't taste it. What am I drinking?"

Owyn took a sip of his, trying to puzzle out the flavors. "Mint, I think. Thyme? And...is that redbark?"

"Mistress Ambaryl says that mint and thyme kill the sickness, and that redbark is good for bringing on sweats to break a fever," Esai offered. "It's her 'cures what ails you' tea. But a bunch of us just like the taste. There's mallow in it, too."

"Which is good for sore throats and coughing," Alanar said. He took another sip. "And elderberry? If she's using the common herbs."

"Pretty sure, yes." Esai took another cup of tea and sat down in another chair. "Supper will be soon, I think. Then an early night. You wanted to push through to Terraces tomorrow, Fireborn?"

"Please, my name is Owyn," Owyn said. "And yes, if we can."

Esai looked up at the sky. "The weather should hold. It'll be a long day. A hard one, too. Are you both up for that?"

Owyn looked up at Alanar, who shrugged one shoulder. "I'll probably sleep most of it," the healer said. "You should ride at least a bit of it. You don't have to sit in the coach with me."

"I want to sit in the coach with you," Owyn protested.

"It'll be safer, too," Esai added. "You're not armed—"

"He is," Alanar interrupted. Then he frowned. "You are, aren't you?"

"I have my whip chain," Owyn answered.

"A whip chain?" Esai gasped. "Really? I've read about those! I've never seen one!"

Owyn smiled and looked back at her. "Do you want to?" He took the whip chain out of his pouch and passed it to her. "This is mine. Memfis made it for me."

She ran the links through her hands. "This is it?" she asked, looking up. "It...doesn't seem like much of a weapon."

"It is," Alanar said. "And Owyn is very good with it." He grinned. "Not so good with a crossbow—"

"Hey!" Owyn protested, and Alanar laughed until he started coughing. "Drink your tea and stop making fun of me," Owyn grumbled. He turned back to see Esai smiling at him. "You want to see?" he asked, and held his hand out. She handed the whip chain back to him, and he got to his feet. He draped the chain over his shoulders, taking the blade off the end and replacing it with the ball. Then he looked around. "All right. I'm going on the other side of the coach. You all don't go any further than the coach to watch me. Understand?"

Esai nodded, her eyes wide. "We'll stay back. But you changed the tip—"

"I can still bash your skull in by accident, so stay back," Owyn repeated. "Denis? Stay with Alanar, please?" He walked away from the fire, past the coach, and out to the open area of grass. He turned in a circle, seeing the guards arranging themselves on either side of the coach. None of them came past it, and he nodded. He closed his eyes, took a deep breath, then snapped the chain forward, listening to it sing. Distantly, he heard shouts and cheering, but the music of the whip chain slicing through the air. It felt good to move, to dance, and he let himself flow with the chain, letting it wrap around his body, then whipping it out before the ball could break his bones. He spun, throwing his whip hand forward, then snapping it back and hearing the ball whistle past him. He started to slow, hearing the whip's song deepen and soften as he drew the chain in wider, lazy circles, until it was slow enough that he could let it wrap around his other arm. He fell still, breathing hard.

The cheering was startling, and Owyn jumped as the guards rushed toward him, all of them talking at once. Esai reached him first.

"That was amazing!" she gasped. "I've never seen anyone move like that! And you couldn't see the chain at all! I...how can anyone stand against that?"

Owyn sniffed, unwinding the chain and folding it back up. "Someone took me down with a polearm," he answered. Then he realized what he'd said. It had been one of Mannon's guards who had taken him down. One of Esai's companions, maybe one of her friends. He swallowed. "I...yeah."

He must have blushed, or gone pale, or something, because Esai rested her hand on his arm. "What's wrong?" she demanded. "You all of a sudden look like you're going to pass out." She looked around. "Someone bring some water!"

"No, I'm fine," Owyn protested. Fuck, if Alanar thought he was going to be sick..."I'm fine, Esai!" He looked around. "It's just...look, don't kill me, okay? Mannon will get mad at you."

"What?" Esai looked confused. "What are you talking about?"

Owyn grimaced. He was surrounded. "If you do...leave Alanar alone?"

"Owyn!" Esai grabbed him by the upper arms. "Will you please explain?"

Owyn swallowed. He looked past her, past the other guards, and saw Alanar standing with Denis. "Just..." Owyn stopped. Closed his eyes. "Promise me, Esai."

"No one is going to hurt you or Alanar or anyone!" Esai said, her voice firm. "That's a promise. Now what is it?"

"The one who took me down with the polearm," Owyn said slowly. "He was a guard. One of you lot."

Esai blinked. "And...what happened to him?"

"He and his squadron were all killed," Owyn answered, keeping his voice low.

Esai looked even more confused. She looked around. "Did...did we have a squadron go missing? And I missed it?"

The surrounding guards looked at each other, all talking at once. Finally, they fell silent, and another guard shook his head. "No. No squadrons missing. When was this? And where?"

"Mid-autumn, and south of Terraces." Owyn answered. "Ummm...there's a little village down there. Cliffside? You know it?"

"A day's ride south of Terraces?" one of the guards asked. "Yeah, that's Cliffside. My mother lives there. We don't patrol that far south. Haven't for years."

Owyn stared at him for a moment, then looked at Esai. She nodded. "We don't patrol past Terraces. You don't see guards down there unless we're heading to Forge, and then we go by ship."

"Then...who tried to kill us? Because they damn near did kill our Water, and they tried to take my head off." Owyn looked around. "Any of you have uniforms missing?"

"Owyn," Alanar called. "Remember that Mannon said that there were some guards who threw their lot in with Risha? Maybe they were more of hers?"

"You can hear me, way over there?" Owyn called back.

"Your voice gets louder when you're excited," Alanar answered. "And I could hear all of you better if you came closer."

A chuckle ran through the group of guards, and they walked back to the fire. Owyn sat down at Alanar's feet again, tucking the whip chain back into his pouch. "So, you never had troops south of Terraces?"

"Not for years and years," the guard who'd spoken earlier answered. "There's no forage there, and the hunting is awful. The farming gets worse and worse every year. I keep trying to get my mother to come and live in the Palace, but she won't. My fa is buried out there. She won't leave him."

"You're Earthborn," Alanar said.

"All through," the guard agreed with a grin.

"So, if there weren't any guards south of Terraces, then those guards must have come from Terraces. But...if they came from Mannon's guard originally, wouldn't you all have known them?" Owyn asked, looking around. Some of the guards frowned. Others started whispering to each other, gesturing as they spoke in low voices. Owyn tipped his head back against Alanar's knee, suddenly tired. He closed his eyes. "You wouldn't think I'd slept all day, as tired as I am now," he murmured, and smiled as Alanar ran his fingers through Owyn's hair. "How are you feeling?"

"Worn," Alanar answered. "Everything aches, and my breathing is tight. I want to be home."

Owyn reached up and took Alanar's hand. "Tomorrow, love. We'll be home tomorrow. We'll be in our own bed tomorrow night."

"No, I won't," Alanar said. "Jehan will make me spend at least the night in a ward room, in deep trance to make sure my lungs aren't damaged. The night after, we'll be in our own bed." He squeezed Owyn's hand. "I'm sorry."

"It's not your fault, Allie," Owyn said. He turned around onto his knees, kneeling between Alanar's legs. "It's not your fault you took sick. We'll get home tomorrow, and everything will be all right."

"Healer Alanar, here." Denis came up next to them, carrying a pair of flasks. "It's the tonic that Ambaryl sent. Then you can have some soup, and we'll see you off to bed." He put one flask into Alanar's hand, then handed the other to Owyn. "You should drink it, too. We don't want you to get sick as well."

Owyn took the flask and sniffed the contents. The scent made his nose tingle. What was in this? "I'm feeling fine," he protested, and tried to hand the flask back. "Save this for Alanar, for tomorrow."

"I have six more flasks just like this for tomorrow," Denis replied. "Three for you, three for Alanar. So drink it."

"Try it, Wyn," Alanar suggested.

Owyn stretched up and kissed him, then tapped his flask against Alanar's. "Well, here's to our health, then."

The first thing that Owyn noticed when he took a drink was that the tonic was alcohol-based. Brandy, he though. It burned his throat when he swallowed. He coughed.

"Wyn?"

"Wasn't ready for it," Owyn answered. He looked at the flask. "What is in this?"

Alanar took another sip. He shook his head. "My head is too stuffed up for me to answer. Denis?"

"I have no idea," Denis answered. "Ambaryl doesn't tell anyone her tonic recipes. But she did tell me once she learned them in her healer training. She just doesn't have the gift."

Alanar nodded. "She'd mentioned that she was a healing assistant. So this is a standard healing tonic, Owyn. We'll probably be able to find the recipe when we get home."

Owyn nodded. His face already felt warm. "Do I have to drink it all?" he asked. "I'll get drunk. Especially since we haven't eaten yet."

"I'll get you some food," Denis said, and walked toward the fire. Owyn corked the flask and turned, sitting down between Alanar's legs. He tipped his head to the side, resting his ear on Alanar's thigh.

"I feel fine," he grumbled. "If I get drunk, I won't feel fine."

"Pour it out," Alanar murmured. "Otherwise, he'll keep after you all night to drink it."

Owyn looked up. "You sure?"

"Yes," Alanar said. "Pour it out before he gets back. Drink the tea."

Owyn looked up, checking to see where Denis was. The servant's back was to them, so he quickly took the flask, pulled the cork, and poured the contents out into the dirt underneath Alanar's chair. He took his cup of tea and poured it into the empty flask, and took a long drink just as Denis came back toward them. The servant smiled and handed a bowl and spoon to Owyn.

"Eat all of it," Denis said, and gave another bowl and spoon to Alanar.

"You know, my fa is back in the Palace," Owyn pointed out. "I don't need another one."

Denis chuckled. "I apologize. I do tend to get over-protective when I'm serving on a personal level." He walked away, came back with two cups. "More tea?"

"Please," Alanar said.

They ate without talking, and Owyn listened to the conversations flare and fade among the guards. Esai sat closest to them, and kept glancing at Owyn. He smiled at her, and she blushed.

"Your heart rate just sped up," Alanar murmured. "What is it?"

Owyn tipped his head back. "One of the guards is interested in us," he whispered, keeping his voice pitched for Alanar's ears alone.

"Interested?" Alanar repeated. Then he grinned. "Oh? And, is the interest being returned?"

Owyn laughed. "No, love. Not by me. Now, if she's interested in you—"

"Unlikely," Alanar interrupted. "They all know I'm sick. Unless she intends to make plans for the future, it's you she's looking at."

Owyn snorted. "Well, I'm not looking at anyone but you." He looked down at his bowl, scraping his spoon against the bottom to get the last drops of broth. "I'm done. Are you done?"

"I didn't eat much," Alanar admitted. "I'm not very hungry. I am thirsty. Is there more tea?"

Owyn set his bowl aside and got up. "I'll get some more, and then I'm putting you to bed."

"Yes, Fa," Alanar said. Owyn laughed and headed toward the fire with their cups. He refilled them, and nearly ran Esai over when he turned back toward Alanar.

"Can I help?" she asked.

He shook his head. "I've got it, thanks. And I need to get Alanar to bed." He frowned. "Wait, actually. Yes. You can help. Can you bring another two cups of that tea? Alanar needs to keep drinking."

She smiled. "I'll follow you."

Owyn nodded and walked around her, back to Alanar. He handed a cup to the healer. "Drink that. Then it's time for bed."

Alanar took a sip, then turned his head. "Where's Denis? He's not fussing over us?"

"Denis went to find a convenient bush," Esai answered as she joined them. "How are you feeling, Healer?"

"Like I need one," Alanar answered. "We'll be home tomorrow, and I'm glad of it. If a patient came to me telling me that their chest felt the way mine does, I'd have them in a healing trance faster than you could blink!"

Owyn hesitated. "It's that bad?" he asked. He looked around, then turned to Esai. "There's no way we can travel all night, can we?"

Esai grimaced. She looked up, studied the sky for a moment, then shook her head. "It'll be harder at this phase of the moon," she answered. "It'll be dark. We'd risk breaking an axle on the coach."

Alanar chuckled. "My timing sucks," he laughed. The laughter turned to wet-sounding coughing, and when the coughs finally stopped, Owyn could clearly hear Alanar's breath whistling.

So could Esai.

"The moon should rise in a few hours," she said. "We'll head out then. Go get some sleep. We'll wake you when it's time to go."

CHAPTER EIGHTEEN

Owyn wasn't expecting to sleep at all. He'd already slept for hours, and he didn't feel tired. He tucked in with Alanar anyway, because he knew that the healer wouldn't settle if Owyn wasn't in bed. He lay in the dark, listening to Alanar struggle to breathe. He could hear the guards outside the tent. Some of them were probably packing up the camp, getting things ready to ride out when the moon rose.

He fell asleep trying to puzzle out how long it would take them to make it to Terraces if they started at moonrise.

And he woke to the sounds of shouting, and steel crashing and grating on steel.

"Fuck!" He rolled out of bed and grabbed for his trousers, tugging them on and stamping into his boots.

"Owyn?" Alanar sounded panicked. "Owyn, what's wrong?"

"Attack!" Owyn answered. "Stay here!" He grabbed his pouch and pulled the whip chain out, draping it over his shoulders. He turned, and the tent flap swung open; Denis rushed inside.

"Bandits!" he shrilled.

"I figured," Owyn said, keeping his voice level and calm. "Stay here with Alanar. Allie, do you have your staff?"

"No," Alanar answered. "And I couldn't use it if I did. Not with my head like this. Owyn, be careful."

Owyn nodded. He crossed over to the bed and leaned down, kissing Alanar hard. "I'll be careful," he said. "Stay here." He turned and ran out of the tent.

The fighting was being kept well back from the tents — the attack must have come up from the beach. He could see the guards, and thought about joining them. Then he realized that if he did, he ran the risk of being misidentified as another attacker. Better to guard the tent. He draped his whip chain over his shoulders, realizing that he hadn't replaced the ball after he'd shown off for the guards.

"Fuck," Owyn breathed, and pulled the blade out of his pouch. He watched the fighting in front of him, stepping back into the shadows...

And something sharp dug into his back.

"Don't shout," a voice hissed in his ear. An arm snaked out and encircled his neck, pulling him back. "Drop the chain, or you're dead."

He recognized the voice. *Teva*! He swore, then stabbed backwards with the blade, feeling it bite, hearing Teva shout. Pain ripped through his ribs, but he tore away from Teva's grip and rolled, coming up with the chain whistling. Teva staggered out of the shadows, blood running down his leg. He glared at Owyn, then whistled. Owyn saw a flare of light, and a stranger carrying a torch stepped into view from the far side of the tent. Owyn's mouth went dry.

"No!" he shouted, and snapped the whip chain into motion. The torch-man fell with a heavy thud, the torch landing in the dirt. Owyn whirled, the whip chain singing, looking for a target. Where was Teva?

Something hit him in the back, hard enough to knock him forward. The pain hit a heartbeat later and drove him to his knees. The whip chain fell from his fingers as he grabbed at his shoulder, stabbing his palm on something sharp and metal and wet with his blood. It took him a moment to realize that he'd been shot.

"Secure him," Teva shouted, his voice barely audible over the pain screaming in Owyn's ears. "Get them out of the tent and secure them, too."

Someone grabbed Owyn's arms and pulled them behind his back. He screamed, and heard Alanar calling his name. He forced himself to look up — Alanar looked like he had only just gotten his shirt on, and hadn't finished wrapping it. It hung open and hid nothing. His hair hung wild and loose around his shoulders. One of the men had him by the arm, dragging him away from the tent. Another man had Denis, who was clearly terrified, sobbing in his fear.

"Owyn!" Alanar called again.

Owyn heard Teva laugh. "Alanar! Well, it's good to see you again. And so much of you, too."

"Leave him alone," Owyn growled, pulling against the cords that someone was tightening around his wrists. "Teva, leave him alone!"

"Oh, I'm not going to touch him," Teva said. "Not without heavy gloves, anyway." He nodded toward the man holding Alanar. "Don't let him touch your bare skin."

Alanar stopped and turned toward Teva. "You think that's going to stop me?" he asked softly, in a voice that made Owyn's blood go cold. He turned his head slightly, and the man holding his arm went pale. He gurgled once, then dropped bonelessly to the ground.

"Allie, no!" Owyn shouted. He tugged against the cords and tried to get to his feet, but the man behind him held him in place. Alanar turned toward his voice, and started walking toward him.

"If you think I won't kill you, Teva, you're wrong," Alanar said. "You killed Virrik. You've hurt Owyn. I will make you pay for that."

Teva snorted. "Really?" he asked. Then he laughed. "I've changed my mind. You're not worth the trouble to keep. Kill him."

"No!" Owyn shouted. But it was too late. He heard the snap, the wet sounding thump as the quarrel struck Alanar and knocked him off his feet. He didn't move. He didn't make a sound. Denis wailed, pulling free from his captor and crawling across the dirt toward Alanar.

"No!" Owyn struggled against the hands holding him back, trying to get to his feet. Trying to get to his Alanar. He could feel the tears starting. "No! Alanar!"

Dimly, he heard Teva snapping orders. "Kill the rest of them. We have what we came for. And put him down!"

More hands grabbed at Owyn, pulling him back, throwing him onto the ground. He stopped fighting, let them do what they wanted. His lack of resistance didn't make them any gentler, as they bound him tighter. They seemed to be expecting him to start fighting again.

There didn't seem to be a point anymore.

He knew now what the Mother hadn't wanted him to see when he went looking for visions.

He'd secured Aria's throne...and lost Alanar in the process.

He closed his eyes as someone held a cloth over face. He smelled dreamflower, and welcomed the dark.

Maybe he wouldn't wake up.

"I TOLD YOU I SAW FIRE last night!" Evarra swung down from her horse. "Look, that looks like it was a tent. It must have gone up like a torch. And...was that the coach?"

"Looks like it. See the wheel rim? Never been so glad of a broken saddle girth." Garrity dismounted and followed her, his crossbow held ready. "This was their camp. Look at the uniforms. What in the Mother's name happened here?"

"Bandits?" Evarra drew her sword. "I don't think there's anyone alive here, Gar."

"We'll search anyway. See if you can find Owyn or Alanar."

They spread out, searching among the bodies. Then they went back and searched again, working together to drag all of the bodies into a line. By the time they were done, the rising sun was over the horizon, and there was no sign of Owyn or Alanar.

"You don't think they were taken prisoner, do you?" Garrity asked, mopping his face with his sleeve.

Evarra shook her head. "I don't know. Let's check where that tent was." She turned and headed toward the remains — ashes and burnt timbers that were still smoking in places. Halfway there, she tripped on something in the grass.

"Evarra?" Garrity trotted over to her, and saw metal glinting on the ground. He picked up the long length of chain. "This is Owyn's! And there's blood on it."

Evarra came over to him, then turned in a circle. "I don't see any other bodies. Maybe...is there any place to hide?" She glanced at Garrity. "I don't think there are any bandits in earshot, do you?"

"They're long gone," Garrity said. He took a deep breath, then shouted, "Owyn! Alanar!"

For a moment, all they heard was the wind and the distant waves on the beach. Then a thin voice called, barely audible, "Help!"

"That's a woman!" Garrity whispered, and started forward, toward the beach. "We hear you!" he called. "Keep talking! We're coming!"

"Help!" the woman called again. "Help us!"

Evarra tapped Garrity on the arm, pointed, and they started toward the voice, splitting up so that they were coming at it from two different directions. There was a high point, topped with waving grasses, and Evarra reached the top to see that it was a sheer drop of a man's height down to the sands below. And she could see a booted foot sticking out from under an overhang.

"I see you!" she called. "We're coming. Garrity, there's a trail, that way!"

They made their way down to the beach. Evarra gestured for Garrity to stop, and walked forward, her hands held wide. "My name is Evarra," she called. "I'm from Terraces. I rode to the Palace with Owyn Fireborn and Healer Alanar. Do you know me?"

The woman whimpered. Then she answered, "Yes. Help us."

Evarra crouched to better see into the small space under the overhang. The woman was young, her thin face pinched and pale. She had a crossbow in her hands, but didn't look as if she was strong enough to lift it. And behind her...

"Alanar," Evarra breathed.

"He's been shot," the woman blurted. "I did what I could, got us down here. But he won't wake up."

"It's all right. We're here now." Evarra forced a smile. "What's your name?"

"Esai."

"Esai. All right. My friend is Garrity. He's going to help us. How badly are you hurt?" Evarra shifted closer, held out her hand. "Let me have the crossbow."

"It's useless. The limb is broken. I blocked a sword, and it cracked. When I tried to shoot someone, it snapped."

Evarra weapon out of Esai's hands. "All right. How badly are you hurt?"

"Deep gash in my leg," Esai answered. "Made it worse getting Alanar under cover. They thought he was dead, I think. Thought we were all dead." She frowned. "Are they all dead?"

Evarra nodded. "Yes. Who, Esai? Who did this?"

"They came up from the beach," Esai answered. "I...I heard Owyn call one of them Teva?"

"Oh, fuck," Garrity breathed. "Evarra, which way? North or south?"

Evarra looked over her shoulder at him, then back at Esai. "How badly hurt is Alanar?" she asked.

Esai looked as if she was going to cry. "He took a shot to the chest. He's coughing blood. He's going to die."

Evarra swallowed. "Garrity, get the horses. We're going north."

"He needs a healer!" Esai cried.

"And we can't get him south on these roads in time!" Evarra snapped back. "But Mannon can take us by ship. It's our only choice. We go north."

Garrity nodded and ran back up the trail. Evarra helped Esai out of the tiny cave, then crawled in to examine Alanar. Even in the dim light, the healer looked ashen, and there was blood on his lips. She studied the quarrel that was still embedded in his chest.

"I tried to pull it out—"

Evarra looked back at Esai. "It's a good thing you didn't. The only thing keeping him from bleeding out is the quarrel plugging the wound." She turned back. "I'm trying to think how we can move him without killing him." She crawled out of the cave. "He can't ride—"

"The cart didn't burn," Garrity called. "Is your horse double duty? Mine isn't."

"Neither is mine," Evarra answered. She swore softly. "We need to get moving. Let's get him out of here. Ah...give me your cloak."

They managed to use the cloak as a stretcher, carrying Alanar up the trail and laying him out on the ground. While Garrity went back for Esai, Evarra went to the cart. There were scorch marks in places, but it seemed to be intact, and the harness was laid in neat piles nearby. But they needed cart horses, or mules. There had been mules, hadn't there? Had the attackers killed the animals, or just scared them off?

One way to find out. Alanar had been riding a double-duty horse, one that had been broken to both saddle and harness. And all horses in Terraces had a common signal they were trained to respond to. She dug through her belt pouch and came up with a slender whistle. She blew it — one long blast, three short, and one long. Then she waited.

A few minutes later, she grinned as a familiar horse appeared, walking toward her.

"Meadowfoam?" she called. She held her hands out, and clicked her tongue at him — he came toward her and rubbed his nose on her sleeve, then stood docilely while she examined him. The horse seemed to be unhurt, and she dug a piece of dried apple out of her pocket and fed it to him. "Well, you're a welcome sight," she murmured. "Let's get you harnessed."

She was still adjusting the harness when Garrity carried Esai to the cart. He set the injured guard down in the cart-bed, then came over to help Evarra.

"He came when you called him?" he asked. "I heard the whistle."

"It's a damn good thing that they put Alanar on a double-duty horse," Evarra said. She cinched the last strap, then scratched Meadowfoam under his mane. "All right. Let's get Alanar into the back. Do you want to drive, or am I driving?"

"You've a better hand at driving than I do."

Getting Alanar into the back of the cart was nightmarish — the healer woke screaming as they finished maneuvering him up and into the back. Garrity pinned him down, shouting his name.

"Alanar! Alanar! It's me! It's Garrity! We're here. You're safe. We're taking you someplace safe." He glanced at Evarra, then focused back on Alanar. "You have to lie still!"

"Owyn," Alanar croaked. "Where...where is Owyn?"

Evarra hissed, then mouthed the word *lie*. Garrity grimaced.

"Gone on ahead," Garrity answered. "We need to get you moving. Esai is here. She's going to sit with you."

Alanar groaned. "Garrity. I want Owyn. I want Owyn with me when I die."

Garrity caught Alanar's hand. "You're not dying, Alanar. Not if I can help it." He looked up. "Evarra, tether the horses to the cart, then drive. I'll stay back here."

Evarra hurried to collect her horse and Garrity's. She moved their packs and weapons to the cart, secured the horse's reins to the back of the cart, then climbed up into the driver's seat and picked up the reins. And tried not to worry about if they'd reach the Palace with three passengers...or only two.

They were, by Evarra's reckoning, about halfway back to the Palace when she heard what sounded like the roar of thunder coming closer. She drew the coach off to the side of the road, looked up the hill, then turned. "Garrity, give me a crossbow."

He passed one up to her, and set the other on the side of the cart. Evarra raised the crossbow and waited, listening to the thunder growing even louder. Then the horsemen appeared over the crest of the hill. Mannon was at the head of the charge. He drew in his horse when he saw them, his jaw dropping.

"Owyn's horse came back to the Palace. We thought the worst," he called as he reached them. "What happened?"

"The worst," Garrity answered. "We need to get Alanar back to Terraces now."

Mannon peered over the edge of the cart and swore softly. "Calix, ride back," he said without turning. "Find the harbormaster and tell him I want the flagship ready to sail as soon as we arrive. Tell Memfis to be ready to leave when we get there."

The rider galloped off, and Mannon's frown deepened. "What happened? Esai?"

"Ride alongside," Evarra said. "We need to move."

Mannon turned his horse, keeping pace with the cart as they started moving again. "Esai?" he repeated.

Evarra didn't turn, but she could hear Esai's voice clearly. "We made camp on the dunes just north of the ruins. We were going to rest, then ride on when the moon rose. Healer Alanar's breathing was getting worse. Just before moonrise, they came up from the beach. They overran the sentries. Their leader...Owyn called him Teva."

"Teva?" Mannon repeated. "You're sure of that?"

"Yes, sir," Esai answered. "And he and Alanar both knew him. He wanted Owyn and Alanar, and when Alanar killed one of his men—"

"Alanar did *what*?" Garrity yelped.

"Killed one of Teva's men. Without touching him," Esai answered. "That's when Teva ordered him shot. He told his men to kill the rest of us. Any who were left. I played dead, and when they were gone, I thought I'd try to make my way back to tell you. But I couldn't walk well, and they'd scared all the horses off. And then I found Healer Alanar was still alive and I had to protect him. So I managed to hide him in the dunes. That's where Evarra and Garrity found us."

"And Freckles might have run off to the Palace, but Meadowfoam is a Terraces-bred horse, and knows to stay where he is and come when he's called," Evarra said. "And he's broken for saddle and harness, thank the Mother."

Mannon nodded. He looked at the cart, then at Evarra. "The tide will be going out in about three hours. If we miss it, we'll have to wait until dusk. Think we can make it back to the Palace in two?"

DESPITE HIS WISHES, Owyn woke up to find himself face down on a wooden floor. The sun was warm on his back, and the wind in his face smelled of the sea. Owyn frowned slightly and started to sit up. As he pushed up onto his hands and knees, he realized there were manacles on his wrists, and a short chain between them. His pledge bracelet was gone. He stared at his wrists, trying to make things make sense. His shoulder didn't hurt anymore, and the wound was closed. Healed. Who had healed him?

Wait. It was Teva that took him. Which meant he knew exactly who had healed him. Risha was around here somewhere. But why kidnap him? Why not just kill him?

And...was the floor *moving*?

"So, you're awake?" Boots moved into his line of sight, and he looked up to see Teva stood over him.

"Why am I still alive?" Owyn asked softly.

Teva smiled. "Because I wanted you that way. You're mine now."

Owyn snorted. He pushed back to sit on his heels, looking past Teva. Wide wooden floor, out in the air? Where...

His mouth went dry, and he couldn't breathe. Wide, wooden, *moving* floor. "Where are we?" he gasped, and staggered to his feet.

He couldn't see anything but sky. There was nothing beyond the low wooden walls at the edge of the floor. He headed toward the closest one, weaving like a drunkard, hearing the clink of chain as he walked to the wall.

There was nothing beyond it. Nothing but water. He couldn't see anything but water until it reached the sky. He moaned, and backed away from the rail, bumping into Teva.

"You've got nowhere to go, Owyn," Teva crooned. He slid his arm around Owyn's neck, pulling him back against him. "Nowhere to run. You're mine now."

Owyn snarled and drove his elbow back into Teva's gut, then spun and lashed out, using the chain that connected his wrists as a flail. Teva fell backward, howling in pain, his hands clasped to his bleeding face. Owyn backed up to the rail and looked down at the water. He died out here. He *knew* that.

But he couldn't make himself jump.

"You don't have to jump, Owyn. I've told him that he's not allowed to harm you."

Owyn knew the voice, so he didn't bother to turn. "You've got fucked up ideas of what harming people is, Risha."

He felt a warm hand on his shoulder. "I've told him that if he attempts to force you, I'll geld him. Permanently."

That got Owyn to look at her. "You told him that?" he asked. "That...why?"

She smiled. "Because regardless of what you think of me, I do have my standards. He will not try to force you. If you go to his bed, it will be of your own volition. Now, I need to go put Teva back together." She gestured. "Take Owyn to Teva's quarters and secure him there."

Two men came forward and took Owyn's arms, pulling him away from the rail, then shoving him toward the rear of the ship. Owyn looked up to stare at the high sails and the mast.

Where the fuck had Risha gotten a ship like this?

CHAPTER
NINETEEN

Memfis stood in the corner of the harbor master's office and tried not to scream. The office was barely more than a shack built on the docks, already cramped by a single desk and chair, and unbearably crowded by the addition of three men.

"Tell me again," Mannon said slowly. His voice was quiet, but the man who stood in front of him flinched. "Brothi, I need you to explain to me just how you somehow managed to mislay my flagship?"

Brothi swallowed and stammered, "She had a writ, Lord Mannon. Your signature and seal! A list of the crew—"

"Which should have been a clear signal that all what not what it seemed," Mannon interrupted. "I've never handpicked a crew. You know your men far better than I." He closed his eyes and took a long breath through his nose. "We'll discuss this more later. And at length. I want to know why this is the first I'm hearing of it. But I don't have time for an explanation today. Do you still know where the cutter is located?"

"The cutter, Lord Mannon?" Brothi asked. "I...of course."

"Of course, he says," Mannon spat. "I want it ready to sail immediately. A man's life hangs in the balance, and we should have sailed an hour ago." He waved one hand, and the harbormaster fled the shack. He took another deep breath and turned. "Memfis, I wish I could do something more."

"Two men's lives," Memfis said. "My son is out there somewhere." He frowned, closing his eyes. When he opened them again, it was Mannon who flinched. "He's not coming back, Mannon," Memfis finished.

"We'll find him, Memfis—"

"Do you know what a waking vision is? Did your father's Fire ever tell you?"

Mannon looked startled at the interruption. He frowned. "I...I shouldn't, but yes. Toman did tell me. The first thing a Smoke Dancer sees. Their death."

"Owyn's waking vision was of drowning," Memfis said softly.

Mannon stared at him for a moment, his mouth hanging open. "His...and he was *willing* to go on board a ship?" He scrubbed one hand over his face. "And that's why Alanar refused, I'm assuming? He knew?"

Memfis nodded. "He must have. I can't imagine Owyn keeping it from him. Not when they were to be married. He told Aria and Aven." He looked down, his guts churning. "My boy. My son. I...I was horrible to him, the last time I saw him in Terraces. I said things that were inexcusable. We never really cleared the air between us. I apologized, but...it wasn't enough. I never asked him to forgive me." He turned away, shaking his head. "I was supposed to see him marry. You should have let me go with him."

"And lose you, too?" Mannon asked. "Memfis, what could you have done?"

Memfis closed his eyes. Mouse. His Mouse. "I would have died first. I wouldn't have to live with the fact that my boy is going to die alone," he answered without turning.

A heavy hand squeezed Memfis' shoulder. "Your other boy needs you. Alanar needs you. Don't give up on him." He moved to stand next to Memfis — Memfis could see him out of the corner of his eye. "They can't be far from shore, Memfis. There's not a Waterborn navigator in the entire navy — they won't serve me. Never thought it was a good thing until now. I'll send ships out. We'll find them. We'll find him."

Memfis took a long, shaking breath. Then he turned and looked at Mannon. "There had better not be any alcohol on that cutter."

Mannon nodded. "I'll pour it all out myself. Come on. We need to go."

They left the harbor master's office, and walked back off the dock, toward the cart where the others waited. Evarra was leaning against the side of the cart, her head resting on her folded arms. Garrity had his back against the side of the cart, and his chin tucked down to his chest. In the back of the cart, Ambaryl sat with Esai and the unconscious Alanar — she had dosed him with dreamflower so that they could move him without hurting him. Memfis went to the side of the cart and reached down, brushing hair off Alanar's face. His skin was cool and bloodless.

"We'll be leaving shortly," Mannon said. "They're preparing the cutter. We'll be to Terraces in an hour or two."

"He's fading, sir," Ambaryl said. "I don't know if he has an hour or two."

Mannon looked at Memfis, then nodded slowly. "Do what you can, Baryl," he said, and walked down the dock.

"Ambaryl, how long do you think he has?" Memfis asked.

"He's fighting, Memfis," Ambaryl answered. "But he was already sick when he left. I'm worried that it's undermining his strength."

Memfis nodded. "He'll make it. He's overcome so much already. He'll make it." He tried to sound convincing. From the look in her eyes, he'd failed miserably. She sighed and looked down at Alanar, and he turned and looked at Esai.

"How are you feeling?" he asked.

The young guard shook her head. "I failed them," she answered, her voice broken enough that he could hear the tears in it. "I should have—"

"You saved Alanar," Memfis interrupted. "At the risk of damaging your leg."

"Damn my leg," she spat. "If I'd been paying more attention to my duties, and less to my fantasies, I'd have been able to do more to save them!" She looked up at him, then blushed a deep crimson. "I...fuck."

Memfis smiled slightly. "Don't worry. I won't say anything. Nor will Ambaryl." He glanced at the older woman, who tutted gently and laughed.

"Not a word, dear," Ambaryl agreed. "And I don't blame you. They're lovely young men, the pair of them." She sat up straighter. "And once we get to Terraces, Alanar will be fine. And Lord Mannon will find Owyn. And they'll both know what you tried to do for them."

Esai shook her head, letting it hang. "And they'll both know I failed them."

Memfis sighed. There wasn't much he could do to console her. Not when he was feeling much the same way. He looked away, and saw Mannon coming back up the dock. There were four men behind him, who came to the cart and surrounded it. One of them was carrying a long bundle that proved to be a litter.

"We're to take the healer on board," he said. "And the injured guard."

"You'll need help," Garrity said. He raised his head and turned. "You'll all four of you need to carry Alanar. I'll get Esai."

The guard who had spoken nodded, and they carefully shifted Alanar onto the litter and carried him away. Memfis helped Ambaryl out of the cart, and took her arm as they followed the guards down the deck to a ship with a single mast. It was smaller than the ships

Memfis could see further out in the harbor, and he slowed his pace to let Garrity and Evarra pass. Garrity had Esai cradled in his arms, and was talking to her in a low voice.

"— I'm sure your leg is going to be fine," Memfis heard him say as they went past. "And the Senior Healer is a good man. I'm sure he'll—"

What Jehan was going to do was lost to the wind as Garrity moved out of earshot. Memfis started walking again, seeing Mannon standing near the ship.

"Why are we taking a little one?" Memfis asked as he and Ambaryl reached Mannon.

"Because this one is lighter and faster," Mannon answered. "It's the fastest thing in the fleet."

"Then why did you want your flagship?" Memfis asked.

Mannon actually looked sheepish. "Because I like my flagship," he admitted. "It's comfortable. But it's also slower than the cutter. So come aboard, and we'll get underway." He turned and raised his voice. "Captain Destria, what's the fastest you've ever made it to Terraces?"

"Haven't berthed at Terraces in years," a woman shouted back. "But I've made Serenity Bay in under two hours without pushing."

Mannon turned to help Ambaryl onto the ship, then held his hand out Memfis. Memfis took it and stepped into the craft. Mannon nodded and looked back at the captain.

"There's a dying man in your cabin, Destria. I want him to live. If we can make it to Terraces in an hour, there's a bonus in it for you and your crew."

She looked thoughtful. "What sort of bonus?"

"A big one," Mannon answered. "An hour. Can you do it?"

She grinned. "Let's find out."

THE CUTTER PRACTICALLY flew over the waves, wind whipping over the deck in icy gusts. Memfis stayed in the cabin with Ambaryl for a time, then went back out onto the deck. He found Mannon standing near the front of the ship, his hands on the rails. His hair was blowing wildly, and he was smiling. Memfis came up next to him, and Mannon looked at him and nodded.

"I thought you'd stay below," he shouted over the wind. "This is a bit much if you're not used to it."

"You seem to enjoy it," Memfis said.

Mannon grinned. "I do. I love being on the water. Legacy of my grandmother, I assume."

Memfis rested his hands on the railing. "You have Water blood? I thought you were Fire and Air." He turned to see Mannon looking quizzically at him.

"You're pure Fire, aren't you?" Mannon asked. When Memfis nodded, Mannon nodded in return. "I thought so. In the tribes, you can have pure bloods. You don't find that when you've got the blood of the Firstborn in your veins." He looked back out over the water. "We're supposed to balance the tribes — we're made up of all of them. I've Water blood in my veins, from my grandmother. Fire and Air, from my parents. Earth..." He frowned. "Three generations back? That sounds right." He shrugged. "I wonder, sometimes, if the reason for the Companions isn't to make sure that the Firstborn is always from all the tribes. So that we don't just cleave to our own, the way that Air and Water tend to do."

Memfis snorted. "Air and Water tend to stay among their own because Earth and Fire tend to look down their noses at them. Tell me I'm wrong."

Mannon laughed. "You're not wrong," he admitted. "And it's getting worse. But to push away those tribes is to push away part of ourselves. Having the Firstborn be from all the tribes means that we have to accept all the tribes, or reject our Firstborn."

"Tell that to Risha, will you?"

"Before or after I wring her neck?" Mannon asked. "No, no, during. Definitely during." He looked back out over the water. He pointed. "See that stone pillar? That's the marker for Shadow Cove. Destria is going to break her record. It won't be under an hour, but we'll be at Terraces soon."

"Good," Memfis said. He looked back at the deck, seeing men and women going this way and that.

"I wonder," Mannon said. "If the role of the Firstborn isn't so much to rule as it is to balance us out."

Memfis looked at him. "What do you mean?"

Mannon shrugged. "Late night thoughts, really. The Firstborn always has all four bloodlines. It's a question as to how much, but they always have a bit of each. They speak to all the tribes, and tribes listen, because they all know that the Firstborn is one of them, to some degree. The Firstborn brings balance to all four tribes. I think that's the heart of it. And...I think that's the heart of the problem." He sighed and smiled ruefully. "I didn't understand this before, you see. And when I...well, I threw everything out of balance. And it's only been getting worse, no matter how I try to fix it. Because I'm not balanced."

"But Aria is," Memfis said. Mannon shook his head.

"She's not, though. She's Fire and Air, just like me. At least, I think she is. Liara was pure Air, wasn't she? And Milon was Fire and...I'm forgetting. Varia was what?"

Memfis frowning, thinking back. "I never knew Varia," he said. "She died before I met Milon. But I think she was pure Fire."

Mannon nodded. "And so was Milon. Aria isn't balanced. But her children will be, especially if it's a child by Aven. He's Water and Earth—"

"And Fire," Memfis added. "You claimed him as kin. Jehan is half Fire—"

"Which Pirit denies," Mannon pointed out. "She says he's pure Earth, for all that Father claimed him in the Book of Silver. I don't know why she doesn't just confirm who sired Jehan."

"Because it doesn't matter to her? Or there was no one else to do the testing? How many fifth level healers were around then?" Memfis offered. Mannon shrugged.

"I don't know. Regardless, if she's right, if Jehan is pure Earth, then any child of Aria and Aven will be all four tribes, in equal amounts. Complete balance. Hopefully, it'll be enough to put things to rights. I hope I'm around to see that child." He smiled. "Now, speaking of balance, tell me about the Heir's Tower. How go the reinforcements?"

Memfis scowled. "I don't have my notes," he grumbled. "And honestly, I'm having a hard time trying to plan on how to reinforce and stabilize the tower when I can't inspect all of the damage. When do I get inside?"

Mannon shook his head. "It's too dangerous," he said. "I won't risk you, Memfis. Aria would never forgive me." He looked out over the water. "Nor would Owyn," he added. He looked back at Memfis and smiled. "I like your boy, Memfis. I will do whatever I can to get him back safely."

"Thank you," Memfis answered. He looked out over the water. "And my other boy? How much longer before we reach Terraces?"

"Not long, I don't think." Mannon pointed. "You can see the lowest terrace from here."

Mannon was right, and it wasn't long before the ship was being tied off at a stone dock.

"You owe my crew a bonus, Mannon," Destria called as she joined them. "Now, do you know the way up?"

"I do," Garrity said. "We used to come down here to fish. It's rough, but I know the way." He took off his leather coat and passed it to Evarra. "And I'm faster."

"Hurry," Mannon said.

Garrity took off running.

"LIDL IS COMING ALONG nicely," Jehan said, rubbing his forehead. "But Tancis need a little extra tutoring. Who can we spare to help him?"

Pirit looked down at the papers on the table in front of her. "Malani perhaps. If we can convince him that she's teaching him and not flirting with him."

Jehan sniffed, considering the healer-in-training. "So, Beryn, then?"

His mother chuckled. "I'll rearrange their schedules—" She stopped, turning in her seat as someone outside the office shouted Jehan's name.

Jehan bolted out of his chair and was halfway to the door when it opened. He blinked in shock. "Garrity? When did you get back?"

"No time," Garrity panted. "You have to come now. Alanar is dying. Down on the low docks. Hurry!"

"The low docks?" Jehan repeated, but Garrity was already gone, running back out of the healing complex. Jehan followed, hearing people behind him, but not looking back as he followed Garrity into the tunnels. Alanar dying? On the docks? How had he even gotten there?

By the time that the tunnel opened up to reveal the ship berthed on the low docks, Jehan was focused on two things — Alanar, and the fact that he was too blasted old to run through partially collapsed tunnels like a boy.

"Where is he?" he shouted.

"Captain's cabin!" Garrity shouted. He went to his knees on the dock, panting heavily. Jehan ran past him, pushing past people and jumping from the dock to the ship with practiced ease. The rocking under his feet was a comfortable thing, something he'd missed without realizing. He looked around, saw a door, and headed for it. It opened, and a woman looked out at him.

"Are you the healer?" she asked. "He's coughing blood—"

"Let me in!" Jehan demanded. The woman stepped out of his way, and he entered the cabin. He could smell blood and sweat, and something sweet...

"Dreamflower? You've been keeping him sedated?"

"He's in so much pain, and he's fighting us," she answered. "He caught the winter ague, and it got bad very fast. Then he was shot, and he's coughing blood—"

Jehan turned to kneel by the bed and tuned out the world. He rested one hand on Alanar's forehead, the other on his chest. Then he closed his eyes and let his power flow, assessing the damage. Alanar's lungs were full of fluid from the ague and blood from the pierced lung; his chest rattled as he struggled to breathe. So deal with that first; Jehan poured power into Alanar, burning out the sickness that had been killing the young healer, then slowly drawing out the quarrel, painstakingly healing the wound as he worked, until the arrow lay on the bloody sheet, and there was only a small, red scar on Alanar's skin to show where it had been. Jehan took a breath, then went back to work, clearing the mucus and blood out of Alanar's lungs.

Finally, he opened his eyes. Pirit stood on the other side of the bed, one hand held out flat over Alanar's abdomen.

"You dealt with that nicely," she murmured. "He'll need to be monitored for a day or two, but he should be fine."

"Thank you," Jehan croaked.

"You didn't pay any attention to who was on this ship, did you?" she asked. "You were so focused on the patient?"

"I..." Jehan frowned, thinking back. He'd pushed past two men on his way in here. And one of them...he went cold, and pushed himself up to his feet. He swayed, and a hand on his back steadied him.

"You never did know when to stop," a familiar voice said. It had been too long since Jehan had last heard it, and he looked up at Memfis in shock.

"You got old, Mem," he said. He smiled up at Memfis. Then he realized there was something wrong. "Where did you come from?" he demanded. "And where were you? You were missing..." He stopped. Looked around. "Where's Owyn?"

"It's a long story, Jehan," Memfis said. "To keep it short...we don't know."

"I see." Jehan turned to face the man standing in the open door. "And did you have anything to do with this?"

"Not a blasted thing," Mannon answered. "We have a lot to talk about, Jhansri."

"I don't have a single thing to say to you," Jehan snapped.

"Jehan, he got us here to save Alanar's life," Memfis said softly. "He's going to help us find Owyn." He rested his hand on Jehan's shoulder. "Let him talk."

Jehan looked back and glared at Memfis. "You're on his side now?"

"I've heard what he has to say," Memfis answered. "You want to hear this."

Jehan turned away, looking back at the bed. Alanar was still pale, still quiet. "I have a patient. It will have to wait until he's stable."

"Of course," Mannon agreed. "If you'd rather I wait here, I will. Or I'll come with you. In custody, of course."

"In...in custody?" Jehan stammered. "I..."

"Jehan, I will deal with Mannon," Pirit said. "You have a patient. We'll meet you in your office when you're done."

Jehan dragged his focus back to Alanar. "I'll need attendants—"

"There are sailors waiting to help," Mannon interrupted. "And a litter."

Jehan nodded. "Send them in."

IT WAS DARK OUTSIDE when Jehan finally left Alanar under the care of a healing attendant. Alanar still hadn't opened his eyes, but Jehan wasn't sure if that was because of the dreamflower, or because Alanar was refusing to admit that he was awake. He suspected the latter; he'd come back and check later. For now, he walked down the corridor, through the entry hall and around the corner to his office. There were two of Pirit's guards standing outside — one of them nodded to Jehan and opened the door for him. He entered, and heard the door close behind him.

His office wasn't small, usually. Today, though, it felt tight. Too close, too cramped. Too full of the one person that Jehan had absolutely no desire to spend time with. Mannon sat in the chair facing Jehan's desk, his back to the door. Memfis stood with his back against the side wall, his arms folded. Pirit was nowhere to be seen.

"Your mother looks good," Memfis said as Jehan came in. "She's off seeing to the guard that was injured saving Alanar."

"You didn't tell me there was a second patient," Jehan replied.

"Esai wasn't hurt as badly," Mannon said, turning in his chair. "Alanar needed to be your focus. I have something to show you. And Aria, if you can convince her to come and speak to me."

"That's not as easy as it sounds. Is it something I want to see?" Jehan asked.

"Yes," Memfis said. "You want to see this."

Jehan looked at Memfis, but there was no hint of what to expect. He came around the desk and sat down. Mannon met his eyes, and laid something on the desk. Jehan's jaw dropped when he saw the Air gem.

"Where did you get this?" he asked.

"It's mine," Mannon answered, his voice quiet. "Yana gave it to me."

Jehan let the words sink in. He reached out, waiting until Mannon nodded before he picked up the gem. He turned it over in his hands, then huffed out a brittle laugh.

"She chose you. After all that...you finally got what you wanted."

"And realized that I'd lost everything to get it," Mannon added. "Is Aria coming? I want to show this to her. And then tell her the message that Owyn was carrying when they were attacked." He took the gem from Jehan's hand, sat up straight, and met Jehan's eyes. "I'm abdicating. The throne is hers. And then...well, whatever she decides."

"What happened to Owyn?" Jehan asked.

"I found out only a few hours ago that Risha and Teva stole my flagship after they escaped from you. I had sent Owyn and Alanar back, because Alanar was so ill. Esai said that they stopped to rest, and were attacked from the sea. And that Owyn called one of the attackers Teva. They took him, Jehan. And I'm going to find him." He looked up at Memfis, then back to Jehan. "Where's Aria?"

Jehan closed his eyes and rested his hands on the desk. It took him a moment to order his thoughts and decide to answer. "Not here," he said. "She's not in Terraces. She left a few days ago. The day before Owyn and Alanar left, actually."

"Where is she?" Mannon asked.

"On her way to Forge, to Lady Meris," Memfis answered. Mannon turned in his chair.

"You knew?" he demanded.

"Owyn told me. And asked me not to tell you. He wasn't sure of you."

"And you are?" Jehan asked.

Memfis frowned slightly. Then he nodded. "I think I am."

Jehan stood up. "Then we need to move. How soon can your ship get us to Forge, Mannon?"

CHAPTER TWENTY

A deep breath confirmed to Alanar that he wasn't in his own bed, nor back at the Palace. The bed in the Palace had smelled of sweet chandan incense, beeswax, lavender and soap. And their entire house smelled faintly of spices and yeast, and their pillows smelled faintly of red-bark and cloves and mint. They were the scents that he had come to associate with Owyn. Owyn himself always smelled like bread and yeast and spices, with a faint undertone of iron.

This bed, however, smelled of soap and the harsh cleaners they used in the healing complex. Therefore, he was in the healing complex. How had he gotten here?

He could ask. There was someone in the room. Alanar could feel her there. He could sense her. She was scared, worried. She was breathing wrong. Her heart rate was elevated, the pressure too high.

He knew who it was.

"Why are you here, Rhexa?" he asked softly. "And why am I here?"

"I thought you were awake," she answered. "You were sick, and injured. Jehan saved your life. I didn't want you to wake alone."

"Doesn't matter what you want," he muttered. "I am alone."

A cool hand rested on his shoulder. "You're not alone," Rhexa said gently. "And Owyn is coming home. Mannon's promised that he'll find him—"

"Owyn is dead," Alanar snapped, and rolled away from the hand, putting his back to Rhexa. "His waking vision was of drowning. Did you know that?"

"I don't know what a waking vision is," Rhexa answered. "Alanar, we don't know that he's dead."

"He's dead," Alanar repeated. "And it's my fault."

"It isn't!" Rhexa protested. "How could it be?"

"Because he wanted to take me back by ship," Alanar said, feeling his throat growing tight. "I wouldn't let him. I knew about the vision. He told me about the vision. I wasn't going to let him anywhere near a ship. We came over land...and now he's dead."

"He isn't dead."

Alanar sat up at the sound of Jehan's voice. "Why didn't you let me die?" he asked.

"Because Owyn would have found creative ways to murder me if I had," Jehan answered, his voice sharp. "Now, are you ready to listen?"

Alanar closed his eyes. "What?"

"Owyn isn't dead," Jehan repeated. "His Fire gem is still on the nightstand where he left it." He paused. "Look. This is Companion lore. And I don't know if it's supposed to be told outside of the Companions, but I'm telling you. We're taught that if a Companion dies, their gem returns to the Mother. She will send it back to the Firstborn or the Heir when they're ready to choose again."

Alanar raised his head. "Really?"

The bed shifted and creaked, and when Jehan spoke again, it was clear that he'd sat down. "It's never happened, not in all our history, but that's the lore as we were taught it. Owyn's gem is here, so Owyn is still alive. Mannon's promised to find him and bring him home. He wants to see you, by the by."

"Not yet," Alanar said. "I...not yet."

"Fine. You will have to talk to him soon. Especially if you come with me."

"Come with you? You're leaving? To go where?" Alanar asked. "Where are you going?"

"Mannon is taking me to Forge by ship. We're leaving tomorrow morning with the tide. We're going to get Aria. You can come with me, or you can stay here and help Mother."

Alanar frowned, counting days. Had he missed a day? Maybe. "Owyn said it took them twelve days to get to Terraces from Forge. Will Aria be there tomorrow?"

"She should be," Jehan answered. "So, are you coming or staying?"

"You should stay," Rhexa said gently. "You should rest."

Alanar frowned. "How long before Mannon starts looking for Owyn? If he's taking you to Forge, he won't start for days."

Jehan snorted. "He started immediately, actually. He asked to talk to Owyn's friend who talks to birds. Turns out, he uses messenger birds. He asked Marik to send messenger birds to someone named Nestor, with orders to send his ships out on the next tide. How did he know about Marik?"

"Owyn probably mentioned him." Alanar closed his eyes. "And, if he's searching already, I'll stay. They'll find Owyn, and bring him here. I'll be here to meet him."

"And you can stay with me while we wait," Rhexa said. Her cold hand settled on his shoulder. "If you want the company. But for now, you need to rest. Sleep, Alanar."

Alanar closed his eyes and lay back down, arranging himself on his side. He wasn't sure if he would be able to sleep — until he felt Jehan's hand on his arm, the warmth of his power.

"Go to sleep, Alanar. I'll come back before I leave."

TREESI ROLLED HER SHOULDERS and yawned, grimacing at the odd scent of sulfur in the air. Her back ached, and her hips hated her. Driving a cart was one thing. Riding for days on end? She purely hated it. She'd never spent as much time in the saddle as she had over the past fourteen days, and she never wanted to again.

The worst of it was that she now understood what Owyn was feeling. She was *lonely*. At home, she had Owyn and Alanar. Here...Aria had demanded that she come on this journey, only to ignore her completely. Anise and Jillia, the guards who rode with them, were nice, but they weren't her Heir.

"Treesi?"

Treesi looked up in shock. It was the first time Aria had said her name in a day and a half, since before they'd entered the forest that Jillia called the Ashen Woods. Awkwardly, she urged her horse forward so that she was knee to knee with Aria, studying her Heir as closely as she could without being obvious. Aria's wings were folded tightly to her back, but Treesi had seen that her feathers were starting to come back in. She looked happier. Healthier. Maybe she'd been right. Maybe leaving Terraces had been for the best.

But Treesi was still lonely.

"Yes?" Treesi asked.

Aria turned and smiled at her, and Treesi's heart started to race. Only to plummet when Aria looked away and pointed. "There's Forge. That's the wall, and the northern gate. We'll be there soon."

"And then what?" Treesi asked. "Aria, what do we do when we get to the walls? We can't just go into the city, can we? Won't they stop us?"

Aria frowned slightly. "I have been asking myself that. I am...somewhat obvious. We can't just ride through the city. Someone will tell the guard, and word will get back to Mannon that I am in Forge. I was thinking that perhaps we'd send in either Anise or Jillia. Have them go to my grandmother and have her send a carriage."

"My Heir?" Jillia rode up next to Treesi. "Healer Treesi? There's someone coming from Forge. We should get off the road."

Treesi turned and looked, and saw the single rider on the road, coming toward them at a fast pace. "It's one man."

"Still, we should try not to be seen," Jillia insisted. "Off the road."

Treesi sighed and turned her horse's head so that the little mare followed Jillia and Aria as they rode off the road and toward a dying copse of trees. Just before they reached it, a man's voice rang out.

"Aria!"

Aria turned in her saddle, and burst out laughing. "Trey?" She urged her horse forward, and Treesi followed her. "Trey, it is you!"

"What took you so long?" Trey asked. He glanced at Treesi and smiled, but the smile faded from his face when he looked back at Aria. "We expected you two days ago!"

Aria looked shocked. "Expected me? How...how did you know? Oh, did my Grandmother see it in the smoke?"

Trey grimaced, dragging his fingers through his hair. A heavy bracelet on his wrist caught the sun and threw it back. A pledge bracelet? It looked like the one that Treesi had helped Alanar choose for Owyn. "Something like that. It's safe for you to ride through the city. It's empty."

"Empty? Why is Forge empty?" Aria looked shocked. "Trey, what's happening?"

"A lot since you left," Trey answered. "Ah...would you let your guards know I'm not going to eat you?"

Treesi looked over her shoulder to see that both guards had raised their crossbows.

Aria looked, too, and laughed. "Anise, Jillia, this is Trey. He's a guard in Forge, and a friend of ours." She turned to Treesi. "And this is Healer Treesi, my Earth."

Trey grinned at Treesi. "Aria caught herself another cute healer? I'm jealous." He turned back to Aria. "You look tired. Different. Are you all right?"

"I am fine," Aria answered. "There has been a great deal happening to us since we left you. But this is more important. Tell me what's happening in Forge. Is my grandmother all right?"

"She's fine," Trey answered. "Look, let me keep this simple, while we ride." He didn't start talking again until they were all moving, heading toward Forge. "The Smoking Mountain is getting worse. And the Council fell apart, so Lady Meris has been running the city for months now. She's made sure everyone gets out and gets to safety. We've sent the last few groups out over the past couple of days. Now, the only ones left in Forge are me and Karse. We're not leaving Lady Meris."

"Trey, what do you mean the Smoking Mountain is getting worse?" Aria looked toward the wall that was growing slowly closer. "What are we riding into?"

Trey clicked his tongue, then frowned. "How to explain...the Smoking Mountain has always been the sleeping bear, you know?" he said. "Everyone who lives in Forge knows it might go up, but it never has. Not since before Forge was Forge. But this past winter was hard, and since the rains stopped, we've had regular tremors. The vents aren't safe anymore. And..." He paused, then sighed, "And the fire mice are gone. They're all gone. We don't know where. But if they've left, then it'll be bad when it finally goes. We're just not sure how bad."

"We haven't felt any tremors in Terraces," Treesi said. "Is that unusual?"

"How far is Terraces from here?" Trey asked. "I'm not clear on it, for all that I looked at the maps."

"Well, we were supposed to be here two days ago, according to you," she answered, and he laughed. "Which is my fault. I'm not a good rider. We had to stop a lot."

Trey chuckled. "First time on a horse?"

Treesi nodded. "I can drive a cart, but carts are slow. I've never ridden before."

"You're probably no worse than I was, or Wyn, back when we both started riding. Back then, Wyn thought the horse was going to eat him!"

Aria sniffed. "Why do I doubt that, Trey?"

"Because that might have been me?" Trey replied slowly, and Aria giggled. "No, he took to riding like he'd been born doing it."

Treesi nodded. "He's got the Earth sense with animals, so that's not surprising."

Trey turned to look at Treesi. "Earth sense? Owyn?" His jaw dropped. "You found his kin? And he's Earthborn? But he's a Smoke Dancer!"

"According to the healers, he is part Earth, and part Fire. According to his aunt, his mother was an Earthborn healer, and his father a Smoke Dancer," Aria said.

"An aunt?" Trey rode in silence for a while, then snorted. "Did she know the rest of his damned song?"

Treesi giggled. "It's called *The Stars Dance*, and yes. It's a very popular children's song in Terraces."

Trey grinned. "He used to sing it to me. What he could remember. I'm glad he found the rest of it. And answers." He looked down at his hands. "I'm sorry you came all this way to find out that part of the world is blowing up. But we can be out of here as soon as you're rested."

"I was coming to stay," Aria said softly. "I need to be away from everything for a time."

"I understand that," Trey replied, his voice gentle. "There are times when I want to hide under the bed and not come out. Let Karse poke food underneath with a stick. But I have a job to do." He sighed. "And so do you. Besides, it's not safe to stay here. We need to be gone, and soon. We'd have been gone ourselves if we hadn't found out you were coming."

"You could have just met us on the road," Treesi said. Trey didn't answer. He didn't seem to hear her, which struck her as odd. She studied him, then looked closer. He wasn't close enough to touch, but she could feel his quick heartbeat even at this distance. He was either nervous or he was scared, and she wasn't sure which. Maybe scared. Living underneath a volcano that was waiting to explode would definitely make someone scared. She looked up at the mountain, and the plume of smoke rising from it.

"Is it always like that?" she asked. "We really can't see it from Terraces."

"Like what?" Trey asked.

"All that smoke," Treesi answered, pointing.

"No," he said, drawing his horse in so that he was riding between her and Aria. "No, there's definitely more smoke these days. And you can smell it more. Used to be, you could only smell it in the vents, but now you can smell it even at Lady Meris' house." He shuddered. "Rotten eggs, all the time."

"I noticed. It's so appealing," Treesi muttered.

Trey chuckled. "I know. But you get used to it. If you're here long enough. Which, hopefully, you won't be."

Treesi nodded and studied Trey. He caught her looking, and arched a brow in question. "I shouldn't stare," she said. "But you're Owyn's Trey. He talks about you."

Trey glanced at her. "He does?"

"He says you're a friend. A good friend."

Trey smiled. "I'm glad he thinks that. I think that, too. I miss him."

They rode through the gates, and through the streets. Empty windows looked down onto silent streets, and their horses' hooves echoed. It was enough to make Treesi shiver and keep looking back over her shoulder. The guards, she noticed, were both on high alert.

"There's no one here," Trey said. "Tannery Row has been empty for weeks."

"I remember this street," Aria said. "This is where we found Aven, after he got away from Fandor."

"It was?" Trey asked. "Here?"

Aria nodded. "You were not with us. Karse was." She looked around. "We are going that way, aren't we? Turning there?"

Trey chuckled. "You did this once, and you already know this city?"

"It's very similar to Terraces," Aria said. She looked at Treesi. "Isn't it?"

"It's bigger than Terraces," Treesi said. She swallowed, and urged her horse closer to Aria's. If she got separated here, she'd never find her way!

Aria seemed to understand immediately what Treesi was doing and why. "Do you want me to take your reins?"

Treesi felt her shoulders relax. "Please?" she answered. "If I get turned around here, you'll never find me."

Aria reached out. Not for the reins — instead, she took Treesi's hand. "I will always find you, my Earth," she said. "I've been terrible. I know. But I will try to do better." She let go of Treesi's hand and took the reins from her.

They rode for a while, turning down a street and passing buildings that gradually changed from shops to houses. From small houses to larger ones, with walls and gates of their own. None of them seemed to be inhabited.

"There's really no one here?" Treesi asked. Trey shook his head.

"Not a soul, save for Lady Meris, and me and Karse. We weren't leaving her. I promised Owyn I'd look after her."

"That's right," Treesi said. "She's his grandmother, too. For someone who had no family, he has an awful large one."

"Family is what you make it," Trey said cheerfully. "He made his. I've made mine." He drew his horse to a stop at a gate, and reached out to ring a bell hanging from a post. It echoed through the empty streets. Almost immediately, a man appeared in the courtyard beyond. "Karse!" Trey shouted. "I have them!"

"It's about time!" Karse shouted back. He trotted across the courtyard and unbarred the gate, pulling it open.

Trey led them through, and Treesi looked up at a house that was easily four times as large as the one she lived in with Owyn and Alanar. She heard the gate clang closed, and scrambled down to the ground when Aria dismounted.

"Karse," Aria said as the older man came closer. "It is good to see you."

"It's surprising to see you," Karse said. He grinned and held his hand out, then tugged Aria into a quick embrace. "But it's still good. I hear you're turning the world upside down."

"Which is quite exhausting," Aria told him. "I needed some time, and I wanted to see my grandmother."

Karse looked over at Trey. Trey shook his head, ever so slightly. Karse nodded. "She's not alone in there. There's someone who needs to talk to you." He held his arm out. "Come on. She's waiting. Been waiting, for days. Once you have this out, we can get out of Forge."

Aria looked at Treesi, then at the guards. "Trey said there was no one else in the city. Who is here?"

"Just come see," Karse said.

Aria frowned, but took his arm. He led her toward the house. Trey offered his arm to Treesi, and they followed. Treesi could hear

Anise and Jillia behind them as they entered the house and walked through wide hallways, up to a set of double doors. As they reached them, the doors opened.

"Jehan?" Aria gasped. "What are you doing here? How did you get here first?"

Jehan smiled. "Come inside. We have a lot to talk about, and not much time." He stepped back so that they could enter.

Aria and Karse passed through the door, and Treesi heard Aria cry out. She dropped Trey's arm and ran through the door, only to stop in shock.

"Memfis?" she gasped. "What...how?" She looked at Aria, and realized that her Heir wasn't looking at Memfis. She was staring at the other man in the room, and she had her crossbow raised.

"Have you all betrayed me?" Aria demanded. "Where is my grandmother? And what is Mannon doing here?"

CHAPTER TWENTY-ONE

Jehan stepped between Aria and Mannon. "Aria, I brought him here. Do you trust me?"

Aria glared at him, cold and hot and terrified all at once. "I do not know any more," she answered. "You brought him here. Can I trust you? Where is my grandmother?"

"I went to get something for you to eat." Meris' voice came from behind Aria. She moved into sight, and put the tray she was carrying down on a table. "I thought you would be hungry. Aria, darling, put the crossbow down and listen. He's unarmed. And in chains. I allowed him to be here. But he's not a guest. He's a prisoner."

Aria stepped back, bumping into Treesi. Treesi had something in her hand — a small tube? No, a blow-pipe. Aria wondered for a moment what was on the dart, then looked back at Mannon, and saw that he'd raised his hands. It was a defensive gesture, but the chain between his wrists wouldn't let him spread his hands wide enough to be an effective deterrent. He looked older than the last time she'd seen him. Older and more tired.

"He surrendered," Memfis said quietly. "To your will."

"And if my will is to kill him immediately, for what he's done to us?" Aria asked.

Mannon lowered his hands and sighed. "Then is it your will," he said. "I will ask only one last thing. Let Lady Meris show you what I've given her."

Aria hesitated. He'd brought something? Surely it wasn't anything she wanted to see. But curiosity won, and she looked at Meris. "Grandmother?"

"I have it here," Meris answered. "Put down the crossbow."

Aria didn't immediately comply. "Anise?" she said. "If he moves, kill him."

"Yes, my Heir," the guard answered. Satisfied, Aria lowered her arm. She looked back at Treesi and saw that she had tucked away the blow-pipe. She reached for the healer's hand. Treesi smiled and laced her cold fingers with Aria's, and they stepped to the side to see what Meris was holding.

Meris smiled up at Aria. "It's good to see you, darling. Introduce me to your Earth?"

"I can wait," Treesi blurted. "What have you got? That's more important."

Meris chuckled. "I like her already," she said to Aria. Then she picked up a small leather pouch. She opened it, and shook a pendant out into her palm. She held it out and Aria felt the world wobble. Almost automatically, she reached for a pouch on her belt, the one that held a similar stone. That still held that stone.

"What is that?" she asked softly. "Whose is that?"

Meris sniffed. "You know the answer to that, Aria. And you know who brought it."

Aria let Treesi's hand fall. She reached out and took the Air gem from her grandmother's hand, studying it for a moment. It was different from the one that her mother had worn. Different from the one in her pouch. She turned and looked at Mannon, to find him looking at her.

"Did Yana give this to you?" she asked. "Or did you take it from her the way you would have taken the Diadem from me?"

He nodded. "You can believe whatever you like about me, Aria. But I loved Yana with all my heart. She gave that to me."

She could see the truth in his eyes. And the pain. "You were her Air. Why did you not stand down for her? Why didn't you let her be the Firstborn she was supposed to be?"

Mannon took a deep breath. "Because when she was brought to me, she was injured. A head wound. She was brought to me unconscious, and I didn't think she'd wake. Not at first. When she did, she had the mind of a child. But she looked at me, and she laughed, and she called me hers. And...I was. Completely. Totally. I did everything I could to protect her. But in the end, I failed her."

"Did she have other Companions?" Treesi asked. "What happened to them?"

"She had one," Mannon answered. "Delandri. Her Fire. He died in the battle that took Yana's wits. I don't know if she ever knew he was dead. She talked about him as if he'd just stepped away for a moment. As for the others — taking her out to find her other Companions, as damaged as she was? People would have rioted. I made the choice to protect her. It might have been the wrong choice. I don't know anymore." He paused, then looked up. "She couldn't rule. That much was clear. So I held the throne, and ruled for her. I had hopes that her son would be the one to wear the Diadem next, until—" He paused again, then cleared his throat. "You should know that Del is named after his father."

Aria stared at him for a moment. For a moment, his words made no sense. Then she understood. "Del is not your son?"

Mannon looked startled. Then he turned in his chair to look at Jehan. "Owyn didn't know that either. You've been with them for months. You've been involved since nearly the beginning. Why doesn't Aria know this?"

Jehan snorted. "Because even though I would cheerfully use your guts as bait, I will not violate my oaths as a healer. Confidentiality—"

Mannon burst out laughing. "Even for me? You'd keep that fact confidential, even for me?" He shook his head. "Jehan—"

"Now that you've brought it up, tell them," Jehan interrupted.

Mannon turned to Treesi. "You're Aria's Earth. That would make you...is it Treesi? Healer Treesi?"

"Yes," Treesi said slowly. "How do you know my name?"

"My steward Nestor mentioned you. Owyn told him about you, about you being Aria's Earth. From what I've heard of you, she chose well," Mannon said. "If you please, Healer, tell the Heir what happens in serious cases of mountain fever?"

Treesi frowned. "I...are there not-serious cases of mountain fever? Ever? I've never heard of any. Most of the time, catching mountain fever means death," she answered. "And if the healers get to them immediately, there's still damage. There can be hemorrhaging. Intestinal perforation, kidney failure, test—" She stopped, her face going pale under her freckles. "Testicular atrophy. You're *sterile*?"

Mannon winced slightly, then shrugged. "I've known for years." He nodded toward Jehan. "He saved my life. He couldn't save my future."

"You know that's probably why you weren't chosen?" Jehan murmured.

"I know," Mannon agreed. "And...I'm not sure how much of what happened after was because of the loss compounding the disappointment. I wanted a family. I wanted children. I was thirty-five, and I was courting a young woman in my father's court. She died from mountain fever, and I..." He took a deep breath and let it out. "Del is my son in name only. And he will always be my only son."

Aria closed her eyes, her wings pulling close as she wrapped her arms around her chest. "I...I sent him away. I told him I wouldn't have him. I hurt my Aven, because I wouldn't have your blood near me."

"I know," Mannon admitted. "Owyn told me. And you should know that, for all that Jehan is listed as my brother in The Book of Silver, for all that I acknowledge him as my brother and Aven as my nephew, Aven may very well not be my blood at all." He looked up at Jehan. "Pirit never did admit you were Elcam's, even though he claimed you were."

"She was never sure," Jehan said. "She said it was either Elcam or Hargat, the Palace healer, and it didn't matter to her which."

"You're not helping, either of you," Treesi snapped.

Aria listened to Treesi scolding them. Then she realized something and turned. "You met Owyn. You met my Owyn. You've spoken to him. Enough that he'd talked of Treesi. That he told you what happened. Where did you meet him?"

It was Memfis who answered. "They were going north, to tell Alanar's family that he and Owyn were getting married—"

"What?" Aria gasped. "They're *what*?"

"Alanar finally asked him?" Treesi squealed. "Oh!"

"Owyn said you didn't say no," Memfis said slowly. "You didn't say no because you didn't know?"

"I...no," Aria whimpered. She stumbled away from them, to a couch in the corner. She sank down into it and covered her face with her hands.

"Aria?" Meris' voice was soft and gentle. "Aria, darling, what is it?"

Aria shook her head, and felt the couch shift as Meris sat down with her. Arms encircled her, and Aria broke, sobbing in her grandmother's arms. She felt Treesi's hands on her knees, heard her Earth's voice, but not the words. The words didn't matter. None of it mattered.

She'd ruined everything.

"Aria."

She shuddered at his voice, looked up to see Mannon on his knees in front of her, his hands resting on his thighs. She sat up, wanting more distance between them.

"Is it that bad?" he asked.

"You have no right to ask me that," she snapped. "You have no right. It is your fault that it is this bad!"

He winced. "I've no doubt about that. But I'm trying to make it right."

"There is nothing you can do to make this right." Aria wiped her face and got up, her wings flaring. "You stole a throne that wasn't yours. Your greed and your arrogance destroyed the woman who would have made things right. You murdered my father—"

"I didn't!" Mannon protested.

"You murdered my mother," Aria continued as if he hadn't spoken. "And the first time you saw me, you were going to force me—"

He winced again. "Del lectured me about that. For days, until his fingers cramped. It wasn't what I meant."

"What did you mean?" Meris asked, her voice cold. "Because this is the first I'm hearing that you threatened to assault my great-granddaughter."

Mannon turned red. "I was going to marry her off to Del," he said slowly. "After Risha...after what she did to him, I held no hopes that he would ever hold the Diadem. I was hoping that you could help him to heal. And I ruined that, too." He sat back on his heels. "I'm trying to make it right the only way I know how. The message that your Owyn was supposed to be carrying to you is that I am abdicating. I will hold the throne until you go north and claim the Crown. Then...what happens to me is up to you."

"Owyn was carrying a message?" Treesi said.

Aria wiped her face and looked around. "Where is Owyn?" she asked. "Is he here?"

Silence, as the men in the room all looked at each other. Treesi moaned softly.

"Where is Owyn?" Aria repeated.

Mannon answered. "I met them on the road. Memfis told me where, because I'd already told him my plans and he said he would help me if it meant you would hold the throne without more bloodshed. I offered Owyn and Healer Alanar the Mother's Peace and brought them to the Palace. I gave Owyn a letter for you, explaining that I was going to abdicate. We started making plans. He has fantastic ideas, your Owyn. Then Alanar got sick. Winter ague, and it got very bad very quickly. He needed a healer. I offered to send them back by ship. They'd have been in Terraces in a few hours. Alanar refused to go that way. They left by coach. They were waylaid..."

"Are they dead?" Treesi croaked. Suddenly cold, suddenly terrified, Aria put her arm around Treesi's shoulders.

"Are they?" she echoed.

"Alanar is alive," Jehan said. "Although it was a near thing. They were attacked when they stopped to rest. The attack came from the sea."

"Waterborn?" Treesi asked.

"Risha," Mannon spat. "That's why none of my men have been able to find the bitch. She stole my flagship. She has a crew made up of men I thought were loyal to me. And now, she has Owyn." He raised his hands, dragged his fingers through his hair. "I sent messenger birds back to the Palace, to Nestor. Once I knew that Alanar would survive. My ships with my loyal men are searching the coast. We'll find him." He looked back at Memfis. "We will find him."

"But...he was leaving me..." Aria started.

Jehan shook his head. "The story about them going north to meet Alanar's kin was a ruse," he said. "He was trying to make contact with the Waterborn. He was trying to get word to Aven that he and Del need to come back. He was trying to fix the Companion Bond, Aria. And for that, you need the Heart."

Mannon looked up, a puzzled expression on his face. "I thought Aven was on his season?"

Jehan was silent for a moment, and Aria watched his jaw clench. Then, slowly, he growled, "Your bitch broke my son."

Mannon shook his head and let it hang. "I understand. She's made a habit of doing that."

"It's not funny!" Aria snapped.

"And I'm not laughing!" Mannon retorted. "There's nothing worth laughing at now." He growled softly. "Nothing that she did to Aven was by my orders. Nothing that she did to you was by my orders. She's under a death sentence, should we take her alive. And I make one request of you." He lurched to his feet, and Aria saw Anise raise her bow. She shook her head, and Anise lowered the weapon once more.

"What request?" Aria asked.

He met her eyes evenly. "If you decide that a death sentence will be my fate as well, let me go last." He swallowed. "Del is my son. He is the only child I will ever call my own. She murdered his mother, and she almost murdered him. She butchered him, and he has never been the same. Let me see her burn before I die."

Aria took a deep breath. She could almost feel the pain rolling off of him. "If it is that important, and if I so decide, I will grant that request. Now, tell me what happened to Yana."

He swallowed, going pale. He cleared his throat. "I...I knew you'd ask me that. I didn't tell Owyn. I had Nestor tell him. It's hard for me to talk about." He paused. "I promised her that I would always care for her. And when Risha lured her up to the tower, I wasn't there. I wasn't there to save her." He swallowed again. "She didn't fly, after she was hurt. She forgot how. So she couldn't teach Del. I was going to find him a teacher, but there was an uprising. I left them. I was gone for a week. And I came back to find my Yana dead, to find my son half-dead and mutilated, and Risha swore to me that Yana had been trying to escape from me. I knew she was lying, but the only person who could tell me otherwise was locked inside his own head. He couldn't tell me the entire story for years. Not until I found someone willing to teach him and me Water signs."

"He told us," Treesi said gently. "About what happened. He wrote it all down."

"He did?" Mannon looked remarkably cheered by that. "Oh, that's good." He smiled broadly. "That's very good."

"Why?" Aria asked.

"Because he never would write it. He could. Even at six, he could write. But he wouldn't put what happened on paper. Not in words, not in drawings. He was past ten before he wrote a single word again. He was sixteen before he could finally tell me what happened. And then it was because he finally had the signs to do it. For him to write it out? That's..." He laughed. "You did more for him in a day than I managed in years!"

"Did you know that he was hurt when he came to us?" Treesi asked. "He had an arrow in his shoulder."

The joy vanished from Mannon's face. "It hit him? I saw the shot. I didn't think it hit him. I broke the jaw of the guard who fired the shot."

"It was superficial. He's fine." Treesi looked at Aria. "The last time I saw him."

"He's with Aven. I know that." Mannon frowned. "But Aven isn't on his season, you said. He left."

"Because I wouldn't have someone of your blood by my side or in my bed," Aria said. "My first mistake. My worst mistake."

"But not irreparable," Treesi said, taking Aria's hand. "They'll come back. And...and we'll find Owyn. And you'll..." She stopped, biting her lip. "And it'll all be fine," she finished.

Aria looked at her, knowing that Treesi had caught herself before saying anything about the baby. Treesi blushed, turning her face into Aria's arm. Aria put her arm around Treesi's shoulders and turned back to the men.

"And you've been at the Palace the whole time, Memfis?" she asked. Memfis smiled.

"Not entirely," Memfis answered. "Risha had me kept prisoner in the green levels. Then Mannon found out and I was brought north. Once he convinced me he was serious about abdicating, I've been..." He paused, looked at Mannon. "Adviser under duress?"

Mannon snorted. "You have such a way of putting things." He went back to the chair and slumped into it. "Memfis has been helping me," he said. "The Palace took a great deal of damage this past winter. I want to turn it over to you in as good condition as I can."

Aria sat down facing Mannon. She opened the collar of her coat and wiped sweat from her brow. It was too warm in the room, but she couldn't take off her loose coat.

Not here. Not yet.

"What plans did you and Owyn make?" she asked.

Mannon nodded. "I brought my notes. We can review them on the way back to Terraces."

Aria frowned. "I...I hadn't planned on going back to Terraces yet. I wanted time to think. Time where I was not the Heir. Time where I was only a granddaughter." She looked up as Meris came to stand next to her chair. "I needed to be able to think of what I needed to do next. The trip here helped somewhat. But it wasn't enough. I wanted...no. I needed more time."

"It isn't safe to stay, Aria," Meris said gently. "We waited only because Jehan said you were coming. Karse and Trey and I would have been gone days ago if not for that. Everyone else is gone. The ship is ready."

Mannon coughed gently. "The tide isn't," he added. "We can't go just yet. The tides won't be right for us to leave until tomorrow."

Jehan looked at him in clear surprise. "What? When did you—?"

Mannon just smiled. "You're not the only one who likes Water, Jehan. The tides are going out now. Destria won't be able to get the cutter out until high tide—"

"Which will be the middle of the night," Jehan finished.

"Exactly. If we want to sleep, we won't be able to sail until high tide, about midday tomorrow." He looked down at his hands, then up at Karse. "Well, Captain? Am I to be locked away again?"

"Just for the night," Karse answered. "Aria, mind if I borrow your guard?"

"I have to ask one question first," Aria said. "Anise, I told you that if he moved, you were to kill him. Why didn't you?" She turned to see Anise had turned bright red.

"Ah...the truth, my Heir," the guard stammered. "Ah..." She snorted, then laughed. "Honestly? If I had killed him right off, I'd never have seen the Usurper crawl like a dog. It was worth disobeying you."

CHAPTER TWENTY-TWO

Once Mannon was taken away, Meris gently but firmly made Aria eat, serving the food on the tray to her and Treesi. Then she walked them to a familiar room. The last time Aria had been here, she'd shared the wide bed with Aven and Owyn. Now, the room and the bed both looked empty and cold.

"I'll leave you both to rest," Meris said. "You've had a long journey. Thankfully, tomorrow the return trip won't be nearly as long." She smiled. "I've never been on a ship before. I wonder if I'll like it?"

"You haven't?" Treesi asked. "But you were a Companion, weren't you? I remember your name."

"I was, but I always traveled over land. I've never been on the sea before. Our Water Hara was always telling me I was missing something special. Now I'll be able to find out if she was right. Goodnight, my dears."

Aria turned and kissed Meris' cheek, then watched as her grandmother left the room, closing the door behind her.

"This is a nice room," Treesi said. "Nice big bed. Owyn would like this."

"He did," Aria said absently. "Treesi—"

"They'll find him," Treesi blurted. "He'll be fine."

Aria shook her head. "Did he tell you about his waking vision, Treesi?" she asked. She turned to see Treesi looking at her with a puzzled expression. "I see. It's something about being a Smoke Dancer. He described it as the price we pay for being able to see forward. The first thing we see is where we will die."

Treesi's jaw dropped. "He...and you...you both know when you're going to die?"

"Not when. Where," Aria corrected. "And Owyn told us that his death is in deep water. Salt water."

"No," Treesi breathed. "No, he can't...he can't die out there! We need him!"

Aria turned away. "Do we?" she asked softly. "He was leaving me—"

"He was not!" Treesi protested.

Aria sniffed, then gasped as Treesi grabbed her arm and turned her around. The healer had to jump back to avoid being hit by Aria's wing, but she stepped forward again, her fists planted firmly on her hips.

"He was not leaving you," she repeated. "He was lonely. And Alanar loves him."

"But he is mine!"

"And where have you been?" Treesi snapped back. "You've been in the same room as the rest of us, but you were never there. You claimed him, but you act like you don't want him. Or me. We've all been lonely, Aria. But he's feeling it most, because he's been with you longer than I have. But you've closed him out. You've closed both of us out." She paused, then blurted. "He wasn't leaving you. He loves you. But you're killing him."

Aria stared at her. "I...I am what?"

"I've been trying to tell you this since before we left Terraces. You weren't listening then." Treesi sighed. "Are you going to listen now?"

"I am listening," Aria answered. "I know I've ruined so many things. What else have I done?"

"You haven't been paying any attention to Owyn. At all. You don't know how he talks when he doesn't say a word," Treesi said. "Owyn takes care of people. It's how he shows them he loves them. He's been trying to take care of you ever since Aven left. And you won't let him. He cooks for you and you won't eat. He does little things around the house and you never notice. The only thing he's done that you responded to was that blasted rose, and then you went back to ignoring him! He's learning, and growing, so that he can be the Companion that he thinks you deserve. And you turned your back on him. You left him behind without a word. Without any explanation. He didn't leave you, Aria. You left him. You left all of us." She looked down, then turned toward the door. "I...should probably find someplace else to sleep, shouldn't I?"

"No," Aria answered. "No, you belong here. You're right. I did leave you all. I'm sorry." She perched on the edge of the bed, pulling her wings in close as she clasped her hands in her lap. "I don't know how to fix it. How to fix anything."

"You can start by stopping," Treesi said gently. Aria looked up at her, and she smiled. "Stop hurting the people who love you. Let us help you."

Aria swallowed. "Do you love me, Treesi? Even after everything I've done? You love Owyn. I know you do."

Treesi blushed slightly. "You never really let me close enough to love you. Not the way Owyn did," she answered. "I like you a lot. A whole lot. I could tip over into love really easy, if you let me. And...let's start fixing things. But first, you need to sleep."

Aria sighed. "I don't know if I can. Not here. This...we were happy here. Owyn and Aven and I. Owyn was safe here. He woke up here, after Aven and Trey rescued him from Fandor. We all slept in this bed."

"And we will again," Treesi said. "It's certainly big enough." She giggled. "We need a bed like this. Our bed at home isn't this big!"

Aria smiled. "The bed you have with Owyn and Alanar?"

"You were always welcome there, you know," Treesi said. "We'd have made room."

Aria shook her head. "I wasn't ready for that. I wasn't ready to share my bed with anyone. Not after what happened the first time." She looked up at Treesi. "I promised Owyn that if he was patient, if he waited until Aven and I — Treesi, what do I do if Owyn doesn't come back?"

"Don't say that!" Treesi gasped. "Don't think that! He's coming home!" She gnawed on her lower lip. "He has to come home," she added. "He...he can't die. Not so far from us. He's supposed to be here. With us. Forever."

Aria closed her eyes. "They both were. They all were. And I ruined it. For all of us." She felt the tears starting again, and sniffed. Then jerked, as something fluttered in her stomach, feeling very much like small wings. "Oh!"

"What?" Treesi asked. "What's wrong?"

"Something..." Aria rested her hand on the hidden swell of her belly. "I...Treesi...something...something moved."

"Moved?" Treesi repeated. Then she laughed. "You felt the baby move?"

Aria gaped at her. "That...that was the baby?" She looked down at herself, then up at Treesi. "My baby?"

"Well, it certainly wasn't mine!" Treesi laughed.

Aria stared at her, then gasped, "Treesi?"

"What?" Treesi looked puzzled, then realized what she said. "No! No, I'm not. Not yet, anyway. We haven't even talked about it." She dropped to her knees in front of Aria. "It's called quickening. You're feeling the baby move."

Aria looked down again, then slowly opened her coat. "I...that means the baby is healthy, doesn't it?" she asked as she rubbed one hand over her stomach. The fluttering started again, and she smiled.

"Aria, I'd have told you if the baby wasn't healthy," Treesi chided. "The baby is perfectly fine."

"And moving. I can feel them moving." She hiccupped. "I want Aven. I want Owyn. And Del. I can't do this alone. I was wrong. I want them back."

"They'll come back," Treesi said. "You heard them. Mannon has his ships out looking for Owyn. And Aven will come back soon. You'll see. And they'll forgive you—"

"Will they?" Aria murmured.

"Of course they will," Treesi said. She got back to her feet. "They love you. Now you need to get some rest."

"You don't love me," Aria said as she stood up. She let Treesi help her with her coat. "You said that."

"I said not yet," Treesi answered. Then she grinned. "Give me until tomorrow. Because I'm taking you to bed tonight."

"To bed?" Aria blinked, looking at the wide bed. "I...Treesi, I don't know—"

"I do. And I remember. You said I would be your first woman. So don't worry. I'll take care of you." She held out her hand. "We'll be all right, Aria. You'll see."

A LIGHT TAPPING AT the door woke Aria, who found herself sleeping with her head pillowed on Treesi's arm. The healer was still asleep, her fiery curls wild on the pillow. Aria leaned close to kiss Treesi, then slipped out of bed. She went to the door and softly called, "Who's there?"

"It's Trey. We're starting to get ready to leave. There'll be food in a few minutes."

"We'll be out shortly," Aria said, and heard footsteps moving away from the door. She turned to see Treesi had sat up. Her curls now fell around her shoulders, and she smiled as she stretched.

"Did he say food?" she asked.

"He said food in a few minutes, and then we'll be leaving. There's a bath through there." Aria pointed at the door. "There's room for us both," she added, and held out her hand. Treesi clambered off the bed and took her hand, then moved closer and stood on her toes to kiss Aria on the lips.

"Good morning," she chirped. "I love you."

Aria giggled, feeling her cheeks warm. "I love you, too. Let's get ready." She led Treesi into the bathing room, and they quickly washed up and dressed.

"Do you want your coat?" Treesi asked as she picked the garment up off the chair where it had been tossed the night before.

"I'll carry it," Aria answered. She looked down at herself. "I'm more noticeable, aren't I?"

"That you're pregnant? Yes," Treesi answered. "I think you're going to surprise everyone out there except Jehan." She looked thoughtful. "Do you think he told anyone?"

"He didn't tell us that Mannon could not sire children," Aria pointed out. "I do not think he would violate his oaths to tell Mannon that I can bear them."

"Truth," Treesi agreed. "All right. I'm ready."

They walked down the corridor hand in hand, and Trey met them where the corridor turned. "There you are," he said. "I was just coming to fetch you. Lady Meris couldn't remember if you'd been to the dining room yet. She thought you might get lost." He smiled, and Aria watched as his eyes trailed downward. His jaw dropped slightly. "Oh. Is that what's different?"

Aria smiled. "Yes, it is."

"I would never have guessed that," Trey said as they started walking. "Not with that coat you were wearing. I could use it as armor on the training grounds."

Aria giggled. "It isn't that thick!"

"If it's hiding that much?" Trey countered. "Sure it is."

They turned into the dining room, and Aria heard someone gasp. She wasn't sure who — Mannon and Memfis both sat on the side of the table facing her, and both looked as stunned as if they'd flown into their first downburst.

"Aria!" Meris cried. "You didn't tell me!"

"I have not told anyone, Grandmother," Aria admitted.

"All the more reason for you to eat so we can be away from here," Meris said. "We sent the pregnant women and young children out first — the air here is bad for them." She took Aria's arm and led her to the table. Treesi let go of her hand, but followed and took the seat on Aria's left. Aria looked up and smiled at her table-mate.

"If you are not careful," she said. "You will catch flies."

Mannon closed his mouth. Then he chuckled and shook his head. "I should have been talking about the entire world righting itself and the Mother to walk Adavar once more. Shouldn't I?" He nudged Memfis with his elbow, making his chains rattle.

"You were talking of this? Of me?" Aria asked. "Did Owyn tell you?"

"No, he most certainly did not!" Memfis answered. He sounded almost indignant, and Aria tried not to smile.

"Did he know?" Mannon asked. "Because the impression I got of him was that he couldn't tell a lie if his life depended on it."

"He can't," Memfis grumbled. "He never could. He's as transparent as glass." He snorted and picked up his cup. "He used to be, anyway. When did you teach my Mouse to lie, Aria?"

"I did not," Aria answered, picking up her own cup. "He has many skills, my Owyn." She looked at Mannon. "And you are doing what to find him?"

"I told you last night. I sent messenger birds to the Palace, ordering my steward to have loyal men launch the rest of the fleet. They'll be sailing up and down the coast to find him, Aria." He paused. "I liked him. Quite a bit. I like a man who'll tell me exactly what he's thinking. And who thinks." He looked to his side. "You raised a good man, Memfis."

"Thank you," Memfis said. "Just be sure I'm not burning one."

Mannon winced. "I should have insisted. I should have made them go back by ship. If they hadn't been on the road—" He stopped. "I...I hadn't given it any thought. Not yet. But how did she know?" he asked slowly. "How could she have known? To attack that party, at that place...how?" He closed his eyes and groaned. "She must still have eyes and ears in the Palace. Someone...Mother of us all, they must have used my messenger birds!"

Memfis went ashen. "How could you have missed that?"

"I thought I found them all," Mannon answered. "I thought I'd gotten all of her traitors and dealt with them." He rested his hands on the table top. "One more thing to add to my list of wrongs."

"Make it right, then," Treesi said, her voice firm. "You're the all-powerful Usurper, the one who said that he was right and the Mother Goddess was wrong. So, make it right."

Mannon looked at her. Then, to Aria's surprise, he smiled. "You have good Companions, Aria. They're afraid of nothing."

"Not true," Treesi answered. "I'm afraid we're not going to see Owyn again. I'm afraid of what will happen to Alanar if Owyn doesn't come back." She turned to Aria. "I hadn't said anything about that to you. I should have."

"You are telling me now," Aria said. "What do you fear? What do you think would happen?"

When Treesi didn't answer, Mannon closed his eyes for a moment. "His lover, the one that Risha killed. The name was...Vir? No, that's not right. Virrik."

"He told you about that?" Aria asked.

"He asked me to be sure that Risha paid for his death," Mannon answered. "I assume what's worrying you is something that happened when Virrik died—"

"That's just it," Treesi interrupted. "We didn't know he was dead. He vanished. Alanar thought he'd been abandoned. And he got really dark. He...well, he hid. He stopped coming out of his room, he barely ate. He lost a lot of weight. He stopped going on rounds, stopped studying. He..." She paused, bit her lip. "I didn't want to lose him, too. So I picked the lock on his door and wouldn't leave. He was...pretty awful to me. He kept on trying to drive me away. I wouldn't go."

"He didn't hurt you, did he?" Mannon asked.

"No," Treesi answered. "No, he was hurting. I knew he wouldn't hurt me. So I wouldn't leave him, and I let him yell at me until he cried. Then I held him when he cried. Then...well..." she shrugged. "I'm a healer. Some of what we do is horizontal."

"And now you're worried about what will happen to Alanar if he loses Owyn the way he lost Virrik." Mannon rubbed one hand over his face, his chains rattling. "I'm not sure what else I can do! The Water tribes won't deal with me at all. I have no contacts with them."

"But we do," Aria said. She looked at Jehan. "Your sister—"

Mannon coughed. "Sister?"

"Danzi," Jehan answered. "The youngest. She built a canoe with a Water boy. Her son is Marik."

"The one who talks to birds," Mannon said, nodding. "I met him. And she has contacts in the canoes? Will they be willing to help me?"

"No," Aria answered. "But they'll help me." She nodded slowly. "Once we get back to Terraces, we can send word to Danzi. When can we leave?"

"Eat first," Meris said. "Then we'll talk while the men prepare the carriage."

———— ❧ ————

"ARIA, BEFORE WE LEAVE, walk with me. We never did have our walk in the garden."

Aria looked up from her empty plate and smiled. "Of course, Grandmother." She rose from the table, gently brushing her fingers over Treesi's shoulders before following Meris out of the dining room. Meris took Aria's arm, and led her out to the walled garden. The air was smoky, and smelled strongly of sulfur, and the light of the sun was sickly and weak.

"Oh, it's worse today. We won't stay out here long," Meris said. "I wanted to talk to you without the men around. Aria, when were you going to tell me you were pregnant?"

Aria bit her lip. "Once we were alone, Grandmother."

"And is it Owyn's child, or Aven's?" Meris asked. "Not that I mind either way. They're both wonderful men."

Aria looked down at herself, at the swell of her stomach. "It's Aven's. Grandmother, I wasn't ready for this."

"No mother ever truly is, my dear."

"No," Aria protested. She looked away. "I didn't want a child. Not yet. Not until my rule is secure. Aven and Owyn agreed with my reasoning. So we decided neither of them would be in my bed until we were certain I would not come away pregnant. When Risha learned of that, she offered to set a block. But she didn't. I think she did the opposite."

"Oh," Meris breathed. "Oh, Aria. Does Aven even know?"

Aria shook her head. "No. He was gone before we realized what had been done. Treesi noticed first, and she brought me to Jehan."

"Oh, Aria," Meris repeated. "And...living with healers, I know you had options. You didn't have to bear this child."

"Jehan offered. I refused," Aria said. She rested her hand on her belly, felt another flutter. "This child may be all I have of Aven. I don't know if he'll forgive me. I was so horrible to him."

"He'll come back—"

"Eventually, I think he will," Aria said without looking at Meris. "But will he forgive me?"

"I didn't know Aven for very long, but he didn't strike me as being an idiot," Meris answered, her voice tart. "He's had plenty of time to realize that if he wants an apology, he has to come to you to get it. He'll be back. And he'll forgive you. Because he loves you. Now, let's go inside. We need to leave."

CHAPTER TWENTY-THREE

Meris insisted that Aria and Treesi ride in the coach with her down to the shore. They sat next to each other, with Meris on Aria's right, and Treesi on her left. They faced Jehan, Mannon and Memfis across the coach. Jehan had his head tipped back against the wall of the coach, seemingly asleep. Memfis stared out the window, looking like he was trying to ignore the world and failing miserably. And Mannon sat with his head bowed, his fingers laced together. As the coach started moving, Aria thought back to the day before, and to everything that Mannon had said.

"Tell me something," Aria blurted. "Mannon, tell me this. What happened to my father?"

"He killed him," Memfis growled.

"I keep telling you! I did not!" Mannon snapped in reply.

"You said that yesterday. You said it when we first met, as well," Aria pointed out. "If you did not, then tell me what happened."

Mannon took a deep breath. "He wasn't supposed to die," he started, then looked at Memfis. "You probably don't believe that. But I gave orders that he be spared. That the Heir and the Companions be taken alive. I don't know who disobeyed. I never did find out. We found Milon alone in a locked room, barely alive. I ordered him taken to the healers, and we kept searching. We found the passage through the servant tunnels, but by the time we did, the Companions were gone. When I went back to the healers later that day, they told me that Milon never woke." He looked at Memfis. "I did not kill Milon. I did not order him killed. If I knew who had done it, I'd have seen them punished."

Memfis studied him for a moment. Then he nodded, once.

"And what about Liara?" Jehan asked.

"I do know who killed Liara," Mannon said. "An upstart officer who thought that she knew better than I did, and who considered my orders suggestions only. She'd been insubordinate once too many times, which was why she was out at the Temple ruins, guarding a pile of rocks. It was a punishment duty. She's dead now." He reached up and scratched his chin. "She reminded me of myself at her age. Ambitious. I think she might have been on her way to following my example," he added. "If I'd let her be, I probably wouldn't have survived the year. She had cohorts, all of whom eventually confessed to me their undying loyalty."

"After she was executed?" Jehan asked dryly.

Mannon chuckled. "I didn't have the chance. She died at sea, in the storm that blew the ship carrying Aria off course. The survivors told me what happened, and pledged themselves to me. Not that I trust any of them. They're serving where I can keep an eye on them. I learned that lesson, at least." He shook his head. "There are many things laid at my feet that were expressly counter to my orders. But, since they were all done by my men, I must claim responsibility. But I want you to know that they were never by my orders."

The coach rattled over the rough road for a few minutes, and Aria could hear voices from outside the coach. Trey was laughing. She wondered what had happened to make him laugh. Treesi took her hand, and Aria turned and smiled at her. Then she looked at Mannon again.

"The ship I was on, it wasn't going to you. It wasn't bound for the Palace."

Mannon looked startled. "Is that why they were so far off course? I'd wondered how they'd lost their bearings so much. The survivors told me that they were further south than they should have been when the storm hit, and they couldn't make it to safe harbor. Where was it going? Do you know?"

"Forge," Aria answered. "It was going to Forge. And there was a cargo of inferno oil. They were going to burn the city—"

"They were what?" Mannon gasped. "Inferno oil? That..." He turned and looked at Jehan. "Is *that* why your canoe went up like a torch?"

Jehan's brows rose. "You didn't know about that, either?" he asked. "Mannon, correct me if I'm wrong, but weren't you supposed to be ruling?"

"That's what I thought, too," Mannon said. He snorted, then shook his head and looked at Aria. "I told Owyn that I wanted to hand the Palace over to you in proper condition. I'm afraid I can't do the same for the rest of Adavar." He shrugged and sighed. "Father would be very disappointed with me."

"Father would have kicked your arse from the Palace to Forge without bouncing. Then from Forge to the Solstice Village. Then back. And for good measure, he'd have done it all again," Jehan said. He looked archly at Mannon. "Tell me I'm wrong."

Mannon glared back at Jehan, and for a moment, the similarities between the two men were clear enough that Aria wouldn't have needed the *Book of Silver* to tell that they were related.

"You're not wrong," Mannon admitted. He tipped his head back. "You're definitely not wrong."

"You truly are related, aren't you?" Treesi asked, echoing Aria's thoughts.

Jehan shrugged. "At some level, perhaps. Mother says that my father was either Elcam, or the Palace healer when she served there on rotation. That healer shared a grandmother with Elcam. Mother never went further with it, and I never cared. It wasn't important."

"Until it was?" Mannon asked. Jehan shrugged again.

"Once we get back to Terraces, what then?" Treesi asked. "Are we staying there, or are we going to the Palace?"

Aria frowned slightly. "When your people find Owyn, where will they bring him?"

"Terraces," Mannon answered. "I told them to bring him to Terraces. He'll probably need looking after, and that's the best place for it. And there's the fact that Aven knows you're there. If...."

"When," Jehan murmured. "There are no ifs where my boy is concerned."

Mannon smiled. "When he comes back, he knows to go there. The Palace isn't going anywhere."

"What's it like?" Treesi asked. "Is it very big?" Her eyes widened, and the look she gave Aria was pure panic. "I'm going to get lost!"

"Lost?" Mannon repeated.

"I have trouble with lefts and rights," Treesi said. "I get lost easily. And I reverse letters."

Mannon nodded slowly, looking thoughtful. "I'll think on it. See what I can come up with. There has to be some way to address that, other than sending you out with a guide. Although that is an option, and I have a very contrite young guard who might appreciate the company of a pretty young healer while she recovers. She was the only other survivor of the party that accompanied Owyn and Alanar, and she risked irreparable damage to her own leg to save Alanar's life."

"Is it?" Aria asked. "Irreparable?"

Jehan took a long breath through his nose. "She was in healing trance when we left Terraces. I don't know how she responded to it. We'll find out."

"If she cannot continue as a guard, then we'll find another place for her," Aria said. "She risked everything to save someone I care for. I won't let that go unrewarded. She'll be welcome with us."

Mannon smiled. "Her name is Esai. She's a good girl. Fantastic guard. You'll like her."

Aria nodded. "I look forward to meeting her."

Outside the coach, the sound of the wheels on the road changed, and the coach slowed to a stop. Aria heard a heavy thump, then the door to Aria's left swung open. Karse stood outside, smiling.

"The dinghy is here," he said. "Looks like they're ready to start ferrying. Baggage first?"

Aria followed Treesi out of the coach, looking around. She wasn't sure, but this could have been the beach where she'd found Aven after they'd escaped Mannon's ship so many months ago. The air was just as thick here as it had been in her grandmother's garden, and it smelled just as strongly of sulfur.

"Is it snowing? This late?" Treesi asked. She held her hand out, and Aria could see black flecks on her palm. "Black snow? Is it dirty? Because of the volcano?"

"Black snow?" Memfis came over to them and looked at the flakes in Treesi's hand. He dragged one finger over one, and it smeared. "That's not snow," he said in a low voice. "That's ash. We have to get off this beach now!"

"Memfis?" Meris asked.

"Ash fall!" Memfis shouted back. "Get to the dinghy! Karse, never mind the baggage. Take it with you! Get moving!"

Karse and Trey ran for the coach. As they drove off, Aria saw her grandmother sway. She ran to her side. "Grandmother?"

"Ash fall," Meris whispered. "I've always...we have to go, my dear. Now." She frowned. "Six of us. There won't be enough room in the dinghy." She looked at Aria. "Can you still fly?"

Aria gaped at her for a moment, then looked out over the water at the ship. "I...I think I can make that. It's getting harder to fly distances. What is ash fall?"

"It means that our worst fears are coming to pass," Meris answered. "The Smoking Mountain is going to erupt. Now."

"Lady Meris," Jehan called as he came trotting up the beach toward them. "You need to come now. We're going in two shifts. You're going first, with Aria and Treesi. We'll follow—"

"I will fly," Aria said. "You take my place, Jehan. Terraces needs you."

Jehan blinked. Then he frowned. "Aria—"

"I can still fly that far. Go! I will follow!" Aria watched his face harden, and folded her arms over her chest. "That's an order, Senior Healer."

He blinked. Then he smiled. "You're not Firstborn yet, heart-daughter. But I'll listen. Lady Meris, if you'll come?"

Aria followed Jehan and Meris down to the dinghy. Memfis had already put Treesi into the boat; he nodded to Aria as she joined them.

"You'll sit next to Treesi —"

"No, Jehan will," Aria said. "I will fly. If we need to go quickly, then it is better that way." She looked at the boat, watching as Jehan settled Meris next to Treesi and took the space next to the crewman manning the boat. "There is no room for you or Mannon."

"I'm going last," Mannon said. "If it's the Mother's will that I die in the fires that made me, then so be it. Memfis, you should go."

Memfis shook his head. "I'm not leaving you alone here. Mother alone knows what mischief you'll get up to." He looked at the crewman on the dinghy. "Get them out of here."

The crewman nodded. "There and back...ten minutes?"

"Then you'd best get moving," Memfis said. "Mannon, help me push."

The two men got behind the dinghy and pushed it out into the water, wading out up to their thighs, then splashing back to the shore. Mannon looked up at the sky and shook his head.

"We should have insisted you go, Aria. It might not be a good idea to fly," he said. "The air is bad. And Smoking Mountain could start throwing stones at any moment if it's already throwing ash." He shook his head. "I read the legends about this. I never thought I'd see it."

"Why, though?" Memfis said. "Why now? Things have been out of balance for twenty-five years. Why now?"

"Because now, what's out of balance is getting worse," Mannon answered. "Because—" His voice trailed off, and he was cut off as the ground rumbled and rolled beneath them, making a sound like thunder. Aria flared her wings as she struggled to keep her balance, and Mannon and Memfis both fell to the ground. The shaking seemed to go on and on, and Aria was considering taking to the sky when it finally slowed and stopped. But the noise kept going, long, low roaring that was punctuated by moments of louder, deeper percussion.

Mannon looked up at her, and she could see that his face had turned pale. "You need to go. Get to the cutter and tell Destria to go. Now."

"Why?" Aria asked. "What is it?"

He raised his chained hands and pointed; Aria turned, and saw what was causing the percussion.

The Smoking Mountain was throwing plumes of fire into the skies.

"Rocks soon," Mannon said. "Mark me on that. Destria needs to get that cutter out into deep water, out of range."

"Mother of us all," Memfis breathed, staggering back to his feet. "Aria, go! Now!"

"But what about you?" Aria demanded. "Memfis, we can't leave you!"

"Never mind us," Memfis said. "You're the important one. You and that baby. Get out of here. Tell Owyn I love him and I'm sorry for everything."

Mannon nodded slowly as he rose. "Tell Del that I love him and I miss him. Tell him to be happy." He smiled slightly. "Be gentle with him, will you?"

Aria nodded slowly. "I will tell them if you cannot. But I would rather you both tell them yourselves." She looked out toward the ship. "Can you swim?"

Memfis coughed. "No," he said. "And the ship is too far out. We'd never make it. But we might be able to catch Karse and Trey, if we hurry."

Mannon looked at him, then held out his hands. "Take these off me," he demanded. "We don't have time for you to worry about doing it later, and I'll need both hands. Aria, get out of here!"

Aria turned and ran for the shoreline, her wings beating hard as she took flight. She circled, seeing Memfis and Mannon below her — Memfis had unlocked one of the manacles, and was working on the other. He looked up and waved a hand at her, shooing her off. She took the hint and wheeled, turning toward the water and the cutter. The dinghy was only halfway to the ship — Jehan was working at the oars with the crewman. Aria circled over them for a moment, then headed toward the ship, her wings and back aching already. This would be her last flight until after she gave birth. Hopefully, she wouldn't need to fly again any time soon, and thankfully, she didn't need to go much farther.

She back-winged, and landed on the deck, grimacing at the cramping that she could already feel in her back and shoulders. A woman hurried toward her. She wore the uniform of Mannon's guard, but had more braid on her sleeves.

"My Heir," she said, and bowed. "I'm Captain Destria." She rose, and her jaw dropped. "Should...should you even be flying?"

"There wasn't much choice. And I do not think I will be flying again," Aria answered. "Thank you, Captain." She went to the rail. "Is there another boat? A...what is it? A dinghy? Not everyone could fit."

"We only carry one. No room for a second one. Who's left on shore?" Destria asked. She joined Aria at the rail, squinting slightly. "I can't see in the haze."

"Mannon and Memfis are on shore. They are going back to Forge — they're going to try and catch Karse and Trey and my guards. He says that you should sail for deep water as soon as everyone is on board."

Destria grunted. "There are faster ways to commit suicide," she muttered. She leaned on the rail and shouted, "Put your back into it! We need to get out of range!"

If there was an answer, it was lost in a deep rumbling that seemed to be coming from somewhere far beneath them. Aria remembered Aven saying something about Father Adavar rolling in his sleep. How they didn't want him to wake. Suddenly, she knew why, as the ship began to roll; she grabbed onto the rail and watched in horror as the dinghy bobbed violently. They were close enough that she could see her grandmother clinging to Treesi's arm.

"Stand back," Destria ordered. She'd grabbed a rope — where from Aria had no idea. She went to the rail and tossed the weighted end toward the dinghy. It splashed just short of the small boat, and Destria swore and reeled the rope back in. She tossed it again, and this time, Jehan dropped his oar and caught the rope, tying it off to the prow of the dinghy as Destria and two other crewmen started to pull the boat in. Aria tried to stay out of the way, but hurried to the rail when the dinghy finally drew alongside the cutter. The crewmen helped Meris onto the cutter, then Treesi, and Aria barely let the crewmen clear before she rushed in to embrace her grandmother and her Earth.

"Hara was wrong," Meris murmured. "I am not enjoying this. At all."

"I'm going back for the others," Aria heard Jehan call, and raised her head to look at the dinghy.

"There's no time!" Destria protested.

"Mannon said he wanted us to leave as soon as you were on board," Aria said, raising her voice to be heard. She looked up at the volcano, at the spraying fire and the smoke. "They've gone to catch Karse and Trey. They are not on shore anymore. We must go!"

Jehan swore vehemently, then clambered up onto the cutter. He turned to help the crewman secure the dinghy. Destria nodded, and came over to Aria.

"My Heir, your family will be more comfortable in my quarters," she said. "We'll sail as soon as the dinghy is secure."

Aria looked at Meris. "Grandmother, you should go."

"Will you come with me?" Meris asked.

"Not yet," Aria answered. "I will join you shortly."

"I'm not going. I'm staying with you," Treesi said. She swallowed. "I...I don't think I like being on a boat, Aria. It moves. The ground isn't supposed to move." She clung to Aria's arm. "I don't like this."

Aria put her arm around Treesi's shoulders. "I did not like it either, my first time. This is not usual—"

"It's not unusual, either," Jehan said. He came over to them, looked at Treesi, then put his hand on her arm. "You're not likely to ever be comfortable at sea," he added. "But I can keep you from having to hang over the rail."

"Hang over the rail?" Aria repeated. Jehan grinned, and she realized what he meant. "Oh. Treesi, perhaps you should go lay down?"

"You should all go below," Destria ordered. "We're going to go fast. And deep. We're heading out to deep waters."

"If you need help with navigation, I've learned a thing or six over the years," Jehan offered.

"I might take you up on that." Destria turned and shouted, "Get us underway!"

"The cabin is that way," Jehan said. He pointed, and Aria turned to see.

So she missed the moment when the Forge side of the Smoking Mountain exploded outward.

CHAPTER TWENTY-FOUR

Owyn curled into a tight ball in the corner of the cabin, hearing the chains at his wrists and ankles clink as he moved. It was morning, at least. At least, he thought it was still morning. He wasn't sure. Wasn't sure about anything anymore. He no longer knew what day it was, nor how many days it had been since he'd been taken. He hadn't been outside this cabin since they'd brought him in here. He'd been in the cabin...or in the box.

He closed his eyes. The box stood in another corner of the cabin. It wasn't very big, nor was it very tall. It wasn't even big enough for Owyn to sit in. The sides of the box squeezed his shoulders, and he had to keep his head ducked down to his raised knees. There wasn't enough room for him to move, and he could barely breathe inside of it. There were no gaps in the wood, no spaces for light to get in, and the sides were thick enough that sound didn't penetrate easily.

It had taken three men to get him into the box the first time.

It had taken five the second.

The third time? Teva had given him a choice. He could go to the box, or go to Teva's bed.

It wasn't really much of a choice. Owyn went into the box. And Teva left him there, locked in the dark until Owyn was sure that he'd been forgotten. He had no way to know how long he'd been inside. Hours, maybe days. Probably days — when Teva had finally released him in the dim hours before dawn, Owyn was weak with hunger and thirst, and his throat raw from screaming.

"Are you ready to be reasonable?" Teva asked as Owyn toppled out of the box and onto the floor. "I know you're stubborn, Owyn, but really. You could be so much more comfortable."

Owyn glared up at him and croaked, "No."

Teva snorted. "I'm not surprised. Stubborn and stupid," he said. He picked up another length of chain, this one tethered to the bed, and locked it to the chain at Owyn's ankles. "This is your last chance, Owyn. You can stay out, for now. But when I come back, I'm asking you again. And if it's still no, then you go back into the box and I nail it shut and throw it overboard." He turned and walked out of the room, and Owyn heard the lock snapping shut. He stayed where he was, watching the sun rise through one of the windows, slowly stretching out as his cramped and aching muscles relaxed. When he could move again, he'd crawled to the corner and fell asleep.

Now he was awake again, listening to his stomach rumbling as he watched the patterns of light dance on the ceiling. He wondered how long he'd slept. How much longer he had to live. The idea of dying didn't frighten him nearly as much as it once had — it wasn't like he had anything to live for. The only person who really seemed to love him anymore was dead. Would anyone else care that he was gone?

Treesi would. And Mem. They would mourn him. But that was it. Aria had already shown she didn't care. And Aven? He'd never know.

They'd failed. He'd failed. And nothing mattered anymore.

But he could die on his own terms. He wasn't a whore. Not anymore. He'd learned his own worth. He wasn't going to bend for Teva. And it wasn't like he didn't know he was going to die out here.

Drowning would be quick, wouldn't it?

He heard someone shouting, an urgent sound from the other side of the locked door. Then, someone else shouting. But that voice came from outside the window. Owyn looked, and felt a flare of curiosity. Was someone out there? He got up and staggered to see.

Canoes. Dozens of them, ranging around the ship as far as he could see. Were they surrounded? Surrounded by Waterborn?

Was Aven out there?

For a moment, Owyn felt a flare of hope. Aven had saved his life before. He could do it again. But he had no idea that Owyn was a prisoner on this ship, and there was no way to tell him. Unless Owyn could get a message out to them. He tried the windows, but they'd been nailed closed. Clumsily, it looked like. Done in a hurry? Probably.

Owyn hadn't searched the room yet. He hadn't had time. Was there anything that could he use to pry the bent nails out? He took a step, and the heavy chains that bound his ankles clanked. He looked down at them, and at the similar heavy chains on his wrists.

Catching a bent nail in a link of chain was easy. Getting the angle right so that he could rip the nail out of the wood was more difficult. The topmost nails were simple— he could use his weight, and the weight of the chain. The lower ones were harder. He didn't have the same leverage. But he finally managed to pull the last nail out, and the window swung outward, letting in a cold salty breeze. Owyn leaned out, and took a deep breath. The canoes weren't close enough for him to call for help without having someone come. And he couldn't jump out to them. He couldn't get out of the room at all, but maybe there was another way.

He searched the room, but found nothing to write on. Nothing to write with. So he dragged one of the sheets off the bed and laid it on the floor. Then he picked up the bent nails, closed his eyes, and sliced open his palm. He had to keep the message short — he didn't want to bleed to death calling for help. So in long, bloody smears, he wrote: *Mouse here. Tell Aven.*

He tore off a strip of the sheet and bound his bleeding hand, then gathered the sheet and hung it out the window, stabbing through the cloth with the bent nails to hold it in place. He saw a commotion on one of the canoes, one of the men pointing. Pointing at the window. At Owyn. Owyn raised his arms, waved, and saw the man wave back before he dove into the water and vanished.

Owyn considered taking the sheet back in, then decided it wasn't worth it. Something would happen. Or, it wouldn't, and he'd die. He closed the window, went back to his corner, and sat down again to wait.

He'd just closed his eyes when the door slammed open, hard enough that Owyn felt the impact of it hitting the wall. He jumped, opening his eyes to see Teva stalking toward him, clearly furious.

"What did you do?" he demanded. "How do they know you're here?" He unlocked the tether from Owyn's ankles, then dragged him to his feet and out of the cabin. Owyn stumbled along with him, blinking in the bright sun, and caught himself on the rail when Teva shoved him forward. He gathered himself, then froze.

Aven.

Aven was standing on one of the larger canoes, looking up at the ship. He was wearing only a kilt, and his arms and chest now boasted dark tattoos. His face was completely expressionless, until he turned to speak to a woman who stood next to him. As he moved, Owyn saw the mask slip, saw the fear. Aven said something, and the woman nodded as he turned back. He met Owyn's eyes, and nodded slightly. Owyn shivered in response. Aven was here. He was going to be all right.

"You have no place out here, Risha," the woman shouted. "These waters are ours. The only reason you still live is standing next to you. Give us the prisoner, and we will allow you to pass."

Owyn looked to his right, where Risha had joined him at the rail. She laughed. "And if I refuse? Why should I deal with a fish?"

"Because this fish has warriors below your ship, ready to cut holes in your hull," the Waterborn woman answered. "If you refuse to hand him over, then we will take him once we sink your ship."

Owyn blinked. If Risha handed him over, they'd let her live? They'd let her *leave*?

"No!" he shouted. "Sink the ship! Sink the fucking thing!"

A familiar footstep behind him was the only warning Owyn had before Teva hit him, hard enough that he staggered and nearly fell, catching himself on the rail. Teva grabbed him by the hair, pulling him upright, and Owyn felt cold metal at his throat.

"They want him?" Teva asked. "They didn't say how."

Owyn reacted without thinking, doing exactly the same thing that he'd done to Teva when he'd first awakened on this ship. He drove his elbow back into Teva's gut, then spun and lashed out with his chained wrists, catching Teva in the jaw. Teva staggered backwards, his hand going to his face. When he lowered it, Owyn saw blood and bone.

"I'm going to throw them your corpse!" Teva snarled.

Owyn stepped back. He looked at the rail, at Risha's shocked face, and knew in his bones.

Now.

Fear vanished. There was only calm resignation, and a deep-seated need for revenge. When Teva rushed at him, he sidestepped, and dropped the chain between his wrists over Teva's head.

"I may be dying out here," he growled, looping the chain around Teva's neck and pulling it tight. "But I'm taking you with me."

Then he tumbled backward over the rail, dragging a screaming, struggling Teva with him as he fell. He heard Risha scream, heard Aven's voice, shouting his name.

Then he hit the water, hard enough that he gasped. Ice and salt filled his mouth, his nose. Just the way he'd known he was going to die.

At least Teva was going to die with him. Revenge for Alanar almost made dying worth it.

ALANAR REACHED UP AND touched the gem that he wore underneath his shirt. Before he left, Jehan had said it wouldn't hurt anything if he wore Owyn's Fire gem. It was a comfort, a promise that his lover would return. Alanar closed his eyes, offered up another in a long litany of silent prayers, and went back to his charting. Distantly, he heard a low rumble, and set down his cords. What was that?

The rumble got louder, and he started to feel it through the floor. No, through the ground. A tremor? Old instructions rose to the surface — if the ground shakes, get outside. Don't be in a building or underground if you can help it. He'd learned it since he was small. But he'd never felt a tremor before. He got up quickly, hurrying for the door.

"Alanar!"

Alanar kept moving — the voice was in front of him. "Rhexa," he called. "Is everyone evacuating?"

"We're moving patients out into the open right now," Rhexa answered. "I'm not liking this at all. There's never been a tremor this far north."

"Do we know what happened?" Alanar asked, turning to go out into the air. "Something happened."

"Clearly," Rhexa muttered. "But...Mother of us all!"

"What is it?" Alanar repeated.

Rhexa didn't have a chance to answer — a sound like the loudest thunder Alanar had ever heard boomed out, loud enough to be painful. People screamed, and Alanar's ears rang hard enough that he staggered back under the sheer force of the sound.

When Alanar could hear again, he heard Rhexa shouting, "I want sentries, up in the topmost Terraces! Get up high! I want to know what that is!"

"Rhexa, what happened?" Alanar shouted. "What—" He stopped.

The weight around his neck was gone. He fumbled with the collar of his shirt, looking for the cord. But his neck was bare.

"Rhexa?" he called. "Rhexa, it's gone."

"What?" Rhexa asked. "What's gone?"

"The Fire gem," Alanar said. He ran one hand down his chest, searching his shirt. But it wasn't there. "He...it's gone." He stopped. He knew. He *knew*. "He's gone. He's dead. Owyn's dead."

"OWYN!"

Aven watched in horror as Owyn fell from the ship's deck, dragging a screaming Teva with him. He was moving even before the splash, even before he heard his mother shouting, "Aven! Go!" He dove into the water, bracing himself for the pain of his change. He saw the streak of someone else diving in after him, and a third. One was his cousin Othi. The other was his water-cat Melody. By the time Aven had his tail, they had both outstripped him, diving deep to chase after Owyn. Aven kicked hard, trying to catch up, ignoring the pain in his desperate need to reach Owyn before the Smoke Dancer's waking vision became truth.

What had happened on land? How had Owyn ended up a prisoner on a ship? Aven couldn't imagine what had led to this. He'd have to get Owyn to tell him. He kicked harder, and drew closer to Othi. Othi looked back over his shoulder and pointed; Aven nodded, and the two of them dove deeper. He could see Melody, swimming in tight circles around something.

Around Owyn. Melody was keeping him from sinking further, but Aven could see that Owyn's body was limp. And he was alone. Where was Teva? He looked toward the surface, and saw the man swimming back toward the air. Aven trilled, then waved his arm toward Teva. Melody circled Owyn once more, then surrendered him to Othi and streaked through the water after Teva.

Othi swam up to meet Aven, holding Owyn under his arms. When Aven went to take Owyn from him, he shook his head, then nodded toward the surface. Aven frowned, and Othi shifted, signing awkwardly with one hand.

I carry. You heal.

Aven nodded, and they swam slowly upwards, the light growing closer and closer until the water around them was white and gold, and they broke through to the air.

"Here!" Aven heard Aleia shout. "Bring him here!"

Aven lifted himself out of the water as Othi passed Owyn's limp body up to the canoe. Aven saw Del shoving his long hair down the back of his vest, and dropping to his knees. When he covered Owyn's mouth with his own, Aven slapped the deck.

"Shift him over!" Aleia shouted. "Let Aven work."

Del pulled back as Owyn was moved. Aven waited until Del started to breathe for Owyn once more, then rested his hands on Owyn's chest and opened himself completely to his healing power.

There was no heartbeat.

"No," Aven growled, his voice not yet fully returned. He closed his eyes and focused, commanding Owyn's heart to start once more. He couldn't have been underwater long enough to drown! But his lungs were full of water, and there was no heartbeat. Aven changed position, balancing on his hip so that he could get both hands on Owyn's chest. He started pumping, forcing the heart to beat. He could hear Del panting, heard Neera tell him to move so she could take his place. Aven closed his eyes, forcing everything he had into his healing.

"Ven, he's dead," Aven heard Othi said softly. "I'm sorry. I wasn't fast enough."

No. No, he wasn't. Aven squeezed his eyes tighter, worked harder, pushed more power into healing.

"Not...dead," he gasped. "Not until I say so." He growled, deep in his throat and sent up a silent prayer. *Mother, please!*

Almost as if in answer, Owyn's body spasmed. Under Aven's hands, his heart started beating. Aven pulled back, seeing Neera do the same as Owyn wheezed, gasped, and vomited up seawater. Hands pushed him onto his side, and held him there until he went still once more.

"Ven?" Othi whispered. "Did...did you just *heal* a dead man?"

"No," Aven answered, feeling his head spinning. "Stole him back." He reached out and rested his hand on Owyn's hip, sending Owyn into a healing trance. Once it was done, he lay back, closing his eyes. "He's asleep. He'll sleep for a while. Take him into my canoe. Someone needs to watch him." He opened his eyes and looked around. The ship was gone. "Did she get away?"

"She won't get far," Aleia answered. "Not with the holes we left in the hull."

"Good," Aven murmured. He stretched out on the deck and closed his eyes. Then he opened them again and raised his head. "Where's Melody?"

Othi stood up and looked out over the water, shading his eyes with his hand. He grinned. "Suppertime, I think."

Aven smiled. "Good girl."

———— ❧ ————

OWYN WOKE UP. THAT surprised him enough that, for a long moment, all he could do was stare at the shadowed ceiling over him, marveling at the experience of just breathing. He'd woken up. That meant he was alive.

How the *fuck* had that happened?

He lay still, studying the darkness above him. It wasn't completely dark — there were tiny pinpricks of light that looked like stars. A thatch roof? Seemed to be. Where was he? Not back on the ship, that was certain. But the room was rocking gently. That meant...a canoe?

"Aven?" he whispered, and sat up, a thin blanket puddling around his hips. When he moved, a shadow in the corner uncurled. And kept uncurling, revealing itself to be something sinuous, and about twice as long as Owyn was tall. It undulated toward him, and he was about to scream when he remembered a long-ago description. He swallowed, trying to slow his heartbeat.

"Hey," he said gently. "Hey, there. Are you Melody?" He held his hand out, noticing for the first time that his wrists were bare of manacles. He only had a moment to think about that before Melody sniffed his fingers, then bumped her head against his hand, clearly demanding to be petted. Owyn chuckled, stroking and scratching her smooth, leathery skin, the same way he would have petted Granna Meris' cat. Melody crooned softly, twining around him and dropping her heavy head on his legs.

"Before you get yourself all comfortable, where's Aven?" Owyn asked. In answer, the water-cat snorted, unwound herself from around Owyn, and loped out of the shelter through a curtained doorway. Once she was gone, Owyn took stock of himself. The chains were gone. His wounded hand was healed, although he could feel a ridge across his palm that was probably another scar. He could live with another scar. He was as naked under the blanket as he had been when he'd dove off the ship. He looked down at his bare wrist, and closed his eyes. He had no idea what had happened to Alanar's pledge bracelet. He rubbed his wrist, finally allowing himself to feel the weight of the loss. His last link to Alanar, gone. He had nothing left. But at least Teva was dead.

Wasn't he?

The curtain moved, and a slender figure slipped into the shelter. Before the curtain fell back into place, Owyn saw a bright glint of sunlight on golden hair, enough to identify who had come inside.

"Del!" Owyn said. "Been hearing about you. Del the Silent, they call you. Said you were a good trader."

Del opened the curtain enough to let some light in. Then he came over to sit cross-legged on the floor in front of Owyn. He was dressed very similarly to what Aven had been wearing when Owyn first met him — a kilt and an open vest, with a carry-bag slung across his chest. And there was a dark mark on his right shoulder, something that Owyn couldn't really make out in the dim light. A tattoo? He smiled at Owyn, reached across the space between them and tapped Owyn on the chest, then cocked his head to the side, brows raised.

"What, how am I feeling?" Owyn asked. When Del nodded, he grinned. "Surprised that I'm not dead. I'm supposed to be dead. Why am I not dead?" He stopped and bit his lip. "And how are you supposed to answer? I don't know water signs."

Del laughed, and reached into his bag. He took out something that looked like a book, which opened to reveal a creamy white slate. He went back into the bag, and pulled out a piece of charcoal.

"*We can talk like this,*" he wrote. "*And the War Leader is coming. You're not dead because Aven and Othi pulled you out of the water. Neera and I breathed for you while Aven started your heart beating again.*"

"Started my..." Owyn stammered. "You mean I was dead?"

"For at least a minute," a woman said as she came through the curtain. "But Aven wasn't going to let you go as easy as that. He'll be along shortly. He was with the Clan Mother on the other side of the city."

"The city?" Owyn realized what she meant. "The Floating City? Really? You have all the canoes put together out there? Can I come see it? I've read about it, but I never thought I'd get to see it, and...and I don't know you. Sorry. I'm Owyn. Owyn Jaxis, son of Dyneh, Huris, and Memfis."

She looked startled, then smiled. "I knew you were Memfis' boy. Aven told me. But I don't think he knew the entire thing. And it's a pleasure to meet you. I'm Aleia."

Owyn's jaw dropped. "You're Aven's mother! We thought you were dead!" He looked at Del, then back at Aleia. "You're the War Leader?"

Aleia nodded. "And when the time is right, we'll show them that I'm very much alive, and very much in command. Now, how do you feel?"

Owyn considered the question, thinking about what he now knew. "I was supposed to die out here. My waking vision...d'ye know about that? You were a Companion."

"I still am a Companion," Aleia said. "Yes, I know. Yours involved drowning?"

"In salt water," Owyn answered. "When I ended up out here, I knew my time had come. It's why I jumped. So I wasn't expecting to wake up." He frowned slightly, looking down at his wrist. "Not sure I wanted to."

Aleia came over and sat down next to Del. She looked troubled by his words. "Why?" she asked gently.

Owyn took a deep breath, trying to figure out how to answer the question. Then he heard footsteps. Uneven footsteps, punctuated by the even thump of a walking stick. Del looked up at the sound, then touched Aleia's arm. She must have read something in his expression, because she got gracefully to her feet.

"We'll talk later," she said. "You're welcome here, Owyn Fireborn." She turned and escorted Del out of the shelter.

A moment later, Aven limped inside.

CHAPTER TWENTY-FIVE

With the curtain open behind him, all Owyn could see of Aven was a silhouette. But he'd know that shape anywhere. He rocked up onto his knees, and found he was shaking too hard to get to his feet.

"Aven," he breathed. "I...I knew you'd save me. You always save me."

Aven came closer, and went to his knees in front of Owyn. He rested his hand on Owyn's chest, and Owyn felt warm. He closed his eyes.

"I missed you," he murmured. "I've been trying to get messages to you for weeks."

"I know," Aven answered. "I've gotten some of them. Only in the past few days, as the canoes came together. But I've gotten some of them." He lowered his hand, and Owyn opened his eyes.

"Was I dead?" Owyn asked. "Your mother says I was."

"No heartbeat," Aven said. "No breathing. Not sure if there was anything happening in your brain..." He paused, then grinned. "But I've never been sure of that."

Owyn giggled. "Fuck you, Fishie."

Aven arched a brow. "Right now?"

Owyn caught his breath. He looked at Aven, then smiled. "Yeah. Right now."

Aven laughed, and reached for Owyn. "That's what I hoped you'd say."

OWYN WOKE UP AGAIN to find himself draped over Aven, who was lying on his back. He could hear Aven's heartbeat under his ear. He closed his eyes and sighed, then squirmed a little as Aven started tracing his fingers up and down the length of Owyn's spine.

"I missed you," Aven's voice was rumble in Owyn's ear. "Mouse, what happened? How did you get out here?"

"Long story," Owyn said. "And it's the end of the long story. Let me start at the beginning. You need to come back."

Aven snorted, bouncing Owyn gently. "She doesn't want me, Mouse."

"She does," Owyn insisted. "She was wrong, and she knows it. She wants you back. She needs you back. She's going to shatter like glass without all of us." He paused, then used the only coin he had. "Aven, she's pregnant."

Aven's hand went still. "Well," he murmured. "Congratulations."

"Congratul— no!" Owyn raised his head and looked Aven in the eyes. "It's not mine. She hasn't been in my bed. She hasn't been in anyone's bed since you left. The baby is yours, Fishie."

Aven stared at him for a moment, then sat up, spilling Owyn off of his chest. "Mine?" he gasped. "But—" He stopped, frowning. "Risha...she did something. Not what she was supposed to do. She didn't block the pregnancy. She...she made it happen?"

Owyn sat up and folded his legs. "I think so. And Aria...it's tearing her up. Your Fa said that he offered to end the pregnancy—"

"He did *what*?" Aven looked stunned.

"She said no," Owyn said. "She wants this child. Your child. But she's tearing herself up. Literally, Aven. She's pulling out her own feathers."

Aven closed his eyes. "Owyn, did she tell you that she wants me back?"

Owyn snorted. "She didn't even tell me she was leaving Terraces. She left me behind, too."

"Leaving Terraces? To go where?"

"Forge," Owyn answered. "She went to Forge, and Alanar and I headed north to try and contact as many canoes as we could. And...well, shit happened. And I think I need to tell your Ma this part, too. Because I met Mannon—"

"And he sent you out with Risha?" Aven asked.

"No. He abdicated." Owyn grinned at the stunned look on Aven's face. "At least, he will when we get back." He frowned. "Look, if I'm going to tell the rest of this story, I'd rather just do it once. It...it don't end well."

Aven slowly got to his feet. Now that his eyes had adjusted to the darkness, Owyn could see that tattoos covered Aven's back, his chest, his left shoulder and his left arm. There was a smaller one on his right arm.

"I need to see you in better light," Owyn said. "You got all the tattoos your grandmother wouldn't let you have?"

Aven looked down at himself and nodded. "All of them. I spent a lot of time lying on my front while someone went at me with a hammer. My cousin Neera is Clan Mother now. She welcomed me as a full member of the family practically the minute we got here. Del, too."

"Oh!" Owyn gasped. "I saw he had something on his shoulder. The right one." He tapped his own. "Is that what you've got? A family tattoo?"

"Come out into the light," Aven said. He picked up his discarded kilt and opened the curtain.

"Hey!" Owyn yelped. "I need clothes!"

Aven looked back over his shoulder. "You don't, if you don't want to wear them."

Owyn gaped at him for a moment, then swallowed. "I...let me start slow, yeah?" Aven came back inside, going to a basket in the corner. Owyn watched him, then looked around. "This is yours?"

Aven nodded, coming back with another kilt. He leaned in close and wrapped it around Owyn's waist. "No one told you? Yes, this is mine. Mine and Del's."

Owyn blinked. " Oh. And...you and he paired off?" he asked.

Aven shook his head. "No. You said Aria hasn't been in anyone's bed since that night? Neither have I. Not for lack of invitations, but...I didn't feel right doing it." He met Owyn's eyes and smiled. "Not until today."

"I...well," Owyn breathed. "I'm honored. Or something. Why not with Del?"

"Because Del isn't interested," Aven answered. He wrapped his own kilt around his waist and nodded. "Not in men or in women. He's had plenty of invitations, too."

Owyn frowned, trying to make sense of it. "Not interested in sex?"

"At all," Aven agreed. "And if you want to ask him about it, he has his tablet. And we can start teaching you to use signs." He gestured to the curtain. "Come on."

Aven led Owyn out into the light, and Owyn got his first good look at Aven's tattoos. They were dark, with the sharp look of new tattoos, and he wondered what the ink was that they used. He walked a slow circle around Aven, studying them. "This is the family mark." he said, tapping Aven's right shoulder. "Then what's the left?"

Aven held his left arm out. "Warrior's marks," he answered. "And then there's this." He held his right hand up, the back of it facing Owyn. There were lines tattooed there, and dots.

Owyn studied them, then whistled. "That had to hurt like fuck," he murmured. "And...those are what?"

"Navigator marks," Aven said, and Owyn could hear the pride in his voice.

"You been busy, haven't you?" Owyn said, and Aven laughed.

"It gave me something to do. Now come on. Let's go find Ama." He reached out and grabbed a club that had been leaning against the shelter wall. No, not a club. A walking stick, and Aven leaned on it as they started walking. "Watch your step here," he added as they reached the edge of the canoe. Aven stepped easily from one canoe to the next. Owyn hesitated, seeing the water between them. Then he swallowed and stepped across.

"How's the leg?" Owyn asked as they started walking again. "And tell me to fuck right off if you don't want to talk about it."

Aven smiled, but there was a tension to it that hadn't been there before. "Not getting any better," he answered. "Walking hurts. Changing hurts. Swimming hurts. Some days, breathing hurts. Fair warning — I can get snappish at the end of the day."

"Understandable," Owyn said. "And that's the point someone tells you to go to bed?"

The smile was real this time. "Del, usually. If he's busy, then my cousin Othi or my mother."

"Othi. Del said he was with you when you pulled me out." He turned and looked around, at the expanse of water that surrounded the canoes. "Aven, where's the ship?"

"The warriors who followed it to make sure it sank haven't come back yet. But they put some good sized holes in the hull."

"And...what happened to Teva? Did I kill him?"

"Almost," Aven said. "Melody finished the job."

Owyn nodded, feeling his stomach churning slightly. "I wish I'd done it. But I'll accept that it's done. And honestly, he deserved worse." He looked down at himself. He didn't feel different. Did he? "I really was dead?"

Aven nodded. "I should warn you," he said. "My cousins are going to treat you like you're the embodiment of Father Adavar. They think you rose from the dead."

"And how are they treating you?" Owyn asked. "I mean, you rose me."

Aven snorted. "I think you left your grammar in your other life," he teased. "And no one is complaining about the Mudborn anymore. There's no one avoiding me. Treating me like I'm not worth anything. Not anymore."

They moved from one canoe to another, and Owyn slowly got more comfortable with it. The canoes were anchored close enough that you could step from one to the other without stretching too far or going off balance. Really, it was like walking in the coal fields — you had to keep an eye on your footing, but the ground was solid. Even though it moved, it all seemed to move together.

"You're relaxing," Aven said. "That's good."

"I'm getting used to the movement," Owyn answered. "Where are we going?"

Aven stopped and pointed to a larger structure on the next canoe. "There. That's Ama's headquarters."

"And...she's really the War Leader?" Owyn asked. "I mean, we've heard about her. The Waterborn that came to trade with Serenity told me about the War Leader. But we didn't know the War Leader was a her, and we didn't know it was your mother."

"She's really the War Leader," Aven agreed. "That started before Del and I got here. She's united the entire Water tribe under her banner, and the warriors will be heading to shore when the time is right. And once we do, there won't be a ship in Mannon's navy safe from us."

"Listen to him boast!" a cheerful voice called. "You'd think we'd already won." The owner of the voice came out of one of the other shelters, ducking underneath the low doorframe as he did. He had to duck — he was taller than Aven by easily the length of Owyn's arm from fingertip to elbow.

"Aven?" Owyn whispered, trying not to stare. This man was at least two Avens lumped together into one massive person. Maybe three. "Tell me he's unusually big?"

"No," Aven said with a laugh. "I'm considered small for Water. This is my cousin, Othi."

"Othi," Owyn repeated, looking up at the man as he stopped next to them. "Del told me you pulled me out of the water. Thanks."

Othi laughed. "You're welcome. I know you're Owyn. I've heard your name a lot over the past couple of months. Didn't think I'd get to meet you. At least, not until we got on land. Ven says you don't swim, and you don't do boats."

"I don't swim," Owyn said with a nod. "And I didn't do boats. Not until I was forced on to one. Hey, how'd you get the chains off?" He held up his hands.

Aven grinned and looked at Othi, and the both of them answered at once, "Del."

"Really? He picks locks?" Owyn snorted. "Right. Umm...you said Melody did for Teva. Did...did she happen to spit up a bracelet?"

Aven looked at Othi. "Did you see one? I was busy."

"I didn't, but that doesn't mean he didn't have it. But if he did have it, it's probably down in the deeps," Othi said. "Melody didn't leave much, and that was in pieces."

Owyn shuddered. "I was hoping. But it's all right. I should thank her, when I see her next." He looked up at Aven and Othi. "Right. Where are we going?"

"Inside," Aven answered, and led Owyn to the large shelter. He drew the curtain back, and gestured for Owyn to enter.

The shelter was well-lit, and dominated by a single table in the center of the space. As Owyn walked closer, he realized that the surface was a map.

"I thought you didn't do flat maps!" he said, going to the table. To his shock, the map wasn't drawn in ink — it was created from a variety of colors of sand. "Oh, this is beautiful," he breathed. Then he covered his mouth. "If I sneeze, you all will kill me!"

A woman laughed, and Aleia came up behind him, placing her hand on his shoulder. "The sand is glued down. And no, we don't usually use flat maps. How did you know?"

Owyn lowered his hand. "Aven told me. I asked him how you navigated without roads. He told me about winds and waves and stars."

Aleia squeezed his shoulder. "I'll make a navigator out of you yet. Now, you have something to tell me?"

Owyn swallowed. "Yeah. Just...it'll take a while. You might want to sit down."

"...AND WHEN WE STOPPED for a rest, that's when Risha and Teva attacked. And they killed my Allie." Owyn looked down at his hands, folded in his lap. He was sitting cross-legged on the floor, his back against a support post. Aven was on his left, and Del on his right. "When I woke up again, I was on a ship, my pledge bracelet was gone, and Teva told me I was his. That by the time he was done, I'd be begging to be in his bed." He shook his head. "I was going to die first. I mean, I knew I was going to die out here. It was my waking vision. And...I did, didn't I? I died out here. But now..." he frowned. "Am I still a Smoke Dancer? Do I get another waking vision?"

Aleia looked thoughtful. "Milon and Memfis, they never really talked about the arcana of being a Smoke Dancer. I don't know. I don't know if there's ever been another Smoke Dancer who's died and come back. You may be the first."

Owyn chuckled. "I'm the first, huh? Does that mean I get a title or something? Owyn, the Ever-living?"

Aleia smiled. "If you like. Now, tell me more about this abdication."

Owyn nodded. "First off, do you know about Yana?"

Aleia nodded. "The Heir before Aria, and Del's mother. Aven told me."

"Mannon was Yana's Air," Owyn said, and heard everyone in the room gasp. Aleia raised one hand, and waited until silence fell.

"How did he prove this?" she asked.

"He still has his Air gem," Owyn answered. "He told us that Yana chose him after she was hurt, and after her Fire died. Her Fire was Del's father." He glanced at Del, who nodded. He raised his hands and started signing. Owyn watched him for a moment, trying to understand what the signs meant. There didn't seem to be a pattern that he could follow...

"He says that he's seen the gem, that Mannon used to let him wear it after his mother died," Aven said, his voice low. "He says that he remembers his mother calling Mannon her Air."

Aleia nodded slowly. "Well," she murmured. "That's interesting. When you told me that there had been an Heir before Aria, I didn't realize that she had any of her Companions."

"I don't think anyone knew," Owyn said. "Mannon said he decided that he couldn't take Yana out to find her Water or her Earth, because of how badly she'd been hurt. He said there'd have been riots." He shrugged. "He said it might not have been the best choice, but it was the one he made. He says he's done the best he could, and that he knows he's fucked everything up. He wrote out his entire abdication plan, including that he was surrendering to Aria's will." Owyn grimaced. "I...I had it when we were attacked. I—"

Aven shifted, putting his arm around Owyn's shoulders. "You were marrying Alanar?" he asked gently.

"Yeah," Owyn answered. "He...nobody was making him love me." He looked up at Aven. He felt hollow. Brittle, like badly worked metal or glass. "I mean, I do love you, Fishie. And I know you love me. But we talked about this. About the Mother forcing us all together, because there's no time to let us grow together the usual way. Alanar was different. Nobody was *forcing* him to want me. There weren't no goddess saying that I was going to be his forever. He wanted me because he wanted me. He loved me without being told to. The usual way." He closed his eyes, felt his breath hitch, and his walls shattered. "And it got him killed!" he sobbed.

Arms closed around him — Aven's, and another set from behind. Owyn was beyond thinking, finally giving in to his grief. "He shouldn't have been there!" he gasped between sobs. "He wouldn't let me go alone because he was afraid I wouldn't come back. He shouldn't have been there!"

Owyn wasn't sure how long he cried, but Aven's arms never loosened. He heard Aven whispering soft somethings, but never registered what the words were or what they meant. It didn't matter. It didn't help.

Until something did register.

"Did I make a mistake?" Aven asked. "Bringing you back?"

Owyn sniffed and tugged out of Aven's arms. "What?"

Aven met his eyes. "Were you trying to die, Owyn?" he asked gently. "When you jumped? I thought you were trying to escape. Was I wrong?"

Owyn scrubbed his hand over his face and looked down at the arms that still encircled him from behind. "You can let go, Del," he murmured. And felt Del shake his head no, his cheek rubbing against Owyn's bare back. Despite himself, Owyn laughed. Then he looked at Aven.

"No," he answered. "You didn't make a mistake. I..." He paused and scrubbed his hand over his face. "I don't know where I'm going now, though."

"Back to land?" Aleia asked. "With us?"

Owyn looked at her, at the sympathy in her eyes. "You're going?"

She nodded. "We'll stay here for a day or two, until the warriors who followed the ship report back that it's sunk. Then we'll go ashore. You were admiring my map. Where would you say would be the best place to go ashore?"

Owyn sniffed and rubbed the back of his hand over his nose. "I...best place? Ummm...there was a tunnel, they told me. In Terraces. The Waterborn who lived there used to use them. They told me the tunnel collapsed. But they told people a lot of the tunnels collapsed, when really they were being used by Pirit and her army."

"Pirit?" Aleia repeated. "Has an army?" She snorted. "Pirit was an army all by herself."

"She is that," Owyn agreed. "So there might be a place to dock in Terraces, but I don't know the way through the tunnels. If you've got anyone here who used to live here, they might know."

"Assume we don't," Aleia said. "Where would be your second choice?"

Owyn frowned, thinking. Then he looked over his shoulder. "I need to stand up. Now you have to let go."

Del nodded and released him, and Owyn turned and kissed him on the cheek. "Thank you," he said. He went back to the table, studying the coast. It confirmed what he already knew.

"It'll be a long walk to get to Terraces, but here," he said, pointing. "Serenity Bay. You've got a sister who lives there. Danzi. She's head-woman.

Aleia frowned, then blinked. "Jehan's sister? That Danzi? Head-woman?"

"She married a Water. Her son Marik is a friend of mine."

"I told you about Marik, Ama," Aven volunteered. "He talks to birds."

Aleia nodded. "I remember now. All right. I'll confer with Neera—"

"I heard my name?" A young woman came into the shelter. She was as tall as Aven, and as pretty. She smiled when she saw Owyn. "Ah. I'm glad to see you well, Twiceborn."

CHAPTER TWENTY-SIX

"Twiceborn?" Owyn echoed. "Me? I...what does she mean, Twiceborn? Aven? What does that mean?"

"You haven't told him?" Neera asked.

"He knows," Aven answered. He slowly got back to his feet, leaning on his walking stick as he straightened. "But I didn't tell him what people were calling him."

"People?" Owyn repeated. "You mean, more than just her? There are people calling me Twiceborn? Why?" Del poked him in the shoulder and scowled at him. "What?" Owyn demanded.

"He's telling you not to be rude," Aleia said. "Neera is Clan Mother."

"No!" Owyn blurted, looking back at the young woman. "She's too young!"

Aven snorted. "Owyn, you need to stop now. She's got a nasty backhand."

Owyn gaped at him for a moment, then laughed. "No! No, that wasn't what I meant. I mean...Clan Mother, that's like Lady Meris. Or...or Pirit."

"I understand what you mean," Neera said. "It's not that I'm too young to rule the tribe. It's that I'm young enough that I don't appear to have the life experience to do it well."

Owyn nodded agreement. "Yeah, that's it. They said Clan Mother, I was expecting someone old enough to be a mother."

Neera snorted. "I am that, Owyn. Old enough, I mean. And I shouldn't be Clan Mother. Not yet. But my grandmother and mother both died in the Mother's Rage. That big storm last winter. I already know I'm too young to be Clan Mother. But I am what we have. Aunt Aleia is better suited to be War Leader."

"And Neera has done very well for us," Aleia said. Neera smiled, her face turning ever so slightly red.

"I had excellent teachers, and a wonderful role model," she murmured. "Now, do you really need an explanation, Twiceborn?"

"Owyn," Owyn said. "My name is Owyn. And...umm...yes?"

Neera chuckled. "I see why you like him, Aven," she said. "You were Fireborn. Then you were born again from the Water. That makes you—"

"Steam," Owyn interjected. "That makes me steam."

Neera looked at him for a moment, then started to giggle. Giggles turned to full laughter, and she ended up leaning on the table, trying to catch her breath. "Oh," she gasped. "Oh, my."

"Should I apologize?" Owyn asked, looking up at Aven.

"No, I think she needed that," Aven answered. He draped one arm over Owyn's shoulders. "I told them they were being pretentious."

"Are they right, though?" Owyn asked. "Am I...well, not Fireborn anymore?" He frowned. "I...am I not a Smoke Dancer anymore? Or Companion?"

Aven tensed. "I...I don't know."

"I'm not Water, am I?" Owyn asked. He reached up and touched his throat. "No gills. And I can't swim. I don't think. Do you know that without being taught?"

"No, we learn it early," Neera asked, finally having composed herself. "Regardless of what you are, Owyn, you are welcome here."

"I need to know, though," Owyn said. "I was a Smoke Dancer. I need to know if I still am. I mean, I died. Does that change anything?

How can I tell? I don't have my blades. My whip chain is gone. I can't dance." He wrapped his arms over his chest, his fingers digging into his arms. "I need to know."

Warm hands slid up his arms, then started kneading his shoulders. "Do you remember when you danced for us, on the beach?" Aven asked.

"When I saw Del the first time?" Owyn asked. "Yeah. Why?"

"You don't have your blades," Aven answered. "But I have mine. Remember, I told you that you reminded me of the way we sword dance?"

"I..." He twisted and looked at Aven. "You think that will work?"

"It's worth a try," Aven said. He looked over at Del, who nodded, then darted out of the shelter.

"He going for the swords?" Owyn asked.

"Yes. And we'll meet him on the dancing floor." Aven stepped back, then held his hand out to Owyn. "Come on." He looked over his shoulder. "Ama, are you coming with us?"

"Yes," Aleia answered. "It's been a long time since I last saw someone dance for a vision." She smiled. "And it was your father, Owyn."

Owyn grinned. "He taught me. Taught me everything."

"Memfis was always a good teacher."

They walked out of the shelter and out into the sun. Owyn blinked and squinted, looking around. There were more people around, and all of them seemed to be looking at him. And from behind him, he heard a low whistle.

"When are we getting him warrior marks, Neera?" Othi asked. "With scars like that? He's seen battles."

"First, we welcome him to the canoe," Neera answered. "And give him the family mark. Then, if he wants them—"

"Warrior marks?" Owyn gasped. "Me? But..." He paused, then said, "Aria called me her Warrior."

Othi laughed. "If the Heir says you're a warrior, then you can have any warrior mark you want. Where are we going?"

"The dancing floor," Aven answered. "Owyn's going to try and catch a vision."

Othi's brows rose. "What kind of net do you need for that?"

Owyn burst out laughing, and heard Aven chuckling next to him. Othi grinned. "Good. Looks like you needed that. Mind if I come watch?"

"It might not work," Owyn said slowly.

Othi shrugged one shoulder. "So? Isn't that how most things are? It either works or it doesn't. Don't know until you try."

They started walking, moving from one canoe to the next. Owyn watched Aven as they walked, studying the limp. Aven's stiff movements fairly screamed that he was in pain. All at once, Owyn realized that he'd never seen Aven sword dance. They'd talked about it. But there had never been a chance. Would he ever? Maybe. Once they got back to Terraces, maybe Jehan and Pirit could put Aven to rights. And Teva had paid for it, and for everything else he'd done. That was something, at least.

It should still never have happened.

They finally stopped on the edge of what looked like about a dozen small canoes tethered together to make one large, flat surface. The dancing floor, Owyn guessed. Del was already there, kneeling next to an open case. He looked up at Aven, then took out two familiar blades — the hook swords that Memfis had given to Aven.

"Fishie, I've never danced with swords," Owyn said slowly. "I'm not sure if it'll work."

"It won't hurt to try," Aven answered. He squeezed Owyn's shoulder gently, then leaned down and took one of the swords from Del and handed it to Owyn.

The sword was lighter than Owyn expected, and he gnawed on his lip as he shifted his grip. "It's different from my smoke blades," he murmured. He took the other one from Del, testing the weights, the balance. Then he nodded. "All right. I'll try it. Stay back. I'm not used to doing this with something sharp."

Aven leaned down and kissed Owyn gently. "We'll be here when you come back."

The words sounded familiar, and it took Owyn a moment to remember — Alanar had said much the same thing the last time Owyn had gone seeking visions. He shivered, and Aven frowned.

"What?"

"It's...no, I'll explain later. Let me do this, or I'm not going to do it." Owyn forced a smile, then turned and walked to the middle of the dancing floor. The canoes had been tethered together so securely that there was no space between them, and Owyn could barely tell which seam in the wooden planks was the space between one canoe and the next. He looked up, checking to see how far he was from everyone. Far enough. He took an experimental swing with the right hand sword. Then another. He nodded. Then he closed his eyes, took three deep breaths, and started to move. It was awkward at first — the swords didn't flow the same way that his smoke blades did. He stopped, resettled himself. Another deep breath. A second. A third. Then he started moving again.

And the vision closed over him like salt water, dragging him under.

He was lying on a soft bed, a heavy blanket covering him to the chest. There was a pattern of tiles over the bed — abstract swirls in blue, gold, red and orange, like flames swimming in still waters. He was warm, and comfortable, and so unbelievably tired.

"Owyn? Jaxsyn is here. He's brought Avram."

He turned his head, trying to understand why it felt so heavy. Sitting next to the bed was an old woman, and standing behind her was a man with hair like Treesi's, who was carrying a small child. For a moment, he thought the woman was Meris. Then she smiled.

Treesi!

The shock of seeing Treesi as an old woman was enough to throw Owyn out of the vision. He gasped and went to one knee, trying to catch his breath.

What had he seen? Treesi, only old. How had she gotten so old? And...she was talking to him.

That meant he'd been old, too.

Suddenly, he understood. Why he'd been in bed. Why he'd felt so tired.

He'd been *dying*. In his own bed. With people he loved around him. Jaxsyn. Had that been his son? His son with Treesi?

He looked up to see Aven coming toward him.

"Owyn? Are you all right?"

"I..." Owyn swallowed. "I had a vision. I had a waking vision. I'm still a Smoke Dancer. And..." He got to his feet and looked at the water that stretched as far as he could see. He felt...almost giddy. Like he was drunk. "Aven, teach me to swim."

"What?" Aven gaped at him for a moment. "Owyn, what?"

"You heard me," Owyn said. He looked up at Aven. "Teach me to swim. You told me that if I asked you, you'd teach me. I'm asking."

"Actually, you're demanding," Aven said slowly. "Owyn, what did you see? Can I ask?"

Owyn grinned. "Well, someday I'm going to have a son." He paused, realizing something. "And a grandson!"

"I NEVER THOUGHT SWIMMING was so much work!" Owyn panted as he followed Aven back to the shelter. Water dripped from his kilt onto his bare feet as he walked. "I mean, you and Aria make it look easy!"

"It is easy," Aven said. "You're just new to it. And you did well."

"I sank!"

Aven laughed as he ducked his head and entered the shelter. Owyn followed, hearing Del's soft step behind him.

"You sank because you're all muscle," Aven said. He stripped off his own wet kilt and slowly lowered himself to sit on the floor. He winced, and Owyn felt a pang.

"And now you're hurting," he said. "Because of me. I'm sorry—"

"I hurt all the time, Mouse," Aven interrupted. "It's not your fault." He stretched out on his back and laced his fingers over his stomach, closing his eyes. "You did well," he repeated. "You're floating. That's the first step. You just need to relax."

"Kinda hard, since I've been scared of salt water for years," Owyn said, taking off his kilt and sitting down next to Aven. "Is there anything I can do?" he asked. "Anything that helps?"

Aven shook his head. "Nothing helps for very long."

Owyn heard a soft snapping noise. He turned to see Del standing behind him. Del held his hands up, fingers splayed wide, then started opening and closing his hands. He stopped, arched a brow.

Owyn frowned. Opening and closing his hands? He looked down at his own hands, repeating the movement. "Oh," he murmured. "Massage? That it?" He looked up to see Del's wide smile. He laughed. "See? Sign language isn't that hard." He turned back toward Aven. "Roll over, Fishie. Let me work on that hip."

Aven grunted and rolled onto his stomach, pillowing his head on his arms. "I didn't know you know massage," he mumbled.

"I know a lot of things. And not a lot of other things," Owyn answered. He ran his hand down Aven's back and over his hip, tracing the lines of his muscles, learning how they lay over the bones. Thinking about what he'd picked up from the brothel boys about massage. Trey had been good at it. But this wasn't muscle or tendon. This was bone not sitting right. Could he ease the tension in the muscles around the bone? Maybe. He started gently, working to relax the muscles made tight by the pain. After a few minutes, he heard

Aven sigh. Good. He shifted onto his knees, leaned over Aven, and dug into the muscles hard. Something popped under his hand, and Aven yelped. Owyn jumped back.

"Fuck! I'm sorry!" he gasped. "I...I thought it would loosen the—"

"Tendons," Aven finished. He rolled on to his right side, then sat up. "I...I think it did. It feels looser. Where did you learn to do that? And why didn't you ever show me?"

"Forge," Owyn answered. "Trey taught me. The brothel boys, they learned shit like this. Some of the customers liked it. He thought it might be good for me to learn, too." He looked up at Del. "Did you try it?"

Del held his hand flat and wiggled it, and Owyn grinned. "Not so much, or not as much?"

"He doesn't mass enough to put that much pressure on the hip," Aven answered. "You didn't answer why you never showed me."

"Because we never had time," Owyn answered. "Because we were on the run, or on the road, or you were living with the trainees." He reached up and scratched the back of his neck. "And it goes both ways. I still haven't heard you sing. Or drum. Or—" He stopped.

He'd been about to say *dance*.

Aven grimaced, but didn't seem to realize what Owyn had stopped himself from saying. "We'll have time for that before you go with Ama."

Owyn looked at him in shock. "Before I go? What about you?"

Aven shrugged. "I'm not sure I'm going back to shore. I mean, she told me flat out she didn't want me."

"She didn't mean that!" Owyn protested. "And you might not be. Mannon says you might not be his kin. So does your father."

"Aria thinks I am," Aven said. "If she doesn't want me because of that, how do I nay-say her?"

"You tell her that she's being stupid?" Owyn suggested. "Like I did?"

Del snickered, coming over to sit down next to Owyn. He tugged his tablet out of his carrybag, scrawled something on it, then passed it to Aven.

Aven scowled and handed it back. "That's not it."

Del made a rude noise, and Aven lurched to his feet. "I'm going to go swim," he declared, and walked out. He wasn't limping as badly as he had been.

Owyn twisted to watch him leave, then turned to Del. "What did you say?" he asked.

Del passed the tablet to him, and Owyn read the single word. *Pride.*

He looked up at Del. "Is that what you think?" He frowned. "No. I don't think so. I don't think it's pride. I think he's scared. He got hurt. Then Aria hurt him again. It's not pride. It's fear."

Del shrugged. Then he looked up and got gracefully to his feet. As Owyn turned, Aleia peered through the curtain. Owyn stared for a moment, then reached out and grabbed his wet kilt, dragging it over his lap.

She smiled. "I apologize. I should remember you're not used to us. I saw Aven leave. He looked upset." Del gestured, and she nodded. "I see. Well, deep thoughts are best in deep water. I'll step out so that you can dress, Owyn." She closed the curtain, and Owyn stood up and wrapped the kilt around his waist.

"You could warn me, you know," he grumbled to Del. Del made a face at him, making Owyn laugh. "Deep water for deep thoughts, huh? What helps deep fear?" He turned toward the door and stepped outside, nearly bumping into Aleia.

"Good question," she said. "I was wondering if you saw it."

"That he's scared?" Owyn snorted. "I'd be as blind as Alanar if I didn't. Will he really stay behind?"

Aleia started walking, and Owyn hurried to catch up with her. "I hope he doesn't. He's come a long way back from the shattered man who came back to us after the storm. But he's not ready to take that last step." She paused. "I want you to see something."

"All right," Owyn said. "Where are we going?"

She didn't answer. She led him past shelters to the edge of the canoes and the wide expanse of sea. There were others there, looking out over the water. In the distance, Owyn could see a dark cloud on the horizon.

"Is that a storm?" he asked, squinting to try and get a better look.

"No storm I've ever seen," Othi murmured, coming up behind Owyn. "And it's in the wrong place."

"What does that mean?" Owyn looked up.

"It's not over open water," Aleia answered. She stretched out her arm, holding her hand at an angle, then shook her head. "It's south of here. South and east. It's in the wrong place."

"South? And east. What's south and east of...oh." Owyn went cold. "And it's not over water. Oh...oh, fuck. Oh, fuck." He turned and looked at Aleia. "That's the Smoking Mountain, isn't it? It erupted?"

Aleia took a deep breath. "I think so. Yes."

"Meris said it would," Owyn stammered. "She said it would go, because everything was out of balance and getting worse. The droughts and the crop failures were only the beginning. She said..." His voice trailed off as he realized something. "Aria and Treesi are in Forge," he said softly.

Aleia turned and looked at him for a moment. Then she turned away and started shouting orders. Owyn stepped back to avoid being run over, and bumped into someone. He turned, expecting Othi.

It was Aven. There was water pouring from his hair, beading on his body. "What's got Ama stirred up?" he asked, his voice sounding not quite right. "Is it something to do with why the water tastes odd?"

Owyn pointed. "The Smoking Mountain blew. Just like Granna Meris said it would."

Aven looked. He frowned, then went stiff.

"Aria's in Forge," he whispered. "You said—"

"I think we're leaving now," Owyn interrupted. "I don't think we're waiting for the scouts."

Aven looked at him. He closed his eyes. Then he nodded.

"Yes," he murmured. "It's time to go back."

CHAPTER TWENTY-SEVEN

Aria stood at the very rear of the ship, watching the sunrise illuminate the plume of smoke and fire that didn't seem to grow any smaller, no matter how far they traveled. They'd sailed far out to sea, the better to avoid rocks and ash and embers. Then they'd sailed north, traveling slowly through the night. Now, with the sun rising, the land was a distant smudge on the horizon, a line abruptly punctuated by a tower of destruction far to the south.

"You should go inside. The ash isn't good for you to breathe."

"Inside Treesi and my grandmother are both being ill, and Grandmother sent me out." She looked up at Jehan. "I couldn't sleep anymore anyway. We're far enough that the ash isn't an issue. Or is it?"

He sighed. "Not yet," he admitted. "But it will be. Wind and water will carry it. Eventually, it'll be good for the land. The ash will help revitalize it. But until it settles, it'll block the skies."

"And without sun, there will be no crops," Aria murmured. "Will it kill the fish?" She frowned. "Will it hurt the Waterborn?"

Jehan shook his head. "Not at this range. There aren't any canoes that I know of that range this far south. They're all north of here, and further west. Deeper. They'll be able to tell it's happened, taste it in the waters, but it shouldn't hurt them. It might kill fish, this close in. But out in the deep? No."

Aria nodded. She looked back to the south. "Do you think they survived? Memfis and Mannon?"

"You're worried about Mannon?" Jehan asked.

"I'm not sure what I am," Aria admitted. She hugged herself. "I did not sleep much last night, thinking about this. About him. He crawled to me. He begged my forgiveness. And he is giving the throne to me. He is nothing like the man we met last year on his ship. And he confuses me. He was Yana's Air. How could he have been Yana's Air after doing what he did?"

Jehan sighed and shook his head. "I don't know. I had no idea that Yana existed until just recently. I definitely didn't know that she'd had the horrific taste to choose my brother—"

"You're really not sure?" Aria interrupted.

"It never mattered enough to me to find out," Jehan answered. "Mother raised me outside of court. I knew Elcam might have been my father, but I never knew him as more than a name and a possibility. I didn't know for certain until Milon chose me and I came to the Palace. That was when I met Mannon the first time. I had no idea I even had an older brother until he introduced himself to me as such, and showed me that Elcam claimed me. When I asked her why she never confirmed it, she told me that she didn't want him taking me from her. He'd have brought me to live in the Palace if she'd acknowledged me as his. She didn't want to give me up."

"Showed you?" Aria asked. "How?"

"The *Book of Silver*," Jehan answered. "There's a duplicate copy in the Palace. It's the duty of the Council in Forge to keep it updated quarterly." He frowned. "Although I don't know when that was last done. Not with the way things are now. And I don't know if the actual book made it out of Forge. The most recent records may be lost."

"Ask my grandmother," Aria suggested. "She should know. She may have it in her baggage." She frowned and looked back. "Which means it may be lost after all. The baggage didn't make it to the ship, did it?"

Jehan shook his head. "No. It went with Karse. Mother, I hope they made it. I liked him."

"He knew you, he told us," Aria said. "He knew Memfis, even when Memfis was using a false name. And he said he knew you. He was a child in the Palace, and you healed his arm when he fell out of a tree."

"Fell out of a..." Jehan repeated. Then he laughed. "No wonder he looked so familiar. He looks like his father. Makarsh was assistant to the major-domo. His father was a good man."

Aria nodded and looked back out over the water. "He is a good man. Karse and Trey are both good men." She frowned. "Mannon has it in him to be a good man, I think. Perhaps. I don't know. He confuses me."

"I think he's confused, period," Jehan said. He sighed and turned around, squinting slightly. "We'll be heading back to shore as soon as the sun is fully above the horizon. I'll need to go navigate." He paused, then added, "I wonder if they felt the eruption in Terraces?"

"Do you think they would have?"

He nodded. "They might have. Might have heard it, too. How are your ears, by the way?"

"Still ringing," Aria admitted. "I have never heard anything that loud before. Would they really hear it in Terraces? I had not thought the sound could travel that far."

Jehan chuckled. "Sound travels farther than you think. And underwater, it travels even more. I'm not sure why that is, but the Waterborn can hear for miles underwater." He slipped his arm around Aria's shoulders, carefully avoiding her wings. He frowned slightly. "Your back hurts? You didn't tell me you were in pain."

She laughed. "I flew when I should not have. My back is displeased at me. It will pass, and you were busy with navigation and with taking care of Treesi and Grandmother."

"Being seasick is wretched," Jehan said. "Especially your first time. You still should have told me."

"It's nothing. But I will not be flying again for some time. Not until after the baby comes." She leaned into his side. "Jehan, what do I do now?"

He hugged her. "You be the Heir. And let the rest of us help you. Trust your Companions."

"That's the one I need to work on most, I think," she said. "I did not, and now I may not have them."

"They'll come back."

"And Owyn?" she asked, looking up. "What about my Owyn?"

"Mannon's men will find Owyn." Jehan sounded certain. Aria looked away, wishing that she could be that certain.

"I've made a mess of everything," she said softly.

"Then you know what you have to do," Jehan replied.

She nodded. "Clean it up."

He hugged her again. "You'll do just fine. Let me see to your grandmother and to Treesi before I have to take us in."

THEY DOCKED IN THE late afternoon on a stone pier that ended in a wide-mouthed cave. Aria looked around curiously. "Where are we?"

"Underneath Terraces," Jehan answered. He held a hand out to Meris, who still looked uncomfortable. "It's an easy step, Lady Meris."

"I am never going on a ship again," Meris declared. "Ever."

"Me, either," Treesi grumbled. She swayed next to Aria. "I don't think I'm ever going to be able to eat anything again."

Aria put her arm around Treesi. "You will be fine once you're on land."

"And I'm never going off land again. Never," Treesi said vehemently. Aria smiled and helped her to the rail, letting Jehan steady her as she stepped down onto the dock. Treesi looked down at her feet, then back at Aria. "It's still moving. The ground is still moving! That's not right! It shouldn't do that!"

"It'll stop," Jehan assured her. "Your balance will adjust. I..." He stopped and turned, looking toward the cave. A moment later, Garrity appeared at a run.

"You made it!" he gasped. "We saw the sail, and I came down as soon as I could."

"Report," Jehan snapped. "What's happening?"

"We had tremors, and then something exploded. We've had some tunnels fall in, but no one was hurt. We started having people coming in through the upper tunnels late yesterday, and Pirit and Rhexa are handling them, getting them settled. I think everyone is coming here. And...Senior Healer—" He stopped and looked past Jehan at Treesi. "Something is wrong with Alanar. Rhexa thinks he's lost his mind."

"What?" Jehan gasped. "What happened?"

Garrity dragged his fingers through his hair. "It was after the first tremor. We were all outside, the way we're taught. And just after the explosion, he started swearing that Owyn was dead. That the Fire gem was gone, and Owyn was dead. Rhexa tried to talk him out of it, but he won't listen. And..." He paused. "Pirit has him sedated in the healing center. He was starting to talk about throwing himself off the lowest level."

"No!" Aria gasped. "No. Jehan, why would he think that?"

Jehan turned to look at her, and his pale face made her suddenly frightened. "You have the gems with you," he said, his voice hoarse. "How many?"

"I have Aven's Water gem and Del's Air," Aria answered. She touched the pouch on her belt. "Here."

Jehan closed his eyes. "Open the pouch."

Mystified, Aria opened the pouch and slipped her hand inside. And touched three carved stones. She pulled them out, staring at Owyn's Fire gem.

"How..." she gasped. She looked at Jehan. "Jehan, I didn't take this with me."

Jehan nodded. "I know," he murmured. "It's...we're taught that when a Companion dies, their gem returns to the Heir. Or the Firstborn."

"No!" Treesi moaned. "No, you said that we'd find him! That we'd save him! No!"

Aria looked down at the stone in her hand, feeling the world shaking around her. "No," she whispered. "He isn't dead. I'd know if he was dead." She looked at Jehan. "Wouldn't I?"

"The gem knows," Jehan said. "The Mother knows. She sent the gem back to you."

"So that I can replace him?" Aria spat. "No. I refuse. I will not have another Fire. Owyn was my Fire, and he is still my Fire. I will not have another."

"Be careful what you say, Aria," Jehan warned. "The last time you said something like that—"

"I know what I said!" Aria snapped back. "And I know what I am saying now. My Owyn is not dead. I will not believe it. Not until I see his body for myself." She closed her hand around the gem, feeling it digging into her palm. Then he put it back into her pouch and stepped onto the dock. She took Meris' hand, noticing that her grandmother was crying. Of course. She was Owyn's grandmother, too.

"He is not dead," Aria repeated. "And we have work to do."

— ⟨⟨⟩⟩ —

WALKING OUT INTO THE light revealed more people than Treesi ever remembered seeing in Terraces. For a moment, she forgot her discomfort.

"So many people!" she breathed. "Will we have room for all of them?"

"We'll make room," Jehan answered. "Treesi, I hate to ask this of you, but I'm going to need you—"

"That's not even a question," Treesi interrupted, waving one hand. The movement made her sway gently, and she squeaked. "Can you even me out, though? If I'm walking like I'm drunk, no one will trust me!"

Jehan came over to her, taking her hand. His power flowed up her arm, warm as creeping sunlight, and she closed her eyes and let it wash over her. When he let her go, the ground had stopped moving under her feet.

"Thank you," she said. "Where do you want me to start?"

"With Alanar."

Treesi looked up at him. "What do I need to know?" she asked. "Why does he think that Owyn is dead?"

Jehan took a deep breath, then let it out in a blast. "Because I told him about what Companions are taught happens if one of us dies," he admitted. "It's never happened. Not in all our history. There's never been a Companion die before their Firstborn. But we're taught that if it does happen, our gem goes back to our Heir, or our Firstborn, so they can find someone to replace us." He grimaced. "And I told him that it was fine if he wore the gem while we waited for Owyn to come home. It seemed to help settle him."

"So he was wearing the gem when it disappeared," Aria said. "And when it came back to me. He knew the moment it happened." She covered her face with her hands. "I should have been here. I should never have left."

"There's a great deal of '*should have, could have, would have*' that you can punish yourself for, my dear," Meris said. "But it won't help at all. You have to work with what you have. And right now, you have people who need to see you. They need to know that they have an Heir. You're their hope."

Aria nodded. "I will take you to our house, then go and find Rhexa and Pirit, and see where I can be most useful, then." She turned to Treesi. "I'll come and see Alanar later."

"I'll tell him," Treesi said. She turned back to Jehan. "Shall we?"

She started walking toward the healing complex, hearing Jehan behind her. He caught up with her before she'd gone a dozen steps.

"What are you going to do?" he asked, falling in beside her.

"Not sure yet," she admitted. "I need to see him. Talk to him. He wasn't this bad when Virrik disappeared. He never talked about killing himself before. It might be enough to hold him while he cries, and give him an orgasm or two. That worked before." She shook her head. "If it's as bad as Garrity says, that might not be enough."

"I should never have told him about the stones," Jehan muttered.

"What did Meris say? About the should haves?" Treesi asked. "Does that also cover should not haves?"

Jehan snorted. "If he decides to die, if we lose him, I'll be punishing myself for this particular should not have for the rest of my life," he said.

"Then I'd better not let him go," Treesi said, and walked into the healing complex. Malani was at the front desk, looking unusually somber.

"I missed you," the assistant said. "You've been gone too long."

Treesi nodded as she went to the fountain and started scrubbing her hands. "I know," she answered. "But my Heir needed me."

"Is she better?" Malani glanced toward the door. "She's not pulling her feathers out anymore, is she?"

"You knew about that?"

"I saw it, once," Malani whispered. "When she came to read to the children. I wasn't sure what I was seeing, until I asked Marik about why a bird would have bald spots. Since I didn't think you'd let her get mites, I figured it had to be that she was pulling her feathers out from stress." She frowned. "You didn't know?"

"Not until just before we left," Treesi answered. "She hid it from me."

"Because she knew you'd sit on her to make her stop." Malani brought Treesi a cloth to dry her hands. "Alanar isn't well."

"I heard from Garrity. Where is he?"

Malani grimaced. "Secure room six," she said, lacing her fingers together and twisting her hands. "But Pirit is starting to talk about transferring him to green."

"Transfer to green?" Treesi gasped. "Why?"

"Because he can't be controlled, and I can't keep him under sedation without hurting him." Treesi turned as Pirit came in behind her. The older healer looked tired. She shook her head and sighed. "I can keep him in healing trance, or I can use dreamflower. But I can't do either for very long, and if he's not sedated, he'll put everyone around him to sleep and try to get out of the complex."

"Alanar wouldn't—"

"He's done it twice," Pirit interrupted Treesi's protests. "Do you have any suggestions, Healer?"

Treesi bit down on what was left of her protests. "Twice?" she whispered. "And...why didn't you let him go? If he wants so badly to die, shouldn't we help him?"

"If he was rational, and wanted to die, and could explain his reasoning to me, then I would certainly help him," Pirit said. "But he is not rational, and I can't be certain he's making the choice to die in his right mind. Until I can be sure that he isn't insane, then I will protect him from himself."

Treesi nodded, her mind racing. It didn't sound like Alanar. But at the same time, she remembered how badly he'd reacted when they had thought Virrik had left without saying goodbye.

"Well?" Pirit asked. "Any suggestions?"

"Let me talk to him," Treesi said. "Let me see if I can reach him."

Pirit nodded. "Be careful with him," she said. "I'll walk with you, and wait for you. And I'll tell you about his injuries. He's lucky to be alive."

Treesi nodded. "Jehan told us they were attacked on the road, and that it was a near thing."

"He was shot, at close range, with a crossbow," Pirit said. "It punctured his lung. Compounded with the winter ague he contracted—" Pirit sighed. "If they'd been another hour, he'd have been too far gone to save."

"But he's fine now?" Treesi asked. "No residual damage to the lungs?"

"None. His body is completely healthy, if a little weak from the extensive healing. I'm more worried about his mind." Pirit stopped walking and turned to face Treesi. "This is a heavy load to put on you, Treesi. It won't be easy—"

"I know that," Treesi interrupted. "I've gone through this with him before. This time, though...this time we know that Owyn isn't coming back. We know that he didn't abandon Alanar. That might help."

Pirit looked skeptical, but didn't say anything. Instead, she took a key from her pocket and handed it to Treesi. "Secure room six," she said. "Be careful."

"I will be," Treesi said as she took the key. "Will you stay and listen?"

Pirit smiled. "Did you think I wouldn't?"

Treesi handed the key back to Pirit. "Then you hold this. Just in case."

CHAPTER TWENTY-EIGHT

Treesi let the door close behind her, hearing the lock snapping home. If she raised her voice, Pirit would come in. She knew that. But she also knew that if Alanar wanted to hurt her, he could do a lot before Pirit could stop him.

But she had to do something. She stepped further into the room. The narrow bed was empty. There was no other furniture. She turned. He was standing in the corner where he was hidden by the open door, his arms folded over his chest.

"Allie?" she said. "Allie, what are you doing?"

"Listening," Alanar answered. "Waiting. When did you get back?"

"Just now," Treesi said. "I came straight here. Allie—"

"You know he's dead."

She flinched at the pain in his voice. "Yes. Aria has his gem. She doesn't think he's dead. She says she's not going to believe it until she sees his body. But Jehan explained it. Allie—"

"It's her fault," Alanar said. "She drove him out."

Treesi frowned. "I..." She paused. Then she sighed. "You're right. She drove them all out. All she has left is me." She swallowed. "Allie, I'm going to miss him, too."

"You have Aria," Alanar snapped, and moved away from the wall. He ran his fingers along the wall until he came to the corner, then turned toward her. "Owyn was all I had. All I had left. He died because of her. And because of me. Because I insisted we couldn't go by ship. We had to go by land. I wanted to keep him safe." Alanar ran his hand over his face, then through his messy, tangled hair. "I got him killed. It's her fault. But it's mine, too."

"Allie, it's not your fault!" Treesi protested. "You didn't know you were going to be attacked. And they told us they attacked from the water. There was nothing stopping them from doing the same thing if you sailed. And then we'd never have known what happened to him. Or to you."

Alanar frowned slightly. It looked like the idea hadn't even occurred to him. Then he shook his head. "So?"

"So?" Treesi repeated. "So you'd have left us wondering what happened to you both, the same way you and I wondered about Virrik."

Alanar shrugged. "Virrik is dead. Owyn is dead. It doesn't matter if I die, too. And he's waiting for me. They're both waiting for me."

"It matters to me." Treesi moved closer. "You know it matters to me."

Alanar looked puzzled. "Does it?" he asked, and pushed off the wall. "You never said goodbye."

It took Treesi a moment to realize what he was talking about. "We didn't tell anyone we were going," she answered. "We didn't say goodbye to anyone."

"I noticed," Alanar said, his voice dry. "And I also noticed that I matter so much to you that you left me behind without a word." He moved to the bed and sat down. "Are you here to try and talk me out of suicide?" he asked.

Treesi knelt in front of him, resting her hands on his knees. "Or help you, if you convince me that it's what you really want."

Alanar covered her hands with his. "Really? You won't just knock me out the way Pirit's been doing?"

"No," Treesi answered. "But I need to know that it's what you really want. So if you want to die, convince me."

He smiled slightly, running his nails over the backs of her hands. "Thank you," he murmured. "For not lying. Trees, I don't know what I want. Except him. I want him, and he's gone. And he should never have been there. I should have listened to him. I should have listened to him, and to Mannon, and gone by ship. But I was trying to protect him —" He frowned. "I might have killed him, Trees. No, no. I definitely killed him." He shook his head. "It wasn't Aria. Ignore I said that. Don't tell her that I blamed her. The truth is it was all me. It was all my fault."

"I don't understand why it was your fault, Allie," Treesi said. She started running her hands up and down his thighs, gently massaging. "Explain?"

"He didn't tell you about his waking vision? About how he was going to die?"

"Aria told me. When we found out that he'd been taken."

Alanar took her hands in his. "I didn't know if you knew. Owyn explained it to me when he told me why he didn't want to go north by ship. When he told me that, I knew I wasn't ever going to let him go onboard a ship. Then I got sick, and he was willing to get on a ship to help save my life." He let her hands go and clasped his own in front of him. "I fought him. I refused to go on a ship. I wouldn't listen to him or to Mannon. I insisted we had to go by land. I killed him, Treesi. It's my fault. I put him where they could take him. My choice to try and protect him is what killed him. And that's my reason. That's why I want to die." He lowered his head. "I cost myself everything."

"Are you so sure that they wouldn't have attacked by sea?" Treesi asked. "And killed the both of you?"

"They were going to kill the both of us anyway. Teva shot me, did they tell you?" Alanar said softly. "Esai saved my life, they told me.

You should meet Esai. She's nice. Blaming herself, they told me. She doesn't need to. Tell her that, will you?"

"They told me. And you can introduce me to her later," Treesi said. "Alanar, Aria isn't convinced Owyn is dead. She says she won't choose another Fire until she sees his body for herself."

Alanar snorted. "Aria is good at making definitive statements like that. Definitive, wrong statements—"

"We don't know—"

"Does she have his gem?" Alanar interrupted. "Did it return to her?"

Treesi bit her lip, then sighed. "Yes," she admitted. "She has it."

"He's dead," Alanar said, his voice flat. "And she's in denial. I'm not. He's dead, and it's my fault because I wouldn't listen to him." He stood up so abruptly that Treesi fell over backward. Alanar stepped away from the bed, stopped, then turned back. "I knocked you over. I'm sorry." He held his hand out. Treesi took it, and let him pull her up to her feet. He ran his hands up her arms. "So why are you really here, Treesi?" he asked. "In this room. Now."

"Because I'm worried about you," Treesi answered. "Because I want to be sure this is what you really want. I want to help you."

"Help me? Or help Pirit keep me alive?" Alanar's fingers dug into Treesi's arms. "I want to die, Trees. But she won't let me." He frowned. "And even if you do help me, she's right outside. I can feel her there. She'll stop you. Stop me. She'll bring me back. She's not going to let me die because I'm valuable. She kept telling me that the Earth tribe needs me. That she won't let me die because they need me."

Treesi blinked, stunned. "She...she wouldn't do that!"

"I tried already, Trees. Twice—"

"They told me," Treesi said. "That you'd put people to sleep so you could get out. Why?"

He smiled, sweet and sad all at once. "I'm going to fly one last time, Treesi. I've realized that I've forgotten what it feels like. I'm going to fly again before I die."

"Allie!" Treesi breathed. Then she winced, as his fingers tightened on her arms. "Allie, that hurts."

"You said you were going to help me," Alanar said. "Then help me leave here. Now."

Treesi looked up at him. "Allie, if I say no, what will you do?"

Alanar frowned. "You said you were going to help me."

"Answer the question," Treesi insisted. "If I say no? If I ask you to stay? If I ask you to let me take you to bed?"

Alanar snorted. "That's not going to help me this time, Treesi. Although I appreciate the offer. Why am I staying? Not for the Earth tribe. Not for Pirit. Why? What is there for me?"

"You're part of Aria's family—"

"And she turned her back on me when she turned her back on Owyn. Try again."

"And I love you."

Alanar paused. He frowned. Then he shook his head. "But you're not mine. Not anymore. I don't know that you ever were. I wasn't yours."

"We were important to each other, for a long time," Treesi said. "Doesn't that count for anything?"

Alanar let his head fall forward, and his breathing shook. "I...it's not enough, Trees. Especially...Virrik is dead. Owyn is dead. And I told you. They're waiting for me. I can hear them."

Treesi blinked. "Hear them?"

"Calling me. They want me to join them," Alanar answered. "Owyn's annoyed at me. I think because I'm making him wait. He's mine, and he's waiting."

"Allie, that makes no sense," Treesi said. "And you still didn't answer me. What will you do if I say no?"

Alanar closed his eyes. Then he dropped his hands. "Get out, Treesi."

"What?"

"You're not going to help me. So get out." Alanar went back to the bed, stretching out on his side with his back to Treesi. "I'm coming, love. I'll be there. I'll find a way."

Treesi stepped toward the bed. "Allie, who are you talking to?"

"Owyn," Alanar answered. "I told you. He's waiting for me."

Treesi took another step. "And...you're hearing him? He's talking to you?"

Alanar snorted. "I'm not hearing him with you chattering away at me," he snapped. "Go away if you're not going to help."

Treesi moved next to the bed, and put her hand on Alanar's shoulder. "Allie—"

She didn't expect him to move, to roll on to his back and lash out with his fist. It caught her in the shoulder, driving her backwards as she yelped, more from shock than pain.

"Allie!"

"I told you to go away!" he shouted, getting up from the bed and looming over her. "You left me already. Why won't you leave us alone now?"

"He's not here!" Treesi gasped. "Allie, he's dead!"

"I know he's dead!" Alanar yelled back. "I knew before any of you! He's dead, and he's waiting for me to come meet him! And if you won't help me to go, then I'm going to find a way to get there myself!" He paused. "You have the keys."

"I don't," Treesi said. "They're outside."

"Then you're locked in here with me," Alanar said, and smiled. It wasn't anything like his usual smile. This one was small, quiet. Terrifying. "And if they want you back in one piece, then they'll have to let me out." He reached for her, and she yelped and darted backward, away from his outstretched hand.

"Pirit!" she shouted. "Help!"

Alanar just laughed. "Can they get to you before I do?" he asked, and lunged again. Treesi jumped back, and slammed into someone. She screamed, twisting to see that it was Jehan.

"Enough," he thundered. He put his arm around Treesi's shoulders. "Alanar, I'm sorry."

"Then just let me die," Alanar said. "All will be forgiven."

Jehan sniffed. "No. I'm sorry I have to do this." In one smooth motion, he brought up a short blowpipe. He aimed, and blew, and a dart blossomed in Alanar's chest.

Alanar gasped, reaching for it and plucking it out. "What is this?" he asked, frowning. He raised the dart and sniffed it, and one brow rose. "There's nothing on here?"

"There's a reason I'm the Senior Healer, Alanar," Jehan said. "And part of it is that I know a lot more than you."

"There's nothing on here!" Alanar insisted. Then he blinked and shook his head. "I— what is this?"

"It's concentrated oil of brown seaweed," Jehan said. "It's almost as powerful as dreamflower, and much safer. And you've never heard of it. No one outside of the Water tribe has." He sighed. "Go to sleep, Alanar."

Alanar took a step forward, then slowly crumpled to the ground. Treesi stared at him for a moment, starting to shake.

"He was going to hurt me," she whispered. "Jehan—"

Jehan pulled her into his arms and held her tightly. "I wasn't going to let him, sweetheart," he murmured into her hair. "I wasn't going to let him hurt you."

"He's gone insane."

Jehan sighed. "Completely." He let her go, turning toward the door. "Come and get him. Treat him gently, and take him to the green level. We'll work out a watch schedule."

Four men walked in. Treesi couldn't tell who they were — they wore heavy coats with long sleeves, thick gloves, and hoods that covered their heads and necks. She couldn't see any visible skin. They carried a litter, and gently bundled Alanar onto it, cinching heavy straps around his body before carrying him out.

"Will I be on that watch schedule?" Treesi asked softly.

"I'm not asking that of you," Jehan answered. "Not after this. I'll see to him personally." He rubbed one hand over his face and sighed. "Go home, Treesi."

Treesi looked up at him. "There's nothing I can do to help?"

"I want you recovered from this before I put you to work," Jehan answered. "Go home. Tomorrow is soon enough."

JEHAN WALKED TREESI to the door of the healing complex and waited until she was gone. Then he turned and sprinted back down the hall. He turned the corner, and nearly barreled into Pirit.

"I dealt with it," she said softly. "Brown seaweed? Really?"

Jehan snorted. "I had to tell her something. And brown seaweed does have sedative properties."

"Whatever this was wasn't a sedative," Pirit answered. "It was a toxin. I had to work fast to flush it from his system, even with your warning. So what was it?"

Jehan swallowed, then met his mother's eyes. "Spine fish venom."

"Jhansri!"

"It's diluted!" Jehan protested. "It's less than a tenth the potency that the Water tribe uses when they hunt wolf-singers."

Pirit shifted to stand in front of him, her fists on her hips. "You could have killed him!"

"That's why I warned you!" Jehan snapped back. "And it wasn't like I had a choice! You saw him. He'd have killed Treesi to get what he wanted. He's gone, Mother. And I don't know if we can get him back."

Pirit closed her eyes and shook her head. "It's done. For better or worse, it's done. We'll monitor him. Make sure there's no residual damage. How do we proceed?"

"Restraints," Jehan answered. "Constant monitoring. Protective gear on the monitors, so even if he gets out of the restraints, he can't touch skin." He frowned. "Boots."

"Boots?"

"Alanar can't use his air sense if he's not barefoot," Jehan said. "I don't want him able to navigate freely. If he does manage to get past his monitors, I want him at a disadvantage."

Pirit nodded. "I'll see to it, and assign monitors." She sighed. "What a blasted waste."

Jehan stared at her for a moment. "He's more than his healing ability, Mother. He's more than just my protege—"

"He's your surrogate son," Pirit finished. "I've noticed. And I approve. I had his initial training, Jehan. I'm fond of him." She shrugged slightly. "As fond as I am of anyone, really. You know it doesn't come easily to me."

"I'd never noticed," Jehan muttered dryly. "Yes, he's like a son to me. And I never should have told him he could wear the blasted Fire gem. Or what it meant if it disappeared."

"But you did," Pirit said. "You can't change that. We had no idea he was so fragile. That losing a second lover in the space of a year would shatter him."

Jehan took a deep breath. "All I can do now is take care of him. Until he's rational again. Then...we'll see what he wants."

Pirit rested her hand on his arm. "It isn't your fault, Jehan," she said gently.

"Keep telling me that. Maybe someday I'll believe it."

CHAPTER TWENTY-NINE

It took a day before they left, as the Floating City dissolved into separate canoes. They sailed away in small groups, until there were only two left — Aven's canoe and the large canoe that had been at the center of the Floating City. That one was Aleia's center of operations, and would be the last to sail. Owyn found it deeply fascinating to watch as the separate families took their leave, some to head back out to the deep, others to sail to shore with Aleia.

"How did they decide who went which way?" he asked, sitting next to Del in the shade of the shelter he now shared with Del and Aven. Del gestured, and Owyn watched his hands intently, trying to remember the lessons he'd taken with Del and Neera the night before. "Wait. Do that last one again?"

Del repeated the gesture, and Owyn nodded. "So...kids and old folks went out deep? And the sick? And some warriors to take care of them? Did I get it?"

Del laughed and nodded, and Owyn grinned. He heard a splash from behind him, and the canoe rocked harder than usual. The first time this had happened, he'd panicked, thinking that something had happened, and that they were going to sink. But it had just been Melody, jumping up onto the canoe. She came around the shelter and bumped her head against Del's arm, then twined her body around Owyn and settled her heavy head in his lap.

"I'm going to be jealous one of these times, you know," Aven said, coming over to slowly lower himself to the ground next to Owyn. He reached over and scratched Melody's head, and she crooned in pleasure. "You're her new favorite."

"That's because she knows that I think she's the prettiest thing in the water," Owyn said. He ran his hand over Melody's long body. "Don't you, Melody?" Melody trilled gently, and he laughed. "I keep wondering what she'd think of Trinket. What Trinket would think of her."

Del made a small, sharp gesture, and Aven chuckled in response.

"I don't think Melody would know what to do with Trinket," Aven said. "I don't think she'd recognize a fire-mouse as a snack. But we'll keep them apart, just in case." He stretched his legs out in front of him. "We're setting out."

"What about the scouts?" Owyn asked. "I thought we were waiting—"

"They came in," Aven interrupted. "Ama is with them now. And from the tone, she's not happy."

"Not...oh, you're not telling me that Risha got away?" Owyn demanded.

"I'm not telling you anything," Aven answered. "I didn't hear. I just heard the tone, and she's not happy." He leaned back on his elbows, tipping his head back. "It's going to be strange, going back. I didn't think that I would."

"We're needed," Owyn said. "She needs us. Well, she needs you."

Aven turned to look at him. "She needs us."

"I'm not sure I'm still her Fire," Owyn said. "I was dead. Doesn't that end it?"

"We don't know. It's never happened before."

Owyn twisted to see Aleia coming onto the canoe. Aven sat up and turned to face his mother.

"And?" he asked.

"And the ship had sailed inland, far enough that it was in Mannon's travel lanes. It was foundering when it was challenged by another of Mannon's ships. Apparently, they were out hunting for it. For her. The scouts decided to leave the ship to Mannon's men, and came back. They didn't bother to confirm what happened to Risha before they left."

"So they don't know what happened?" Owyn asked. Aleia shook her head, and he breathed, "Fuck. They could have been his men. Or they could have been more of hers."

"I've let them know that I'm unhappy with them," Aleia added. "But we're leaving, and I'm not having them go off and find out which it was. It doesn't matter. We control the waters. And when we're close enough to shore, there isn't a ship in Mannon's navy that will sail without our say so."

"But for now, she's off who knows where, doing who knows what." Owyn scowled. "She's supposed to be shark shit."

Aleia burst out laughing. "How did you know that?"

"Your man told me," Owyn answered. "After Ketti told me that she wanted what was left of Risha, for what they did to Virrik."

Aleia smiled. "Ketti told me about that. And about what you did for Virrik."

Owyn snorted. "All I did was not puke. It was Aven that did all the work." He reached out and poked Aven in the shoulder.

Aven laughed and poked him back. "When are you getting your marks, Mouse?" he asked. "Neera said you're part of the tribe. They're yours, if you want them. And Othi can do it. He did mine."

"Do we have time?" Owyn asked. "I thought I might wait, since we won't have time." He looked around at the water. "How long will it take us to get to land? And which way is land?"

Aven pointed. "That way. See where the sea touches the sky? That's where we're going."

"And we're about six days out. Maybe seven," Aleia added. She tipped her head back, closing her eyes. "With this wind? Six."

"And then what?" Owyn asked. "They'll see us coming, I think. They can't help but see us coming, if they're watching from Terraces."

Aleia came over and ran her fingers through his hair. Owyn sighed and leaned into her hand.

"We'll find out what happens when we get there," she said. "And we'll deal with it. But you don't need to worry, Owyn. No matter what, you have a place with us."

Owyn smiled. "Thank you."

"Owyn?" She didn't say anything else. Not until he tipped his head back and looked up at her. "You know I can hear you thinking it? You can say it, if you want to."

Owyn looked at her for a moment, puzzled. Then he coughed. "But—"

"It would be my honor, Owyn."

He bit his lip and looked at Aven. Aven smiled, reaching out to squeeze Owyn's knee.

"If you want my permission, then yes. I'll share."

Owyn hesitated, then looked back up at Aleia. "Thank you, Mama."

AFTER TWO DAYS, THE line where the sky met the sea started showing a soft smudge that looked to Owyn like a faint charcoal line that had been smeared to show shadow. It wasn't nearly as dark as the still-growing cloud of smoke and ash far off to his right, but it was still there.

Land.

On the third day, the smudge became more distinct. It was still too far to see detail, but it was more than a shadow.

On day five, he could see details. He could see what had to be the cliffs where Terraces stood, rising over the sea. And off to the left, he could see a shining something that he suspected was the Palace.

On the morning of day six, he saw the ship. Distant, but definitely there.

"Aven!" he called. "That's a sail, isn't it?"

Aven looked where Owyn was pointing and nodded. "Yes," he said, and took in the lines, steering the canoe toward Aleia's larger one. Owyn glanced over, saw Othi wave and point. He turned, apparently listening to something. Then he dove into the water.

"They've seen it," he called to Aven. "I think Othi is coming over."

"Good," Aven called back. "Let's see what Ama wants to do."

A moment later, Othi surfaced and pulled himself out of the water onto the deck of the canoe. He grinned at Owyn, then leaned back and closed his eyes. Owyn looked back at the distant sail.

"It's coming toward us, isn't it?" he asked. He looked over at Del, and was unsurprised to see that the other man had gone to fetch his barbed spear, and had also brought out the short club that Aleia had given to Owyn. He handed it to Owyn. "I see. That's a yes."

Del nodded and went to stand near Aven.

"Del, toss the lines to Neera when we're close enough," Aven said. "You know how. Othi, you finished yet?"

"Almost," Othi croaked at them. "Nearly there."

Del passed his spear to Owyn and went to get the lines out of the storage compartment in the deck. He fastened one end down, then tossed the other across the gap between the canoes. Neera caught them and drew them in slowly as Aven steered his canoe alongside the larger one. She tied them off, then waved.

On Aven's canoe, Othi slowly got to his feet and chuckled. "I should have waited where I was," he said. "You're quick."

"What does Ama say?" Aven asked. "That's one of Mannon's ships. It has to be. No one else would have something like that on the water."

"She agrees that it's one of his, and that it's heading for us. It's small. Fast, too," Othi said. "Moves like a cross between a canoe and one of those floating behemoths. Aunt Aleia says we're going to wait on them. See what they want. And I'm to go below with a boring tool, just in case." He grinned. "Either they deal, or they sink."

Aven nodded. "Sounds good. Where does she want us to wait?"

"With her. Come over."

Owyn followed Aven and Del over onto the larger canoe, and moved into the shadow of the shelter to watch and wait. The approaching ship was just as fast as Othi said. Over the next hour, it grew larger and larger, until Owyn could see a banner that snapped in the wind from the top of the mast.

"What's that flag?" he called.

Aleia shaded her eyes with her hand. She looked for a long moment, then lowered her arm. "Well."

"What?" Aven asked. "What is it?"

"Things have changed on land," Aleia answered. "That's the Heir's banner. That ship sails in Aria's name."

Aven straightened, looking out over the water. "Do you think she's aboard?"

"I think we'll find out soon enough," Aleia answered. "Othi, I think you can stay above."

Time seemed to crawl as the ship grew bigger. Grew closer. Owyn could see people now, moving back and forth on the deck. One of them in particular looked familiar.

None of them had wings.

"She's not on board," he said at last. "But...Aven, is that Marik?"

"I think it might be," Aven said. "Ama, you might be meeting your nephew today."

"A family reunion is a lovely thing," Aleia replied, sounding amused. "But we'll wait."

They didn't have to wait long before a familiar voice rang out over the waves. "Hail, the canoes!"

Aven broke into a wide grin. He glanced at Aleia, who nodded. Then he called back, "Hail, the ship!"

Laughter rolled back toward them. "Aven! I was hoping! Permission to come closer?"

"Granted!" Aleia shouted. "And to come across."

The ship maneuvered closer, drawing alongside the canoes. Marik appeared at the rail. He frowned slightly, then jumped, landing hard on the deck of the canoe.

"Marik!" Aven gasped. "What are you doing? You almost missed!"

"Still learning to judge distances," Marik said with a laugh. He got up, then sobered. "You didn't know about this," he added, waving his hand at his face. "Sorry to surprise you." He held his hand out, and laughed again when Aven hugged him. "It's good to see you! Even if I'm only half-seeing you." He looked Aven up and down. "You're more decorated than when I saw you last. It suits you."

"Thank you. It's good to see you, too. The eye was that bad?" Aven asked.

"Yeah. And your fa, he's good, but he couldn't do anything to save it. One of these days, Teva will get what's coming to him."

"He already did," Owyn said, coming toward them. Marik turned toward him, and his face went as white as milk.

"Owyn?" he whispered. "But...no, that's impossible! You're dead!"

"How did you know?" Aven asked.

"What?" Marik stared at Aven. "I...what?"

"Owyn was dead. For at least a minute." Aven looked over at Owyn. "But how did you know?"

"Long story," Marik said. He moved away from Aven, took a step closer to Owyn. "You're really alive?"

Owyn nodded. "Really alive, yeah," He smiled. "And Teva is really, really dead."

"He is?" Marik looked stunned. "I...thank you. And...and you're not dead. You need to come back. You need to come back now. Today."

"Why?" Aven asked. "Marik, what's wrong?"

Marik closed his eye and swallowed. "You know the Smoking Mountain erupted, right?"

"We can see it," Aleia said. "Marik, sit before you fall down."

"No, let me stand on my feet and say this," Marik said. "Thank you. Jehan had gone to Forge to fetch back Aria and Treesi—"

"They're safe?" Aven interrupted.

"They're fine," Marik answered. "We don't know about Mannon or Memfis, though. Aria says that Mannon gave up his seat in the dinghy to make sure Jehan got out. He and Mannon went to try and catch others. Men named Karse and Trey. But those two arrived yesterday and said they'd never seen them." He frowned. "I'm getting twisted. Ah...before he left Jehan told Alanar—"

"*What*?" Owyn yelped. "Alanar is *alive*?"

Marik nodded. "They barely got him back to Terraces, but yes. But...damn it, Jehan let him wear your Fire gem. And when you died, it vanished. Showed up in Aria's pouch with the other gems. And...fuck, there's no easy way to say it. Alanar's gone insane." He looked down, shifting uneasily from foot to foot. "They've had to lock him up in green to keep him from hurting himself or anyone else."

Owyn stared at Marik. "But he's alive. Really. He's alive." He closed his eyes and swallowed. "I...oh, fuck. He's going to be so angry. I lost the pledge bracelet. He gave it to me, and I lost it and—" A hand closed on his shoulder, and he turned to see Del, a worried expression on his face. Owyn tried to smile. "It was special," he stammered. "Allie picked it out for me, and he's blind, so it wasn't an easy thing. And I lost it, and he's going to be mad because it was special and I—" Del stepped closer and wrapped his arms around Owyn, who took a shuddering breath. "He's *alive*," he whispered. "Mother, he's alive!"

"And he's crackpot insane," Marik said. "Owyn—"

"That don't worry me," Owyn said. He patted Del's arm, then straightened. "D'ye know how many street boys were crackpot insane? Fuck, for a long time, they all thought I was crackpot insane. I can deal with crackpot."

"He's tried to kill himself," Marik insisted. "He's tried to hurt his monitors. He tried to hurt Treesi!"

"Oh, now that I won't stand for," Owyn breathed. "No, no. No hurting himself. No hurting anyone else. Especially not Treesi." He frowned. "What's he done?"

"I don't know all the details," Marik admitted. "Except that Jehan is looking after him personally."

"That's good," Owyn said. "I mean, isn't it? He'll get better. Jehan will make him better."

"That's not good," Aven said gently. "If the Senior Healer is taking care of him personally? It's not good." He frowned. "Marik, what else is happening on land?"

Marik shrugged. "Lots of people coming in from the south. We're seeing a lot of people who got out of Forge ahead of the eruption. The houses are starting to fill up." He grinned. "I finished that report, Wyn. Just in time, too."

Owyn nodded. "Knew you would. What else?"

"Aria...she's settled down. Woke up. She's thinking again, and she's being...well, impressive. And did you know she's pregnant?"

"I found out right before I left," Owyn answered. "And Aven found out he's gonna be a father...what, six days ago?"

"Still hasn't sunk in," Aven muttered. "She's really doing better?"

"She's stepped up to be the Heir people need. She's doing a lot. Taking control. Making sure folks have what they need. And...she's got a weird theory." Marik rubbed his hands together. "Risha, she tried to kill you, Aven. And we had that big storm. Right?"

"I remember," Aven growled.

"And Owyn, he died. And—" He gestured toward the south.

"And the Smoking Mountain erupted," Owyn finished. "Fuck. You think it's related?"

"She thinks it might be. Lady Meris says things are dangerously out of balance. That's the root of the theory."

Aven looked over at Aleia. "Ama?"

"It's an interesting idea," Aleia said slowly. "And one that I'd have liked to discuss with the priest in the Mother's Womb, if there was one."

"When there is one, we can ask them," Owyn said. "For now...how long will it take us to get to shore? And from Serenity to Terraces?"

"You don't need to go to Serenity," Marik said. "That's why we came out to meet you, Destria and I. There's anchorage underneath Terraces. We'll guide you in."

THEY DREW UP TO THE stone dock as the sun was setting, and Aven started tying down the sail. He did it slowly. Carefully. Trying to calm the water-cats swimming attack patterns in his belly.

Too slowly and carefully, it seemed.

"You're as scared as I am, aren't you?" Owyn asked.

Aven smiled slightly. "Am I obvious?"

"To me, yeah," Owyn answered. "To Del, probably. To your ma? You're most likely clear as glass."

Aven laughed. "Well, not so much scared as nervous. I don't know how she'll react. What she'll say. What I'll say to her."

Del tapped Aven on the arm and pointed. Aven looked and saw the people standing at the end of the dock. His father. And her.

"Time to find out," Owyn said softly.

Aven almost didn't hear him. It felt like the world stopped. He couldn't breathe. He couldn't move.

"Go on, Fishie," Owyn urged.

Aven nodded. He fumbled for his walking stick, almost dropping it before Del grabbed it and put it into his hand. Slowly, he stepped onto the dock, standing still for a moment. Then he drew himself up and started forward.

Aria didn't give him a chance to take more than a step. She ran to him and threw herself into his arms, hard enough to knock him back and make him drop his stick. He gathered himself and wrapped his arms around her, and said the only thing he could think of.

"I'm sorry."

Their voices harmonized as they said the words in unison. He pulled back slightly, looked in her eyes, and they both burst out laughing. Aven felt as if a weight was lifted from his shoulders. He started to say something...

Then she kissed him, grabbing his hair in her fingers and holding tight. The world stopped again; he tightened his arms around her, lifting her off the ground as he kissed her back with the intensity born from months of missing her. Her body against his, the swell of her belly pressing against him. He could feel the pounding of her heart, and the distant, faint fluttering of the baby's heartbeat.

She drew back to breathe, and he set her on her feet. "Mother of us all, I missed you," he whispered. "So much."

"You have your marks. You have all your marks." She looked up at him, and he could see the tears in her eyes. "But you're missing something. I have it for you," she said. "You left it."

"It was a mistake to leave it," he said. He tipped his head forward, resting his forehead against hers, his nose to hers, breathing in the breath from her lungs. "It was a mistake to leave you."

"No, I was horrible," she protested. "And I hurt you. And I'm sorry."

"I forgive you." He straightened, letting her go as she tugged back. She reached into her pouch and took out his gem. He let her fasten the cord around his neck, the gem nestled against the base of his throat, and he realized that, after months of a vague sense of missing something, he was finally complete.

"I have Del's gem," Aria said. She turned toward the canoe, and froze. "Owyn?" She looked at Aven, then back at the canoe. "Owyn? Is it...it can't be! You're dead!"

Owyn stepped off the canoe and walked over to Aria. He took her hand and put it against his chest. "You think that would stop me from coming back to you, my Heir?" he asked.

She whimpered, then pulled him close and hugged him. "How?" She stepped back and held Owyn at arm's length, then looked at Aven. "How?"

"He was dead," Aven said softly. "For almost a minute."

"You brought him back to life?" Aria gasped.

"He's stubborn, my son," Aleia said as she joined them. Neera and Othi trailed behind her. Aleia held her hands out to Aria, then hugged her tightly. "Look at you," she said fondly as she let Aria go. "Oh, my heart-daughter. Milon would be so proud."

"This is her?" Othi asked. "This is our Heir?"

"And you are?" Aria asked. Othi and Neera both bowed in unison.

"Aria, may I present my niece and nephew?" Aleia asked. "Neera is our Clan Mother. Othi is her brother and her Second."

Aria bowed her head slightly. "It's a pleasure to meet you, Neera. We'll be working together, I trust?"

"The canoes of the Waterborn are united in your name, my Heir," Neera replied. She smiled and quietly asked, "And I wonder if you could be convinced to lend me your Air? When you're not needing him?"

"Lend you Del?" Aria looked around to see Del still on the canoe, bundling something into one of the compartments. "Why?"

"Because Neera is sweet on him, and he won't build a canoe with her," Othi whispered. Neera jabbed him with her elbow, and Othi laughed.

"Calm down, you two," Aven called. He grinned and nodded to his mother. "We can discuss that later. Or not. Ama, there's someone waiting for you," Aleia nodded and walked the rest of the way up the dock. Aven put his arm around Aria, and watched his parents embrace.

"That's a good thing," Owyn murmured. "That's a real good thing."

Aria nodded. She looked at him and smiled. "I have something of yours."

"Is it?" Owyn asked. "Is it still mine?"

"Did you think it wouldn't be?" Aria asked as she took the Fire gem from her pouch. She put the cord around Owyn's neck, then straightened the stone into place.

"Well, I was dead. It sort of ends things," Owyn said. He grinned. "Now do Del!"

Aria turned toward the canoe. She held her hand out, and Del took it and stepped up onto the dock.

"I'm sorry, Del," Aria said. "I'm sorry I rejected you. I was wrong."

Del smiled, took her hand in his and turned it, kissing her palm. She laughed. Then she tugged her hand free and took the Air gem from her pouch. She fastened the cord around Del's neck, then looked from him to Owyn to Aven.

"We just need Treesi with us, and we'll be complete."

"Then let's go find her," Owyn said. "And...then I need to see Alanar."

Aria frowned. She looked up at Aven. "We have to go through the tunnels. Will you be all right?"

Aven snorted. "After everything else?" he asked. "I'll walk the tunnels blindfolded." He reached for her hand. "As long as you're with me."

CHAPTER THIRTY

Treesi was finishing with a patient when she heard the distant commotion. She looked up, then shook her head.

"Someone is certainly excited," she commented, tying off the ends of the sling. "Now, the bones are still healing, so keep your arm in the sling for another day. Tomorrow, you come back to me and I'll make sure the healing is complete." She smiled at the boy. "And no more climbing chokeberry trees. The fruit isn't even ripe yet."

The boy laughed. "Yes, Healer."

Treesi ruffled his hair and held her hand out. "Come with me. I'll take you to your mother."

They walked out of the examination room and down to the waiting area where Treesi surrendered the boy to his mother. Then she kept going toward the front desk, walking into the ongoing commotion. People laughing, people crying. People talking, all at the same time. She saw Rhexa, sobbing and embracing someone whose back was to Treesi.

She knew the pattern of scars on that back better than she knew the lines on her own hands.

"Owyn?" she gasped.

He pulled himself from Rhexa's embrace and turned. He smiled, and Treesi burst into tears and ran to him, throwing her arms around his neck and sobbing. He held her tightly, whispering into her hair.

"It's all right," he murmured. "I'm fine. I'm back. I'm fine."

"You were dead!" Treesi wailed. "How are you fine?"

She heard him laugh. "Because Aven is a stubborn man," he answered. "He brought me back. He saved me. And now I'm home."

Treesi hugged him harder. "I'm never letting you leave, ever again."

She felt him kiss the top of her head. "I'm never leaving, ever again," he said. "At least, not unless you and Allie are with me."

"Allie...Owyn—" Treesi looked up at him to see his unusually serious expression.

"I know," he said. "I'm going to see him. See if seeing me helps snap his wits back into place." He frowned. "We've got work to do, Trees. The lot of us. And I need Allie with me." He paused. "You and Allie. And everyone else."

"Everyone?" Treesi stepped back and looked around. Rhexa was still standing close. Jehan was nearby, with a strange woman on his arm. And behind them...

"Aven?" Treesi gasped. He smiled at her, and she laughed. "I almost didn't know you! Look at you!"

Aven came closer, and Treesi bit her lip when she saw how badly he was limping. He shook his head. "It's not important, Treesi."

"But your leg—"

"Fa says you can help him with fixing my leg, once we see to Alanar. I can wait." He held his hands out to her. "Do I get welcomed back?"

She ran to embrace him, pressing her cheek against his bare chest. "You look so good," she said. "You have all your marks!"

He hugged her tightly and kissed the top of her head. "All of them. Owyn will have some, too. He's been adopted."

"Clan Mother says they'll all be adopted, if they want to be," someone said from behind Aven. Aven turned, and Treesi found herself looking up at the biggest man she'd ever seen.

"Trees, this is my cousin, Othi."

"His sane cousin, Othi," Othi added. "Ven, what were you thinking, leaving beautiful women like this behind?" He winked at Treesi. "Now, I've met the Heir. That would make you Treesi? The Healer?"

"Othi." There was a definite hint of warning in Owyn's voice, and he rested his hand on Treesi's shoulder.

Othi rolled his eyes. "Oh, can't I even look? She's so cute and little!" He grinned at Treesi again. "I could put her into..." He stopped. "Ven, what are they called? The pouches in those things?" He pointed at Jehan.

Aven chuckled. "Pockets. Pockets in trousers."

"Cute and little?" Treesi repeated. "Me?" She giggled, and felt Owyn's hand tighten slightly.

"Right. Pockets." Othi grinned. "It's all fun, Owyn. Really. So stop glaring at me. I know she's not for me."

Treesi looked over her shoulder at Owyn. "Really, Owyn. He can flirt all he wants. I don't mind. Flirting is fun, and it doesn't mean anything. Besides, I don't think I've ever been cute and little before. That's new." She stepped back and slid one arm around Owyn's waist. "You're being awfully possessive," she added in a soft voice. "That's not like you."

Owyn grimaced. "Sorry. Just...I've had enough of losing the people I love —"

Othi snorted. "Well, she *is* tiny! I suppose it's always possible I might misplace her..." he drawled, then laughed when Owyn made a rude gesture at him.

"And speaking of," Owyn continued, "I need someone to take me up to the green levels."

"Are you sure you want to do this now, Owyn?" Jehan asked, coming toward them. The woman with him smiled at Treesi.

"Aven," she said. "Introduce me?"

"Healer Treesi," Aven said instantly. "May I present you to my mother, Aleia, daughter of Arana, Companion of Milon, and the War Leader of the Water tribe?"

Treesi looked at Aven, then back at Aleia. "You're the War Leader? Oh, I'm so glad!"

Aleia arched a brow. "That I'm War Leader?"

"That you're alive!" Treesi answered. "We were worried that Risha had done something horrible to you."

Aleia nodded. "So Owyn said. I regret that I made you all worry so much over me. I was safer than the rest of you." She looked up at Jehan. "Take Owyn to the green levels."

Jehan frowned. "Owyn, you're sure?"

"Now," Owyn said. "Right now. He needs me."

RIGHT NOW TURNED INTO fifteen minutes which were spent at the house, because Jehan insisted that Owyn change from the Water tribe kilt into clothing more suited for dealing with a potentially violent Healer before they went to the green levels. So when they set out, Owyn was wearing well-worn trousers, a long-sleeved shirt, and boots.

"How bad was it?" he asked Jehan as they walked.

Jehan glanced at him. Then he sighed. "Bad. He's hallucinating. He says he hears you and Virrik, telling him to join you. So he's insisting that he's going to fly one more time before he dies."

"Fly...he's planning to jump? Off the low terrace?" Owyn whistled. "That would do it."

"He tried to get there twice before we got back, when he was still being held in a secure treatment room," Jehan continued. "And he's tried two times since to get out, and once to just kill himself in his cell. That was three days ago, and we had to change how he was being secured."

Owyn nodded. "And...are you going to tell me what I can expect?"

Jehan took a deep breath. "When we get there, stay quiet. I'll let you see him through the viewing port. And you can decide what you want to do."

"Jehan, what aren't you telling me?" Owyn asked. Jehan just shook his head, and said nothing more. They entered the tunnels and started down halls Owyn remembered running through last fall. He'd found Jehan imprisoned down one of these halls.

They stopped at the end of a corridor, where a young man in training gray sat at a small table, reading. Jehan nodded to him. "Caron, take a walk."

The healer-in-training nodded and rose, leaving his book behind. Jehan waited until he was gone, then took a key from his pocket. "Now, not a word until I close the viewing port. I don't want him to hear you yet."

Owyn nodded, watching as Jehan opened the little door that covered a wire grating. He moved in closer and looked, and felt his mouth go dry. He nodded slowly, and stepped back so that Jehan could close the door. They retreated down the hall, and Jehan leaned against the wall and rubbed one hand over his face.

"You cut his hair," Owyn whispered. "You cut off his hair!"

"No choice," Jehan said, sounding tired. "He tried to hang himself with it." He met Owyn's eyes, and Owyn could see the regret and the pain there. "He braided his hair and tried to hang himself with it. Owyn, I have never seen someone so determined to die before."

"Then why are you keeping him alive?" Owyn asked. "Really?"

"Because he's not in his right mind," Jehan answered. "Because I don't think he really wants to die. I think he's hurting so much that his mind broke. Until he heals enough to be rational, I can't let him die."

"And if he was rational, and wanted to die?"

"I'd help him. But without pain, without fear. I'd send him to sleep, and he wouldn't wake." Jehan closed his eyes and swallowed. "I've done it before."

Owyn took a deep breath and looked at the door. "Let me in, will you? And...be ready to get me out. If he's as far gone as you said...he might not know it's really me."

"That's one thing I'm worried about, yes."

"You're only worried about one thing?"

"It's one thing, Owyn, but it's one thing on a very long list." He took the key from his pocket again. "Let's go."

He unlocked the door and opened it, stepping out of the way for Owyn. Owyn walked into the small room, and heard the door close behind him. He glanced back to see that Jehan was inside with him. He turned back to Alanar. His Alanar, who was sitting on the floor in the corner. His hair was cut almost as short as Owyn usually wore his own, but his beard and mustache were longer, and looked ragged. Alanar's upper body was wrapped in some kind of binding that looked like canvas, and that secured his arms tightly to his body. He wore soft leather boots on his feet, with locking straps wrapped around his ankles so that he couldn't kick them off. Alanar had his head tipped back against the wall, and his eyes were closed.

"Allie?" Owyn said softly.

"Don't yell at me, Wyn," Alanar answered. "I'm trying. I just...I don't know what else to try."

"You could stop trying," Owyn said. He stepped closer. "Allie, I'm not dead. Honestly, I thought you were. I thought I'd lost you."

Alanar frowned and opened his eyes, turning toward Owyn's voice. "That's a new one. You haven't said that before."

"Because I haven't been here. I'm really here, Allie. I'm not a voice in your head. No more whispers in the dark. I'm here. I just got back. I'm here." He moved another step closer, and went to one knee. "I lost the bracelet. I'm sorry."

"Lost the bracelet?" Alanar's frown deepened. "No. You're not here. Teva killed you."

"Teva is dead. Teva is very dead. Teva was torn to pieces by a water-cat." From behind him, Owyn heard a soft laugh.

Alanar's eyes widened. "You're not alone?"

"No," Owyn answered. "You can't tell?"

"We've got him on a mild sedative, to keep him from using his healing abilities," Jehan said. "He's aware, but not quite drunk on them."

Owyn snorted. "Well, not quite drunk is no fun at all," he said. He reached out and ran his fingers through Alanar's short-cropped hair, which was short enough to curl. Owyn wound one of the short curls around his finger. "Oh, Allie."

Alanar jerked at his touch, sitting up straighter. "You touched me," he breathed, his voice faint. Then he blinked and leaned forward. "Do it again."

"Touch you?" Owyn repeated. He ran the fingers of both hands through Alanar's hair, down over the back of his head, stopping with his fingers laced behind Alanar's neck. Then he leaned forward and kissed him. "I thought I lost you," he whispered.

To his shock, Alanar started shaking. Owyn looked back over his shoulder to see Jehan had moved away from the door. He shook his head, and Jehan stopped. Owyn turned back to Alanar, straddling his legs, leaning in close to him, and kissing him again, catching short blond hair in his fingers as he tried to pour weeks of loss and regret into a single kiss. He felt Alanar's shaking growing stronger, and Owyn broke the kiss and wrapped his arms around him.

"I'm here," he repeated. "I'm here and I'm never leaving you again. I'm sorry."

Shaking turned to crying, great hooting sobs that wracked Alanar's body and threatened to shake Owyn off of his legs. Owyn held on, clinging tightly to him, whispering in Alanar's ear. "I love you. I'm sorry. I'm here."

As the sobs eased, he could hear Alanar repeating his name, over and over. "Owyn. Owyn. Owyn."

"I'm here," Owyn repeated. "Allie, I'm here."

He felt Alanar nod, his beard scraping against the fabric of his shirt. "I know. I know. How? You were dead. Your gem—"

"Is a rock, and can't tell the difference between really dead, and only dead for a minute," Owyn interrupted. "I was dead, Allie. For under a minute. At least, that's what Aven tells me." Alanar sat up, sniffling. Owyn wiped tears from his face with his thumbs. "You still hearing voices, Allie?"

"Right now, all I'm hearing is my heartbeat," Alanar answered. "You were dead. You drowned."

"I drowned. In salt water. Aven and his cousin pulled me out, and Aven brought me back." He looked over his shoulder. "There such a thing as a level six healer? I mean, if someone can bring back a dead man, he's more than a five, right?"

"I think Aven had extra incentive," Jehan said, sounding like he was trying not to laugh. Owyn grinned and turned back to Alanar.

"So...if I undo that thing, you're going to stay with me, right? No more one-way flights?"

"I don't need to," Alanar said. "I was trying to fly to you."

"And...I heard Virrik was in your head, too. Tell him his time is over. You're mine now, and we've got a wedding—" Owyn grimaced. "I lost the bracelet. I'm sorry."

Alanar closed his eyes and smiled. "You can make new ones. For both of us. You promised me, remember? You said you were going to spoil me rotten."

Owyn laughed, remembering the day they'd ridden out of Terraces. "I remember. I've done a horrible job of it so far."

"Well, you're forgiven because you were dead," Alanar answered. "And..." He frowned, "Virrik says he doesn't mind."

Owyn blinked. "Virrik...is still in your head?" he asked slowly.

Alanar nodded, still looking distant. "He's not at loud as you were when you were dead," he said. "Maybe because he's been dead longer. He says he doesn't mind that we're marrying. He wants me happy."

Owyn licked his lips and nodded. "Well, I'm glad he approves, then. And I'm sorry I never got to meet him in person. When he was breathing, anyway."

Alanar nodded. "He appreciates that," he said. "Can I get undone now? I want to stretch."

"Jehan? We can let him out now, right?"

"I just need to know one thing," Jehan said slowly. "You're not going to try to jump—"

"Fly," Alanar interjected.

Jehan nodded. "Fly. You're not going to try to fly again. Are you going to try to hurt anyone?"

Alanar's cheeks turned red. "I have a lot of apologizing to do, don't I?" he asked. "Mother of us all, is Treesi ever going to forgive me?"

"Of course she will," Owyn said. "You're just going to have to grovel. A lot."

Alanar chuckled. "I can do that. So can I have this off?"

Jehan hesitated, then nodded. Owyn shifted off of Alanar's legs, then helped him to move so that he could reach the buckles that ran down the length of Alanar's spine. He sniffed, then murmured, "Don't get any ideas, love. You're not getting this on me."

Alanar shook his head. "I wouldn't. It's been wretched. My nose itched the entire time."

Undoing all the straps took several minutes, unbuckling and unwinding, until finally the binding opened up, revealing that it was very much like a coat worn backwards. Owyn tugged the sleeves down Alanar's arms, and tossed the heavy canvas contraption onto the bed. Then he sat back on his heels and watched as Alanar gingerly raised his arms over his head, stretching until Owyn heard his spine crackling.

"I'm stiff," Alanar grumbled. "How can I be this stiff from not moving?"

"We'll loosen you up," Owyn said. He got to his feet and touched Alanar's shoulder. "Give me your hand. I'll help you up."

"I want the boots off, too." Alanar got gracelessly to his feet. He swayed in place for a moment, then grimaced. "I don't know where I am."

"I don't have the keys for those with me," Jehan answered. "They're in my office. Let Owyn take you home, and I'll meet you there." He smiled, but Owyn noticed that the smile didn't reach his eyes. "Go on, Owyn. Take him home."

Owyn nodded slowly, taking Alanar's hand. "Come on, love." He smiled. "It's going to take me a while to get used to the short hair."

Alanar reached up and ran his fingers through his curls. "It'll take me forever to grow it out again. You'll have to be patient."

"I can be patient, as long as you don't start listening to Virrik and not me." He squeezed Alanar's hand and led him toward the door. As they walked toward Jehan, he started to sign. Simple signs, like the ones that Neera and Del had taught him.

We will talk later.

Owyn nodded, making an affirmative gesture with his free hand. Jehan smiled and stepped out of their way, and Owyn led Alanar out into the corridor.

"Easy now," Owyn murmured. "Nice flat floor, no steps for a bit." He looked up at Alanar as they walked. It hadn't been that long since the night on the beach, he didn't think. But Alanar looked different. He looked fragile. Alanar had only ever looked fragile when he was sick.

"You were dead," Alanar said after a moment. "Really dead."

"So Aven says, yeah," Owyn answered.

"What was it like?"

Owyn frowned. "I...I'm not sure. I don't really remember it. I just...wasn't. Like when you sleep, I think. I hit the water. It was cold, and I tasted salt, just like I remember from my waking vision. And I remember thinking it was worth it, because I was killing Teva, too. It was worth it to die, because I was killing the man who killed you." He stopped to guide Alanar down a flight of stairs. "Then I woke up, enough to know that I was puking up about half the sea, it felt like. That's all I remember, until I woke up again for real."

Alanar nodded slowly. "I'd wondered if there was anything after. I mean, there has to be. Virrik is still talking to me."

"Allie, you had me talking to you, too. And I'm not dead. You just thought I was." Owyn gnawed on his lip. "I'm not sure Virrik is actually in there. I think you're imagining it."

"No," Alanar answered. "It's too real. I know he's dead, but he's still talking to me. He's still here with me."

Owyn bit his lip to keep from arguing. Alanar, his Alanar, was still crackpot insane.

But it didn't matter. So long as he didn't try to hurt anyone, or fly off the lowest terrace, Owyn could deal with crackpot insane.

"They told me that they don't know what happened to Mem, or to Mannon," he told Alanar as he led them out into the open air. "But Karse and Trey are here somewhere. I have to introduce you to them."

"Trey?" Alanar repeated. "Your Trey? Is here?"

"Marik said so. I haven't seen him yet. I really want you to meet him." He squeezed Alanar's fingers. "No getting jealous now. I've known him forever. He's a friend."

"Who was your lover."

"He wasn't my lover," Owyn protested. "We fucked. Because we were both street boys, and that's what we knew. When we knew better, we stopped. You're my lover. Because I love you."

Alanar smiled. "I missed hearing that."

"Oh, I'm going to make you tired of hearing it," Owyn said, laughing. "Steps coming up."

"Tired of hearing your voice?" Alanar asked as they walked down the stairs and out into the streets of Terraces. "That won't happen. That will never happen." He smiled. "Owyn? How soon can you make the pledge bracelets?"

Owyn frowned. "I...I'll have to ask Persis when I can borrow his forge again. But the actual work? It'll take me a week or two to get it right, I think."

Alanar nodded. "Then we have a week or two to plan the wedding."

Owyn stopped. He turned and faced Alanar. "You want to get married that soon?"

Alanar frowned. "You don't?"

Owyn laughed. "I did not say that!" he protested. "I never said that. I just...can we do it that fast in Terraces? In Forge, it takes a month to get the bloodlines researched, and that's before you even can draw up the contracts!"

"I'm fairly certain we're not related," Alanar said, sounding amused. "And there are no contracts in Terraces. We stand up before our friends and family, and we swear to each other."

"Is that all?" Owyn started walking again, leading Alanar along toward the Northwest spoke. "That's barely anything. Yeah, we can do that. I just thought it would take longer to plan." He paused, then stopped again. "Are you sure you want to wait that long? We could get pledge bracelets tomorrow."

"We could," Alanar agreed. "But you promised to make them. I can wait."

"Then I'll talk to Persis tomorrow," Owyn said. "Let's go home and tell the others."

CHAPTER THIRTY-ONE

The house at Three Northwest was more crowded than Owyn had ever seen before. There were people on the front walk and in front of the door. The front room was full enough that it was hard to walk without bumping into anyone. Pirit was there, and Marik. Garrity and Evarra, flanking the chair where Esai sat. Othi was there, taking up a larger percentage of the room than seemed possible for one person. Neera stood with him, talking animatedly to Aleia and Rhexa, and a woman who Owyn recognized from the Palace. What was her name? Oh, right. Ambaryl. He wasn't sure what she was doing here, but she seemed to be standing awfully close to Rhexa. He grinned and looked away. Aven and Del stood near the fireplace with Meris, Treesi and Aria. There were two men with them, their backs to the door. Owyn frowned — they looked familiar, too. Then one turned slightly, and Owyn saw his profile.

"Trey!" Owyn called.

Trey whipped the rest of the way around, burst out laughing, then made his way through the obstacle course of bodies to greet Owyn with an enthusiastic hug.

"There you are!" he crowed. He held Owyn at arm's length, then hugged him again. "We got here, and they told us you were taken, and I..." He stopped, looking past Owyn. "And you're Alanar. If I offer to shake your hand, will you hurt me?"

"Do you want me to?" Alanar asked. He smiled and held his hand out. "I've heard a lot about you. All of it good."

Trey laughed and clasped Alanar's hand. "Hoping we can be friends. Anyone that can turn Wyn's head enough to pledge is someone I want to be friends with."

Alanar's smile grew broader, and he tapped the back of Trey's wrist; Owyn heard a soft thump.

"Who turned your head?" Alanar asked. "Owyn, he's wearing a pledge bracelet, did you see?"

"I didn't!" Owyn gasped. He reached over and pushed up Trey's long sleeve. "Trey, did you finally—?"

"Nah, he didn't," Karse said, coming up behind Trey and draping one arm over his shoulders. "I finally saw what was in front of me. That and Lady Meris demanded to know if I was ever going to put him out of his misery."

Owyn laughed. "Yeah, she'd do that. Congratulations, the both of you." He looked around. "No word about Mem?"

Karse shook his head. "We didn't even know they were missing until we got here. Had no idea they came after us. If I'd known, we'd have gone back for them."

Alanar slipped his arms around Owyn, pressing against his back. "How long would it take to walk here, do you think? Assuming they didn't have horses?"

Karse looked at Trey. "Took us and Aria's guards six days by coach, but we pushed hard. Damn near killed the horses."

"And when we came here, it took us twelve days. Mannon said that was because we were going really slowly," Owyn added. "Remember? We talked about it in the Palace?"

Alanar nodded. "So...something longer than twelve days? When does that mean we should start watching for them?"

Trey frowned. "In three days. That's twelve days. But I think we should double it, really. It's a long way to walk, and neither of them is young."

"You're talking about Memfis and Mannon, aren't you?"

Owyn smiled and turned to hug Meris. "Yes, Granna," he answered. "And if you'd have told me a year ago that I'd be standing here worried about Mannon, I'd have laughed at you."

"We all would have laughed," Meris agreed. "Now, introduce me to your intended."

"How did you know?" Owyn asked.

"Jehan told me," she answered. "I'm so pleased. You've found your Heir, and someone who will stand by you as your husband? Doubly blessed!"

"Yeah, I guess I am." Owyn smiled up at Alanar. "Allie, I want you to meet my grandmother. Adoptive grandmother. Not real grandmother, like she is for Aria. This is Lady Meris, Senior Smoke Dancer of the Fireborn."

Alanar held his hand out, and bowed over Meris' hand. "I am honored," he said.

"My dear Alanar," Meris said. "That is the last time you're allowed to be formal with me. You'll be my grandson, too. Eventually."

"As soon as Owyn finishes the bracelets," Alanar said.

Meris' brows rose. "And how soon will that be?"

Owyn shrugged. "If I can borrow space in a forge? Two weeks, maybe?"

"So soon?" Aria asked, joining them. She slipped her arm around Owyn and leaned into his side. "I thought of this a few days ago, Owyn. We share a grandmother. Does that make us related?"

"After the way you've kissed me? Fuck no!"

"Owyn, stop that," Meris chided. "And no. Not even the most convoluted reading of The *Book of Silver* would judge you related.

Aria, you are my great-granddaughter by blood. Owyn is the grandson of my heart. I never adopted Memfis as my own. Milon wouldn't have it. He fully intended to ask Memfis to marry him someday." She looked wistful for a moment. "So, no. You are not related."

"Good," Aria said. "Because I promised, and I've been remiss." Her arm around Owyn's tensed, just a little. "I've treated you horribly, my Fire, my warrior. None of this would have happened if I had been a better Heir to you. I'm so sorry."

Owyn turned and hugged her. "Thank you. I won't say it's nothing, cause it wasn't. But I forgive you. And we'll do better now." He turned his head to look at Alanar, then turned back to Aria. "You...you don't mind that I'm getting married, do you? You weren't here to ask, and—"

Aria stopped him with her fingers on his lips. "You have my blessing, Owyn. And Alanar. I already welcomed you as one of mine, and as part of my household. This only confirms it."

"We'll just have to be sure that Owyn gets enough sleep," Alanar said. He moved behind Owyn, resting his hands on Owyn's ribs, his body heat radiating warmth even through Owyn's shirt. "And I suppose we can set up a schedule as to whose bed he's in on what night—"

"Or we could just put a bunch of mattresses on the floor of a big room," Owyn said. "That way, we won't have to choose. We'll just all bed down there."

"Mattresses on the floor sounds uncomfortable. How about a really, really big bed?" Alanar suggested.

"Hmmm...like the one in my grandmother's house," Aria agreed. "Owyn, the bed in our room there. Remember?"

"Yeah, I remember. But that one wasn't big enough for six," Owyn said slowly. "Not even if we're all friendly. We'd end up sleeping like puppies, and that won't be comfortable when you're bigging up, Aria."

Aria shrugged. "We have time to decide. For now, we have room here for everyone. And beds enough. And we can make a schedule."

Alanar laughed, leaning down and kissing Owyn's cheek. "Mine first? Or shall we flip a coin?"

"Hey!" Owyn laughed. "I get to choose. And I'm not choosing now! Allie, come meet Aven's mother."

There seemed to be no conscious choice — the informal gathering simply turned into a party. It was partly a celebration of Owyn and Alanar's upcoming wedding, partly a celebration that Owyn was alive. And, in Owyn's mind, it was entirely a celebration that the Companion bond had been reformed and completed. They were all here. They were all together.

They were one.

IT WAS LATE, AND DARK out, and the party had settled into a quiet communion of the renewed bond. The Heir and her Companions were sitting on the low couches in the front room, all of them together, as close as they could be without sitting on top of each other. Aven on one side of Aria, and Treesi on the other. Owyn sat between Treesi and Alanar, and Del was on Aven's far side, his head resting on Aven's shoulder. Karse and Trey left to return to the house they'd been assigned, and where they lived with Meris. Rhexa escorted Neera and Othi to a guest house, and had not returned. Ambaryl had left with Rhexa, and Owyn wondered just when his aunt was going to tell him that she had taken a partner. Not that he minded — Ambaryl seemed like a nice enough person. Pirit had returned to her caves and the guards had gone...somewhere. Owyn wasn't sure where, but he'd been amused to see that Esai had left on

Marik's arm. Aleia and Jehan were still here, but were sitting outside. So for the moment, it was the Heir, and her Companions.

"Aria?" Owyn asked. "Now what?"

"Hmm?" Aria asked, her voice a sleepy hum. "Now what...what?"

"What do we do now?"

"Sleep?" Aven suggested. "That seems like a good thing." He grinned at Aria. "Or maybe not sleep?"

She giggled. "I do not think that is what Owyn is asking."

"It's not," Owyn agreed. "What do we do now? We're all of us here. And Mannon...well, he's abdicated. And he might very well be dead for all we know. What do we do now?"

"You made plans, he told me," Aria said. "What were they?"

"Ahhh..." Owyn hummed softly. "I had them written down. But I don't think they came with me when we left the Palace."

Aria nodded. "Then once you are wed, we will go north. We will go to the Palace. We will settle there. And once we are able, we will go into the mountains."

"To the Temple?" Aven asked.

Aria nodded. "I am the Heir. But that won't be enough for some. I need to be Firstborn. Which means I need claim the Crown."

Aleia appeared in the doorway. "I'm not entirely sure you're going to find it, Aria," she said as she came back in. Jehan followed her, leaning against the wall and folding his arms over his chest.

"Why not?" Aria asked.

Aleia took a deep breath. "You have a lot of time to think, when you're swimming alone in the deep. I was alone, for weeks, swimming back to the canoes. And I realized something. I'm no longer convinced Milon is dead."

Aria sat up straight, her wings flaring behind the low back of the couch. "What do you mean?"

"You went to the Temple, and you found the Diadem," Aleia said. "Before you, Yana went to the Temple and found the Diadem. Neither of you found the Crown. But there was no Firstborn."

"Or we just thought there was no Firstborn," Alanar said softly. "But if he lives, somewhere..."

"How?" Aria demanded. "How could he? It's been twenty-five years!"

"You heard Mannon," Jehan said. "He said they found Milon barely alive, and that he gave Milon to the healers to save. The healers told him that Milon never woke. They didn't tell him that Milon died."

Aria went pale. "You think they lied?"

"Aleia told me her thoughts, while we were outside," Jehan said. "And...I was a half-trained healer and terrified out of my mind. I had no idea what I was doing when I put him to sleep so that he wouldn't die in pain." He dragged his fingers through his hair. "And Mannon said they found him like that. In deep trance. The healers could have told Mannon the truth. Milon didn't wake. Until after they had him hidden away as a prisoner."

"But to hide him for so long, even from Mannon?" Treesi asked. "How?"

"It would be really easy," Owyn said. "There was a bunch that Mannon didn't know. A lot of things. How much did Risha hide from him, just here?" He coughed. "Was...was she one of his healers, then? Did she answer to him back then?"

"Where are you going, Mouse?" Aven asked.

"If she was his healer, even then, and she was here in Terraces already? You...you need to check here. Now. Because she's been gone for months, and if her folks were gone, too..."

Aleia went pale. "Mother of us all."

"No, it's not possible. Pirit ordered a search of the whole of the green levels after we took Terraces back," Alanar said. "There were no hidden prisoners there. Well, there were, but there aren't anymore." He shrugged. "And Risha...she would have been a trainee then, wouldn't she?"

Jehan nodded slowly. "Mother would know exactly. I don't remember her from my year at the main healing center, before we went to the deep. But I was focused on finishing my studies. I'll ask Mother tomorrow."

"Maybe I'll take a look tomorrow, too. Take my blades and go down to the lowest terrace to dance," Owyn said. He yawned, feeling his jaw crack. "Or the day after. I might sleep tomorrow."

"And not sleep tomorrow?" Alanar murmured.

Owyn chuckled and leaned into his side. "Maybe."

"Before you head off to bed," Jehan said. "May I have a word?"

Owyn nodded, remembering the simple signs in Alanar's cell. "Sure. I'll be right out." He untangled himself from the others, then took Alanar's hand. "Come on. I'm putting you to bed."

"But you're not joining me?"

"I'll be a few minutes." He led Alanar down the hall to the room they shared with Treesi, closing the door behind him. "Allie, you get comfortable. I'll be back as soon as I see what Jehan wants."

Alanar laughed. "He wants to warn you that I'm still insane. I thought he might."

"What?" Owyn gasped. "No—"

"I am," Alanar insisted, sitting down on the bed. "I know I am. I mean...I have a dead man whispering in my ear. How am I not insane?"

"Well...he's not telling you to fly off the lowest terrace anymore, is he?" Owyn asked.

"No. No, right at the moment he's telling me to tell you to stop worrying about Memfis. He's fine. He'll be here."

Owyn nodded. "That doesn't sound insane, love. That sounds like me, when I've been dancing. It sounds like some of the Smoke

Dancers I've talked to. Granna Meris heard voices when she danced, she told me."

Alanar looked startled. "So I'm not hearing Virrik? I'm having visions?"

"Maybe? And you're just hearing them in Virrik's voice," Owyn answered. He scratched the back of his neck, feeling the cord of his gem under his fingertips. It made him smile. "We can talk to Granna tomorrow and ask her."

"I'd like that," Alanar said. "I like her."

"She likes you," Owyn told him. "Just don't be all formal at her. She hates that."

Alanar nodded. "I'll try to remember. Go see if I was right about what Jehan wants."

Owyn smiled. He stood in front of Alanar, leaning down to kiss him. "You know that doesn't matter to me, right?" he asked.

Alanar tipped his head back. "I know."

Owyn kissed him again, then left the room. The front room was empty when he got there, so he kept on going, heading out to the front of the house. There was a bench in the front of the house, underneath a grape arbor, and that was where he found Jehan.

"You know he's insane, right?" Jehan asked without preamble.

"You know I don't give a fuck, right?" Owyn answered.

Jehan snorted. "I knew you'd say that."

"Here's the thing," Owyn added, sitting down next to Jehan. "I'm not sure he is. He told me what Virrik is telling him. He's not just hearing Virrik. He's having visions. Only thing is, he can't see them. So he's hearing them."

Jehan was quiet for a moment. Then he huffed softly. "Is that even a thing?"

"I'm not sure. I'm going to ask Granna in the morning." Owyn leaned forward with his elbows on his knees. "I wish Mem was here."

"So do I," Jehan breathed. "So do I. I wish he was here to poke holes in Aleia's theories. But he isn't, and I can't. I think she's right."

"What, that Milon is alive, and that's why Aria didn't get the Crown right off?" Owyn nodded. "It makes sense. But where would they have hidden him?"

"The question I'm asking myself is how did my mother not know," Jehan said. "Or does she?"

"Oh," Owyn murmured. "Oh, fuck."

"Exactly." Jehan sighed, then rubbed his hands together. "Go to bed, Owyn. It's late. Alanar is waiting for you, and Aleia is waiting for me."

Owyn nodded. "And you've been waiting for her for a lot longer. Go on. See you tomorrow." Owyn watched as Jehan headed out into the street, heading back toward the healing complex. Once the older man was out of sight, Owyn turned and went inside. Aven was waiting for him.

"Thought you'd gone to bed," Owyn said.

"We had, but we were missing you," Aven answered. "Come be with us. Treesi went to get Alanar."

"Your bed isn't big enough!" Owyn said with a laugh.

"It's just to sleep." Aven held out his hand. "We're all tired. We just want to be together. Come be with us."

Owyn smiled and took his hand. "Love you, Fishie. You can come to our room."

"I love you, too, Mouse. We all do." He glanced back over his shoulder. Owyn looked, and saw Aria standing in the doorway. She held her hands out to him and to Aven.

"Come to bed, you two," she said. "We'll work out the schedule tomorrow."

CHAPTER THIRTY-TWO

O wyn woke up in the middle of a tangle of arms and legs and wings and hair. It took him a moment to make sense of which arms and legs belonged to which body — Alanar was behind him, pressed hard up against his back. In front of him was Treesi, and behind her was Aria. Del was sprawled across his legs and Alanar's, boneless as a rag-doll. And Owyn's head was pillowed on Aven's stomach, and he could hear the inner churning and growling that told him clearly that Aven was going to be starving when he woke up.

Fuck. Breakfast. He needed to get up and cook. He raised his head and looked at the tangle.

Nope. That was not happening. Not without waking every other person in the bed.

He put his head back down and closed his eyes. He needed to talk to Granna Meris today. And Persis. He needed to design the bracelets, and see what he'd need in materials. He needed to go spend some time with his aunt, and collect Trinket. They needed food...

"Stop thinking so hard," Treesi whispered. "You'll wake people."

Owyn chuckled and opened his eyes. "How'd you know I was awake?"

Treesi giggled. "I'm a healer, and you've got a lot of bare skin up against mine. I knew the minute you woke up."

Owyn smiled and pulled her closer, enjoying her warmth against him. "I was thinking I needed to get up and make breakfast. But I'd wake everyone if I moved."

"But isn't someone cooking?" Treesi asked. "I mean, I smell something."

Owyn raised his head. "Now that you mention it," he murmured. Yes, he did smell food. But who...?

There was a light tapping at the door. It opened, and Rhexa peered inside. "I thought I heard voices. Breakfast will be in a few minutes," she whispered. "If you can get up for it."

"Auntie?" Owyn asked, loud enough that Alanar grunted and rolled onto his back. It let Owyn shift to better see the door. "You're cooking for us?"

"Baryl and I are," Rhexa said. Then she blushed. "She thought it would be a nice thing to do for you, since you've had no time to get supplies."

"That is a very nice thing," Aria said. "Thank you." She raised her head and pushed hair out of her face. "It smells wonderful."

Rhexa smiled. "We'll have everything on the table in the front room when you come out." She closed the door. Owyn glanced over his shoulder to check for room, then rolled onto his back. And found himself immediately covered by Alanar, who rolled onto him and pinned him to the bed. He grinned, his nose almost-but-not-quite touching Owyn's.

"Pay the toll," Alanar growled, his voice still raspy from sleep.

Owyn squirmed, then laughed. "There's not enough room in the bed to wrestle right now," he said. "So come down here."

"You gave up far too easily," Alanar grumbled, and leaned down to kiss Owyn. He'd barely begun to stop time when he yelped and rolled away, rolling off the bed and landing on the floor with a thud and an 'oof!'

"What the—?" Owyn sat up, and was immediately faced with a stunned and blushing Del. He looked over the edge of the bed at Alanar, who was laughing and looked unhurt. Satisfied, he looked back at Del. "You poked him, didn't you?"

Del nodded.

"In the ribs?"

Another nod.

Owyn burst out laughing. "You had no way to know he's ticklish!" He rolled to the edge of the bed and looked down. "You okay, Allie?"

"I'm fine. And that wasn't fair," Alanar protested. "I want a rematch."

"Later," Aven called as he sat up. He winced and shifted. "Alanar, are you going to be able to help today?"

Alanar sat on the edge of the bed. "Help with what?"

"Fa wants to try and put this hip of mine to rights. He thinks that if we take it slowly, and reshape the bone little by little, it will work. And he said something about asking you and Treesi."

"He hasn't yet," Alanar said. "But we were busy last night. Of course I'll help. I don't like you being in pain. It makes me itch." He stood up and ran his fingers through his short hair. "I can't get used to this."

"It looks very nice," Aria said. "And it will grow out again. Now, there is breakfast."

Sorting through discarded clothes took several minutes and a lot of laughing, so by the time they filed down the corridor to the front room, everything was on the table, and Rhexa and Ambaryl were waiting with Jehan.

"Where's Ama?" Aven asked as he slowly lowered himself into a chair.

"She went down to the water with Neera and Othi. They wanted to go out to the rest of the canoes, have them spread out up and down the coast." Jehan sat back in his chair and sipped his tea. "Alanar, are you available this morning?"

"Aven already asked if I would help, and I'd be glad to," Alanar answered. "Do you think we can reform the bone?"

"I think we should be able to, if we work carefully. And slowly — I'm thinking four to six individual sessions, with a few days between to make sure that the changes hold. But I'm not sure how many of us it will take. Treesi—"

"Of course I'm helping!" Treesi blurted. "Who's going to cover rounds?"

The conversation among the healers turned to things that Owyn wasn't sure he wanted to know, so he turned back toward the other end of the table, where Rhexa and Ambaryl were sitting.

"So...something you want to tell me, Auntie?" he asked slowly.

Rhexa laughed. "Baryl and I were girls together, and we entered training together. Neither of us had healing potential, so I went into administration, and she went off..."

"And ended up in the Palace as housekeeper," Owyn finished.

"Eventually, yes." Ambaryl nodded. "I came back with Alanar, because I knew enough to care for him on the trip. And I was so surprised to see Rhex again—"

"Rhex?" Owyn echoed, and watched his aunt blush.

"We've been catching each other up on everything, and she told me you were Dyneh's son. I had no idea!"

"Neither did I, really," Owyn admitted. "Not until I came here. My parents died when I was small, and I don't really remember them at all." He shook his head when Ambaryl paled. "I'm fine with it. Really. That sounds kind of heartless, but I am. You can't miss what you don't know."

"I suppose not," Ambaryl said, nodding. "It's still sad, though. Dyneh was a lovely girl."

"And Owyn takes after her," Rhexa said, reaching out and resting her hand on Owyn's. "Now, before I forget, Trinket has set up housekeeping in my stove. Once you're settled, I'm sure she'll be happy to see you. And I'm managed to keep your bread starter alive—"

"Barely," Ambaryl muttered.

"It's doing better now that you're here," Rhexa added, and Owyn grinned.

"Sounds like I'm not the only one getting married?" he drawled.

Ambaryl turned pink and Rhexa lowered her eyes. "We've waited this long," she murmured. "Longer than you've been alive, Owyn. I made the mistake of not asking Baryl a long time ago, and I'm not making it again. But we can wait to see you wed."

"Auntie, you don't have to wait!" Owyn protested. "Not for me! Look, you should be happy. I want you to be happy. And if being happy means you get married today, then we'll get you married today. However you do it here. Alanar says there aren't any contracts like in Forge. You just stand up in front of your friends and family." He looked around the table, saw Aria smiling at him. "Well, we're all here."

Rhexa squeezed his hand. "You're very sweet, Owyn. Let's get you and your Alanar settled first. You've only just come back." She bit her lip, looked down at the table, then lowered her voice. "Is he all right now?"

"Yeah," Owyn answered. "And he can still probably hear you. He's got really good ears."

"I do," Alanar agreed. "And I am, thank you." He turned and smiled at Rhexa. "And I don't mind either. If you want to get married first, we'll just have a much longer party."

Rhexa burst out laughing, and Owyn turned his attention to his breakfast, thinking about the rest of his day. He glanced to the other end of the table, and realized that Aria had gone back to paying close attention to the healers, which left Del sitting alone. He was looking down at his plate, but he didn't appear to have eaten anything. Owyn reached over and poked Del in the shoulder. "Hey, you doing all right?'

Del shrugged one shoulder, turning slightly toward Owyn.

Owyn nodded. "Feeling like the fifth wheel on the wagon?" he asked. That got a grin from Del. "I know. It's weird. You'll get used to it. Used to us. Now eat something." A thought occurred to him, and he turned back to Rhexa. "Auntie, could you take Del to the dispensary? He needs clothes and...well, just about everything else. Him and Aven both. I think they'll need to measure Aven again."

"He does look like he's broadened across the shoulders," Rhexa agreed. "Well, Del? Think you can put up with an old lady for a few hours? I don't know how to read Water signs, but I have plenty of paper in my office."

Del smiled and bowed his head. Then he looked at Owyn and gestured, one of the signs that Owyn knew.

"Me? I've got to arrange for a forge, and for materials to make the pledge bracelets. And I have to design them, which means sitting and sketching things out. And I wanted to get my blades and go see if I can catch a vision. Maybe give us an idea what to expect when we go back to the Palace. Maybe see if both our fathers are all right. Allie says Mem is, but he didn't say anything about Mannon. Oh, and I have to ask Lady Meris to talk with Allie about visions."

"Is he having visions?" Ambaryl asked. "I thought only Smoke Dancers had visions."

"So did I, but he's sounding just like a Smoke Dancer, so I figure having him talk to one would be a good thing. Granna Meris is the best there ever was. And Granna should also talk to Aria, who actually *is* a Smoke Dancer. She needs training, and Mem never had a chance." He looked over at Alanar, noticed that the healer had his head cocked slightly. "You're listening to both conversations, love?"

"I heard my name," Alanar answered. "That's a question I'd like answered. Are there any visionaries who aren't Fire? Because I'm not. Not even a little."

Own shrugged. "I have no idea. Maybe Granna knows. Once you're done with Aven, we can sit down with her."

Alanar nodded and turned back to the healing conversation, and Owyn looked down at his plate. As he ate, he categorized what he needed to do. Dance first. Take something with him to eat so that he'd be grounded to go on to talk to Persis. Then he'd have until Alanar was done to work on designs. He nodded and started eating.

ONCE BREAKFAST WAS over, the healers left. Owyn wished them luck, then went to fetch his smoke blades and the bag that contained his book. When he came back to the front room, only Aria was there.

"Del went with your aunt and Ambaryl," she said. "Rhexa says to come later to pick up Trinket."

Owyn nodded. "I'll do that. Aren't you going with Aven?"

She shook her head. "No. I will be in the way, and there is nothing I can do to help. He asked me to go with you, to make sure that you're taken care of after you dance. So I have something for you to eat after." She raised a small bundle. "Where are we going?"

"The lowest terrace. And thank you."

They walked out of the house and down toward the lowest terrace. Owyn kicked off his boots while Aria took a seat on one of the covered benches.

"Someday, I will learn to do this," she declared. Then she looked down at herself. "After the baby is born and I can fly again."

"For now, I'm happy to go hunting visions for the both of us," Owyn said. He closed his eyes, shook his head, then rolled his shoulders and started to take his three deep breaths. The blades felt good in his hand when he started moving. He felt his skin prickle, and the vision closed over him.

Ruins. He wasn't sure where they were, other than ruins. Shattered columns and toppled walls that bore black scorch marks, and broken tiles and glass under his boots. Aven was off to his left, his hook swords bare in his hands. Del was on Owyn's right, carrying a crossbow. He looked at Owyn, and they walked forward, toward a door that swung lazily on its hinges. From somewhere, he heard a baby crying.

Then the door opened....

Owyn opened his eyes to see grass. He shook his head, trying to clear it. He was on his hands and knees, his blades resting next to him. He shook his head again, and sat back on his heels.

"Is that all?" he called. "That's not enough to tell me anything!"

"What was it?" Aria asked. She came over to him and handed him the bundle. "Eat. Then tell me."

He unwrapped the bundle, finding inside flat biscuits. When he bit into one, he tasted honey and spices. "These are good," he mumbled around a mouthful. "Where did these come from?"

"Rhexa brought them to me when you went for your blades, because she heard you were going to go dance. I think Ambaryl made them." Aria sat down with him and reached out to take a biscuit. "Will you tell me what you saw?"

Owyn finished his biscuit and started another one. "I'm not sure," he answered around mouthfuls. "Me, Aven and Del. We're all armed. We're someplace in ruins, and we're heading for a door. I can hear a baby. The door opens, and that's when I fell out of the vision. I don't know what was on the other side of the door. Or who."

"A baby?" Aria asked. "My baby?"

Owyn shook his head. "No idea. Just...a baby crying." He frowned, thinking about other details. "I don't know where those ruins were. It wasn't any place I've been before. Fire damage, knocked down walls and columns."

Aria blinked. "Was one of the columns cut off at a sharp angle?" She held her hand up, tipping it. "Like this? It would have been the one on the right as you were looking at the door?"

"Yeah!" Owyn gasped. "You're been there!"

"You saw the Temple," Aria answered. "At least, I think you did."

Owyn nodded. "Give me a minute. Let me see if I can still get it down." He took his book and a piece of charcoal out of his bag, opened it to a blank page, and started to sketch, laying the image that he'd seen so clearly down on paper. When he was done, he tipped the book so that Aria could see.

She nodded. "That is the Temple." She pointed to the door. "That is the door to the crypt."

Owyn nodded, picking up another biscuit. He ate it, chewing slowly. "So...we get there. But why are we all armed?"

"And where am I? Or Treesi?" Aria added.

Owyn nodded again. "See? No real answers. Just questions." He sighed and shook his head. "Come on. It's not enough to worry about."

"I know you. You're going to worry anyway."

"Later," Owyn said as he got to his feet. He held his hand out to Aria and helped her up, then bent to put his book back into the bag. He picked up his blades and looked around. "I'll worry about it later. When I know it's something to worry about. For now? Let's go see if they put Aven's leg on backwards."

THEY STOPPED IN THE house to put away the smoke blades and Owyn's book, then walked in silence to the healing complex. Malani greeted them warmly, and told them that the healers were still working.

"Thank you, Malani," Aria said, and turned to Owyn. "I will wait. You have things to do. Come back when you're done?"

"And we'll all go see Aven in room nineteen?" Owyn asked. "It'll be like old times."

Aria smiled and wrapped her arms around his neck. "Without the missteps that went with those old times, yes." She kissed him, then stepped back. "I'll see you when you are finished."

Owyn grinned as she walked away, disappearing down the corridor. He waved to Malani, then headed back outside, setting out for the steps that would take him up to the higher terraces, and to the northeast spoke of the wheel. Persis' forge was closest to the tunnels that led to the stables, near the very end of the northeast spoke. Owyn could hear the ringing of the anvil long before he reached the building. When he did, he stopped outside the wide, double-hung doors that led into the forge. The tops of the door were open, and Owyn could feel the heat rolling out. Persis was inside, glowering at a glowing horseshoe that he held in his tongs. Even at this distance, Owyn could see that the horseshoe was slightly warped.

"Gonna fit it hot?" he called.

"Gonna have to," Persis answered. He shoved the horseshoe back into the fire-pot and turned toward the doors, wiping his forehead with the back of his wrist. "Well, you're looking good for a dead man. Were you really?"

"According to Aven, for nearly a minute."

Persis snorted. "That must have been something. So what can I do for you, dead man?"

Owyn grinned. "I was hoping to borrow the forge?"

"What are you making this time?" Persis asked. "Another rose?"

"This time? Pledge bracelets. Not sure what all I'll need yet." Owyn hesitated, then scratched the back of his neck. "Figured I'd talk to you first."

"Pledge bracelets?" Persis said, and whistled. "You don't want to be talking to me. You want to be talking to Tassali."

Owyn frowned. "Have I met Tassali?"

"She's down the way a bit. You passed her shop."

Owyn looked back down the street. "Wait, you mean the silversmith?"

"Yeah, that's Tassali."

Owyn coughed, then stammered, "I thought...maybe I could make something nice from bronze—"

"And turn Alanar's wrist green?" Persis asked.

"I promised him I'd make the bracelets, Persis!" Owyn insisted. "I can't not make them! And I don't know how to work silver."

Persis nodded. He walked away from Owyn and shouted to the house behind the forge. "Lixi! Run up to Tassali's place, there's a good girl! Tell Tass I need to talk to her!"

Owyn saw Persis' daughter Lixi running up the street. A few minutes later, she was back with an older woman in tow.

"What is it, Persis?" the woman asked.

"Tassali, this here is Owyn Fireborn," Persis said. "He's a damn fine smith in his own right, but what he's wanting to do isn't in his area, or in mine. It's in yours."

"Yeah, but here's the thing," Owyn said. "I sort of promised my intended that I'd make the pledge bracelets."

"Who's your intended?" Tassali asked.

"Healer Alanar," Owyn answered.

Tassali's brows rose. "He bought a bracelet from me a few months back."

Owyn winced. "Yeah, about that...it's a long story, but that bracelet is at the bottom of the ocean now. I need to replace it, and I need to make a pair, and *I* need to be the one to make them."

She nodded. "All right. Got a design in mind?"

Owyn shook his head. "Not yet, no."

She smiled. "Come on back up to my shop. We'll sit down, and we'll talk. We'll see what we can do."

When Owyn left Tassali's shop an hour later, he was grinning from ear to ear. The bracelets were going to be perfect.

CHAPTER THIRTY-THREE

Owyn smoothed the front of his new shirt and looked at himself in the mirror. The shirt was the dark blue of a twilight sky, made from some material he wasn't even sure of, and it was the nicest piece of clothing he'd ever owned. Aria had given it to him this morning, to wear for his wedding.

He grinned. His wedding. He hadn't seen Alanar yet, wouldn't see him until they met to exchange bracelets and promises down on the lowest terrace. Alanar had spent the night in his old quarters in the healing complex, with Treesi to keep him company. Today, when the wedding parties finally met, Treesi and the rest of the healers would stand with Alanar as his family. With Owyn would be Meris, Aria, Rhexa and Ambaryl.

But not Memfis.

Crafting the bracelets had taken Owyn longer than he'd expected. Today marked twenty-nine days since the Smoking Mountain had erupted. Every evening for the past five days, he'd gone to the tunnels to talk with the guides. He'd gone to the healing assistants who were recording the comings and goings of refugees from the Fire tribe lands, and checked with them. Even though he knew in his bones that someone would have come and found him if Memfis had returned to Terraces, he still went. And came away disappointed.

"That is a very good color on you."

Owyn turned to see Aven standing in the doorway. He was wearing a new kilt, and a vest of the same material as Owyn's shirt. He'd refused a shirt, and the blue material brought out the underlying blues hidden in the tattoo ink.

"It's not a bad color on you, either," Owyn said. He smoothed his hands down the front of his shirt. "Come to fetch me?"

"It's about time to start," Aven said. He took a deep breath. "It feels odd, to be giving you away. I didn't think it would be this odd."

"Giving me away?" Owyn laughed. "You're not! I'm still here. I'm still part of this. And now, Allie will be, too."

"It's still odd," Aven said. He shook his head. "It feels like I'm losing you. Which I don't think I have any right to feel. I left you first."

"You can feel however you feel. It's all right. Just...let us know what you're feeling. So we don't make the same mistakes." Owyn took a deep breath. "Fishie, I still love you. You know that, right?"

"I know," Aven said. "And I love you, Mouse. I'm just...confused, I guess." He smiled. "I'll get my head around it. I do love you. And I do like Alanar. He's a good friend."

"Are you standing with him today, or me?" Owyn asked. "You could be in either place. With me and Aria, or with the healers."

"I'm with you," Aven said. "Because he's a friend. You're more than that." He held his hand out. Owyn took it and let Aven pull him into an embrace. "I want you happy, Mouse."

Owyn leaned into Aven's chest, resting his ear over Aven's heart. "I'm almost happy."

Aven sighed. "I miss him, too."

"I wanted him here for this. He said he'd be here for this. He promised." Owyn stopped, feeling his throat tighten. Aven's arms around him were strong, and he drew comfort from that.

"Mouse, what was his waking vision?" Aven asked.

"Dunno," Owyn answered. "He never told me."

"Fa didn't know either," Aven asked. "Except that Memfis told him once that it was a long time in the future."

Owyn tipped his head back. "You went looking?"

Aven nodded. "I wanted something that might make you feel better. I know it's worrying you, and you shouldn't be worried. Not today."

Owyn smiled. "Thank you." He stepped back, pulling gently out of Aven's embrace. "Allie says that Mem is fine. That he'll be back."

"And what did Lady Meris say?" Aven asked. "I never asked you."

Owyn went back to the mirror. He ran his fingers through his hair, resettled his Fire gem at his throat. Then he turned back to Aven. "She says that she's never heard of a visionary who didn't have any Fire in them. That it's the Fire that lets us see. But she also said that just because she's never heard of it doesn't mean it's not real. So—"

"She's as confused as the rest of us?"

Owyn chuckled. "Yeah. Where's everyone else?"

"Outside, waiting for us." Aven stepped back into the corridor. Owyn followed him as they walked out to the front room. Aven was still limping slightly, but it wasn't nearly as bad as it had been, and there was still one more session of bone reshaping scheduled.

"You never did show me how you sword dance," Owyn blurted.

Aven looked back over his shoulder. "What brought that on?"

"You're walking a lot better. You're not using the stick as much anymore," Owyn answered. "It don't hurt as much anymore, it looks like."

"It doesn't," Aven agreed. "Unless I'm on my feet too long. It barely hurts to change, either. I think the next session will be the last. It's not the way it used to be, but it's better than it was when we came back."

They walked out into the early morning sunshine, and Owyn smiled to see the small group gathered in front of the house. Rhexa and Ambaryl were there, hand in hand, talking with Meris, who was seated on the covered bench. Aria stood nearby with Del, and the both of them were wearing the same shade of dark blue as Owyn. Del had a vest very much like Aven's, which he wore over a simple white shirt and dark trousers. And Aria took Owyn's breath away — her gown was high necked, but left her arms bare, and the skirts hung higher in the front than in the back, just skimming the tops of her boots. It took him a moment of staring to notice that she was also wearing the Diadem.

"Owyn, you look magnificent," Meris said. She got slowly to her feet and came toward him, her hands held wide. Owyn hugged her, then offered her his arm. She just sighed and shook her head. "Oh, my Owyn. I wish Memfis could see you."

Owyn swallowed. "So do I, Granna."

"What do we do now?" Aria asked. She rested one hand on Owyn's shoulder. "They'll be waiting for us."

"Rhexa?" Meris asked. "How do we proceed?"

They started walking — Owyn in front, with Meris on his arm. Behind him, as closest blood kin, was Rhexa, with Ambaryl on her arm. Behind them were Aria, Aven and Del. Owyn glanced back as they walked, then looked forward and smiled.

He was still wishing for Mem, but he knew Memfis wouldn't have wanted him to delay anymore.

They walked down the stairs to the lowest terraces, and saw the group waiting by a canopy that had been hung with spring flowers. Underneath it, Jehan stood by a small table draped in green. Owyn knew what was on that table — the pledge bracelets. He looked around, seeing Aleia, Neera and Othi. Near the Waterborn were a small group of guards, Karse and Trey among them. Marik waved at him, then turned back to Esai. The healers stood in a group, and Alanar was at the center. As Owyn led Meris to the canopy, the group opened, and Alanar walked toward him. Up until that moment,

Owyn hadn't seen Alanar wear anything but Healer white or trainee gray, except for the blue shirt at the Palace. He knew for a fact that the healer didn't own anything in any other color.

Today, Alanar was dressed in unrelieved black — his shirt, the long vest that came to his thighs, and his trousers. There were slight hints of silver embroidery on the vest, like stars at midnight, but all they did was accentuate the darkness. Against Alanar's pale coloring, the black was a striking contrast.

"Oh, you need to wear black more often," Owyn said softly, knowing Alanar would hear him. "That's good on you."

"And it makes it easy to dress myself," Alanar added with a laugh. He held his hand out. "I missed you."

Owyn smiled, leaving Meris to go and join Alanar. He slipped his hand into Alanar's. "It was one night."

"It was the longest night I think I've ever spent," Alanar said. He raised Owyn's fingers to his lips and kissed them. "I still missed you."

Owyn squeezed Alanar's hand and led him underneath the canopy.

Jehan smiled at them, then looked around. "You can all come closer," he said, raising his voice. "That way, I won't have to shout." He waited until everyone moved closer, then chuckled. "My first wedding. And it's this one. Two young men of whom I am very fond. Sons of my heart." He nodded, then cleared his throat. "Who brings Owyn Jaxis Fireborn to this union?"

"I do," Rhexa answered. "His mother's sister, a child of Earth."

"As do I," Meris added. "Son of my heart, a son of Fire."

Jehan nodded, and looked at Alanar. "And who brings Alanar, son of Dantris to this union?"

"His healing family," Treesi announced. "He's one of us, a healer and a son of Earth and Air."

Jehan nodded again, and reached out to take Alanar's left hand and Owyn's right. "And do you both come to this union of your own free will?"

"Yes," Alanar answered.

"Completely," Owyn added.

"Do you understand the responsibilities that lay before you?" Jehan asked. "Those of Healer, and those of Companion? They are neither of them easy roads to take."

Owyn looked up at Alanar. "We're taking the same road. Together. And if we can survive dying, and going crackpot insane, then I'm pretty sure we can handle anything."

Alanar started laughing. Then he bit his lip and nodded. "What he said."

"That's an unconventional answer, but this is an unconventional union." Jehan let their hands go, and took the drape off the pledge bracelets. Owyn heard Rhexa gasp behind him, and grinned.

"Owyn, if you would?" Jehan prompted.

Owyn picked up the bracelet that he'd made for Alanar, opened it, then closed the cuff around Alanar's left wrist, hearing the soft snap as the clasp engaged. "Allie, I love you," he said softly. "There's really not much else to say. I love you. And if you'll have me, I'm yours."

"If I'll have you," Alanar repeated. "I thought we'd covered that." He took the pledge bracelet that Jehan handed to him, and ran his fingers over the textured surface. He looked puzzled for a moment, then smiled. "You...what did you do here?"

"I'll explain it later," Owyn said. "I promise. There's a hinge, and a catch...yeah." He put his left hand into Alanar's right, and tried to control his elation as the bracelet closed around his wrist and the clasp snapped shut. That was it. It was done.

"Does everyone here witness?" Jehan asked.

"We do!"

Owyn clearly picked out Aria's voice, and Aven's. Treesi's, and Trey's. Rhexa and Meris and Ambaryl. Everyone he loved...

Except for one.

"The witnesses affirm," Jehan pronounced. "May I present—"

"Senior Healer!"

Owyn jumped and turned toward the shout, and saw a young woman running toward them. He recognized her from the newer healing assistants, the ones who were working with the refugees. She raced toward them, and came to a skidding stop, tearing runnels in the grass, then falling to her knees. "Senior Healer," she panted. "We need you. We need all of the healers!"

"What is it, Aritty?" Jehan demanded. "How bad?"

"Your brother—"

Jehan was running before she'd finished the word, and Aven and Treesi took off after him.

Owyn stared after them, then turned to Alanar. "Go. I'll follow. They might need you."

"Owyn—"

"Go!" Owyn insisted. "I knew who I was marrying when I said yes. They *need* you. Go!"

Alanar waited only long enough to kiss Owyn, then ran after the other healers. Owyn watched him, aware that Aria had come to stand on his right, and Del on his left. He could feel Del shaking.

"Do you think he's alone?" Aria asked.

"I don't know," Owyn answered. "But I don't want to get in their way." He turned, looking for Aritty. Rhexa had helped the girl to her feet, and was steadying her as Ambaryl offered her a flask. "Was he alone? Was Mannon alone?"

Aritty shook her head, waving off the flask. "No. That's why I came, once we knew who it was that they'd brought in. Mannon is fine. Exhausted, but fine. It's the other man—"

Owyn's heart hit his boots hard enough that he felt it crack. "Other man?"

"Go!" Aria whispered. "Owyn, go!"

Owyn went. He ran blindly up the stairs, up the street, not even knowing which one it was. He didn't care. It didn't matter — all the streets ended at the healing complex, and that was where he needed to be. He dodged people, hearing them shout after him, not stopping to actually hear what they were saying. Seeing only the mismatched bricks of the healing complex as the building grew closer.

He hit the doors hard enough that they bounced open and nearly closed on him before he was through. Malani was behind the desk again, and she jumped to her feet when she saw him.

"Where?" he wheezed.

"The waiting area," she called. "Wait—"

Owyn didn't wait. He ran down the hall toward the large waiting area where people would stay while their families were being cared for. He took the corner too fast and skidded into the wall, which let Del come from behind him and pass him. He hadn't even realized that Del was following him. Del was first into the waiting room, and hit Mannon hard enough to knock the man over. Owyn watched as Mannon stumbled, as he realized just who had attacked him. As he crumpled to the ground, pulling Del down with him.

"Del," Mannon gasped. "My boy. I never thought I'd see you again."

Owyn staggered across the room, feeling as if it was twice the length that he'd just run. He sank to his knees next to them and hoarsely whispered, "Tell me."

Mannon looked at him, then blinked in shock. "Owyn. Thank the Mother. You're alive."

"I'm fine." Owyn decided now was not the time to explain anything. "Where is he? Where's my Fa?"

Mannon closed his eyes. "He saved my life, Owyn. So many times. I told him to leave me, and he wouldn't. He wouldn't. I don't know why."

"Because he's a fucking idiot," Owyn snapped. "Where is he?"

Mannon stared at him for a moment, and Owyn realized that Mannon was struggling just to put two words together. Aritty said he was exhausted. She wasn't exaggerating. Owyn got up and looked around, then went to the door. "Malani!"

Malani rushed toward him. "What can I do?"

"Whatever you can think of to support him," Owyn answered. "All the healers ran off to help my Fa, right? Someone needs to take care of Mannon."

"He told me he didn't want anything!"

"And you listened?" Owyn asked.

Malani blushed. "I'll be back," she said, and hurried away.

Owyn went back inside and crouched down next to Mannon. "Del, help me get him off the floor."

Del nodded, and shifted. Together, he and Owyn got Mannon off the floor and into one of the padded chairs. Malani reappeared, carrying a basket, and with another healing assistant following her carrying a tray. Mannon scowled, and looked as if he was going to refuse, until Owyn cleared his throat.

"You're going to let them take care of you," he said softly. "Or I'm going to let them tie you down and do it."

Mannon looked startled, then sighed. "I'm too tired to fight you," he grumbled.

"Good," Malani said. "Here. Drink this." She handed him a mug, then took a blanket out of the basket.

By the time Aria arrived, Mannon was cocooned in the blanket, and had a mug in each hand. His color was already better. He looked up as Aria came in, and would have stood if Owyn and Del both hadn't made him stay seated.

"Do not stand," Aria said, reinforcing the hands on Mannon's shoulders. "Can you tell us what happened?"

"Did Karse and Trey make it?" Mannon asked. "We never saw them."

"They are here. They are outside," Aria answered. "You walked? The whole way?"

"Ran the first two days, I think," Mannon answered. "It was like running through the heart of the mountain. Fire raining from the sky. I have no idea how we survived that." He frowned. "No, I do. Memfis. He would not let me lay down and die there. Said I needed to keep going. That it wasn't his time to die, so it wasn't mine either. We went to ground...I'm not even sure how many days out. Stayed low until we ran out of water. Then we started walking." He closed his eyes and took a long drink from one of the mugs. Then he sighed. "There was a village. South of here. They were all gone. We stopped there, looking for supplies."

Owyn frowned. "You mean Cliffside?"

"I don't even know, Owyn," Mannon answered with a crooked smile. "I don't think I could find it on a map. I don't think I could read a map as tired as I am now. They'd been gone for a while. Long enough that animals had started setting up housekeeping in the houses. There was a snake in one of the grain bins. Memfis said it was nothing, but by the time dark rolled around, he was running a fever, and his arm had swollen up. I tied off the arm, to keep the poison from spreading, but by morning, he was delirious."

"You carried him here, from Cliffside?" Owyn stammered. "How?"

"Have you ever used a draw-sledge?" Mannon asked. "They're relatively easy to make, and you can pull a load with one, if you can secure it. I scavenged poles, blankets for the basket, and rope. And I started pulling." He shook his head and took another drink. "Took me four days to get him here. And every time I stopped, I thought

I'd find I was dragging a body. But he stayed with me. I couldn't let him die. Not when he wouldn't let me die." He looked up. "We got here, and I told them it was snakebite, and we needed a healer. They rushed us through the tunnels before they even asked my name." He frowned, cocking his head to the side. "You're all dressed up. All of you are. And you match. I...what did I interrupt?"

Owyn covered his mouth with one hand, then sighed. "You were a little late to my wedding. But you made it, so you're forgiven."

"Wedding—" Mannon breathed. "And...and Del is here. You found Aven."

"He found me," Owyn said. "And you need to rest. Malani, can we find him a place to lay down?"

"Not until I know," Mannon insisted. "I need to know."

"Then we will wait together," Aria said. She sat down, arched a brow at Mannon, and added, "Drink your tea."

Owyn sat. He paced. He walked the length of the corridor from waiting room to front hall and back. He sat with Aria, and when Aria left the room, he sat with Del. He was just getting up to pace the corridor for another time when Jehan appeared in the door.

"And?" Owyn demanded. "What took so long?"

Jehan nodded. "Good news, bad news or worse news?"

"The good news had fucking better be that he's alive," Owyn spat.

"Yes, he's alive. And the good news was actually that he's awake and asking for you," Jehan said. "But you're not going in until you get the bad and the worse."

"All right, What's bad, and what's worse?" Owyn felt someone at his back, and glanced back to see Mannon.

Jehan took a deep breath. "You didn't see the snake, did you?" he asked Mannon.

"No."

Jehan nodded. "It was a Widowmaker. That's the bad news."

"Widowmaker?" Owyn repeated. "What is that?"

"Something you don't have in Forge. They live along the coast here. Nasty. Rare, and getting more rare, because anyone who sees one kills it on sight. The venom is necrotic—"

Mannon moaned. "Worse...he lost the arm?"

Jehan nodded. "That's what took so long. We were trying everything we could think of to save his arm. Even in merge, there was nothing we could do. There was too much damage." He pointed at Mannon. "He says that it is not your fault. You did everything you could do. And more. I have never heard of anyone surviving four days after being bitten by a Widowmaker." He sighed again. "He wants to see you, Owyn."

"Lead the way."

Jehan gestured, and Owyn followed him out of the room and down the corridor. They passed room nineteen and turned a corner, and Owyn saw Aven, Alanar, Treesi and Pirit standing outside a room.

"He kicked us out," Aven said. "Said we were fussing at him."

"It's your job to fuss, Healer Aven," Jehan pointed out.

Aven nodded. "That's what I told him. He threw a pillow at me. So he's feeling a little better. And we're monitoring him from here."

"You can do that?" Owyn asked.

"Enough to know he's not in any danger," Alanar answered. He cocked his head to the side. "He's upset, but that's understandable."

"Can I go in?" Owyn asked.

Aven opened the door, and Owyn slipped into the room. The door closed, but he didn't move. Memfis lay flat in the bed, his face turned toward the window on the far wall. The pillow that he'd thrown at Aven was on the floor at Owyn's feet; he stooped and picked it up.

"Fa?" he said softly. "Jehan said you wanted to see me."

"I thought I wasn't going to see you again," Memfis said without turning. "Thought you were going to die out there."

"I...I did," Owyn said. "And Aven brought me back. So...umm...yeah, there's that. Had another waking vision. Don't have to worry about salt water anymore." He stepped closer to the bed. "Fa, I thought I'd lost you."

Memfis turned and looked at him. "I'm not done yet, Mouse. Tell Mannon it's not his fault."

"I don't think I can convince him of that," Owyn said. "I think that's your job." He came closer, stopping next to the bed. "Want this?" he asked, holding up the pillow.

Memfis nodded, and Owyn helped him to sit up, arranging the pillow behind him. For the first time, he really looked at Memfis. At the loose sleeve that hung where his right arm used to be.

"Oh, Mem," he murmured. "We're gonna need to figure things out."

Memfis nodded. "I'll need to learn to write with the other hand," he said. "And I don't know how I'm going to dance. Let alone work a forge."

"We'll figure it out," Owyn said. "We can. Because you're here. You're alive. And I'm alive, and we'll figure it out." He grinned. "And we're all here. All of us. Aven is back. Del is back. It's all fixed."

Memfis nodded. "I knew you would, Mouse."

"Wasn't just me, I don't think." Owyn folded his hands, felt the welcome weight on his left wrist. "You missed the wedding, Fa. We can do it again, if you want."

"Let me see," Memfis said. Owyn held his wrist out, letting Memfis examine the textured metal patterns on the bracelet. "This is your work. I can tell. When did you start working silver?" he asked.

"Twenty-eight days ago," Owyn said slowly. "I had a lot of help."

Memfis let Owyn's hand go. "It's beautiful work, Mouse. You did wonderfully." He smiled. "I knew you would. I always knew you'd do wonderfully." He shook his head. "Go take care of your man. I'm going to sleep. Then...we'll see what tomorrow brings. Tomorrow."

"You sure, Mem?"

"I'm sure. Go."

Owyn helped Memfis lay back down, then moved from the edge of the bed to the chair. He waited until Memfis was snoring before he got up and left. In the corridor, the only person waiting was Alanar.

"He's asleep," Owyn said. "Which you probably knew already."

"I knew," Alanar said. "How is he?"

"That's an odd question for you to ask. Can't you tell?"

"Emotionally, I mean," Alanar clarified. "Losing the arm, that's hard. Trust me, I understand."

"He seems to be doing okay," Owyn answered, taking Alanar's hand. "I don't know if he knew it was going to happen someday. And I don't know if it just hasn't sunk in yet. Might be a bit of both."

Alanar nodded. "The assistants will watch him. And we'll help him. All of us." He fell silent, then sighed. "I'm sorry."

"About what?" Owyn asked.

"We didn't finish the wedding—"

"You're wearing my bracelet, aren't you?" Owyn grinned. "We did the important part." He paused. "The second most important part."

Alanar turned his head, then laughed. "And the most important part?"

"That's later," Owyn assured him. "Then...Mem is right. We'll see what tomorrow brings. Tomorrow."

Don't miss out!

Visit the website below and you can sign up to receive emails whenever Elizabeth Schechter publishes a new book. There's no charge and no obligation.

https://books2read.com/r/B-A-KGBH-YGEFB

Connecting independent readers to independent writers.

Also by Elizabeth Schechter

Heir to the Firstborn
Worlds Begin
Written in Water
Forged in Fire
Bones of Earth

Rebel Mage
Counsel of the Wicked
Haven's Fall
Where Home Lies

Swords of Charlemagne
Hidden Things
The Lady and the Sword
Ashes and Light
Table of Stone
Swords of Charlemagne: The Complete Series

Watch for more at elizabethschechterwrites.com.

About the Author

Elizabeth Schechter has been called one of the top erotica and alternative sexuality writers in the world. Her writing credits include the award-winning steampunk erotic romance *House of Sable Locks*, the Celtic fantasy *Princes of Air,* and the dystopian fantasy *Rebel Mage* trilogy. Her shorter work has appeared in anthologies edited by D.L King (*Carnal Machines*), Laura Antoniou (*No Safewords*), and Cecilia Tan (*Jingle Balls*; *Like a Prince*).

With *Written in Water*, the first in the *Heir to the Firstborn* series, Elizabeth is exploring new ground, with her first new adult romance that was written entirely in real time on Patreon.

She was born in New York at some point in the past. She is officially old enough to know better, but refuses to grow up. She lives in Central Florida with her husband and son.

Elizabeth can be found online at http://elizabethschechterwrites.com, or on Facebook at https://www.facebook.com/Elizabeth.A.Schechter. You can also find her on Patreon, at https://www.patreon.com/EASchechter.

Subscribe to Elizabeth's newsletter at https://www.subscribepage.com/k4u7k2

Read more at elizabethschechterwrites.com.

www.ingramcontent.com/pod-product-compliance
Lightning Source LLC
Chambersburg PA
CBHW020933020726
47495CB00002B/479